Radiant Angel

NOVELS BY NELSON DEMILLE
Available from Grand Central Publishing

By the Rivers of Babylon
Cathedral
The Talbot Odyssey
Word of Honor
The Charm School
The Gold Coast
The General's Daughter
Spencerville
Up Country
The Gate House

John Corey Novels

Plum Island
The Lion's Game
Night Fall
Wild Fire
The Lion
The Panther

With Thomas Block

Mayday

Available from Center Street

The Quest

Nelson DeMille

Radiant Angel

GRAND CENTRAL PUBLISHING

NEW YORK BOSTON

This book is a work of fiction. Names, characters, places, and incidents are the product of the author's imagination or are used fictitiously. Any resemblance to actual events, locales, or persons, living or dead, is coincidental.

Grand Central Publishing
Hachette Book Group
1290 Avenue of the Americas
New York, NY 10104

www.HachetteBookGroup.com

Printed in the United States of America

RRD-C and RRD-H

First Edition: May 2015
10 9 8 7 6 5 4 3 2 1

Grand Central Publishing is a division of Hachette Book Group, Inc.
The Grand Central Publishing name and logo is a trademark of Hachette Book Group, Inc.

The Hachette Speakers Bureau provides a wide range of authors for speaking events. To find out more, go to www.hachettespeakersbureau.com or call (866) 376-6591.

The publisher is not responsible for websites (or their content) that are not owned by the publisher.

Library of Congress Cataloging in Publication data has been applied for.

ISBN (HC): 978-0-44658-085-4
ISBN (LP): 978-1-455-58959-3
ISBN (intl. pbk.): 978-1-4555-8890-9

For Sandy
My Viking shipmate and navigator

PART I

CHAPTER ONE

It was late afternoon, a Wednesday in September, and Colonel Vasily Petrov of the Russian Foreign Intelligence Service sat in his New York office and stared at the red envelope on his mahogany desk. On the envelope's flap was a wax seal, also red.

The envelope had arrived from Moscow an hour before on the Aeroflot flight that carried the daily diplomatic pouch to the Russian Federation Mission to the United Nations on East 67th Street.

Handwritten on the front of the envelope was his code number, 013575, and beneath that the identification number of the message: 82343.

A cipher clerk stood patiently in front of Colonel Petrov's desk, then cleared his throat. "Sir?"

Petrov picked up a pen and signed the logbook, acknowledging receipt of the envelope and also receipt of a sealed satchel from Moscow that the clerk had placed on his desk.

The clerk retrieved the logbook, then gave Petrov another sealed envelope, saluted, and left.

Petrov sliced open the red envelope and flattened the sheet of paper on his blotter.

The communication from Moscow was typed on flash paper,

encoded in four-letter groupings that appeared to be meaningless. Eye charts, they were called.

Petrov opened the second envelope that the cipher clerk had given him and laid the printed paper next to his encrypted message. On the cipher paper was the daily one-time-only code that would decipher his message.

If this message had been sent electronically, the cipher office on the tenth floor would have seen it and decoded it. And this message was not for their eyes. More importantly, electronic messages were routinely intercepted by the American National Security Agency, whose deciphering capabilities were a worry. Thus the message came in the diplomatic pouch, in a red envelope, which meant it was not for the diplomats; it was for the Foreign Intelligence Service—the SVR—which operated out of the Russian U.N. Mission. This was, in fact, a message for Colonel Petrov's eyes only, and it was of critical importance. And Petrov knew it said one of two things: the operation was on, or the operation was off.

He picked up his pen and began to decipher.

It was a short communication, though like many such brief messages, the brevity was in inverse proportion to its importance.

It took him only a few minutes to decipher the communication, and when he was done he put down his pen and looked at the words.

Greetings: You will commence Operation Zero on Sunday.

He read it again.

Like all men from the beginning of time who await their orders and their fates, he was relieved that the wait was over, and he felt a mixture of calm and confidence, along with a sense of anxiety. It was not death that he feared; it was failure and disgrace—a fate far worse than death.

He took a deep breath and thought of his father, a former KGB general who had been awarded the Order of Lenin and who had been named a Hero of the Soviet Union.

On the day that Colonel Petrov boarded the Aeroflot flight for New York, his father had seen him off at the airport and said to him, "The future of Russia has been placed in your hands, Vasily. The history of this century will be rewritten by you. Come home in glory. Or do not come home."

Petrov looked back at the paper. The next two lines were written in a cryptic style to further obscure the meaning of his orders in the unlikely event this message was seen by someone else.

He read: Happiness will be at planned time and place.

The third line read: The fish is swimming, the horse waits, and the bird will fly.

The final line advised: No further communication to or from you after Sunday. Good luck.

The message was not signed, nor did it ask for a reply. Or even an assurance that he was ready at his end. In fact, after a year of planning, there was nothing more to say. The time had come.

Petrov fed both sheets of paper into his cross-cut shredder, then stood and drew the large ballistic nylon satchel toward him. He broke the seal and unlocked the satchel with the key he had brought with him from Moscow. Petrov opened the satchel and saw three 9mm Makarov pistols. He checked that they were the PB model, developed for the KGB with an integral silencer. He also counted ten extra magazines of ammunition, which, he thought, should be sufficient for the number of people to be killed.

At the bottom of the satchel were two objects wrapped in blue gift paper that he knew were the two MP5 submachine guns he had requested and also about twenty extra magazines. And finally, there was an aluminum box—a tool kit, made for only one purpose. He closed the satchel, then locked it.

Petrov went to his window and stared down into the street. He hadn't liked New York City when he'd first arrived four months before. It was too hot and there were too many Africans, Asians, Arabs, and Jews in this city. But now, in September, the weather had cooled. As for the *chernokozhii*—the blackasses—they didn't seem to bother him as much.

What still bothered him, however, was being followed every minute of every day. The American security services knew who he was, of course, and they gave him little opportunity to do his job outside of his office. Well, they could follow him all they wanted. On Sunday he would lose them and they would not even know they had lost him. And then he could do his job. Operation Zero.

He was officially assigned to the United Nations for two years, and he could have tolerated that. But in fact, his posting was coming to an end on Monday. As was the City of New York.

PART II

CHAPTER TWO

If I wanted to see assholes all day, I would have become a proctologist. Instead, I watch assholes for my country.

I was parked in a black Chevy Blazer down the street from the Russian Federation Mission to the United Nations on East 67th Street in Manhattan, waiting for an asshole named Vasily Petrov to appear. Petrov is a colonel in the Russian Foreign Intelligence Service—the SVR in Russian—which is the equivalent to our CIA, and the successor to the Soviet KGB. Vasily—who we have affectionately code-named Vaseline, because he's slippery—has diplomatic status as Deputy Representative to the United Nations for Human Rights Issues, which is a joke because his real job is SVR Legal Resident in New York—the equivalent of a CIA Station Chief. I have had Colonel Petrov under the eye on previous occasions, and though I've never met him he's reported to be a very dangerous man, and thus an asshole.

I'm John Corey, by the way, former NYPD homicide detective, now working for the Federal government as a contract agent. My NYPD career was cut short by three bullets which left me seventy-five percent disabled (twenty-five percent per bullet?) for retirement pay purposes. In fact, there's nothing wrong with me physically, though the mental health exam for this job was a bit of a challenge.

Anyway, sitting next to me behind the wheel was a young lady whom I'd worked with before, Tess Faraday. Tess was maybe early thirties, auburn hair, tall, trim, and attractive. Also in the SUV, looking over my shoulder, was my wife, Kate Mayfield, who was actually in Washington, but I could feel her presence. If you know what I mean.

Tess asked me, "Do I have time to go to the john, John?" She thought that was funny.

"You have a bladder problem?"

"I shouldn't have had that coffee."

"You had two." Guys on surveillance pee in the container and throw it out the window. I said, "Okay, but be quick."

She exited the vehicle and double-timed it to a Starbucks around the corner on Third Avenue.

Meanwhile, Vasily Petrov could come out of the Mission at any time, get into his chauffeur-driven Mercedes S550, and off he goes.

But I've got three other mobile units, plus four agents on legs, so Vasily is covered while I, the team leader, am sitting here while Ms. Faraday is sitting on the potty.

And what do we think Colonel Petrov is up to? We have no idea. But he's up to *something*. That's why he's here. And that's why I'm here.

In fact, Petrov arrived only about four months ago, and it's the recent arrivals who are sometimes sent on the field with a new game play, and these guys need more watching than the SVR agents who've been stationed here awhile and who are engaged in routine espionage. Watch the new guys.

The Russian U.N. Mission occupies a thirteen-story brick building with a wrought-iron fence in front of it, conveniently located across the street from the 19th Precinct, whose surveillance cameras keep an eye on the Russians 24/7. The Russians don't like being watched by the NYPD, but they know they're also protected from pissed-off demonstrators and people who'd like to plant a bomb outside their front door. FYI, I live five blocks north of here on East 72nd, so I don't have far to walk when I get off duty at four. I could almost taste the Buds in my fridge.

So I sat there, waiting for Vasily Petrov and Tess Faraday. It was a nice day in early September, one of those beautiful dry and sunny days you get after the dog days of August. It was a Sunday, a little after 10 A.M., so the streets and sidewalks of New York were relatively quiet. I volunteered for Sunday duty because Mrs. Corey (my wife, not my mother) was in Washington for a weekend conference, returning tonight or tomorrow morning, and I'd rather be working than trying to find something to do solo on a Sunday.

Also, today was September 11, a day when I usually go to at least one memorial service with Kate, but this year it seemed more appropriate for me to mark the day by doing what I do.

There is a heightened alert every September 11 since 2001, but this year we hadn't picked up any specific intel that Abdul was up to something. And it being a Sunday, there weren't enough residents or commuters in the city for Abdul to murder. September 11, however, is September 11, and there were a lot of security people working today to make sure that this was just another quiet Sunday.

Kate was in D.C. because she's an FBI Special Agent with the Anti-Terrorist Task Force, headquartered downtown at 26 Federal Plaza. Special Agent Mayfield was recently promoted to Supervisory Special Agent, and her new duties take her to Washington a lot. She sometimes goes with her boss, Special Agent-in-Charge Tom Walsh, who used to be my ATTF boss, too, but I don't work for him or the ATTF any longer. And that's a good thing for both of us. We were not compatible. Walsh, however, likes Kate, and I think the feeling is mutual. I wasn't sure Walsh was with Kate on this trip, because I never ask, and she rarely volunteers the information.

On a less annoying subject, I now work for the DSG—the Diplomatic Surveillance Group. The DSG is also headquartered at 26 Fed, but with this new job I don't need to be at headquarters much, if at all.

My years in the Mideast section of the Anti-Terrorist Task Force were interesting, but stressful. And according to Kate, I was the cause of much of that stress. Wives see things husbands don't see. Bottom line, I had some issues and run-ins with the Muslim community (and my FBI bosses) that led directly or indirectly to my being asked by my superiors if I'd like to find other employment. Walsh suggested the Diplomatic Surveillance Group, which would keep me (a) out of his sight, (b) out of his office, and (c) out of trouble.

Sounded good. Kate thought so, too. In fact, she got the promotion after I left.

Coincidence?

My Nextel phone is also a two-way radio, and it blinged. Tess' voice said, "John, do you want a donut or something?"

"Did you wash your hands?"

Tess laughed. She thinks I'm funny. "What do you want?"

"A chocolate chip cookie."

"Coffee?"

"No." I signed off.

Tess' career goal is to become an FBI Special Agent, and to do that she has to qualify for appointment under one of five entry programs—Accounting, Computer Science, Language, Law, or what's called Diversified Experience. Tess is an attorney and thus qualifies. Most failed lawyers become judges or politicians, but Tess tells me she wants to do something meaningful, whatever that means. Meanwhile, she's working with the Diplomatic Surveillance Group.

Most of the DSG men and women are second-career people, twenty-year retirees from various law enforcement agencies, so we have mostly experienced agents, ex-cops, mixed with inexperienced young attorneys like Tess Faraday who see the Diplomatic Surveillance Group as a stepping-stone where they can get some street creds that look good on their FBI app.

Tess got back in the SUV and handed me an oversized cookie. "My treat."

She had another cup of coffee. Some people never learn.

She was wearing khaki cargo pants, a blue polo shirt, and running shoes, which are necessary if the target goes off on foot. Her pants and shirt were loose enough to hide a gun, but Tess is not authorized to carry a gun.

In fact, Diplomatic Surveillance Group agents are theoretically not authorized to carry guns. But we're not as stupid as the people who make the rules, so almost all the ex-cops carry, and I had my 9mm Glock in a pancake holster in the small of my back, beneath my loose-fitting polo shirt.

So we waited for Vasily to show.

Colonel Petrov lives in a big high-rise in the upscale Riverdale section of the Bronx. This building, which we call the 'plex—short for complex—is owned and wholly occupied by the Russians who work at the U.N. and at the Russian Consulate, and it is a nest of spies. The 'plex itself, located on a high hill, sprouts more antennas than a garbage can full of cockroaches.

The National Security Agency, of course, has a facility nearby and they listen to the Russians, who are listening to us, and we all have fun trying to block each other's signals. And round it goes. The only thing that has changed since the days of the Cold War is the encryption codes.

On a less technological level, the game is still played on the ground as it has been forever. Follow that spy. The Diplomatic Surveillance Group also has a confidential off-site facility—what we call the Bat Cave—near the Russian apartment complex, and the DSG team that was watching the 'plex this morning reported that Vasily Petrov had left, and they followed him here to the Mission, where my team picked up the surveillance.

The Russians don't usually work in the office on Sundays, so my guess was that Vasily was in transit to someplace else—or that he was going back to the 'plex—and that he'd be coming out shortly and getting into his chauffeur-driven Benz.

Colonel Petrov, according to the intel, is married, but his wife and children have remained in Moscow. This in itself is suspicious, because the families of the Russian U.N. delegation love to live in New York on the government ruble. Or maybe there's an innocent explanation for the husband-wife separation. Like she has an important job in Moscow or they just hate each other.

Tess informed me, "I have two tickets to the Mets doubleheader today." She further informed me, "I'd like to at least catch the last game."

"You can listen to them lose both games on the radio."

"I'll pretend you didn't say that." She reminded me, "We're supposed to be relieved at four."

"You can relieve yourself anytime you want."

She didn't reply.

A word about Tess Faraday. Did I say she was tall, slim, and attractive? She also swims and plays paddleball, whatever that is. She's fairly sharp, and intermittently enthusiastic, and I guess she's idealistic, which is why she left her Wall Street law firm to apply for the FBI where the money is not as good.

But money is probably not an issue with Ms. Faraday. She mentioned to me that she was born and raised in Lattingtown, an upscale community on the North Shore of Long Island, also known as the Gold Coast. And by her accent and mannerisms I can deduce that she came from some money and good social standing. People like that who want to serve their country usually go to the State Department or into intelligence work, not the FBI. But I give her credit for what she's doing and I wish her luck.

Also, needless to say, Tess Faraday and John Corey have little in common, though we get along during these days and hours of forced intimacy.

One thing we do have in common is that we're both married. His name is Grant, and he's some kind of international finance guy, and he travels a lot for his work. I've never met Grant, and I probably never will, but he likes to text and call his wife a lot. I deduce, by Tess' end of the conversation, that Grant is the jealous type, and Tess seems a bit impatient with him. At least when I'm in earshot of the conversation.

Tess inquired, "If Petrov goes mobile, do we stay with him, or do we hand him over to another team?"

"Depends."

"On what?"

"No, I mean you should wear Depends."

One of us thought that was funny.

But to answer Tess' question, if Vasily went mobile, most probably my team would stay with him. He wasn't supposed to travel farther than a twenty-five-mile radius from Columbus Circle without State Department permission, and according to my briefing he hadn't applied for a weekend travel permit. The Russians rarely did, and when they did they would apply on a Friday afternoon so that no one at State had time to approve or disapprove their travel plans. And off they'd go, in their cars or by train or bus to someplace outside their allowed radius. Usually the women were just going shopping at some discount mall in Jersey, and the men were screwing around in Atlantic City. But sometimes the SVR or the Military Intelligence guys—the GRU—were meeting people, or looking at things like nuclear reactors that they shouldn't be looking at. That's why we follow them, though we almost never bust them. The FBI, of which the DSG is a part, is famous—or infamous—for watching people and collecting evidence for years. Cops act on evidence. The FBI waits until the suspect dies of old age.

I said to Tess, "Let me know now if you can't stay past four. I'll call for a replacement."

She replied, "I'm yours."

"Wonderful."

"But if we get off at four, I have an extra ticket."

I considered my reply, then said, perhaps unwisely, "I take it Mr. Faraday is out of town."

"He is."

"Why have we not heard from Grant this morning?"

"I told him I was on a discreet—and quiet—surveillance."

"You're learning."

"I don't need to learn what I already know."

"Right." Escape and evasion. Perhaps Grant had reason to be jealous. You think?

Regarding the nature of our surveillance of Colonel Vasily Petrov, this was actually a non-discreet surveillance—what we call a bumper lock—meaning we were going to be up Vasily's ass all day. They always spotted a bumper lock surveillance, and sometimes they acknowledged the DSG agents with a hard stare—or if they were pricks they gave you the Italian salute.

Vasily was particularly unfriendly, probably because he was an intel officer, a big wheel in the Motherland, and he found it galling to be on the receiving end of a surveillance. Well, fuck him. Everybody's got a job to do.

Vasily sometimes plays games with the surveillance team, and he's actually given us the slip twice in the last four months. He's never given me the slip, but some other DSG teams lost him. And there's hell to pay when you lose the SVR Resident. And that wasn't going to happen on my watch. I don't lose anyone. Well, I lost my wife once in Bloomingdale's. I can't figure out the logic of a woman's shopping habits. They don't think like us.

"So do you want to go to the game?"

Mrs. Faraday had already started the game. But okay, two colleagues going to a baseball game after work is innocent enough. Even when they're married and their spouses are out of town. Right? I said, "I'll take a rain check."

"Okay." She asked me, "You going to eat that cookie?"

I broke it in half and gave her the bigger half.

Surveillances can be boring, which is why some people try to make them not boring. Two guys together talk about women, and two women together probably talk about guys. A guy and a woman together either have nothing to talk about, or the long hours lead to whatever.

In the last six months, Tess Faraday has been assigned to me about a dozen times, which, with one hundred fifty DSG agents in New York, defies the odds. As the team leader, I could reassign her to another vehicle or to leg surveillance. But I haven't. Why? Because I think she's asking to work with me, and being a very sensitive man I don't want to hurt her feelings. And why does she want to work with me? Because she wants to learn from a master. Or something else is going on.

And by the way, I haven't mentioned Tess Faraday to Kate. Kate is not the jealous type, and there's nothing to be jealous about. Also, like Kate, I keep my work problems and associations to myself. Kate doesn't talk about Tom Walsh, and I don't talk about Tess Faraday. Marital ignorance is bliss. Dumb is happy.

Meanwhile, Vasily has been inside the Mission for over an hour, but his Mercedes is still outside, so he's going someplace. Probably back to the Bronx. He sometimes runs in Central Park, which is a pain in the ass. Everyone on the team wears running shoes, of course, and I think we're all in good shape, but Vasily is in excellent shape. Older FBI agents have told me that the Soviet KGB guys were mostly lardasses who smoked and drank too much. But the only kind of bars and clubs these guys from the new Russia were into were granola bars and health clubs. Their boss, bare-chested Putin, sort of set the new standard.

Vasily, being who he is, also has a girlfriend in town, a Russian lady named Svetlana who sings at a few of the Russian nightclubs in Brighton Beach. I caught a glimpse of her once and she looks like she has good lungs.

I did a radio check with my team and everyone was awake.

A soft breeze fluttered the white, blue, and red Russian flag in front of the Mission. I remember when the Soviet Hammer and Sickle flew there. I kind of miss the Cold War. But I think it's back.

My team today consists of four leg agents and four vehicles—my Chevy Blazer, a Ford Explorer, and two Dodge minivans. We usually have one agent in each vehicle, but today we had two. Why? Because the Russians are tricky, and sometimes they travel in groups and scatter like cockroaches, so recently we've been beefing up the surveillance teams. So today I had two DSG agents in the other three vehicles, all former NYPD. I had the only trainee, an FBI wannabe who probably thinks the DSG job sucks. Sometimes I think the same thing.

In the parlance of the FBI, the Diplomatic Surveillance Group is called a quiet end, which really means a dead end.

But I'm okay with this. No office, no adult supervision, and no bullshit. Just follow that asshole.

A quiet end. But in this business, there is no such thing.

CHAPTER THREE

Diplomatic Surveillance Group agents are not typically assigned to only one group of foreign diplomats. I do, however, seem to pull a lot of Russian duty, maybe because the Russians have a very big diplomatic contingent in New York—about two hundred people, including their consulate building up on East 91st. And maybe that would explain why every time Tess Faraday was with me the target was the Russians. Or maybe that didn't explain it. So to clear this up, I asked her, "Is it a coincidence that you're working with me only when I'm following the Russians?"

"I think it's the law of averages." She explained, "The other big targets are the Islamic dips, and someone told me you're not allowed to come within a hundred yards of a Muslim."

I suppose that would explain it—law of averages. But I've also watched the Chinese, the Cubans, and the psychotic North Koreans, and Ms. Faraday hadn't been with me on any of those occasions. But I didn't pursue this and assured her, "I'm currently taking a class in Islamic cultural sensitivity."

She laughed.

In fact, I was told that I needed to remember that most of my targets had diplomatic status, and thus diplomatic immunity, even if they were spies or potential terrorists. That didn't mean they could blow up 26 Federal Plaza with impunity, but it did mean that I needed to be more judicious and less physical in my methods. I did punch an Iranian diplomat in the balls once in Atlantic City, but that was when I was with the ATTF, before the DSG and before I received the proper training in dealing with the diplomatic community. I'm much nicer now.

On a related subject, a lot of people in the intelligence community (and the general public) think of the U.N. as a house of spies, which to some extent it is. But I see it as job security. I mean, if the U.N. was moved someplace else, I wouldn't have this wonderful job. Look at what happened to all the horseshit shovelers in New York when the automobile was invented. On the other hand, I could do without this job and without guys like Colonel Vasily Petrov in town.

On the subject of job security, I asked Tess, "Who's talking about me?"

"Everyone."

"All good, I hope."

"You're a legend."

"Is that why you ask to work with me?"

"I never asked." She chided me, "You have a big ego."

Tess, I reminded myself, was not a kid trainee who just fell off the turnip truck. She was a Wall Street lawyer, probably went to good schools, and she seemed self-assured. She also seemed like a lady who was used to getting her way. I'm surprised we haven't butted heads by now.

So we sat and waited for Colonel Petrov.

I find that the Russians are more of a challenge than the Islamic, Korean, or Cuban targets. The Russians are better trained at spotting surveillance, and as I mentioned, they know how to give you the slip, or send you off on a wild-goose chase.

I've discovered, too, that in some ways the Russians think like us, which the Islamic guys do not. And if they think like us, they can predict our moves, and we can predict theirs. This is what makes following the Russians interesting. Plus, they're more likely than Abdul to wind up in a tittie bar.

"What are you thinking about?"

"This guy I know went into a sex shop and asked the proprietor for a blow-up sex doll."

"Is this a joke?"

"So the proprietor asks, 'You want a Christian doll, a Jewish doll, or a Muslim doll?' And the guy says, 'What difference does it make?' And the proprietor says, 'Well, the Muslim dolls blow themselves up.' "

Tess laughed, then said, "That's terrible." She suggested, "I think you were in the Mideast section too long."

"Apparently." But it wasn't a bad gig, and I of course distinguished myself, though I started to lose my patience with the Muslim gentlemen I was investigating. Also, the political correctness of the ATTF and the FBI was a little hard to take, and maybe I crossed the line now and then.

And, if the truth be known, my presence on the 26th floor of 26 Federal Plaza was compromising my wife's career. Also, some might say, her position saved my ass a few times.

What I like about the DSG is that I'm out of the office most of the time, and I'm my own man, meaning I'm authorized to make quick decisions, and no one is going to second-guess me as long as I do my job. It's almost like being a cop again.

Tess said, "Petrov's driver just got a phone call."

I looked at the Mercedes down the block and saw the driver get out of the car and open the rear door. I recognized the driver, a guy named Dmitry who was competent but not too tricky behind the wheel.

Tess started the Blazer and I blinged a call-out to the team. "Game time."

Each of the DSG vehicles is equipped with what is called the police package—flashing lights in the grille, sirens, tinted windows, and other bells and whistles. We all have D-1 Nikons with zoom lenses, Sony 8mm video cameras, directional listening devices, and other high-tech toys depending on the assignment, like a little gadget that detects radioactive substances in the area. I never want to hear that thing beeping.

The gate of the wrought-iron security cage in front of the Mission opened and out came Colonel Vasily Petrov, dressed casually in tan slacks, a red polo shirt, and sandals not made for running, which was good.

With Petrov were two similarly dressed gentlemen who were carrying large overnight bags. I recognized one of them as Pavel Fradkov, a middle-aged man who was a more recent arrival than Vasily Petrov. The other guy, a big dude with a black crew cut, was unknown, at least to me, but someone might ID him from the NYPD video surveillance tape that was monitored at 26 Fed. Dmitry and the unknown guy put the bags in the Mercedes' trunk, and everyone got in the car, except Petrov, who looked up and down the block, nodding his head like he'd spotted the four surveillance vehicles and the four guys on leg. As I said, it's non-discreet surveillance, and we're not trying to look like lampposts or something.

Petrov got in the rear with Fradkov and off they went.

I radioed the team, "Vaseline on the move in Benz with dip plate CYR-0823. I'll follow with Matt and Steve. Everyone else keep an eye on the store."

Tess fell in behind the Mercedes, and the Dodge minivan fell in behind us with Matt Conlon behind the wheel and Steve Lansky riding shotgun. I Nexteled the team, "The guy with the green shirt is Pavel Fradkov. Anyone recognize the big guy?"

No one did, so I said, "Unknown is hereafter called Igor until we ID him."

Petrov's vehicle turned south on Park Avenue.

Tess said, "Well, they're not going back to the Bronx. Maybe they're going to the Glass House," meaning the U.N. building.

She was picking up the lingo. In another few weeks she'll be swearing like a cop.

Park Avenue is one of the few two-way avenues in Manhattan, divided by a wide median, and thus the only avenue where you can make a legal U-turn. I said to Tess, "Watch for the U-turn."

But Dmitry wasn't doing any escape and evasion, and this looked like it was going to be a Sunday drive.

We took the elevated road around Grand Central Terminal and continued south, which ruled out the U.N. building. Traffic was light on a Sunday, and we made good time down to 34th Street, where the Mercedes turned left and continued on toward the entrance ramp to the Queens-Midtown Tunnel, meaning he was going to Queens, Brooklyn, or Long Island.

Tess pointed out, "They have bags. So maybe they're going to JFK."

"That would be nice." Arrivederci, assholes.

The Mercedes entered the tunnel under the East River and we followed.

Tess asked, "Should we call this in?"

Phone calls mean conversation, and conversation means someone on the other end thinks they need to give you advice or patch you through to a supervisor. So as I usually do, I texted the case agent: Target mobile. 4 pers. Mercedes, dip plate CYR-0823. East in QMT. 2 surv. veh.

A minute later, the reply read: Copy.

Obviously, the case agent didn't give a shit with a response like that, so all is good. I love this job.

We came out of the tunnel into the sunlight, and the Mercedes veered toward a cash-only booth so there would be no electronic E-ZPass record of their travel. Good tradecraft, except they've got two surveillance vehicles up their ass so what's the point?

We used E-ZPass and slowed up until the Mercedes got through the slower toll booth and caught up with us.

And off we went, eastbound on the Long Island Expressway, destination unknown.

Tess asked, "Where else would Petrov be going with luggage?"

"His girlfriend's apartment in Brighton Beach."

"Why does he need the other guys?"

"Maybe they have a nightclub act."

"You're supposed to be teaching me."

"I just did. Here's another lesson. Keep the target in sight and don't speculate. Lesson three—you'll know where he's going when he gets there. Four, if you lose him, you'll be looking for a job tomorrow."

"I won't lose him."

The Mercedes was in the far left lane, what we call lane one, going about 60 mph. I called Matt and Steve in the minivan and said, "Use lane three and watch for the target to swerve toward an exit." I further briefed them, "He's got a girlfriend in Brighton Beach." Meaning, as we say in the business, he's probably following his dick today, but I didn't say that in mixed company.

We continued east through the borough of Queens. We passed the exit that would have taken us south to Brighton Beach in Brooklyn, which blew that theory, then the exit to La Guardia Airport, then the Kennedy Airport exit. We also passed the exit to Shea Stadium, so we weren't going to be watching the doubleheader with the Russians today.

We crossed the city line into suburban Nassau County and continued east.

I didn't know how much Tess knew about the Russians, so I informed her, "The Russian dips have a weekend house in Upper Brookville, not too far from your ancestral castle in Lattingtown."

She ignored my sarcasm and replied, "Well, if that's where they're going, I know the territory."

"And that's as far as they're allowed to go." Upper Brookville is actually a few miles past the twenty-five-mile limit, but if they go directly there without deviation it's okay.

The Diplomatic Surveillance Group also has a confidential offsite office near the Russian weekend house, so maybe we could hand this to them.

I informed Tess of this, and she said, "Great. I can make the game." She asked me, "Are you sure you don't want to go?"

No, I wasn't sure. But I was saved from a bad decision when we passed the exit that would have taken us north to Upper Brookville.

Tess said, "Damn it."

My Nextel blinged and Matt said, "Where the hell is this guy going?"

"I'll bet if we follow him, we'll find out."

So we continued following the Russians, who were now past their allowable radius.

We actually weren't authorized to bust them unless we were told by higher up to do that, so we always let them run, to see where they were going. They might try to use SDR—surveillance detection route, meaning escape and evasion—but their drivers weren't as good as ours. It was when they were on foot in Manhattan or Brooklyn that they'd get tricky with subways and taxis, and sometimes give you the slip. On the open road, however, they were pretty pathetic. So they weren't going to a secret meeting or something; they were off on a jaunt. Maybe the Hamptons.

Tess said, "Maybe you should call this in."

"Later."

She shrugged and continued to follow the Mercedes, keeping a distance of fifty yards, not letting more than one car come between us and the target. She was a good driver. Matt and Steve continued in the slow lane, but now and then they moved to the center lane to catch up.

The only good thing about following the Russians in New York was that they weren't trying to kill people or blow things up, the way the Islamic radicals did. They were mostly into industrial spying, stealing technology, intercepting our diplomatic and intel commo, or trying to recruit people to do all that. Basic espionage as opposed to acts of terrorism. Still, they posed another kind of threat—long-term. An almost existential threat. So they needed close watching.

Colonel Vasily Petrov, however, had a different pedigree. According to the intel on this guy, his old man, Vladimir Petrov, is a former KGB general who was once head of SMERSH, the assassination arm of the old KGB, and, as they say, the apple does not fall far from the tree. Vasily himself has been implicated in rubbing out political foes of his esteemed president, Mr. Putin, and Vasily had also served in Chechnya where the CIA says he ran the mass execution program of Chechen civilians suspected of aiding the rebels. If true, this was a ruthless man, and a cold-blooded killer.

But I couldn't imagine how Petrov's occupational skills could be used here. Well, maybe I could. The Russians had a long history of sending agents out to the four corners of the world to find and kill dissidents and traitors who'd gotten out of Russia. That's what SMERSH was about, and that could explain why Petrov was here. But even though the Russians had whacked dissidents all over the planet, including England, they hadn't done that here, but if they did and got caught, the shit would really hit the fan.

On the other hand, the Russians were getting ballsy again, and Putin, formerly of the KGB, was beating his bare chest and growling a lot. You can change the name of the KGB to the SVR, but that didn't change anything.

All of this, however, is not my problem or my job anymore. Let somebody else worry about what Petrov is up to. My job is to follow the target, record and report. I'm not a bloodhound anymore; I'm the second dog in a dogsled team. Follow that asshole.

And yet…well, Vasily Petrov has aroused my detective instincts. Unfortunately, whenever that happens, I usually get in trouble.

Tess asked me, "What are you thinking about?"

"A pastrami sandwich."

She replied, "A warhorse put out to pasture doesn't think about the pasture."

I didn't reply.

"He thinks about the battlefield."

I suggested, "Pay attention to the target."

"Yes, sir."

CHAPTER FOUR

We crossed into Suffolk County, still heading east toward the end of Long Island, following the Mercedes with Dmitry at the wheel, Igor riding shotgun, and Petrov and Fradkov in the back seat.

Possibly this was a wild-goose chase to draw half the team away from the Russian U.N. Mission. Our Bureau car radios and our hand-helds didn't work out here, but our Nextel radio feature did, so I blinged the other half of my surveillance team who were still on 67th Street, but they had nothing unusual to report. Kenny Hieb, who was my assistant team leader, also informed me that no one at 26 Fed was able to ID Igor from the PD surveillance tape, but they were working on it. The FBI never sleeps, but things move a little slower on weekends and holidays.

I let my team know we were in Suffolk County, following the target, and would not be returning to their location for a while, if at all. I also advised Kenny to request an additional team to make sure the Mission was covered.

We were now beyond comfortable commuting distance to Manhattan and the suburbs began to thin out. I looked at the fuel gauge and saw we could make it all the way to Montauk Point if we had to. I assumed the Mercedes could do the same, so there'd be no gas station stops unless Ms. Faraday had to pee again.

We were now about fifty road miles from Manhattan, and I let

Tess know, "There's a Russian oligarch, Georgi Tamorov, who has a big oceanfront house in Southampton. Petrov has been Tamorov's guest a few times."

"Do we still get relieved at four?"

"We can ask. But it's Sunday and I think we're it."

"What if they stay overnight?"

"We take turns sleeping in the minivan." I asked her, "Haven't you been doing this awhile?"

"I never did an overnight." She informed me, "Grant is flying in tomorrow morning."

I reminded her, "We are protecting the homeland. Sometimes the hours are not convenient."

"Don't be sarcastic."

"Are you sure you want this job?"

"I am."

"And what does Grant want?"

"That's none of your business. But since you asked, he's not happy about this."

"I'm disappointed in him."

She thought a moment, then said, "I'm sure it's easier if both spouses are in the same business."

I didn't reply.

A few miles later, she asked me, "Am I making a mistake? I mean about wanting to be an FBI agent?"

"Look inside. Your inner light will guide you."

"That's stupid."

"That's correct."

We traveled in silence awhile, then Tess informed me, "I've applied for a gun permit."

"Holy shit."

"What is that supposed to mean?"

"Sorry. That just slipped out."

"Be serious, John. I need to know if I have what it takes to carry and use a gun."

"I'm sure you do."

"Have you ever used your gun?"

"Now and then."

"Did you ever... you know, shoot anyone?"

"What do you hear?"

"I heard you were shot three times."

"All on the same day."

"Did you get them?"

"No."

"Do you want to talk about this?"

"Not at this moment."

"Okay." She asked me, "Do you have any tips? I mean for when I go to Quantico and take the Pistol Qualification Course."

"You'll do fine on the Q Course. But here's a tip for when you're going to a real gunfight. Borrow money from the agents with you. It gives them an added incentive to protect you."

She laughed.

"Remember," I continued helpfully, "anything worth shooting is worth shooting twice. Ammo is cheap. And if your shooting stance is good, you're probably not moving fast enough."

Tess nodded, then glanced at me.

I went on, "When approaching a suspect, watch their hands. Hands kill. In God we trust. Everyone else, keep your hands where I can see them. Be polite. Be professional. But have a plan to kill everyone you meet."

Tess again glanced at me, probably wondering how anyone so clever got plugged three times. I wonder about that myself. Shit happens.

I concluded, "Use a gun that works every time. As George Washington said, 'All skill is in vain when an angel pisses in the flintlock of your musket.'"

We continued in silence. Finally, Tess said, "Thank you."

So it's come to this. Giving tips and assurance to a dilettante who's rebelling against her background and her husband. How are the mighty fallen.

We were entering an area called the Pine Barrens, an empty stretch along the Expressway, and traffic was light here.

Tess asked me, "Why aren't we calling this in?"

"We have nothing to report."

"We're a hundred miles from where we started, John."

"Eighty."

"The case agent should know that."

"The phone works both ways."

She stayed silent a moment, then said, "Maybe we should get some backup moving."

"We're not having any problems or issues."

"Maybe they're leading us into a trap."

"I never thought of that."

"I know it sounds crazy, but—"

"It's beyond crazy."

"All right... but don't say I didn't warn you."

"I won't say that."

"Do you have an extra gun?"

"If I did, you're not getting it."

"You'll be begging me to take it if this is a trap."

"Change the subject."

To be fair to Ms. Faraday and her paranoia, Vasily Petrov *was* a killer, but he wouldn't risk carrying a gun. If he did, and we decided to have the local police pull his car over on some pretext, he'd be booted out of the country tomorrow, and that's not what Colonel Petrov wanted. Or what the CIA wanted. The State Department should have rejected his diplomatic credentials and barred his entry into the U.S. But I'm sure the CIA wanted to see what Petrov was up to. I get this. But that's like opening your door to a killer to see what he wants.

Tess suggested, "Maybe we should call for aviation."

"Negative."

"Why are you being stubborn?"

I informed her, "We are being tracked at 26 Fed through our GPS, so anyone there who wants to know where we are can know. We are on a routine surveillance in broad daylight, following one diplomatic vehicle that is probably on its way to their compatriot's beach house. There are no ambushes ahead, and we do not need a spotter craft or a Black Hawk gunship overhead." I suggested, "Just drive."

"Yes, sir." She added, "I hope we get ambushed."

Me, too, if it shuts her up.

If Ms. Faraday thought that I was not in the best of moods, she was right. And if I thought about why, I'd conclude that I might be having some marital difficulties. Nothing major at the moment, except that we seemed to have little to say to each other.

When Kate and I worked together, we fought a lot about the job, but they were good fights and ironically it brought us closer together. Especially when my unorthodox methods led to the successful conclusion of a big case.

Now, however, I had no big cases and never would with this job. Meanwhile, Kate's career arc was rising, and I'm following assholes all day. I don't even carry handcuffs anymore. I'm not even sure I have arrest powers. On the plus side, my NYPD rank follows me for life and I'm still Detective John Corey. Small consolation.

Big egos deflate quickly, and mine even half-deflated is twice as big as anyone else's. But I needed to do something—like get another job commensurate with my skills and experience, and my bloodhound instincts. And my big ego. Maybe something in foreign intelligence. I pictured myself calling Kate from, say, Iran. "I'll just be another few weeks here, sweetheart. Gotta check out a secret nuclear facility and kidnap an atomic physicist. Don't forget to pick up my dry cleaning. Ciao."

The male ego is a wondrous thing.

On that subject, Mrs. Faraday decided to confess, "I have actually asked to work with you." She inquired, "Do you want to know why?"

"No."

"You do. So I'll tell you."

I waited for her to tell me, but she said, "But not today. I just wanted to fess up and make sure you don't mind."

I wondered who the hell she was talking to, and why Howard Fensterman, the FBI supervisor running the Diplomatic Surveillance Group, would even consider her request. That didn't compute. In fact, there were a few things about Tess Faraday that were not computing. For all I knew, she was with the FBI Office of Professional Responsibility—sort of like the NYPD's Internal Affairs

Bureau—and she was writing me up. But that's a little paranoid. More likely, she or her family had some connections at 26 Fed, or she had good persuasive powers with whoever was running the DSG trainee program. Also, I could imagine some tongues wagging when pretty Tess Faraday asked if she could work with Detective Corey again. Like I don't have enough problems at home or at 26 Fed.

"John? *Do* you mind?"

"The pleasure is all mine."

The Manorville exit to the Hamptons was coming up and the Expressway was about to end. The Mercedes signaled and took the exit.

Tess followed, and Matt and Steve fell in behind us.

The Mercedes turned south on Captain Daniel Roe Highway and we followed. Traffic was light, so the three vehicles, all in a neat row, looked like a caravan of friends heading to the beach.

Tess commented, "We've been tailing these guys for over an hour and they don't seem to care."

"They like being followed. Makes them feel important."

"They're fucking up my day."

I was surprised at the unexpected obscenity. I pointed out, "This gives us quality training time together."

She stayed silent a moment, then said, "Grant expects me to meet him at JFK tomorrow morning."

"Worry about it in the morning."

"I'll text him when we see what's happening here."

"Watch what you say." I reminded her, "Whatever happens here stays here."

"Okay." She seemed less worried and said, "I like that. I can't say where I am because it's top secret."

"Saves a lot of marriages."

She laughed.

We continued for a few miles, then turned east onto Sunrise Highway, which would take us to Southampton.

Tess asked, "You think Petrov is going to this Russian guy's house?"

"He's done it before."

"Who is this guy?"

"I told you. A zillionaire oligarch. Georgi Tamorov. Owns half the planet."

"What is their connection?"

"Don't know, and don't have a need to know."

"But I'll bet you'd like to know."

"Please don't try to get into my head. My last two psychiatrists committed suicide."

She laughed again.

Clearly Tess Faraday enjoyed my company. And clearly there was more to her than a pretty face.

CHAPTER FIVE

The Mercedes continued east on Sunrise Highway, then suddenly made a sharp right onto a small side road. Tess hit her brakes and made the turn, as did Matt and Steve.

We stayed close to the target vehicle as it continued south toward the ocean.

Tess informed me, "My parents had a summer house in East Hampton."

"I'm sure they did."

"I know every back road in the Hamptons."

"Where's the ambush?"

She ignored that and continued, "If they're going to Tamorov's, they'll turn left on Montauk Highway toward the oceanfront mansions."

And sure enough, they turned left on Montauk Highway, which was a curving, two-lane Colonial-era road, somewhat picturesque, and slow with local traffic.

The Shinnecock Indian Reservation came up on our right, sitting on a billion dollars' worth of prime waterfront real estate, a perfect setting for a future gambling casino. In lieu of a casino, the Shinnecocks had a trading post on the side of the road. Matt Nexteled, "What kind of Indians are these? Dot or feather?"

"Feather."

"Oh... I was in the mood for curry."

Everyone's a comedian.

Tess asked me, "Where is Tamorov's house?"

"Martini Lane."

"Gin Lane."

"Right."

"Okay, so he's going to make a right, probably on South Main."

"Don't anticipate. Just follow."

"You're lucky I'm with you." She mocked, "Martini Lane. Is that where Gin Lane crosses Vermouth Road?"

"Drive." I hate a wiseass. Unless it's me.

"And for your information, gin is Old English for a common grazing area."

"Everybody knows that," I assured her.

"What's the name of Tamorov's house?"

"Tamorov's house."

"The houses have names."

"Right. The Tides."

"I know it."

"Been there?"

"No."

"You might get your chance today."

She didn't reply.

We continued, and Montauk Highway narrowed as it entered the shop-lined village of Southampton. An historical marker said JOBS LANE, 1664, which let everyone know they were in a three-hundred-percent markup zone.

Tess told me, "I had my first grown-up date in the Driver's Seat—" She pointed to a pub up the road. "Right there."

"How'd that work out?"

"I couldn't get a drink. I was too young."

"Did they let you use the bathroom?"

"Not funny. Now I have to go. Can I pull over?"

"Sure." Maybe she's pregnant.

She double-parked and hit the flashers, then scooted out of the Blazer and hurried toward the pub.

I blinged Matt and Steve, who were behind me. "Quick P-stop. Stay with the target."

"Copy."

The minivan went around me and continued on Jobs Lane, behind the Mercedes.

My Nextel blinged and Matt said, "Target turning right on South Main."

"Copy." Well, that removed any doubt that Petrov was going to Tamorov's house. But why? Probably a party. This was going to be a long day.

Tess reappeared, hopped in the driver's seat, and asked, "Where'd they go?"

"Right on South Main."

"Told you." She put the Blazer in gear and continued on Jobs Lane.

"Did you call Grant?"

"Quick text."

I didn't pursue that, and she turned right toward the ocean and we caught up with the minivan. "Go around."

She passed Matt and Steve and took up a position fifty feet behind the Mercedes.

Tess lowered her window and said, "Smell that ocean."

"Why?"

South Main was lined with Southampton's iconic hedgerows, behind which were broad lawns that led to old, multimillion-dollar mansions.

Tess pointed. "The Raleighs lived there. Friends of my parents."

"They owned the slum I grew up in. Nice people."

"This brings back a lot of memories."

"Glad for that."

"There were no Russians here when I was growing up."

"The world has changed."

"Where do these oligarchs get all that money?"

"When you find out, let me know."

"My father worked hard for his money. He didn't steal it."

"The Russian oligarchs didn't steal money. They stole the country."

"Disgusting."

"The Shinnecocks would agree with that."

We were approaching Gin Lane, which ran along the Atlantic.

Tess asked, "Why do they want to live here?"

"Russia sucks."

"Never been. How about you?"

"Nope. Been to Brighton Beach, though."

The Mercedes took a left on Gin Lane and we followed. There didn't seem to be any other vehicles on the oceanfront road.

As I said, following Ivan is more fun than following Abdul. The Russians partied hard and they usually had some good-looking babes with them. Not that that's relevant to the job. But if you've ever sat outside a mosque for three hours waiting for Abdul...you get my point.

On the right side of Gin Lane, the ocean side, lay huge waterfront mansions behind hedges and high walls. On the left were equally impressive mansions that became beachfront property when a hurricane blew in.

I'd followed Petrov here once, back in June, so I knew that Tamorov's place was at the east end of Gin Lane. I knew, too, that Tamorov threw some wild parties. Petrov and his pals had overnight bags, so I could conclude that I'd be sleeping in the minivan tonight. I hoped Ms. Faraday didn't snore.

I called Matt and Steve. "Target will turn into an oceanfront estate called The Tides. We will not."

"Copy."

I said to Tess, "Bumper lock this guy and when he turns, stop."

She nodded and sat on the Mercedes' tail.

The big double gates of Tamorov's estate were coming up, marked by a brass sign saying THE TIDES. The Mercedes slowed, then without signaling it turned into the gates, which were already opening electronically, meaning the Russians had called ahead to announce their arrival and let the security guys know they were being followed.

Tess stopped opposite the entrance, and I saw two big guys

behind the gates, dressed in black like Batman, and they tried to eye us through our tinted windows. They didn't have visible weapons, but I was certain they were carrying.

The Mercedes stopped just inside the gates, and an arm extended from the right rear window where Petrov was sitting. He flipped us the bird.

Tess said, "That was rude."

I lowered my tinted window just enough to get my arm out and returned the salute, adding, "Yob vas!" meaning, Fuck you.

"What did you say?"

"I wished them a nice day." I instructed, "Continue fifty yards and make a U-turn."

We continued past the estate, then Tess did a U-turn on the narrow sandy lane and stopped, facing the Tamorov estate down the road.

Matt and Steve did the same, and we all got out of our vehicles for a stretch.

A nice breeze came off the ocean and the sky was light blue, spotted with small puffy clouds. Gulls circled over the water looking for lunch, and the sun was slightly west of high noon. My stomach growled.

Matt Conlon, also a former NYPD homicide detective, said, "I can't believe that scumbag gave us the finger."

Steve Lansky, formerly with the NYPD Counterintelligence Unit, said, "They're pissing me off."

I looked down the road and saw that Tamorov's two security guys had walked into the road and were looking at us.

Steve retrieved his Nikon with the zoom lens and focused on them. "They look Russian." He explained, "One looks like my old man." He shot a few pictures of the security guys.

"All right," I said, "my guess is that Petrov is here for the day, maybe the night."

Tess seemed resigned to the possibility that we'd be on surveillance until dawn, though she did ask, "Can we call for a relief team?"

"I need the overtime." I also informed her, "These guys sometimes play a shell game, so if another vehicle exits the estate then we need to get the locals to pull it over and see if Petrov is in it." I reminded her, "Petrov is the target. Not the Mercedes and not the driver."

"How about Igor and Fradkov?" asked Ms. Faraday. "What if they leave without Petrov?"

"Then you can take the minivan and follow them if you'd like."

"Are you trying to get rid of me?"

"I thought you had a game to see and a husband to meet."

"This is getting interesting."

I reminded everyone, "The Russians are a major power, and they're not our official enemy, so we need to avoid causing an incident." Meaning, no punching anyone in the balls. But a "Fuck you" is okay.

Tess suggested, "Why don't you call a supervisor for instructions?"

"I make the decisions in the field based on my estimation of the situation."

"Okay. Have you decided who goes for lunch?"

"No one. I'm going to shoot a few seagulls. You want one?"

She seemed tired of my wit and informed us, "I know a few delis in town that deliver."

Best news I've had all day.

So we gave Tess our lunch orders and she got on her cell phone and found a deli in Southampton that would deliver to two vehicles parked on Gin Lane. She hung up and informed us, "Half an hour."

I hoped lunch arrived before the Mercedes reappeared.

This job gave you a lot of agita, but also a lot of freedom, like a traveling salesman. If your numbers were good, no one in the home office asked what you did all day.

But if you screwed up, as a contract agent, you went right into free fall and there was no one there to catch you. No union, no civil service job-for-life. And that was okay with me.

Meanwhile, my target was behind closed gates, which doesn't mean I lost him—but I couldn't see him. This was a bit worrisome, but it happens, and eventually the guy has to reappear. All I need to do is see him reappear. If, however, the target slips out the back door, we've got a problem. And Petrov had about ten miles of beach to disappear on and a whole ocean for his back door.

I thought about requesting aviation or one of our watercraft that we use for this kind of surveillance. But that could be overkill. Petrov was a person of prime interest, but, unlike some of our Muslim targets, he didn't warrant the whole nine yards. At least that was the thinking at 26 Fed and beyond.

And in this case, things were probably just as they appeared, meaning Colonel Petrov was a houseguest of Georgi Tamorov, and maybe they were having a party and Petrov was looking forward to seeing boobies in the hot tub and having a few vodkas. No big deal.

All we had to do was make sure we didn't miss him when he left. Eventually, he'd head back to the city. Another day in the life of Vasily Petrov and John Corey.

Unless today was different.

CHAPTER SIX

We stood on the quiet road, our backs to the minivan, drinking bottled water and getting some rays. Most of the summer mansions were empty after Labor Day, but the caretakers or occupants are understandably paranoid, and if anyone saw us they might call the cops. Or we might call the cops. We'd worked with the local and State Police on a few occasions relating to the Tamorov house and other matters of national security, and in fact a few of these local and State Police personnel had been trained by the Anti-Terrorist Task Force and were our local PD contacts.

The world had changed and shrunk, and no place was beyond the reach of the bad guys, and bad things could happen anywhere. Even here, among the hedgerows and the mansions of the rich and powerful.

Steve, who like me is not cut out for passive surveillance, decided he wanted to go piss off the Russian security guys. I don't encourage confrontation, but I do like it. "If you shoot anyone, you do the paperwork."

Steve walked down the road, and the security guys retreated behind the gates and closed them.

I texted the case agent: <u>Target vehicle entered Tamorov house Southampton. Any units available for relief?</u>

It takes awhile to get a response when the case agent or anyone at 26 Fed has to answer a question or make a decision, especially on weekends and holidays, so I pocketed my cell phone.

Steve was at the gates now and he was being provocative by snapping photos through the iron bars.

Probably the security guys were yelling at him, though I couldn't see or hear them at this distance, but I could hear dogs barking.

As I said, this is a non-discreet surveillance, so some interaction is inevitable—or necessary—like the time I double-parked next to a Russian dip car and wouldn't let him out until my backup arrived. But Steve was pushing the protocol a bit.

Discreet surveillance and undercover work, on the other hand, requires a lot more skill and stealth, but it can produce interesting results. One of the reasons the DSG switches targets is so our faces aren't known to the same guys, so we can go discreet or undercover if the target hasn't seen us before. In the case of Colonel Petrov, I've followed him before, but I'm fairly certain he's never seen me up close. On the other hand, the SVR may have taken a picture of me with a zoom lens. So maybe we all had pictures of each other taking pictures of each other. There must be a better way of making a living.

Steve was finished annoying the dogs and the Russians, and he walked back to the vehicles and said, "There are about a dozen cars parked inside." He deduced, "It's party time."

Matt informed us, "I used the house next door in July for a surveillance. Nice people. Don't care for their Russian neighbors." He let us know, "The Russkies partied all night. Lots of babes. Topless."

Steve got interested. "You never showed me those photos."

Matt smiled. "They're classified."

Tess was rolling her eyes and probably hoping that FBI agents were more refined than ex-cops. Unfortunately, they are. She'll miss us.

Well, this was going to be a long day. One of the first things you learn with surveillance work is piss when you can. There was a tall clump of bulrushes on the side of the road and the boys watered them. Tess was okay for now.

There was no sign of our deli delivery, but a few more cars turned into the Tamorov estate and Steve took pictures. Then a box van turned onto Gin Lane from Old Town Road and came toward us. Behind the van were two more vans. I could see the word CATERING on the side of one van, and I asked Tess, "How many sandwiches did you order?"

She didn't acknowledge my quick wit.

I stepped into the road and held up my hand. The vans stopped, and on the side of the lead van I saw HAMPTON CATERING.

I went to the driver's door and held up my creds. The window lowered and I asked the guy behind the wheel, "Where you going?"

He pointed. "The Tides."

God was either smiling on me, or He was setting me up for a monumental disaster, which He sometimes does. With my help.

I asked the guy, "You need a bartender?"

"No..."

"Sure you do. What's your name?"

"Dean. Dean Hampton. Same as the town."

"That's interesting. Okay, Dean—"

Tess approached and asked me, "What are you doing?"

"I'm going to work for Dean."

"Are you crazy?"

I already answered that question during my FBI interview. I asked Dean, who was wearing a white smock, "You got an extra shirt or something?"

"Uh...yeah. A few in the last truck. But—"

Matt and Steve joined us, and I said to them and to Tess, "You talk to this gentleman and get him squared away." I unhooked my pancake holster, knowing the Russian security guys checked for guns, and I gave my gun and extra magazines to Steve. I also gave Matt my creds and my wallet in case the security guys asked me for ID.

Matt and Steve didn't seem to think that me helping Dean cater Tamorov's party was a good idea, but I explained, "I don't want to lose the target."

Matt pointed out, "We know where he is, John. This is as far as we need to go until he goes mobile again."

"He could be going mobile out the back door."

Steve volunteered, "I'll go in with you."

"They just saw you up close," I reminded him.

Tess reminded me, "They saw *you* flipping them off."

"They'd only recognize my middle finger."

Tess suggested, "You need to clear this with the case agent."

"To ask permission is to invite rejection." I added, "Objections noted. Debate closed."

Matt also volunteered to go in with me, but I said to my team, "You're the posse. I'll text or call in, say, an hour. But if you don't hear from me in two hours, come get me."

Matt and Steve exchanged glances, and Matt asked me, "Should we call the local PD for backup?"

"Only if you feel you can't handle it. Okay, let's not make the caterers late." I headed toward the last van, and Tess came up beside me.

"I'm going in with you."

"That's not what I just told you to do."

She held my arm and said, "This could be dangerous. They could recognize you. But they don't know me, and they don't know we're together. You need someone to watch your back."

I replied patiently, "This is not dangerous. If I'm recognized, they will just ask me to leave and Petrov will file a complaint with the State Department. They will not shoot me and feed me to the sharks."

"But if they do, I'd like to see that."

Funny. But also annoying. On the other hand, as I said, there was more to Tess Faraday than a DSG trainee and FBI wannabe. And maybe the best way to find out why she wanted to work with me and where she got the balls to go in undercover was to take it to the next level. "Okay. Get rid of your creds."

She went back to Steve and gave him her creds, then reached behind her back and pulled out a pancake holster, which she handed to him.

She caught up to me and I inquired, "Where the hell did you get that?"

"I told you I had a gun permit."

That's not exactly what she said.

Tess and I walked toward the last of the three catering vans and I asked her, "Who are you working for?"

"Hampton Catering."

I let that go and opened the double doors of the last box van. Sitting on the floor among piles of catering equipment were eight ladies, all wearing white smocks. "Buenos días," I said as Tess and I climbed in and closed the doors.

There was a pile of linens in the corner and Tess found two uniform shirts, which we put on over our polo shirts.

The van started to move and we sat on the floor with the possibly undocumented aliens who, if they knew English, would probably have nothing to say to the Russian security guys about the two roadside pickups. I asked Tess, "You got a green card?"

The van turned left and we bumped over the cobblestone entrance to Tamorov's driveway, then I heard the crunch of gravel. The van stopped and the doors opened.

One of the Russian security guards motioned everyone out, and we all piled out onto the gravel drive. The other two vans were stopped ahead of us, and the catering staff was standing in the long driveway while two security guards wanded them down.

Tess said softly, "They're taking cell phones."

And sure enough, the security goons were taking everyone's cell phones. Maybe I should have anticipated that. But would that have changed my decision to go undercover? No. But I wouldn't have let my trainee go in with me.

I counted eight security guys, including the two we'd seen at the gate, plus two black Dobermans.

I took my Nextel out of my pocket and code-locked it so no one could access my texts or directory. Tess did the same, and I moved away from her so it wouldn't appear we were together. Though, to be realistic, not too many of the other fifteen or so catering staff looked quite as tall and pink as we did.

The guys with the wands reached the last van and ran the wands over everyone, finding coins, keys, religious medals, and one pocketknife, but no Glock 9mm automatics.

We all put our cell phones in a basket, and a Russian guy assured us, "You get when you leave."

One of the security goons who was at the gate earlier was eyeballing me, then he looked at Tess as though she were a gumdrop in a bowl of chili.

The guy came over to me and said, "Wallet."

"No wallet."

Without even asking, he patted me down. Asshole.

He looked at Tess again, then at me, as though he'd seen me—or my middle finger—before.

Dean, who'd been briefed by Steve and Matt, saw what was happening and came over to us. He said to the Russian, "We have to get moving." He tapped his watch. "We're late."

The Russian hesitated, then motioned us back in the van.

I made a mental note to put Dean in for the good citizen award.

As everyone was getting back into the vans, I looked at the Tamorov mansion at the end of the long landscaped driveway. It was a three-story contemporary, stark white with huge tinted windows for privacy. Georgi Tamorov did all right for himself. I mean, we're talking about forty or fifty million bucks for oceanfront on Gin Lane in Southampton, and maybe a million bucks a year in property taxes, which the town loved without loving the source. Money may not buy you respectability, but it will buy you respect.

Tess and I got back into the van, the doors closed, and we started moving.

I glanced at Tess, who seemed a bit anxious.

Well, we'd have a good laugh about this when we got out of here. Even Kate, who likes to follow the rules, would give me credit for good initiative. Maybe. More importantly, the job and the day were getting interesting. I can make any job interesting. Or stressful.

CHAPTER SEVEN

The three catering vans backed into a five-car garage that held a Jaguar and Bentley. The garage was connected to the service entrance, and everyone got out and started unloading food and equipment. I hefted a crate of tomatoes on my shoulder and walked through a pantry storage room into an industrial-sized kitchen.

There were a few household staff in the kitchen, mostly Hispanic but also a few Russians, including two security guys from the driveway who were watching everyone.

Tess, carrying a load of table linens, didn't look like she did this often, but she'd probably seen the family caterers arrive enough times so she didn't seem too out of place.

After everything was unloaded, we all got to work, slicing and dicing, firing up the stoves, and all that. Tess was in charge of cucumbers and I washed lettuce. I never knew it had to be washed.

A big Russian lady, who seemed to be the household cook, supervised the making of zakuski—Russian hors d'oeuvres, which unfortunately didn't include pigs-in-a-blanket. What kind of party is this? I was starving, so when the fat lady wasn't looking I scooped up about two hundred dollars' worth of beluga caviar with my fingers and shoved it in my mouth.

Tess and I tried to make ourselves useful, but neither of us knew our way around a kitchen and the fat lady yelled at me a few times. The Latina ladies, however, were kind and helpful. Nevertheless, Tess and I sort of stuck out, and I was afraid that our cover was going to be blown. In fact, the two Russian security guys kept eyeing us.

Dean saw that we were clueless, so he made Tess and me his personal assistants, and showed us how to put garnish on the trays. Tess used the opportunity to pop a hard-boiled egg in her mouth. We exchanged glances and she smiled, though I could see she was still anxious about this unplanned undercover assignment.

Within twenty minutes there were enough trays loaded so we could begin serving, and I whispered to Dean, "We'll help serve."

He nodded and gave me a conspiratorial wink. Dean was probably CIA—Culinary Institute of America. And he was a patriot. Two good citizen awards for Dean Hampton.

Tess and I and four catering ladies, carrying trays, followed the fat lady into a service corridor that led out to a sprawling rear deck overlooking the ocean.

The party had already started, and everyone had a glass of champagne in one hand and a cigarette in the other. I looked around for Petrov, but I was distracted by about two dozen young women in bikinis and skimpy cover-ups. The ladies were mingling with paunchy middle-aged men who were dressed mostly in shorts and Hawaiian shirts. There seemed to be no wives present, though it was nice to see that the men had all brought their daughters or nieces. I noticed, too, that everyone was speaking Russian. We're not in New York anymore.

I counted about thirty men, and I also spotted three men in black who were not drinking. Tamorov had lots of security, which meant that he needed it.

There was a tiki bar set up on the deck, and two bartenders who looked Russian were pouring champagne. In the middle of the hundred-foot-long deck was a swimming pool where a few of the ladies were dangling their toes. At the far end of the deck was a hot tub, but no one was in it yet.

I didn't see Petrov or Fradkov, or Dmitry the driver, or Igor the unidentified guy with them, and this gave me a little worry.

Also, I didn't see Georgi Tamorov, whom I would recognize from surveillance photos.

All the servers put their trays on a table, and the Russian men converged like we'd thrown blood into shark-infested waters. We got out of there before we were eaten and returned to the kitchen.

On the way, Tess whispered, "I don't see Petrov or the others."

"Right."

We got more trays, brought them outside, and removed the now empty trays. After about four trips, the food was coming out faster than the porkers could eat it. The women, however, only nibbled.

Meanwhile, Petrov, Fradkov, Tamorov, and Igor still hadn't shown up, but I saw Dmitry, which was a good sign that his boss was still here. Dmitry was now dressed in shorts and sandals, and he was catching up on the champagne, so I assumed he wouldn't be driving for a while.

We were now doing passed hors d'oeuvres, and a few of the Russian guys were flirting with Tess in English, and I heard one guy ask her if she was an hors d'oeuvre or the main course, which was maybe a great line in Moscow.

I, being the only male server, made it my responsibility to see that the young ladies were attended to. And being the only guy there who was taller than he was wide, I became popular with the female guests, who seemed interested in my zakuski. One of them put her champagne glass to my lips and insisted I drink. This didn't happen much in the Mideast section of the Anti-Terrorist Task Force. In fact, never.

On my fifth or sixth trip from the kitchen to the deck I finally saw Petrov. He was sitting at a cocktail table with Fradkov and Igor, and Georgi Tamorov. They were all dressed in shorts and tropical shirts, but only Tamorov was drinking champagne. Petrov, Fradkov, and Igor were drinking what looked like water, though it could have been vodka. Or not. Always watch the guys who are not drinking. If they're not Muslims or AA guys, they have a reason. I looked at Igor, who was staring off into space with his dark, deep-set eyes. He looked like a killer.

I passed around some more zakuski, then went to the bar and said to the bartender, who spoke some English, "More vodka for those gentlemen."

He informed me, "No wood-ka. *Voda,*" and poured three glasses of Russian mineral water from a bottle.

I didn't want to get that close to Petrov, so I asked a server to deliver the drinks.

Well, you can't make too much of men at a party who don't drink alcohol. Sometimes the guy just wants to be standing at the end of the night without worrying about getting Willie to rise to the occasion and do his duty.

Back in the kitchen, Dean handed me another tray and asked, "How's it going?"

"Great." I asked, "How long are you on?"

"About midnight." He informed me, "When the sun goes down, the party starts to get a little wild. Skinny-dipping and stuff."

"Do we all get naked?"

Dean forced a smile, probably wondering what government agency I was with. I'd have shown my creds again, but I came in here clean. Regarding that, Tess and I had been here about two hours, and I knew I had to contact Matt and Steve or they'd be busting through the gates with the local police.

The two kitchen security guys were sitting at a table, eating pickles and watching a Russian-language soccer match on a flat-screen TV.

I asked Dean, "Can I use the phone?"

"No."

"Can *you* use the phone? Like, what if you needed more pickled herring or something?"

"I guess..."

"I'll give you a number to call. You'll talk to Matt. Tell him about the cell phones and that J&T are okay, and we'll keep Vaseline under the eye until the caterers leave."

Dean glanced at the security guys.

"You understand that this is a matter of national security?"

He nodded.

I gave him Matt's cell phone number and he repeated it.

I took my tray out to the deck, where Tess was now the cocktail waitress, going around with a tray of champagne glasses.

I informed her, "Dean says everyone gets naked later."

"What the hell did you get me into?"

"You volunteered," I reminded her.

She moved off with her tray of bubbly.

Indeed, this was a day of things not being what they seemed. Tess Faraday was not a serving girl, and maybe she wasn't working with me because she liked me. And it was obvious that her frequent trips to the ladies' room while on surveillance were also occasions to make a phone call—probably to her husband, but maybe to someone else. And Vasily Petrov was not a Human Rights delegate to the U.N., and maybe he wasn't here for the party.

At the end of every masquerade, the masks come off and you know who's who. And when you know who's who, you know what's what.

CHAPTER EIGHT

Another hour or so passed, and the gentlemen were getting shit-faced and the ladies were knocking down the bubbly to make these guys more interesting.

I took a break and stood at the rail, looking out at the ocean. A few motor craft and sailboats ran parallel to the shore, and jetliners cut across the blue sky. A biplane flew low, dragging a banner that read SUNDAY NIGHT SUNDOWNERS AT SAMMY'S SEA-SIDE GRILL. I'll keep that in mind.

I was aware that someone was standing to my left, and I glanced over to see a young lady in a cover-up, her elbows on the rail, gazing out to sea, holding a glass of champagne. Her skin was paper white and her long, straight black hair fell past her shoulders.

She looked at me with big brown eyes, smiled, and pointed in the direction we were facing, toward the south. "Rooshia."

I corrected her geography and pointed east. "That way."

"Yes? So long away."

"Right. But Russia is here today."

She laughed. After a moment, she said, "I am Tasha."

"I'm John." I translated, "Ivan."

Again she laughed, but she looked a bit sad or wistful. I guess if I had to sleep with one of these guys, I'd feel a little blue myself.

She held her glass toward me. "Champagne?"

"I'm on duty." I asked her, "How can I contact you after work?"

She gave me her cell phone number.

Before I could ask her if she was a Pisces, I felt a tap on my shoulder and turned to see Tess' unsmiling face. She said curtly, "We need to return to the kitchen."

"I still have zakuski—"

She handed me an empty tray. "Let's go."

I bid Tasha, "Das vidanya," and followed Tess. I explained to Mrs. Faraday, "I was getting her phone number because she's a potential witness to interview tomorrow."

Tess seemed to buy part of that—though it was all true—but she said, "The security guys were looking at you."

"Don't be as paranoid as the Russians."

Back in the kitchen I caught Dean's eye and glanced toward the wall phone. He gave me a nod.

Tess and I grabbed trays, and on the way out I told her, "Dean called Matt from the kitchen phone and relayed my situation report."

"I hope the phones aren't monitored internally."

"Good paranoia." I also informed her, "Petrov, Fradkov, and Igor are not drinking."

She seemed to understand that could have some significance and she nodded.

I told her, "If Petrov is still here when the caterers leave, I'm going to duck into a closet or something and stay here."

"John, they counted everyone coming in and they will count everyone going out."

"True... but—"

"We leave here together."

"Actually, you'll do what I tell you—"

"I don't know how you survived this long."

"Balls and brains." I reminded her, "I am a legend."

"Don't push it."

We came out on the deck and Tess walked away from me and held out a tray of eggs à la Russe to a Russe, who popped one in his mouth and popped another into Tess' mouth. I hoped she was having fun.

I worked the poolside where a few of the ladies, including Tasha, were now lying in chaises, chatting in Russian with one another, probably about what a great party this would be if they didn't have to fuck all the guests.

I offered Tasha my hot kolbasa, but she declined, then pantomimed holding a phone to her ear and mouthed, "Call me." The other ladies giggled.

One of the security guys caught all this, and he fixed me with a stare.

The feeding frenzy seemed to have subsided for now, and a few bloated gentlemen floated in the pool on inflatable rafts. A half dozen men and women went down to the beach and cavorted in the surf. One guy was lying motionless on a chaise in the sand, and a seagull checked him out to see if he was possibly dead and edible.

I suppose you could say that the Russians had a big appetite for life, or you could say they were dissolute and decadent, which was the opposite side of the same ruble. In either case, they were becoming more confident in themselves and their country. Rarely has an empire fallen so quickly, then experienced such an equally fast resurgence. They should be happy with that, and happier that we didn't kick them when they were down. But it seemed to me that Putin and his goons were still pissed off that we knocked them down in the first place. So we weren't going to be buddies soon.

Meanwhile, the diplomatic and security apparatus in Washington was obsessed with Islamic terrorists and distracted enough not to notice all of this. Or if they did, it wasn't a priority. The Russians, however, were making it a priority to fuck America. When I saw people like Petrov, and when I compared them to the Islamists I spent years following and investigating, I had no doubt who was the most dangerous.

The afternoon slipped into early evening, and the sun was dropping into the western sky. I noted that the bartenders were serving mostly hard stuff now, but Petrov was content with nursing his mineral water, as were Fradkov and Igor. Georgi Tamorov, however, was knocking down a few shots of iced vodka, as was Dmitry, who must have known he wasn't driving back to the city tonight.

It was possible, I conceded, that Petrov and his companions were actually just here for the party. That made more sense than anything else I might suspect or imagine. Or, if there *was* something else going on, it would go down later, behind closed doors, and I'd never know about it. Especially since they were all speaking Russian. And whatever they were up to, it would most probably have nothing to do with American national security; it would have to do with money, or with Georgi Tamorov asking Vasily Petrov for a favor, which was usually the deal when a rich oligarch sucked up to someone like Colonel Petrov of the SVR. Tamorov probably wanted one of his competitors to meet with an unfortunate accident. A million Swiss francs should get the job done.

According to the intel on Georgi Tamorov, he was spending more time in New York and London, and he was tied to the economic interests of the West. Money protects its money, and people like Colonel Petrov made people like Georgi Tamorov nervous. And yet they were here together, and not for the first time. Why?

I used to watch Mafia guys when I was on the Organized Crime Task Force, and it was sometimes hard to figure out who was selling and who was buying. So the other possibility here was that Georgi Tamorov was not looking to buy something from Colonel Petrov—it was Petrov who was selling something to Tamorov. Like his life. Like, Georgi Tamorov would be a lot safer if Colonel Petrov was watching his back. Or maybe Petrov was sent here by the Kremlin to whack Tamorov, who had somehow pissed them off.

The possibilities of why the billionaire oligarch and the SVR assassin were palling around were endless. But as I said, thinking about this was not in my limited job description.

I looked again at Vasily Petrov in the fading light. He did not look like a man who'd come for the party. And if he'd made his deal with Tamorov, he should be leaving. But he wasn't. It seemed instead that he was waiting for something, or someone.

My instincts told me that I had made the right move to stick close to this guy.

Petrov caught my eye and held up his glass.

I went to the bar and got him another mineral water and he stared at me as I handed it to him on a tray.

"What is your name?" he asked.

"Johnny Depp."

He kept looking at me, then turned away and said something to Igor in Russian.

Igor nodded and stared at me.

As a former homicide cop, I know a killer when I see one, and I just saw one.

CHAPTER NINE

It was twilight time, and the household staff lit tonga torches and hurricane lamps, illuminating the sprawling deck in flickering light. The sound system crackled, and Bobby Darin started singing, *Somewhere beyond the sea*... Setting the mood for love and romance.

The ladies' tops had come off in the hot tub, and a few of the Russian gentlemen had gone au naturel in the swimming pool. Thank God my wife was not here to see this. Or Grant for that matter, who would not approve of his wife passing drinks to naked men in the swimming pool. One oaf, floating on a raft with his periscope up, tried to grab Tess' arm as she handed him a drink, but she was too nimble for him.

The Latina serving ladies seemed indifferent to the bare butts in the pool and the bobbing boobs in the hot tub; and they went about their business, even as the Russian gentlemen tried to entice the younger of the señoritas into the pool. I mean, there were two dozen Russian ladies who'd been hired for this, but men always want what they can't buy. On that subject, a few of the men had gone into the house accompanied by a young lady, who presumably had been prepaid by the host to provide services.

Tess and I were at the bar, getting drink orders, and she whispered to me, "This is getting a little uncomfortable."

"No job is perfect." I suggested, "Think of it as a Wall Street Christmas party."

"I'm going to stay in the kitchen."

"Whatever makes you comfortable."

She hesitated, then said, "I'll stay with you."

I hadn't seen any sign of drugs and I smelled no pot, and the girls all seemed to be of age, so I assumed that Georgi Tamorov knew not to compromise his U.N. guests. Thus, even if I was on the vice squad, I'd have to conclude that nothing really illegal was going on here—especially if the ladies were doing it for love.

It would be good, though, if we could compromise Petrov and get him booted out of the country, which would make our unpaid labor worthwhile. Meanwhile, I have to serve drinks to topless ladies.

The speakers were now blaring, *Jeremiah was a bullfrog,* and I felt like dancing. In fact, a few corpulent gentlemen were gyrating on the deck with a few of the ladies, who seemed intent on drinking these guys handsome. The bad light helped.

Our drink orders were ready, and as Tess and I moved off with our trays, five ladies, led by Tasha, lined up at the edge of the pool, took off their tops, then slid off their bottoms and dived into the pool in unison, which got a round of applause.

Tess said, "This is too much. John? *John?*"

"Huh? Oh…I can't watch. I need better light."

She made a sound of disgust and walked away from me.

Anyway, the music switched to Russian nightclub music, like Pitbull, the drinking and dancing continued, and more people got naked in the pool or the hot tub. Tasha and a few of the other ladies were now sitting on the hairy shoulders of the guys in the pool, playing some sort of game with a beach ball. I couldn't figure out the rules, but it looked like everyone was a winner.

Tamorov was still knocking down frozen vodka and smoking up a storm, but Petrov and his two companions just sat there, making perfunctory conversation, barely noticing the naked ladies. Clearly they had more important things on their minds. In fact, I noticed that Fradkov seemed almost nervous, though Igor appeared calm and alert, like a pit bull waiting for a command. Petrov glanced at his watch, then checked his cell phone for a text.

Tess came up to me and said, "They're laying out another buffet, so I'm going to the kitchen."

"Okay."

"Are you coming?"

"I'm still on surveillance."

"Take a break, John. You'll get eyestrain and go blind."

"Right. We need more tonga torches."

Naked Tasha was kneeling on a guy's shoulders, her arms outstretched, waiting for a beach ball pass. The pass came, wide, she reached for it and fell into the water, and everyone laughed. I wondered how much of this I should put in my surveillance log. That reminded me that I had to call Tasha tomorrow.

"John? Are you coming?"

"You go ahead."

She turned toward the house, but I said, "Hold on."

"What?"

I tilted my head toward the ocean and she followed my gaze.

Coming toward us were the running lights of a watercraft, maybe a hundred yards from shore, and as the craft got closer I could hear its motor. I also noticed that one of Tamorov's security guys was on the beach, holding a flashing green light.

I looked toward Petrov and saw in the flickering lamp light that he was standing, along with Fradkov and Igor. Tamorov, too, was standing, and he was now barking orders in Russian to his security guys. Dmitry, Petrov's driver, stayed in the pool, as though he'd been pre-instructed to stay put.

Tess asked, "What's happening?"

"Don't know. But Petrov does."

The security guys were quickly rounding up some of the Russian ladies, who were slipping back into their bikinis and cover-ups, grabbing their bags, and assembling near the steps that led down to the beach.

The boat got closer and I could see by the light of the rising half-moon that it was maybe twenty-five feet, with an open deck and a man steering from the covered cockpit, and another man sitting beside him.

Tess observed, "It's heading right to the shore."

"Seems so."

"Who are they?"

"Don't know."

I didn't sense any danger, and it was obvious that the boat was expected. Nevertheless, it was times like this when a boy missed his gun. I said to Tess, "Go back to the kitchen. See if you can get a call off to Matt. We need aviation and harbor units."

She hesitated, then said, "Let me see what's going on so I know what to say."

I didn't want to argue with her, and in any case I doubted she'd be able to use the phone.

The security guys on the deck began motioning to the dozen or so women, including Tasha, to descend the stairs.

I moved nonchalantly toward the women, collecting empty glasses on my way. Tess followed.

Tasha was about to go down the stairs and I got close to her and asked softly, "Where are you going?"

She looked at me and shrugged. One of the security guys came between us and nudged her toward the stairs.

The women all descended the long wooden staircase to the beach. Some of them seemed indifferent, and some seemed unhappy about leaving the party, but most of them appeared to be excited about what looked like a boat trip. Maybe Tasha thought she was going back to Russia.

The security guy motioned for me and Tess to get back to work.

Tess and I moved to the far end of the deck into a dark corner and watched as the women walked across the wide beach toward the water. The boat was about ten yards offshore, and as it got closer, I could see it had a blunt bow and a wide beam—the sort of watercraft that was more of a ship's tender or utility boat than a sports boat.

Tamorov's guests, including the dozen or so ladies who'd been left behind, were now lined up along the rail, chatting away, laughing, waving, and calling out to their friends on the beach, who waved back.

I glanced at where Petrov, Fradkov, and Igor had been standing and they were gone. Then I saw them coming out of the sliding glass doors of the house, dressed now in pants and polo shirts and carrying their overnight bags. Without so much as a good-bye to their host, they headed for the staircase. This was not good.

I looked back at the boat and saw it hit the beach. I expected someone to throw a line to or from the craft, but all of a sudden the boat started to climb the beach and I saw it was an amphibious craft. The wheels kicked up sand as the flat-bottomed craft got traction and drove onto the shore, then stopped. I saw, too, that there were no markings on the shiny white fiberglass hull—no name and no numbers—which was odd, if not illegal, and again I had the impression of a ship's tender.

The security guys herded the women toward the boat and they began boarding via a short ladder that hung over the side. The second guy onboard was helping the tipsy ladies up and directing them to sit on the benches that ran along the sides and stern.

Petrov, Fradkov, and Igor were on the beach now, heading toward the amphibious craft. Within a few minutes they were onboard and the craft made a U-turn on the beach and returned to the water.

Tess said, "I think you just lost your Russian."

CHAPTER TEN

Tess and I moved quickly to the kitchen and I went straight for the wall phone and dialed Steve's number. On the second ring, a hairy hand reached over my shoulder and hit the cradle.

I glanced back at the big Russian and explained, "I need more mushrooms."

"No call."

Yob vas.

Okay, so Tess and I made busy in the kitchen for a minute, then I said to Dean, "We need to split."

He nodded. "Carry those crates of dirty napkins to the truck."

I grabbed a crate and so did Tess, and we headed for the service entrance.

The two security guys gave us a quick glance, then went back to their MTV show.

Outside in the garage, we ditched the linens and considered our next move. There was no way we were getting through the gates, so we had to jump the fence of the adjoining property.

We pulled off our caterer smocks, threw them in one of the trucks, and moved quickly out of the garage.

Tamorov's house was separated from the next beach house by thick shrubs, behind which I could make out a high fence. I glanced down the driveway and saw the two security guys, about a hundred feet away, sitting in chairs under the post lights of the iron gates. The Dobermans were with them.

Tess said, "Go for it."

I dashed across the gravel driveway and into the shrubbery with Tess right beside me. The Dobermans, who were smarter and more alert than their handlers, started barking.

I found my way through the landscaping and reached the wood-slat fence, which was about eight feet high, and Tess and I started climbing it just as the Dobermans got into the shrubbery. I wished I'd thought to bring five feet of kolbasa with me.

Anyway, we got over the fence, and the dogs were left sniffing our trail and letting out a few tentative barks.

The neighboring oceanfront mansion that Matt said he'd used for surveillance looked dark, but some security lighting, probably activated by motion sensors, came on and lit up the area.

I could hear the dogs barking again on the other side of the fence, and I also heard voices speaking Russian.

Tess informed me, "There's a public beach access path to Gin Lane a few houses down."

We ran toward the shore at high speed, angling away from Tamorov's house, then scrambled over a dune and found ourselves on the beach. I looked out at the water, but I couldn't see the running lights of the amphibious landing craft. I glanced back at Tamorov's house, about a hundred yards away, and could make out people moving on his tonga-lit deck.

I didn't see anyone following us, and no one was on the beach. We turned east, away from Tamorov's house, and broke into a trot, as though we were just jogging the moonlit beach.

Tess said, "Past the next house is the beach access to Gin Lane." She reminded me, "I know this area."

She also knew a little about escape and evasion, as though she'd been trained—or maybe she picked it up being married to Grant.

We reached the access path, which took us between two mansions up to Gin Lane. I saw our vehicles still parked where we'd left them, closer to the Tamorov house, and we doubled back toward them.

Steve and Matt jumped out of the van with their guns drawn, then recognized us. "What's happening?"

"Petrov took off in a boat."

"Shit!"

Steve asked, "You being chased?"

"No. Give me your phone."

He holstered his Glock and gave me his Nextel. I accessed his directory, looking for the number of Scott Kalish, a Suffolk County Police captain with the Marine Bureau who used to be one of my ATTF contacts out here. "You don't have Scott Kalish."

Matt said, "I've got him," and speed-dialed Kalish's number and handed me his phone.

Tess suggested, "You need to call the case agent or the duty agent."

"No, I need to find that boat now."

Scott Kalish answered, and I said, "Scott, this is John Corey."

"Hey, John. What's up?"

"I need some help."

"We're here to serve and protect."

"Good. Look, I'm with the DSG now—"

"Who?"

"Diplomatic Surveillance Group."

"No kidding?"

"I'm in Southampton, Gin Lane, following a Russian dip—"

"I'm home watching Law and Order reruns."

"Great. And this dip just gave me the slip."

"That sucks."

"Right." I gave Captain Kalish a short briefing of my long day, then said, "The amphibious craft was heading due south from Tamorov's. White hull, no markings, two-man crew, maybe twenty-five feet, covered cockpit, open deck, inboard motor, making about ten knots."

"He could be a couple miles from shore by now."

"Right. So let's get some of your Suffolk County Marine Bureau units and aviation on it now."

"Okay... and *who* was onboard?"

"Colonel Vasily Petrov, SVR Legal Resident, and two of his guys, Pavel Fradkov and an unknown—"

"I got *that*. Did you say twelve young ladies in bikinis?"

I rolled my eyes. "Right."

"Hey, I'm joining the search."

"Scott—"

"All right, I'll get on it. What's the beef?"

"Just pick up the surveillance. The target has diplomatic immunity—"

"I know." He asked, "Any crime committed or suspected?"

"Well... maybe drugs," I lied. "Maybe a few of the girls are underage. Also the three Russians are past their twenty-five-mile radius without permission." Also, Petrov gave me the finger, but this wasn't a personal beef. Well... all surveillance becomes personal.

"So we just locate and follow."

"Right. No bust."

"Okay. I'll also call the harbor constables in the area."

"Good, but I don't think that craft is going to make port, Scott. I think it's on its way to a big ship."

"How do you know?"

"I didn't see him turn to run along the shore when he left."

"Sometimes a boat goes out to get away from the surf and sandbars."

"Right, but—"

"From what you've told me, John, it sounds like these Russkies are going from one party to another party." He reminded me, "Twelve babes onboard."

"Right. But the party could be on a *ship*."

"Could be," he conceded. "Lots of high rollers out here go outside the three-mile limit. Gambling, drugs, prostitutes. Hijinks on the high seas."

"Right. So let's locate that craft—"

"But it's an amphibious craft, so he could make land anywhere he can climb ashore."

"I know, Scott, that's why it's called an amphibious craft. But I think—"

"I sense some urgency in your voice, John. What's the problem?"

"I just lost the fucking guy I was supposed to be following."

"Right. It happens."

"Not to me."

"Okay…so there's no national security issue."

That was the thing that Scott Kalish, an Anti-Terrorist Task Force liaison guy, would want to know for sure. I didn't want to blow any more smoke up his butt, so I answered, somewhat truthfully, "I have no direct knowledge of that. But Petrov is SVR."

"You said. Okay, I'll give this a high priority and say maybe the SVR guy is up to something and we need to mobilize all resources. But basically, what I'm hearing is that I'm just helping you out of a tight spot."

"Right. I owe you."

"I've already made a note of it." He asked me, "What happens when you lose your target?"

"Professionally, not too much. Personally, I go into a deep depression."

Kalish laughed, then assured me, "If this amphibious craft comes to shore anywhere around here—a marina, a yacht club, a private dock, or even up on the beach like a D-Day landing—we'll find him."

"I know you will. But I'm really thinking the craft is going to rendezvous with a ship at sea." I explained, logically, "If Petrov was going to a party on land, he'd have taken his car and driver. He doesn't need a landing craft, Scott."

"He needs the landing craft to deliver the twelve babes. Or the party's on an island."

"Think ship."

"That would have to be a very big ship to take a twenty-five-foot craft aboard."

"Then look for a big ship."

"Or maybe this craft was just ferrying these people out to a small ship."

"Then look for a small ship."

"Okay. Are you going to ask your people to call the Coast Guard?"

"Let's keep it in the family."

"Right. What the bosses don't know, they don't know." He assured me, "We can handle it for you."

"Good." I gave him Matt and Steve's Nextel numbers, explaining why I didn't have my phone, and told him, "I'll have Matt's phone."

Scott suggested, "Go back to Tamorov's place and squeeze some nuts." He offered, "I can send a few detectives with you based on your suspicion of illegal activity."

I'd thought about that, but I doubted if Georgi Tamorov knew where Petrov was going. SVR guys, like the CIA, do not give out information—only disinformation. And neither would Dmitry know where his boss was heading. But they might know *something.* I said to Kalish, "I'll get back to you on that."

"All right. And thanks for your confidence in the Suffolk County Police Department, and for fucking up my Sunday night."

"Anytime."

"And John...?"

"Yeah?"

"Don't wait too long to call your boss. That's how we get in more trouble than we're in."

I didn't reply and we signed off. Thanks for the tip, Scott.

Well, this was not the first time I engaged in multi-tasking—covering my ass while covering the problem. But this could be the last time. A quiet end, indeed.

CHAPTER ELEVEN

Tess Faraday seemed not happy that I'd called the cops before I called 26 Fed. Steve and Matt seemed okay with that, and they trusted me to do the right thing—which was to cover all our asses.

More importantly, I got the wheels moving, and no one could find fault with that. The Diplomatic Surveillance Group has access to FBI resources, but those resources weren't immediately available out here on the east end of Long Island. And in any case the wheels of the Feds moved slowly—and sometimes in the wrong direction. Captain Scott Kalish, like all local cops, could get things moving, and he knew his beat. In fact, that was the purpose of the Anti-Terrorist Task Force: to form alliances and liaisons between the Feds and the local law enforcement agencies—synergy, they called it—to combat domestic terrorism. True, Vasily Petrov wasn't a terrorist and I wasn't with the ATTF anymore, but Petrov *was* an asshole, and today he had become my hemorrhoid.

Steve said to me, "You made the right move to go undercover, boss. But before too long, we need to call this in."

I didn't reply.

Matt pointed out, "If John hadn't gone in there, we'd all be sitting here waiting for the black Mercedes to come out of Tamorov's driveway." He added, "So we have that going for us, and maybe the Suffolk PD will spot the boat, then we just pick up the surveillance where we left off."

I was also a little pissed off at myself for not covering this with an air or sea surveillance craft. But as I said, the Russians did not get the full treatment the way the Islamic guys did. Scott Kalish, too, didn't get all worked up about the Russians the way he would have about an Islamic intelligence agent going off in a boat. This was a perception problem; the Russians did not murder three thousand people on 9/11. And these three Russians had a dozen babes with them, which looked more like Russian hijinks than a security issue. And probably that's all it was—a party.

I advised everyone, "I'll give it an hour." Cops understand how to adjust the timelines so it doesn't appear that anyone failed to make a timely report. I mean, sometimes you need a little time to cover your butt and get your stories straight. Also, to call the case agent now would start a pissing match between the Feds and the local police—a turf war, which always led to chaos and confusion, and never to synergy. I was working for the Feds, but I was still Detective John Corey.

I looked at Tess, who was not a cop, and who wanted to be a Fed. She could be a problem.

But she's bright and savvy and she understood all of this, so she said, "I have no idea what the protocol is, and I wasn't in the room when you three were talking."

Good enough.

I asked Steve, "You hear from the office?"

"Just a text asking me why you didn't reply to the CA's last text. I said you were catching some Zs. Also we got an ID on Igor. He's Viktor Gorsky, an SVR agent."

"No surprise."

"Right. He just got here, like, two weeks ago, and he works in Petrov's office."

"That sounds like a scary Human Rights office."

"And according to the intel he worked with Petrov in Chechnya."

I nodded, recalling what Colonel Petrov was reported to have done in Chechnya. When bad actors get together, bad things happen.

Steve also informed me and Tess, "The CA will get a relief team out here at first light if we're still here waiting for Petrov to come out of Tamorov's house."

"Okay. And I assume you didn't mention that I was moonlighting with Hampton Catering."

"It didn't come up."

I nodded. My undercover mission, like most rule-bending, showed either poor judgment or good initiative. To be determined. But all's well that ends well. Or it doesn't.

I asked, "Did the deli delivery ever get here?"

"Yeah, but we ate your sandwiches," Matt admitted.

I suggested, "When the catering trucks come out of Tamorov's, about midnight, talk to Dean and tell him he did a good job, but if he breathes one f-ing word of this to anyone, he's toast. And get his personals."

"Right, and maybe some leftovers."

I continued, "If the Mercedes comes out, call Suffolk PD and have it pulled over for some violation, then call me. Same if any other vehicle leaves Tamorov's."

Steve asked, "You going someplace?"

"I need gas." I said to Tess, "You can stay here, or you can come with me."

"I'm yours."

"Okay." I told Matt, "I'll keep your phone."

Tess and I retrieved our creds, my wallet, her bag, and our guns and ammo, and we got in the Chevy Blazer with her at the wheel. I suggested to her, "Tell me about your gun."

She started the Blazer. "I'm licensed."

"By whom?"

"We can discuss this later."

She moved slowly up Gin Lane, past the Tamorov house. The two security guys, now back in their chairs, gave us a look and the Dobermans barked.

I dialed Tasha's number, but the call went right into voice mail—English and Russian. I didn't leave a message and hung up. I got Kalish back on the phone and said, "I have a cell phone number onboard the target craft."

"That makes life easier."

I gave him Tasha's number and Kalish said, "I'll get the location triangulated, but I gotta tell you it's not that easy if they're still on water." He asked, "Whose phone is that?"

"Tasha." I explained my professional interest in Tasha, and also advised Kalish that all the ladies' phones might have been confiscated and maybe had their batteries removed. But to be more optimistic, I said, "Petrov has no idea that two DSG agents saw him take off in a boat, and he has no idea that I have the cell phone number of one of the ladies onboard. So even if he confiscated the phones, he might not bother to remove the batteries."

"We'll give it a try. Meanwhile, I've got boats and aviation rolling."

"Thanks." We signed off.

Tess said, "If Petrov didn't remove the batteries, he needs to go back to spy school."

"I've had suspects who've done stupider things."

"Were they Russian intelligence agents?"

I asked her, "Did you learn your tradecraft on Wall Street?"

"I watch spy movies."

On the subject of cell phones, mine and hers were in a basket waiting for us to reclaim them from Tamorov's security guys. When we didn't—or long before that—they'd realize two catering staff skipped out. But what would they make of that? And would the security guys mention it to Tamorov? Not if they wanted to keep their jobs. That's how the Russkies think and act. Us, too, sometimes.

As for the phones themselves, they were code-locked and useless, but I wouldn't be surprised if I saw them for sale in Brighton Beach.

On that subject, no matter how this played out tonight, I'd have to let 26 Fed know how we'd lost our government Nextels. More paperwork. But more importantly, people couldn't get hold of us, which was not necessarily a bad thing.

I asked Tess, "You want to call your husband?"

"Later."

She drove back to Montauk Highway and pulled into a local no-name two-pump gas station with the highest gas prices in North America. I got out and gassed up on my government credit card. I suggested to Tess that this would be a good time to use the restroom, but she suggested we go to a nearby diner.

She headed west on Montauk Highway and pulled into the parking lot of the Southampton Diner, a twenty-four-hour place that I'd been to, and a place where Tess said she'd had many sunrise breakfasts after an all-night party. Nothing like coffee and bacon fat to sober you up.

We went inside the upscale diner, which was mostly empty on this Sunday night in September. I checked my watch—9:21 P.M. I was deep into overtime with no end in sight.

We got a quiet booth in the corner, but before Tess sat, she said, "I need to use the restroom."

"I'll get you a coffee."

"I need to borrow your phone."

"I have to make some calls. Use the pay phone."

"I want to text Grant."

I handed her Matt's phone and she headed for the restrooms.

Well, by now I'm thinking that Tess Faraday is working a second job. Let's see...she carries a gun, she knows the ropes too well, and she disappears a lot to use the restroom. If she was with the FBI Office of Professional Responsibility, I'd be answering some questions at 26 Fed about how I handled this surveillance.

But I'd been around FBI people for a lot of years now, and Tess Faraday did not strike me as one of the Fabulously Boring Individuals, as the cops called the FBI. She had a different demeanor—a sort of panache—plus she didn't use any mind-numbing FBI jargon.

The waitress came with two menus and I ordered two coffees.

I finished mine and still no sign of Tess, who was either having bladder problems or husband problems. Or neither.

The Southampton Diner had a liquor license, thank God, and I ordered my next coffee with a shot of medicinal brandy. I think you can drink on overtime.

I calculated Kalish's chances of finding that amphibious craft, or finding the ship it rendezvoused with, or the place where the craft had come ashore. The chances were good that the craft would be found, and that Petrov would also be found. But if not, Petrov and his two goons would probably show up back at Tamorov's for a morning car ride back to the city. I mean, his car and driver were at Tamorov's, so why was I overthinking this? The simplest explanation for what you see is the explanation.

And yet...I kept thinking of Petrov, Fradkov, and the newly IDed

Viktor Gorsky, an SVR agent, sitting on Tamorov's deck, not seeming to be in a party mood.

Or I was imagining things—hoping I had stumbled onto something big.

If Kate was here, that's what she'd say. But she'd also listen and evaluate the evidence and play devil's advocate. I thought about calling her, but she'd just tell me to call 26 Fed immediately and ask forgiveness for not calling earlier. She had an FBI head, and now a supervisor's head. Plus, she didn't want to hear anything from me that she might be asked about by her boss, Tom Walsh, who was a certified asshole.

Tess returned and I inquired, "How's the home front?"

"Okay."

"Who else did you call?"

"I said I was texting."

"Right. Who else did you text?"

"I canceled my morning pedicure." She picked up her menu. "I'm hungry."

"When do I find out who you're working for?"

"Are you hungry?"

"I'm hungry for an answer."

She looked up from her menu and we made eye contact. She said to me, "He told me you were very bright."

"*Who* told you?"

"An old friend of yours."

"I asked you a direct question, counselor. Who are you working for?"

"You actually asked me *when* you'd find out. The answer is tonight."

"When tonight?"

"Shortly." She assured me, "You have time for a burger."

"That's the good news."

"That's the only good news."

CHAPTER TWELVE

We both ordered burgers and fries and I told the waitress, "Two Buds."

Tess reminded me, "We're on duty."

"We're on overtime."

The waitress brought two bottles of Budweiser and Tess asked her, "How'd the Mets do today?"

"Won both."

Tess held out her bottle and tapped mine. "Told you."

She looked around the diner, then leaned toward me and said, "Regarding what you said to Captain Kalish, don't be so sure that Petrov didn't know who we were."

I didn't reply.

She continued, "Also, they picked up on your interest in Tasha."

"They would take it as a personal interest."

"Not if they thought you were one of the DSG guys who followed them from the city." She asked, "Don't you think that crossed their minds?"

"Are you suggesting that they took Tasha aboard for that reason?"

She didn't reply directly to my question, but said, "The way I see it, we're lucky we weren't asked to come inside the house for a chat. Followed by a one-way boat ride."

"You watch too many spy movies."

She poured some beer in her glass and watched the foam rise. She said, "The SVR is neither stupid nor forgiving." She smiled. "Maybe I watch too many spy movies."

I changed the subject and asked, "Where do you think that craft was going?"

"I don't know. You could make a case for it rendezvousing with a ship at sea. Or you could make a case for it putting in on shore. In either case, it appears that Petrov was just party-hopping."

"Right. Bring your own babes."

"And he'll be back at Tamorov's later tonight or in the morning."

"Right."

"And," she continued, "if we hadn't gone in there, we wouldn't even know we lost the target and we wouldn't be worrying about it."

"Correct. But we did, and we are."

"You've followed Petrov before." She asked, "Do you think he's up to something?"

"That's why he's here, Tess."

"I understand that. But I mean something *tonight.*"

"I have no direct or indirect knowledge of that."

"But if he was into something very big, what would it be?"

Well, Colonel Vasily Petrov is a killer, but Tess Faraday, DSG trainee, wouldn't know that, though Tess Faraday working for someone else would. And since I didn't know who she was, I replied, "That's way above my pay grade."

"But you worked the Mideast section of the ATTF for many years and your job was to think, to analyze, to make an informed guess about what the bad guys were up to."

"They weren't Russians."

"All bad guys are the same."

"The Russians are a little more subtle than Abdul." I reminded her, "They're not terrorists."

"But you do agree they are the enemy?"

"No one ever used that word in any of my briefings."

"It's understood."

It seemed to me that Mrs. Faraday had something on her mind—like she had learned something during her long visit to the ladies' room that was, as she indicated, not good news. Well, no use wondering about it since I was sure I was going to hear about it soon, so I changed the subject again and asked her, "What did you learn today?"

"Well, I learned that when you have a problem, you call the police."

"Right. And when you *want* a problem, you call the FBI."

She smiled. "You can take a cop out of the street, but you can't take the street out of the cop."

"That's why they hired me."

She sipped her beer, and said, "I like you."

"Is that you talking or the beer?"

"That's me talking to the beer."

I smiled.

She asked, "So what happens if you lose a target?"

"As I told Kalish, not too much the first time. But you shouldn't make it a habit. And you shouldn't lose the SVR Legal Resident anytime."

"You went above and beyond on this one."

"Catering is a bitch," I agreed.

Our burgers came, I ordered two more beers, and we picked at our fries.

Tess asked, "Are you going to call the CA?"

"If this was a training exercise, Mrs. Faraday, and I was your instructor, I would advise you to communicate *up* the chain of command, starting with the guy on the street."

"Show me how it's done."

I texted Steve: Anything to report?

A few seconds later, he replied: Negative.

I then texted Kalish: Anything?

He replied: I'll let you know when there is.

Tess suggested, "You need to *call* the case agent."

"Right." I turned my wristwatch toward me, explaining, "This is a two-way radio." I said into my watch, "Corey calling home base. Come in home base." I listened, but there was no response.

Tess called for the check and said to me, "You're getting yourself in deeper. Just call and explain the situation, and tell them you have it covered. That's all they want to hear."

"I'd like to be able to tell them that the Suffolk PD has located the target."

"I'd like to be five pounds thinner."

I'd like to have a bigger dick. I said to her, "I'm thinking that we should get on a harbor launch or chopper and join the search." I explained, "It looks good."

"If it looks good, it *is* good. But first..." She glanced at her watch. "I'd like to reunite you with that old friend."

I didn't even bother to ask who, where, or why. I paid the bill, and we left the diner and got into the Blazer.

She headed east on Montauk Highway, and I said to her, "This better be important."

"You know it is."

Okay. So my trainee had gone into the phone booth and come out Superman. Amazing.

Obviously there was more going on tonight than even I knew. And I was about to find out what it was. Or did Ms. Faraday have more tricks up her sleeve? Stay tuned.

CHAPTER THIRTEEN

Tess took a right onto a small road and continued past a sign that said SHINNECOCK NATION—NO TRESPASSING.

I pointed out, "You're in Indian territory."

"We're meeting here. For a powwow."

"Okay." The FBI, as I indicated, could be a bit dull, but these people—and I don't mean the Indians—were into drama and stagecraft.

The road was narrow, bumpy, and dark, and Tess slowed down. She said to me, apropos of nothing and something, "The charter of the Central Intelligence Agency expressly forbids the Agency from operating on American soil. Therefore, as you know, when the CIA has a person of interest who lands on American soil, they have to share the case with the FBI. The FBI, on the other hand, can legally operate in foreign countries." She reminded me, "You, for instance, and your wife were posted to Yemen."

I didn't recall telling her that. But I did recall Yemen. And I knew why she mentioned it. And now I thought I knew who this old friend was. So I slipped my Glock out of my pancake holster and stuck it in my pocket.

She continued, "And then we have State Department Intelligence, which confines its activities to diplomatic spying, including so-called diplomats who are actually spies, such as Vasily Petrov."

I inquired, "Is there a point to this monologue?"

She went on, "The CIA, as with any similar organization, is

reluctant to share or turn over important information or important suspects to another agency."

"Reluctant might be an understatement."

"So," she continued, "the CIA has to find ways to operate freely and legally on American soil." She informed me, "Sometimes, if the suspect is a foreign diplomat, they will work with State Department Intelligence, and most times they will work with the FBI." She reminded me, "The Anti-Terrorist Task Force, for instance, has several CIA officers attached to the task force." She prompted, "I believe you knew one or two of them."

"Right." My wife actually killed one of them. And probably slept with that asshole, Ted Nash, before she and I were married. But it wasn't a crime of passion; it was self-defense. Or so it was ruled. But the CIA thought otherwise and they have long memories, as I found out in Yemen. And maybe as I was about to find out here.

Ms. Faraday continued, "In this case, the person of interest, Colonel Vasily Petrov, is a diplomat. And who is it that is watching Vasily Petrov the most closely?"

"His girlfriend?"

She ignored my wit and answered her own question. "Your group. The DSG."

I kind of understood all this oblique baloney—Petrov was a person of interest to the CIA and to State Department Intelligence and they were sharing the case to give the CIA legal cover in the U.S. And my group, the Diplomatic Surveillance Group, would be a convenient and well-placed ally. But rather than ask us for help, the CIA or SDI penetrated the Diplomatic Surveillance Group with one of their people. And, voilà! Tess Faraday was my trainee. I asked her, "So are you CIA or SDI?"

"Does it matter who I'm working for?"

"Why am I asking?"

"It's better for both of us if you didn't know. In case you are asked later."

"Right." I asked another question. "What do you need from me?"

"Well, as it turns out, you set the wheels in motion to find

Petrov, and Captain Kalish, who has lots of resources, is working well with you."

"So I'm the front guy."

"You're the go-to guy." She stopped the Blazer on a lonely stretch of road and glanced at the dashboard clock. "And you're very bright."

I ignored that and asked her, "What is it that Petrov is suspected of?"

"What do *you* think?"

"Well, as you probably know, he's an evil James Bond with a license to kill."

"I know that."

"Good." So, as it turns out, my instincts were correct; I had stumbled onto something big. Something that the CIA and State Department Intelligence were on to, and might or might not be sharing with the FBI. Also, my instincts about Tess Faraday were correct; she wasn't who she said she was. She was, in fact, a plant—sort of like a parasite that attached itself to the Diplomatic Surveillance Group. Well, that might be a little harsh. Also, I was relieved that she wasn't with the FBI Office of Professional Responsibility. The CIA, I could handle. And, finally, I was a little pissed off.

I don't know why I cared, but I asked her, "Tell me about your legend."

She didn't reply for a few seconds, then said, "I'm not actually a lawyer, but it fit the requirement for me to be an FBI aspirant." She confided, "I was a little concerned about that. You're married to a lawyer, and professions are hard to fake."

"Not if you're a lawyer. They fake it every day."

She smiled and continued, "What's true is that I'm from Lattingtown, and my family did actually summer in the Hamptons."

"More importantly, are you a Mets fan?"

"Let's go Mets."

"That's disappointing."

"I think you were on to me."

To burst her bubble, and because I was pissed, I said, "You need to work on your acting."

"It's not my strong point."

"No, it's not. And I have a target to find, and I'm not making any progress here. So—"

My Nextel—Matt's Nextel—vibrated and I looked at the text, hoping it was from Kalish. But all it said was: I'm here.

Assuming this obscure message was for Mrs. Faraday, I showed it to her.

She nodded and said, "Good." Then she said to me, "Also, if you're wondering, Grant doesn't actually exist. But if he did, he'd be the jealous type and I'd have to take calls from him all day and run to the ladies' room to talk to him in private."

I was relieved to hear that her bladder was okay. I advised her, "I don't like being jerked around, Ms. Faraday—if that's your name."

"It's my real name." She added, "I enjoyed our conversations."

"At some point I will need to see identification. Including your pistol license. Or I will confiscate your gun. And place you under arrest."

"My ID is with the man we're about to meet."

"It better be." I informed her, "At this point, I need to call my case agent." I began dialing. "To cover my ass and report my conversation with you."

She put her hand over mine. "That's taken care of. You're covered. But you can call Matt and Steve, and Captain Kalish if you'd like."

"That's very kind of you."

"John…this is sort of out of your hands now. And out of the FBI's hands. But we'd like you to work with us and maintain contact with your team and your guy Kalish."

"Who is *us*?"

"You're about to find out."

"What's in it for me?"

"This is your job."

"You just said it wasn't."

"We're sharing the job."

And, I, John Corey, was a loose cannon who needed to be kept close. "Let me ask you this—do you have reason to believe that Vasily Petrov is on some sort of mission tonight?"

She stayed silent for a few seconds, then replied, "We didn't think he was up to anything in particular tonight. Then, as we both noticed, Petrov, Fradkov, and the guy you call Igor—Gorsky—got really strange at Tamorov's. Then they take off in a landing craft, so we go from routine surveillance to... well, maybe something interesting. Or maybe nothing." She added, "That's why you follow guys like that."

Right. I follow them to see who they meet, who they know, and how they spend their time outside their home and office, and now and then something interesting comes up. And I report it, with photos included, and that's where my job ends and an FBI agent picks it up. Tonight, however, it seemed like I could rewrite my job description. If I wanted to.

I texted Steve: Anything new?

He replied: All quiet.

I texted Kalish: Any luck?

He replied: You'll be the first.

How could a sea-and-air search not find a twenty-five-foot amphibious landing craft that started from a known point at a known time? Maybe the craft was already onboard a ship and covered with a tarp. Or it had come ashore somewhere along a lonely beach. More importantly, what was the purpose of Petrov leaving Tamorov's party in a landing craft? Everything—boats, babes, and booze—pointed to a pleasure cruise, maybe ending on a small bay island, or a party ship. And maybe that's all there was to it.

Tess said, "Just for the record, and to make you a little less angry, I did ask that I be assigned to you rather than any of the dozens of other team leaders who watch the Russians. And now I'll tell you why. Because you're very good at what you do. And I really enjoy working with you."

I didn't reply.

She put the Blazer in gear and we continued down the narrow road.

I asked her, "Did I say I wanted to work with you?"

"Just meet this guy, and listen. Then make your decision." She added, "Time to come in from the pasture."

Well, be careful what you wish for. We continued on the bumpy reservation road to a powwow.

She was peering into the darkness, then the headlights picked out two stone pillars and an iron gate, which was open. She turned between the pillars and the headlights illuminated a row of gravestones.

"This is the place," Tess said. She glanced at the Blazer's compass, then showing good tradecraft she turned the vehicle around toward the exit. She shut off the engine, leaving us in dark silence.

CHAPTER FOURTEEN

Because Ms. Faraday is a pro, she hit the kill switch for the interior lights before opening her door.

Because Detective Corey is also a pro, I said, "Give me the keys and your gun."

She handed me the keys, then hesitated and drew her gun from her holster and handed it to me, butt first.

She carried a .40 caliber Glock, standard government issue. I pocketed her gun and said, "My last piece of gun advice, since you asked, is never go into a situation with an armed person you don't trust."

"Sorry you feel that way."

"Let's go. Leave your door open."

Tess got out of the Blazer, leaving her door open in case one of us—specifically me—needed to make a quick getaway. "You lead."

She moved onto a path between the gravestones, paved with broken seashells that crunched beneath our feet. I took my Glock out of my pocket and followed, keeping five feet between us.

The graveyard was dimly lit by the half-moon overhead, and tall trees cast moon shadows across the graves and paths. A sea breeze rustled the branches, creating the appearance of movement on the ground.

When someone tells you they want you to meet someone, you get the mental image of one person waiting for you to show up. In fact, however, there could be several people waiting for you. And this was not the first time my curiosity got the better of my usually good judgment.

Tess said, in a soft voice, "Straight ahead is Shinnecock Bay. That's where we stop."

We continued on the path. The gravestones were not big enough to conceal anyone, but the tree trunks were wide. Ahead, I could see the moonlight sparkling on the bay.

The ground sloped down toward the water and I closed the distance between us.

Tess glanced back at me and saw I was holding my gun at my side. "Relax, John."

"Keep moving."

She continued toward the bay and we came to the end of the gravestones, about twenty yards from the shore. She stopped, facing the moonlit bay. "It's so beautiful here."

I glanced to my left and right, and behind me, then I looked out at the bay. On the opposite shore, about three miles away, was the Shinnecock Coast Guard Station and the Ponquogue Bridge that connected the mainland of Long Island to the barrier island, along which I could see large waterfront homes.

It occurred to me that Petrov's amphibious craft had hundreds of miles of shoreline where it could make land—beaches, inlets, coves, creeks, and marshland.

But losing Petrov might be the least of my problems tonight.

Tess turned around and faced me, glancing again at the gun in my hand. "You understand that if this is a trap, that's not going to do you any good."

"Wanna bet?"

"And I hope you also understand that…well, that I've grown honestly fond of you."

I had no reply.

"Just to set the record straight, I'm not married. And to be honest, I'm sorry you are."

Well, hey, if I were going to cheat on my wife, it would certainly be in a graveyard with a woman who lied to me for months. And to make it more enticing, I just disarmed her and we were waiting for a mystery man to show up. I wish I'd brought my handcuffs.

The good news, if there was any, was that Ms. Faraday's personal interest in me could not possibly be a prelude to an ambush. Though perhaps she wanted me to drop my guard.

"John?"

"You'll understand that there may be some trust issues here."

"I understand. So let's revisit this later when we get all this behind us."

"Well...I'm happily married."

"Now who's lying?"

That sort of pissed me off, but she had a point—though I didn't know where she got it.

My cell phone vibrated and I looked at the text: I'm behind you. Don't shoot.

I turned, and coming up the path was a man dressed in tan slacks and a dark blazer. As he got closer I could hear his footsteps on the seashells, then I could see his face, and it was none other than Buckminster Harris of State Department Intelligence, who I'd last seen in Yemen, right before he left me to be killed by a gang of Al Qaeda cutthroats.

So now one of us could take care of some unfinished business.

CHAPTER FIFTEEN

"I'm unarmed," declared Buck Harris as he held out his hands where I could see them.

"I'm not."

He stepped closer to me and inquired, "Will you shake hands with me?"

"Why don't I just kick you in the balls?"

"I sense some anger, John."

Tess interjected, "Whatever issues you both think you need to settle will have to wait." She reminded me, "The mission comes first."

I didn't know I was on a mission. I was on a fucked-up surveillance. But I guess Tess and Buck were on a mission.

I stared at Buck Harris in the moonlight. He still looked good for a man in his seventies, though he was pale compared to the last time I saw him with his Yemen tan.

Buckminster Harris was an old Cold Warrior, a leftover from the days when all we had to worry about was nuclear annihilation. He was, I had to admit, a charming gentleman when he wasn't plotting to get me killed.

He said to me, on that subject, "You may have misinterpreted what happened in Yemen."

"Hey, I never thought of that." I said, partly for Tess' benefit, "So even though it looked to me like you and your CIA buddy were trying to get me, Kate, and Brenner whacked, we got it all wrong. Please accept my apology."

"You haven't lost any of your sardonic wit."

"And my aim is still good."

Tess said, "I think you two need to speak alone." She looked at me. "Just listen and decide." She turned and walked toward the bay.

So Buck and I were alone. Maybe. I asked him, "Anyone with you?"

"No."

"If you lie, you die."

"You have my word."

"Me too." I nodded toward Tess. "Who is she?"

"She's not CIA if that's your concern." He tapped his side pocket. "I can show you her credentials."

"Nice and easy, Buck."

He slipped his hand into his pocket and pulled out a cred case.

"Toss it."

He pitched it to me and I glanced at the open case in the dim light. I could make out her photo and name, Tess Faraday, and also the State Department seal. This meant nothing, of course—spooks carry whatever creds they need, and Buck understood I wasn't fond of the CIA, or vice versa. In fact, the Agency considered me—and Kate—unfinished business.

I put Tess' creds in my pocket and said to Buck, "Turn around, hands against that tree, legs spread."

He complied without complaint and I frisked him. In this business, when you declare you're unarmed, you better be unarmed, or the conversation is over. "Turn around."

He turned around, reclaimed his dignity, and took in his surroundings. "This is an appropriate place for a powwow. We will smoke the peace pipe and bury the tomahawk."

"I'd like to bury it in your fucking head."

"You're not getting into the spirit of this place, John."

"Tell me why I shouldn't kill you."

"Because you need to hear what I have to say about Colonel Petrov."

"You have three minutes."

He sat on the ground with his back against the tree. He looked like a tired old warrior who'd been called back to duty because the old enemy had suddenly reappeared.

He invited me to sit, like we were going to smoke a peace pipe or something, but I declined.

I glanced at the bay, where Tess had rolled up her pants and waded into the water up to her knees. These people—and I mean the entire sixteen separate agencies of the U.S. intelligence community—were a little weird. I stuck my gun in my belt and said, "Talk."

Buck began, "Tess has been briefing me on a regular basis, and when she called me from the pub in Southampton I decided it was worth my time to come out here from the city. Then when she called me from the diner, I was glad I did."

"Me too."

"You need to put Yemen behind you."

"I'm about to."

He looked at me and said, "John... you understand that I was just following orders... orders that I didn't necessarily agree with, or feel good about."

"If you're looking for sympathy, you'll find it in the dictionary between shit and syphilis."

Buck's "just following orders" crap didn't work, so he tried out his charm. "I congratulate you on your bold decision to go undercover into Tamorov's party." He let me know, "What you saw changed everything tonight." Buck saw I wasn't charmed and he changed the subject. "How is Kate?"

"You're wasting your three minutes."

He ignored me and said, "I was happy to hear she got a promotion. But I was puzzled by your... taking a position with lesser responsibilities."

"Buck, fuck you."

He continued, "You're a remarkable man, John, but I don't think they appreciated you on the Anti-Terrorist Task Force."

Buck was fluent in Russian, so I tried that. "Yob vas."

He smiled, then went on, "Your supervisor, Tom Walsh, was undermining you. Which is strange, since he is so fond of Kate."

"Are you trying to get me to shoot you?"

"I'm just making an observation." He also let me know, "Tess has become perhaps overly fond of you." He confided, "We almost took her off the case."

"I already did that, and I also took her gun. That's how much I believe her bullshit and your bullshit."

"Even within a masquerade, some things are real."

I strongly advised him, "Get to Vasily Petrov."

"All right. Colonel Vasily Petrov is the son of Vladimir Petrov, a KGB general who once headed SMERSH."

"I know that."

"Then you also know that Junior is in a similar line of work."

"I thought he was a U.N. delegate for human rights."

"Well, he is, but he doesn't know much about that." He thought a moment, then said, "Tess tells me that Petrov and his two companions were acting a bit odd at Tamorov's party."

"Right."

He smiled. "When a Russian isn't drinking at a party, something is not right." He thought again, then said, "And then Petrov, Fradkov, and Gorsky got into an amphibious craft and sailed off."

"Correct."

"I understand you've gotten the county police to mount a sea-and-air search for that amphibious craft."

"Also correct."

"What do you think their chances are of finding that craft, or discovering where Petrov was taken?"

"Chances were good two hours ago. Not so good now."

He thought about that, then replied, "It is my understanding that your only interest in this is to find the surveillance target you lost."

"Right."

"But I think I know you, John. And I believe you've thought about Vasily Petrov and why he may be in America."

I didn't reply.

"Colonel Petrov," he went on, "has as little knowledge of espionage as he does of human rights. He is a killer."

"We all know that, Buck."

"And Viktor Gorsky is also a killer."

"And Fradkov?"

"That's another matter. I will return to Pavel Fradkov later. But for now, I'd like you to continue your efforts with this Captain Kalish to locate our missing Russians."

My next stop was probably Tamorov's house, so I asked, "What is the relationship between Petrov and Georgi Tamorov?"

"Good question. And the answer is, we don't know. But if I had to guess, I'd say it is as it seems—a relationship of mutual convenience. Tamorov wants the friendship of a powerful SVR colonel, and Colonel Petrov enjoys the hospitality of a rich oligarch."

"Petrov wasn't enjoying himself tonight. He didn't even get laid."

Buck forced a smile. "But he did take a dozen young ladies with him. So it appears that Petrov was using Tamorov's beach house tonight as a place where he was to meet this amphibious craft, which was presumably taking him and his friends to another party."

And maybe, I thought, Petrov collected some tools of his and Gorsky's trade at Tamorov's house that they couldn't carry in their car. But that supposed Petrov was up to something. I mean, did he take off out the back door in a boat to give his DSG followers the slip because he was up to something? Or did he take off in a boat because he had another party to go to? That was the question.

Buck closed his eyes and I thought the old guy had nodded off, but he said, "I tried to convince my colleagues that the Russian threat was not being taken seriously. The intelligence establishment and the military and diplomatic community are funneling vast resources into the war on Islamic terrorism because of 9/11. And they are ignoring the awakening bear."

I'd expect that from Buck, whose glory days were behind him. But I agreed with him that the Cold War was back and no one was paying attention.

Meanwhile, he wasn't giving me the promised briefing, so I asked, "Is Petrov going to whack someone tonight?"

"I'll get to that later." He changed the subject and said, "I've also had the Coast Guard alerted, and they've agreed to send some boats and a helicopter to conduct a search. But as I discovered, their resources are limited compared to what the police have at their disposal."

I nodded. Even in this age of counterterrorism and drug smuggling, the United States Coast Guard was being scaled back. The Suffolk County Police Marine Bureau, on the other hand, had about twenty watercraft of various sizes and capabilities and four helicopters for search, rescue, and law enforcement. Plus there were local harbor constables who also had watercraft that could be deployed at sea. Bottom line here, Scott Kalish had more air and sea resources at his disposal than the U.S. Coast Guard. Which was why I called him.

Buck said, "Tess told me that Petrov and his friends carried three overnight bags onboard the amphibious craft."

"Correct."

"Nothing larger? Like a suitcase?"

Before I could ask why he asked, I heard footsteps and saw Tess coming toward us.

She looked at me, then at Buck sitting under the tree.

Buck said to her, "I believe we're almost finished here." He smiled. "John has decided not to kill me."

"Today," I explained.

Tess looked at me. "Do you understand how important this is?"

"Not really."

She looked at Buck, who said, "I haven't yet gotten to Pavel Fradkov."

"Then," I suggested, "let's get to Pavel Fradkov."

Buck stood, looked at me, and said, "I understand that all your surveillance vehicles are equipped with portable radiation detectors."

That is *not* what I wanted to hear.

He continued, "And Ms. Faraday tells me she heard no beeping, even when you were very close to Petrov's vehicle. So I suppose it's already on the ship that Petrov rendezvoused with."

"*What* is on what ship?"

"You know what I'm talking about."

Indeed I did.

There is little that spooks me, but atomic bombs are at the top of my very short list. I cleared my throat and said, "I assume you mean a nuke."

"Correct." He added, "Probably a suitcase nuke."

"Why do you think that?"

"Because Vasily Petrov is a psychotic mass murderer. And he, like his father, and like his megalomaniacal president, yearns for the glory days of the Soviet Empire. And all that stands in his and his president's way is us."

Buck saw I wasn't buying all of this, so he tempered his concerns a bit and said, "We're not sure this is what's happening tonight, but if you put it all together, then what you saw today at Tamorov's party doesn't make sense except in that context."

I thought back to all that had happened since Petrov went mobile, and I couldn't come to any conclusion that involved a nuke. I said to Buck, "There's a piece missing. Fradkov."

"Correct. Pavel Fradkov, whose real name is Arkady Urmanov, is a nuclear physicist." Buck informed me, "He once worked on the Soviet nuclear weapons miniaturization program. Suitcase nukes."

Holy shit.

"Miniaturized nukes," Buck informed me, "are temperamental and need periodic…well, tune-ups." He continued, "The fear that they could get into the hands of terrorists is real. But no one knows if they'd actually detonate if they hadn't been regularly maintained over the thirty years since most of them were made." He concluded, "To be sure of that, and to properly arm the device, it's good to have a knowledgeable nuclear weapons scientist on hand."

Tess added, "Especially one who hasn't had a drink all night."

The evidence, as we say in criminal investigations, was mounting—and pointing in one direction.

I said to Buck, "I assume Petrov and his pals rendezvoused with a Russian ship."

"I would assume so. And on that ship could be a nuclear device." He informed me, "If it's a suitcase nuke, it could be the biggest model, about the size of a steamer trunk, which would yield about ten kilotons of atomic energy." He further informed me, "For comparison, the Hiroshima bomb was estimated to be between twelve and sixteen kilotons."

I glanced at Tess, wondering when she knew all this.

Buck said, "We should also assume that this ship that Petrov and his friends rendezvoused with is heading for New York City."

I didn't reply, but that was a good assumption.

Buck continued, "The ship will enter the harbor, and at some point, before or after docking, the nuclear device will detonate and the fireball will completely destroy everything within a quarter-mile radius and incinerate structures within a half mile of ground zero." He added, "And then there is shock wave damage, radioactive fallout, loss of communication and services, and mass panic." He further added, "Over half a million initial deaths, followed by at least another half million more in the aftermath."

Again, I didn't reply.

He continued, "Assuming the target is Wall Street, the entire southern end of Manhattan Island will be gone, including the financial and government district—along with your offices at 26 Federal Plaza, and also the World Trade Center construction site. Also gone will be port facilities, bridges, tunnels, and subways and the entire historic district, all of which will be a nuclear wasteland for years. Not to mention the Statue of Liberty and collateral damage to the Brooklyn and New Jersey port facilities." He added, "This would be a crippling financial and psychological blow to America, from which it will take decades to recover."

"I get it." I informed him, "It's very difficult—actually impossible—to get a ship that's emitting radiation past the harbor forts that aim radiation detectors at passing ships." I further informed him, "Also, the NYPD Harbor Unit patrol boats have radiation detectors, as do the Coast Guard cutters." I also told him, "And if the Russians tried to get a suitcase nuke off the ship and into the city, they wouldn't get it past Customs, who also have radiation detectors on the piers."

"I'm sure the Russians have a plan."

Indeed they must. But it occurred to me that a Russian ship, such as a cargo ship or a luxury liner, would be subject to extra scrutiny at Ambrose Buoy, the security checkpoint, before it approached New York Harbor. It also occurred to me that the Russians wouldn't want to be caught with a suitcase nuke aboard one of their ships. And if the nuke did go off, it could be determined that the Russian ship was ground zero, and that could start a nuclear war. So some of this wasn't computing.

Also, why did Petrov, Gorsky, and the nuke guy, Urmanov, have to take an amphibious craft out to rendezvous with this Russian ship that had a nuke onboard? They could have boarded the ship in Russia. So maybe Buck got this wrong, and Petrov was now having a vodka on a party boat with Tasha on his lap. And that's what I'd conclude—if it wasn't for Urmanov.

Buck broke into my thoughts and said, "We don't know if Petrov and his friends have a plan to escape the detonation, or if this is a suicide mission." He added, "I think a man like Petrov would like to see the result of his work, so he may have a plan to get clear of the explosion, along with his two companions. But for the young ladies and everyone else aboard whatever ship they rendezvoused with, this is a suicide mission, though I'm sure they don't know that."

And never will, I thought; they will become one with the universe at the moment of the Big Bang. More importantly, I hoped this wasn't a suicide mission for Petrov, because suicide missions, like 9/11, were more likely to succeed than missions where the perpetrators need an escape plan. Lots to think about. Especially the things that weren't computing.

Buck may have thought that I needed more evidence. But he didn't have any, so he told me a story.

"Not far from here," he began, "is a place called Nassau Point." He asked, "Have you heard of it?"

"Been there."

"So was Albert Einstein, who spent the summer of 1939 there in a rented cottage."

"He deserved a break."

Buck continued, "In July of that year, Einstein received a visit from two well-known physicists, Eugene Wigner and Leó Szilárd, who convinced Einstein that he needed to write a letter to President Roosevelt alerting the president to the threat of the German atomic bomb program."

I'd actually read the famous Nassau Point Letter, so I knew where this was going, but Buck likes to tell stories, so I let him continue.

"In that letter, Einstein says something that...well, is a warning from the past to us in the future." Buck looked at me and said, "Einstein wrote to Roosevelt, 'A single bomb of this type, carried by boat and exploded in a port, might very well destroy the whole port together with some of the surrounding territory.'" Buck stayed silent a moment, then said, "I believe that day has arrived."

Well, I thought, the nuclear nightmare seemed to have begun in the minds of scientists long before anyone else even knew what nuclear energy was. Einstein was a smart guy.

Buck said, "Roosevelt took this seriously, and so should we."

That seemed to be the end of the pointed story, and Buck asked me, "Do *you* take this seriously?"

"It's credible."

"Not everyone thinks so."

"I suppose we'll find out soon enough."

He didn't respond to that and asked me, "Any word from Captain Kalish?"

"No."

Tess said to me, "We'd like you to call the Suffolk PD and get some detectives to accompany you and me to the Tamorov house."

"All right." I guess I'm the front guy and the go-to cop. But before going to see Tamorov, I asked Buck, "What do you know about Georgi Tamorov?"

"Not much more than everyone else knows. He's made billions from oil and gas and he has financial interests all over the world, including America. He's close to Putin and he's a globe-trotting playboy. He owns a Falcon 900 that flies him to the playgrounds of the world."

"Does he own cargo ships or luxury liners?"

"Good question, but no." Buck added, "Though I'm sure he knows people who do."

I nodded and asked, "Personals?"

"Tamorov has been married to the same woman for about twenty-five years and they have a son and a daughter, both at university in England."

I said to Buck, "I seem to remember that Tamorov has a place in Manhattan."

"Yes, he has a townhouse in Tribeca and offices near the former World Trade Center."

"He won't have either if a nuke incinerates Lower Manhattan."

"Correct. So I can't imagine that Tamorov knows what his guest is up to." Buck added, "Also, Tamorov's wife is currently in New York."

And Petrov's wife isn't.

So, I was off to see Georgi Tamorov, and also Dmitry the driver, both of whom knew *something*.

Buck gave me the standard warning. "What you've heard tonight is need-to-know and SCI—Sensitive Compartmented Information—not to be repeated to anyone under any circumstances."

I didn't reply.

"We know you can keep a secret, John, as you did in Yemen. We trust you."

Sorry I can't say the same.

Buck said to me and to Tess, "Let's pray that we are wrong, and that we are misinterpreting what we see."

Right. Just like in Yemen. I said, "I will leave you two to pray, and I'll call when I have something." I added, "Good powwow."

Tess said, "I'm going with you."

"You're fired."

Buck interjected, "I'm afraid I have to insist that you take Tess with you."

"Really?"

"Please." He explained, "Tess has contact information for resources that you may need at a moment's notice."

That might be true, but Buck also wanted his colleague to keep an eye on me. So, knowing I could dump her anytime, I said, "All right." Buck wasn't telling me what his next move was, and I didn't ask. Maybe he was going to take a nap.

Buck wished us luck and offered me his hand, but I didn't take it, and reminded him, "We have unfinished business."

Tess and I walked through the graveyard back to the Blazer.

She asked me, "Do you believe what Buck is suggesting?"

"Do you?"

She walked on in silence, then replied, "It's just so beyond anything I can imagine..."

Well, Albert Einstein imagined it long before the first bomb was even built, and that's why we carry radiation detectors. I asked her, "When did you know about this?"

"I wasn't fully briefed until I called Buck from the diner."

That could be true, considering she didn't want me to crash Tamorov's party. The problem with compartmented information is that nobody knows what the hell is going on. Or why they're doing what they're doing. If the police operated like that, they'd never make an arrest.

She added, "When I told Buck that our three Russians took off in an amphibious craft, he suspected something was up."

"He suspected something was up long before tonight. That's why he was in New York and not Washington. And that's why he stuck me with you."

She didn't reply.

I always believed that 9/11 never would have happened if these people talked straight to each other. Now we were looking at something that would make 9/11 look like a bad day at the office.

We reached the Blazer and I said, "I'm driving," and got behind the wheel.

Tess got in the passenger side and reached back into the rear where all the toys were kept, including the pocket-sized portable radiation detector, which she placed on the console between us.

She asked, "May I have my gun back?"

I handed her her Glock and her creds.

I drove back to the road and headed out of the Shinnecock Reservation.

I looked at the portable radiation detector. There are two ways to detect radiation. One of them is with a PRD before nuclear fission takes place, and the other is too late.

PART III

CHAPTER SIXTEEN

As the last of the twilight disappeared on the western horizon, the amphibious craft carrying Vasily Petrov, Viktor Gorsky, and Dr. Arkady Urmanov approached a long white yacht sitting at anchor in international waters, twelve nautical miles off the coast of Southampton.

The yacht was named *Hana,* which Petrov knew meant "happiness" in Arabic. *Happiness will be at planned time and place.*

The yacht's portholes and decks were aglow, and Petrov noticed a green-and-white flag flying from the stern, which he knew was not a national flag, but the personal ensign of His Royal Highness, Prince Ali Faisel of Saudi Arabia.

The helmsman brought the amphibious craft around to the starboard side of the two-hundred-and-twenty-foot super yacht, and the twelve ladies onboard became excited as they realized this was where they were heading. Several of them stood, and the second crewman motioned them to sit.

Petrov said to the ladies in Russian, "If you fall overboard, we will not rescue you."

The ladies laughed, and Petrov smiled.

Viktor Gorsky, the SVR assassin, snapped, "Sit!"

The ladies sat.

Petrov looked at Urmanov sitting across from him. The man

seemed far away, and Petrov said to him, "Doctor, is your mind working on mathematical formulas? Or are you seasick?"

Urmanov looked at his compatriot, but did not reply.

Petrov was annoyed with the man, and more annoyed at the GRU idiots who had chosen Urmanov for this mission. Urmanov was becoming a problem as he understood the reality of what he had agreed to do.

The amphibious craft continued on a course toward the starboard side of the yacht, and as they drew closer Petrov could see a large door in the hull partly below the waterline—what was called a shell door—about fifteen meters from the stern.

As the amphibious craft approached, the door began to open upward, letting the sea into the hull.

This, Petrov had been told, was a unique feature of this ship. Most garage doors were above the waterline, and the tender craft was pulled into the ship's garage by means of a ramp and a winch. But the Italian shipbuilders who had designed *The Hana* had devised a float-in dock for the prince so that the garage could be flooded and a small craft could sail directly in and out of the hull without the delay or discomfort of a ramp and winch. Wonderful engineering, Petrov thought, and as it turned out this special feature solved one of his and Moscow's problems—the problem of how to mask the radiation of the nuclear device that would later come onboard *The Hana*. The device had a lead radiation shield that had once been sufficient, but no longer was because of the more sophisticated American radiation detectors now in use. Thousands of liters of water, however, along with the lead shield, would ensure that the American radiation detectors in New York Harbor would stay dark and silent.

In fact, the greatest fear of the American nuclear security forces was something like this—an explosive nuclear device attached underwater on the hull of a ship coming into an American port. Well, Petrov thought, the Americans' worst fears were about to be realized, though this nuclear device would not be attached to the outside hull of the ship where the Americans had sonar devices to detect unusual shapes on the hull; this nuclear device would be submerged inside the flooded watertight compartment of *The Hana* where it would be undetectable.

Petrov exchanged glances with Gorsky and they both nodded.

The helmsman pointed his bow at the open door, then cut the throttles as the craft slipped through the opening into the flooded garage. There was a dock on either side of the garage and the helmsman steered to the one toward the stern where deckhands awaited them. The opposite dock was empty, Petrov noted, but not for long. Tonight, another small craft, a lifeboat, would be arriving from a Russian fishing trawler—*the fish is swimming*—and that fishing trawler would deliver a small package of death, no larger than a steamer trunk, but with enough atomic energy inside it to level Lower Manhattan.

Petrov looked at Dr. Urmanov, who had been given very few details of the operation, but who knew that the device would be arriving and that his job was to ensure that it was operational and armed. Urmanov had actually designed these miniature nuclear weapons—what the Americans called suitcase nukes—in the 1970s, and they had worked perfectly in tests when new. But they were complex and temperamental, and they needed periodic maintenance and a technician to properly arm them—or the inventor himself, if a major problem was discovered. The device that was to be delivered to the yacht, Petrov knew, would yield ten to twelve kilotons of atomic energy. Petrov would have liked a bigger device, but twelve kilotons was the limit of these miniaturized devices that were designed to be small, relatively light, self-contained, and easily transported—like a steamer trunk, perfect to take aboard a ship or plane. Petrov smiled.

Suddenly a set of underwater lights came on, creating a dramatic effect that excited the ladies, and one of them exclaimed, "Just like in a James Bond movie!"

Yes, Petrov thought, just like in a James Bond movie, and the second act would be even more dramatic.

A deckhand tossed a line to the crewman in the amphibious craft, and he secured the boat as the shell door was closing, keeping out the sea.

The ladies, carrying their beach bags, were helped onto the polished wood dock. They seemed happy and excited as they looked around the well-appointed reception area that opened onto the stern, where a swimming platform was located behind plate-glass doors.

One of the ladies called out, "Viktor! Give us our phones so we can take photos!"

Gorsky tapped his overnight bag, which contained not their phones—he had dropped them overboard—but his weapons, which the ladies would see soon enough. He replied, "There will be time enough to take photos—if you behave!"

"You are a hard man, Viktor."

Indeed.

Petrov, Gorsky, and Urmanov stepped onto the dock unassisted, carrying their bags, and Petrov looked again at the empty dock across the flooded garage. The lifeboat that would arrive from the Russian fishing trawler would be driven by *The Hana*'s new captain, known to Petrov only as Gleb. Gleb had studied the plans and operational specifications of *The Hana*, and he had actually spent a few hours aboard the Saudi yacht in Monte Carlo some months before at the kind invitation of *The Hana*'s captain, an Englishman named Wells, who didn't know that his Russian guest would one day take his place as captain of the prince's yacht.

Petrov had never met Gleb, and Gleb wasn't an SVR agent—he was a former cargo ship officer. But he had worked for the SVR before and Moscow said he could be trusted to do what he was told and to keep his mouth shut. Otherwise, Captain Gleb would share the same fate as Dr. Urmanov, who would not be leaving this ship.

Gleb had assured his SVR employers in Moscow that he could sail *The Hana* by himself, and that he could navigate into New York Harbor without a pilot and anchor off the tip of Manhattan Island. Once they were anchored, sometime before dawn, as the clock was ticking on the nuclear device, Petrov and Gorsky, with Gleb at the helm, would sail *The Hana*'s amphibious craft—which had no markings to connect it to *The Hana*—to a pier in Brooklyn that was unused while it was being rebuilt. On an adjacent city street was a parked Ford Mustang—*the horse waits*—to which Petrov had the keys. He,

Gorsky, and Gleb would drive to Kennedy Airport and, using false passports, they would board a private jet—*the bird will fly*—that would take them to Moscow. And while they were all having breakfast aboard the aircraft, at 8:46 A.M.—the same time as the first hijacked aircraft had hit the North Tower on September 11—the southern tip of Manhattan Island would be engulfed in a nuclear fireball whose source would be the Saudi prince's yacht.

Yes, Petrov thought, it was a very good plan, and though he wished the kilotonnage was larger, it was large enough to kill a few hundred thousand people and cause a multitrillion-dollar crash on Wall Street. He thought of something his father had said to him: "Victory is measured not by the number killed, but by the number frightened." And that number would be three hundred million people.

Petrov watched as a deckhand standing on a catwalk that connected the two docks hit a switch and the water in the flooded garage began to drop. He had been told that *The Hana*'s high-powered pumps could empty seven thousand liters of water a minute from the garage compartment. More importantly, *The Hana* was rated as seaworthy even with the garage compartment flooded, which it would be as it sailed to New York Harbor with the nuclear device submerged in a hundred thousand liters of water.

The water in the garage compartment was nearly gone and the amphibious craft settled into its hull chocks. Sailing *The Hana*'s amphibious craft out of this garage without the assistance of deckhands, Petrov knew, would be a bit more difficult than arriving. But Gleb had assured the planners in Moscow that this would not be a problem. And Petrov hoped that was true—he didn't want to be trapped onboard *The Hana* as the clock ticked down.

Suicide missions, he knew, were much more likely to succeed than missions that included an escape. This was not a suicide mission, though it could become one. The important thing was that the nuclear device detonate in New York Harbor, destroying not only Lower Manhattan but also destroying all evidence of Russian involvement in the attack, which was obviously perpetrated by the Saudi prince.

Petrov looked at Gorsky, who he knew was also thinking about some of this. Gorsky was good at two things—killing people and living to kill another day. Petrov was glad he had chosen his former Chechen War assassin for this mission.

Petrov and Gorsky exchanged nods, then turned their attention to their surroundings. Two staircases, port and starboard, rose to the upper decks, and two deckhands were leading the ladies up the stairs.

A gray-bearded man in full white uniform appeared and said to the three Russians in British-accented English, "Welcome aboard The Hana, gentlemen. I am Captain Wells and I bring you greetings from His Highness."

Petrov replied, "Thank you, Captain."

"The prince will welcome you himself, in the salon, within the half hour. Meanwhile, a steward will show you to your staterooms, where you can freshen up." Captain Wells looked at his new arrivals, expecting perhaps that being Russian they'd been drinking, and he advised them, "Please be punctual."

Petrov replied, "We will not keep the prince waiting."

Captain Wells nodded and motioned to a steward to take the overnight bags, but Petrov said, "We will take these directly to the salon." He explained, "They contain gifts for the prince."

"As you wish."

Captain Wells was about to take his leave of the Russians, but he felt he should further advise the prince's guests, "You are responsible for the conduct of your ladies."

It was Gorsky who replied curtly, "And you, Captain, are not."

Petrov admonished in Russian, "Be courteous, Viktor." He wanted to remind Gorsky that he needed to gain the captain's trust and goodwill so he could easily kill him later—but Dr. Urmanov would not want to hear that, so Petrov said to his assassin, "Save your rudeness for later."

Gorsky smiled.

Captain Wells stared at Viktor Gorsky and thought to himself that the man looked like a thug, though he supposed that all Russian oil men looked like thugs.

Captain Wells said, "Good day," turned and left.

The steward said he would show them to their staterooms, but

Petrov told him to lead them directly to the salon and that they would carry their own bags.

On the way up the staircase to the salon deck, Petrov remarked to Gorsky and Urmanov, in Russian, "I think we are in the wrong business, gentlemen. The real money is in oil, not nuclear energy."

Gorsky laughed.

Urmanov did not.

CHAPTER SEVENTEEN

The *Hana* was underway again, heading west toward New York City.

Colonel Vasily Petrov stood in the yacht's long salon, waiting for the prince to welcome him and his Russian guests aboard.

The salon, Petrov thought, looked as outlandish as the photos he'd seen of it: gilded chandeliers, gold-brocaded furniture, and a floor covered with garish oriental rugs. The walls and ceiling were draped with loose folds of white silk to replicate a tent, a nostalgic reminder, perhaps, of the royal family's nomadic origins. All that was missing was a camel.

A dark-skinned steward offered Petrov, Gorsky, and Urmanov refreshments, but they declined and the young man bowed and left.

Petrov glanced at the three overnight bags that sat on an ottoman and that held his and Gorsky's MP5 submachine guns with silencers and also their Makarov handguns. The satchel that had arrived Wednesday in the diplomatic pouch from Moscow had been sent by courier to Tamorov's house, along with a verbal message telling Mr. Tamorov to put the satchel in Colonel Petrov's guestroom. Urmanov's overnight bag contained the tool kit and also the third handgun from the satchel, though he'd be surprised to discover the gun didn't work.

Petrov opened a door and stepped out to the side balcony. On the lighted main deck below, his twelve ladies had made themselves at home in the upholstered swivel chairs, and a steward was serving them champagne while they smoked. There was a spa pool on the deck, and one of the ladies took off her cover-up and lowered herself into it. The women all looked happy, Petrov thought, and it made him feel better knowing they would leave this life in such luxury.

Petrov looked at the girl named Tasha. A beautiful woman, and perhaps brighter than the rest. Certainly she was the most spirited, and under other circumstances he would have had her for himself, though by choosing her to come with him he had chosen her for death. And he had done this because she had been speaking to the tall caterer, Depp, who seemed out of place among the others, and she had possibly given this man her phone number, which was not allowed.

Gorsky joined Petrov, who commented, "There seems to be alcohol aboard this Islamic vessel, Viktor."

Gorsky laughed and added, "And scantily clad prostitutes."

"We are far from Mecca," Petrov observed, and they both laughed.

Petrov looked up at the top deck where the ship's bridge sat, and where Captain Wells was in command. Petrov said, "It tells you something, Viktor, when these Arabs don't trust their own countrymen to steer a modern ship."

Gorsky readily agreed. "If not for their oil, they would still be living in tents. Now they decorate their yachts like tents."

Petrov smiled and said, "The only use for these people is to make them pawns in the game against the West." He added, "And in this case, to help them become better terrorists."

Gorsky understood Petrov's contempt for the Arabs and Muslims in general. But Petrov's contempt, Gorsky knew, masked his grudging respect for the jihadists and mujahideen whom they had both fought in Chechnya and elsewhere, and whom Petrov's father had fought in Afghanistan.

Petrov looked at his watch. "We will soon have Captain Gleb at the helm."

Gorsky nodded, glad that Colonel Petrov was so confident in this plan. Gorsky thought the plan depended on too many unknown and variable factors, but he had worked with Colonel Petrov for many years, and he had seen how the colonel, through sheer will, intellect, and courage, made everything go well for himself and for their country. Petrov had always said, "Believe in yourself and believe in the cause of a new Russian Empire. The Islamists believe in their god, and that makes them dangerous, but not always competent. The Americans believe in their superiority, but they have no goal other than to remain at the top. And both sides are obsessed with the other, so when all is said and done it will be Russia that will stand on the corpses of Islam and the West. History is on our side."

And, thought Gorsky, Colonel Petrov had no goal other than to please his father, and to be promoted to his father's rank of general. As for the new Russian Empire, Gorsky didn't know how much Petrov believed in that, but Colonel Petrov believed in himself, and that made working with him easier than working with a man who believed in a cause or a god.

Petrov returned to the salon and Gorsky followed.

A steward dressed in traditional Arab garb stood at the aft door of the salon, then, as if he'd received a signal, he opened the door and announced in English, "His Royal Highness, Prince Ali Faisel."

Urmanov rose to his feet and faced the door. Petrov and Gorsky, too, turned toward the doorway.

The prince entered, and the three Russians made a half bow.

Ali Faisel, wearing khaki trousers and a white polo shirt, strode directly across the salon to Colonel Petrov and, smiling, extended his hand and said in English, "Welcome aboard The Hana, Colonel."

They shook hands and Petrov replied, "Thank you, Your Highness, for receiving us."

"Yes, but we are friends, so please call me Ali."

Petrov nodded. In fact, they were not friends, but they had been introduced by Georgi Tamorov some months before at a U.N. reception, where Colonel Petrov had suggested a more private meeting with His Highness at some future time to discuss a common problem—Islamic radicals. Those radicals within the Russian Federation were fighting wars of independence to become free of Russia; those within the Kingdom of Saudi Arabia wanted nothing less than the end of the monarchy, which they saw as decadent and corrupt, to be replaced by a more pure Islamic state. It was ironic, Petrov thought, that their two countries, with nothing in common, shared a common enemy, and that the enemy was Islam.

Petrov had let the prince know at the U.N. reception that he, Vasily Petrov, had come upon some interesting information in Chechnya that the royal family would find useful in their fight against their internal enemies. Petrov had also hinted that he and the prince could discuss another common problem—the price of crude oil, which both countries would like to see rise a few dollars a barrel. Petrov had mentioned their mutual friend, Georgi Tamorov, in this regard, and the prince seemed interested and agreed to meet privately to discuss these matters. Petrov had suggested the prince's yacht, away from prying eyes and ears, and he had also suggested that he could provide some female dinner companions and perhaps something stronger than alcohol. The prince had nodded his assent, and they had both agreed to keep this to themselves.

Ten years ago, Petrov knew, this meeting would have been unlikely. Russia had been broken, chaos ruled, and the people's spirit was crushed. Now, under Vladimir Putin, the humiliation of defeat was being replaced by a new spirit of confidence, and Russia was again taking its rightful place in the world. And thus the Saudis, the Americans, the Europeans, the Chinese, and others were happy and honored to meet with the Russians to discuss the evolving world order.

Petrov had also told the prince that he would like to bring two colleagues with him to brief His Highness, and the prince agreed and asked for their names, as Petrov knew he would. It had been decided in Moscow that Petrov would stay close to the verifiable truth, so Petrov had given the prince Gorsky's name, and he now said to the prince, "This is Mr. Viktor Gorsky, who I told you about. My assistant in the Human Rights office."

The prince had, of course, inquired about Viktor Gorsky, and he was happy that the SVR officer had diplomatic status.

As for Dr. Arkady Urmanov, nuclear physicist, the SVR had transformed him into Mr. Pavel Fradkov of the GRU—Russian Military Intelligence—and Petrov introduced him as such and added, "Mr. Fradkov also works with me in Human Rights, as you may know, and he, too, enjoys diplomatic status, as does his highness." He added, smiling, "So we are all U.N. diplomats, here to discuss world peace and understanding."

The prince returned the smile and invited his Russian guests to sit, and they all made themselves comfortable around an ivory-inlaid coffee table. The prince said, "Dinner will be served within the hour. But perhaps you would enjoy some aperitifs."

Petrov replied, "Just water, please."

The prince said something to the steward, who left the salon.

Petrov looked at his host. Ali Faisel was thirty-one years old according to the SVR biography, with typical Saudi features, including a pronounced nose, which Petrov imagined was a result of royal inbreeding, and Petrov suspected that his royal host was not particularly bright. But Ali Faisel was ambitious, and according to the SVR profile on him, this young prince strove to stand out among the numerous princes in his kingdom. Petrov didn't know why this was so, and he didn't care; but it did make the young idiot open to the suggestion that they should discuss important matters. If the truth be known, the prince's best qualification for this meeting—aside from his gullibility—was that he owned a yacht that sailed regularly to New York City.

Two stewards brought bottled water, sparkling and still, in ice buckets, with lemon and lime wedges, along with crystal glasses that bore the royal emblem.

The prince apologized. "No Russian mineral water, I'm afraid. But will you have French?"

Petrov replied, "We will pretend it is champagne."

Everyone laughed politely at the bad joke.

The steward poured sparkling water for everyone and Colonel Petrov toasted, "To His Royal Highness, the prince, and to his uncle, the king, and to the future cooperation of our two great nations."

Everyone clinked glasses, and the prince added, "And to your president." Everyone drank.

Despite the congeniality, Petrov knew that the prince might have some misgivings about Colonel Petrov of the SVR. For one thing, he, Petrov, had killed many Muslim Chechens, and his father had also killed many of the prince's coreligionists in Afghanistan. But at the U.N. reception, Petrov made it clear that he had no animosity toward Islam, only toward Islamic extremists who were the enemies of both their countries.

And of course, the subject of the Americans had come up, and both men agreed that America, along with Israel, was the cause of much of the unrest in the Middle East. The prince further agreed that the Saudi and American alliance mostly benefited the Americans and the Jews, and needed to be reevaluated, and Colonel Petrov had promised to share with the prince the SVR's thinking on this subject.

In fact, the prince, though he didn't know it, would be an important player in this reevaluation when *The Hana* sailed into New York Harbor and the nuclear device onboard detonated, thus ending the Saudi-American alliance, which was already strained because of the fifteen Saudis who had taken part in the 9/11 attack.

Also, as Petrov knew, Prince Ali Faisel and the monarchy were playing a double game and had given great sums of money to the madrassas—the Islamic fundamentalist schools throughout the Mideast—and this annoyed the Americans, though they were powerless to end this Saudi policy. Thus, when *The Hana* became a weapon of mass destruction, the American government and people would have no difficulty believing that a Saudi prince had obtained a Soviet miniature nuclear weapon on the black market, which Petrov knew were available for the princely sum of a million dollars a kiloton. And the Americans would also have no trouble believing that Prince Ali Faisel, nephew of the king, had become a jihadist and martyr for Islam. Perhaps the Americans would even retaliate with a nuclear weapon of their own.

Petrov delighted in the dual benefit of this plan, which was first suggested by his father. "In a microsecond of nuclear fission," said the general, "the Americans and the Saudis will be split like the atom and both will be badly wounded in the same explosion."

The prince, Petrov recalled, had been flattered to be asked to a secret meeting, though in reality, Prince Ali Faisel had no power; he was, in fact, a decadent royal, a playboy, and a dilettante, playing at U.N. diplomacy. It was ironic that when the nuclear device onboard

The Hana destroyed Lower Manhattan, this wastrel would be hailed by many of his coreligionists as a nuclear suicide bomber, and given more credit than he was ever worth while alive.

Petrov smiled at the prince. "This is a beautiful ship."

"Thank you." The prince informed his guests, "I designed the interior finishings myself."

"You have excellent taste."

Petrov glanced at Gorsky, who understood he needed to say something, and Gorsky said, "Very beautiful."

Petrov knew that Viktor Gorsky made some people uncomfortable. Gorsky looked like what he was—a killer. And he did nothing to soften his demeanor, which annoyed Petrov. But the man was good at what he did, and as far as Gorsky was concerned there was no reason to be polite to someone you were going to kill within the hour.

Petrov looked at Urmanov, who seemed to be lost in thought, though Petrov knew he was in a nervous state. This man engineered nuclear weapons, Petrov thought, designed to kill millions of people, but Urmanov would be sick at the sight of blood.

Petrov knew, of course, that Urmanov had not volunteered for this mission, but the SVR had presented Dr. Urmanov with two choices, as they were good at doing, and Arkady Urmanov had taken the better of the two bad choices.

Also, though Urmanov had not been fully informed of the operational aspects of the mission, he must have known that everyone on this yacht would be dead before too long—everyone, except, of course, Colonel Petrov, Viktor Gorsky, the Russian sea captain, and himself. Though if Dr. Urmanov believed that about himself, he was mistaken.

Petrov said to the prince, "Forgive Mr. Fradkov for his silence. His English is not very good."

The prince nodded, perhaps wondering how this Russian Military Intelligence officer was going to brief him or how he could do his job in America with poor English.

The prince asked Petrov, "How was your voyage to The Hana?"

Petrov smiled. "The ladies enjoyed it."

"Good." He informed his guests, "Hana is Arabic for 'happiness.' "

Petrov replied, "Yes, and an appropriate name."

"Also, it is the name of my wife."

Gorsky asked, "Which one?"

The prince looked at him, then replied, "My first wife, of course." He joked, "Now my other wives want yachts named after them."

Gorsky did not smile, and the prince turned away from him and asked Petrov, "And how was your party at Mr. Tamorov's house?"

"Very enjoyable. He sends his regards and looks forward to seeing you at his home in the city on Wednesday."

"I, too, look forward to seeing him again."

Actually, Petrov thought, Georgi Tamorov knew nothing about a meeting with the prince, nor did Tamorov even know that he, Petrov, was on the prince's yacht. The less Tamorov knew, the better. And if Tamorov suspected that there was a connection between Vasily Petrov and the nuclear explosion in New York Harbor, he would keep that thought to himself. Russia had changed, but the KGB had changed only its name, not its DNA, and even rich oligarchs understood that.

Petrov glanced at his watch, and knowing that dinner would be served shortly, he needed to get to the real business at hand, which was planning how to kill everyone aboard *The Hana*. He asked his host, "And who will be joining us for dinner?"

The prince replied, "I have six other guests onboard, four of whom are my countrymen who I will introduce at dinner. Two are businessmen from China." He added, "Unfortunately, their English is not good."

Petrov joked, "Seat them with Mr. Fradkov," and everyone laughed, except Arkady Urmanov.

The prince assured his Russian guests, "As Colonel Petrov requested, I have not mentioned any of you by name, and I will introduce you all by first name only, and as Russian petroleum executives who are my overnight guests until we dock in New York."

Petrov nodded, thinking that His Highness was enjoying this game of secret diplomacy. He inquired, "Will Captain Wells or the other officers be dining with us?"

"No. They will dine elsewhere."

"And the ladies?"

"I have arranged a buffet for them here in the salon." He added, "After dinner perhaps we can all gather here for some... relaxation."

Petrov nodded as his eyes scanned the long salon, trying to work out the details of shooting the prostitutes in the large room. Perhaps he would leave that to Gorsky, who he noticed was also interested in the room.

He and Gorsky had studied the deck plans of *The Hana* and he was certain they both knew the layout of the large ship well enough to finish their business before anyone could sound the alarm or try to abandon ship or offer armed resistance.

On that subject, Petrov's next question had to be asked in a way that did not seem too inquisitive or unusual. He looked at the prince and said, "I am assuming you have security onboard."

The prince made eye contact with Petrov, then replied, "Captain Wells has a rifle and a handgun, though he keeps them locked and hidden." He added, "We are better armed when we sail in pirate-infested waters, but guns are a problem with American Customs if they come aboard."

Petrov commented, "There are three hundred million guns in America, so I never understood why an honest man could not bring a few more into the country for protection."

The prince had no reply to that, but offered, "One of my stewards, Karim—the one in traditional dress—is my personal bodyguard." He added, "For when we are ashore." He smiled. "I hope I don't need a bodyguard here."

Petrov returned the smile and considered his next inquiry, then said, "I hope my large group did not put an undue burden on your staff and crew."

The prince assured him, "I have seven hardworking Somali stewards, and my French chef, André, has four good kitchen staff who are all Eastern European and they are used to long hours and hard work." He smiled. "The Saudis, I am afraid, have gotten soft and lazy."

As has His Highness, Petrov thought. He observed, "You have a veritable United Nations onboard." He pointed out, "A British captain, a..."

"An Irish first mate, and two Italian officers—the engineer and the navigator." The prince added, "And seven deckhands from all over the world."

Those numbers agreed with the information that Petrov had been given, and he commented, "A Tower of Babel."

The prince assured his guests, "The common language—the language of the sea—is English. So you will have no difficulties in communicating with anyone." He added, "All crew and staff are sworn to secrecy." He joked, "What happens aboard The Hana, stays aboard The Hana."

"Indeed," said Petrov as he tallied the number of guests, staff, and crew whom he and Gorsky needed to locate and eliminate.

Petrov and the prince made small talk for a few minutes, while Gorsky and Urmanov stayed silent and sipped their water.

The prince cleared his throat and said, "As for the ladies..."

Petrov assured him, "They are compliant, professional, and discreet." He suggested, "Your Highness should choose his companion first. Or perhaps two companions. Then we should let nature take its course."

The prince nodded, and his eyes moved toward the three overnight bags.

Petrov further assured him, "We have brought something for every taste."

Again, the prince nodded, then informed his guests, "We will soon stop the ship and spend the night at anchor, then in the morning perhaps you three gentlemen will join me in my stateroom for breakfast and conversation as we set sail for New York." He inquired, "Will that suit you?"

"That is a good plan," Petrov replied, though he had a better one. He asked, "Will we have any difficulties or delays getting into New York Harbor?" He explained, "I have a lunch engagement in the city."

The prince assured him, "We were cleared at Ambrose Buoy when we first arrived on Saturday, and when Captain Wells requested permission for an overnight cruise this morning, he stated that we were not leaving American waters, so there will be no further security check at Ambrose when we return. Captain Wells also assures me he can navigate to Pier 11 without waiting for a harbor pilot. So it will go quickly." He added, "And most likely there will not be another Customs boarding when we re-dock at Pier 11."

"Good," said Petrov, though it would not be Captain Wells who would be steering *The Hana*. And *The Hana* would not be docking at Pier 11.

The important thing, Petrov knew, was that *The Hana* had been previously cleared at Ambrose Buoy to enter the harbor and would not be subject to another security check. Also, *The Hana* was logged into the Coast Guard's Automatic Identification System and would not be challenged to identify itself. This practice of extending some courtesies of the sea to private pleasure craft, especially those from friendly countries, was an American security lapse and also an opportunity that the SVR had discovered and exploited.

So this was all going as planned, Petrov thought, though the prince didn't know that he had aided the plan by taking Petrov's suggestion that they rendezvous in Southampton, away from New York City and the embassy watchers. Now getting back into New York Harbor would not present any problems for *The Hana*—only for the City of New York.

The prince said to Petrov, "I assume everyone's papers are in order so that you and your female companions can disembark and pass through Immigration and Customs."

Petrov replied, "Of course." He joked, "The ladies, too, have diplomatic passports."

The prince smiled, but Petrov saw that his highness seemed concerned about twelve scantily clad prostitutes leaving his yacht at Pier 11. Plus, of course, neither the ladies nor the three Russian men had been on *The Hana*'s original manifest. And in truth, this could be a problem, except that *The Hana* would turn into a nuclear fireball as it lay at anchor in the harbor, which eliminated the prince's problem.

The prince was looking at Petrov, and Petrov assured him, "We will be met at the pier by a high-ranking consulate officer of the Russian Federation." He added, "There will be no difficulties."

The prince nodded, then suggested, "Perhaps you would like to freshen up." He stood and his guests did as well. The prince said, "The steward will show you to your staterooms." He glanced at his watch, which Petrov noticed was a diamond-encrusted Rolex, and informed his guests, "We will have cocktails in the dining room in half an hour." He further advised his guests, "Dress is casual. Come as you are."

As the prince turned to leave, Petrov made a half bow, as did Urmanov, but Gorsky did not, and he watched the prince leave, then said, to no one in particular, "The world will be a better place without him."

Petrov admonished, "Be a good guest, Viktor. It is no fault of his that he was born royal, rich, and Muslim."

Gorsky smiled. "At least our oligarchs work hard to steal their money."

Petrov smiled, too, then looked at Dr. Urmanov, who was not smiling, and wondered if he knew he was a dead man.

Moscow's plan had been to deliver Dr. Urmanov to *The Hana* via the Russian fishing trawler along with Captain Gleb and the nuclear device. But Petrov had insisted that Urmanov be under his control in New York, so that he, Petrov, could evaluate the man and reject him if there seemed to be a question of his willingness to arm the device. Well, Petrov thought, Dr. Urmanov was willing, or he wouldn't have come this far. Also, the promised two million Swiss francs was a good incentive. Siberian exile was an even better incentive.

Petrov recalled that Moscow had been concerned about slipping Urmanov into America under an alias as a U.N. diplomat. But it had been done before, always successfully, and the SVR assured the Kremlin that no one in the American State Department Intelligence office would discover the true identity of this obscure retired physicist during the diplomatic vetting process.

And so, he, Petrov, had gotten his way, and he and Gorsky had taken the opportunity in New York to question Urmanov about the nuclear device and about all the steps necessary to correct any problems that might arise during the arming sequence. In any case, Petrov and Gorsky each had the device's access code and Petrov would actually arm the device himself and set the timer. Dr. Urmanov was necessary only if there was a technical problem. And if the timer clock didn't function, the device had been fitted with a radio signal detonator—a suicide trigger—which Petrov was prepared to use.

One way or the other, Petrov thought, New York would have the dubious distinction of being only the third city in the world destroyed by a nuclear weapon. The Manhattan Project was coming home.

CHAPTER EIGHTEEN

Viktor Gorsky went to Colonel Petrov's stateroom with his overnight bag, which he opened, spreading out the deck plans of *The Hana* on the bed. They had not overplanned this part of the operation, agreeing to wait and see what they found aboard the yacht. Overplanning, as they both knew, left little room for initiative and instinct. But now that they were here, Petrov and Gorsky discussed the most effective method of killing the crew of more than twenty men, as well as the six guests and their host, and also the twelve prostitutes.

They agreed that Gorsky would start on the bridge to be certain no radio message would be sent as the killings proceeded. Petrov said, "Be careful not to damage any instruments or controls."

"Of course."

Petrov continued, "Then you will go to the salon and take care of the ladies."

Gorsky nodded without comment.

Petrov looked at him and said, "This is difficult, I know. But they have served their purpose, and they will die for a good cause."

"We both understand this, Vasily," Gorsky replied, using his colonel's given name, which was permitted in situations such as this.

Petrov said, "I will start in the dining room. That should go quickly. Then I will go to the galley, then to the crew's quarters"—he pointed to the tank deck, which was partly below the waterline—"where I hope to find all of them at the dinner hour."

They studied the plans of the five-deck yacht: the tank deck where the crew lived, and where the engines, fuel, and water were located; the lower deck, which held the guest staterooms and officers' quarters as well as the tender garage and the swimming platform; and the main deck, which held the dining room and bar, the galley, and the prince's suite. Next was the salon deck, which had an al fresco lounge, and finally the smaller top deck where the bridge was located, along with the captain's quarters and the ship's office. Petrov and Gorsky tried to determine where everyone would be during dinner—or where they might be hiding if they became aware of what was happening.

Gorsky reminded his boss, "The crew carries handheld radios for shipboard communication."

Petrov replied, "We will be sure they have no time to communicate." He added, "As always, this business depends on speed, silence, and surprise." He lifted the gift-wrapped object from his bag and opened a taped end of the blue wrapping paper, revealing the barrel of the MP5 submachine gun. "We can silence this"—he tapped the silencer at the end of the muzzle—"but men scream when they are being shot. Women scream louder. So be quick and accurate."

Gorsky nodded.

Petrov further advised, "Try to avoid ricochets and remember that bullets pass through people and we do not want shattered windows for passing ships to see. So fire low for the takedown." He smiled. "We should use our trick of a group photograph whenever necessary."

Gorsky didn't need advice from Colonel Petrov, but he nodded and said, "It will go well. It always does."

Petrov looked at the wrapped submachine gun in his hands. The German-made MP5 was a good choice for this job. This model, with the telescoping stock retracted, was only twenty-two inches long and weighed less than six pounds. It could be held in one hand by its grip and fired as a machine pistol, which was actually what the Germans called it—a Maschinenpistole, Model 5. MP5.

The magazine held thirty 9mm rounds, and though it wasn't an accurate weapon, the cyclic rate of fire of 750 rounds a minute made it a very deadly weapon in close-in situations, which was what one would find on a ship.

Most importantly, it never jammed, and with the silencer it was as quiet as it was lethal. It was a favorite weapon of the American counterterrorist forces as well as over a hundred other countries that used the MP5 for their police and paramilitary forces. Even the Russians bought them, and Petrov had requested two, gift-wrapped.

Petrov looked up from the weapon and said to Gorsky, "Tell Urmanov to remain in his room with his door locked until we come for him."

Gorsky nodded.

The slight vibration in the ship's superstructure ceased, indicating that the engines had been set at idle, and Petrov felt the forward motion of the ship decrease, which he confirmed by looking out the porthole. Soon the anchors would be lowered. He had been assured at his briefing in Moscow that it was standard procedure for a ship that was intending to make a nearby port at dawn to drop anchor for the night at the dinner hour, allowing the deckhands and officers time to eat and rest while the stewards and cooks attended to the guests. And this worked well for Petrov and Gorsky, who would not have to put a gun to Captain Wells' head to make him stop the ship so they could rendezvous with the Russian fishing trawler and take Captain Gleb and his cargo aboard. In fact, when Captain Wells dropped anchor, his and his crew's usefulness was over, as were their lives.

Petrov and Gorsky checked their watches and agreed to meet in the hallway in ten minutes.

But before Gorsky left, he said, "That caterer troubles me."

Petrov assured him, "It is of no consequence now."

"We should have taken him—and that lady who appeared to know him—inside to question them."

"Then you create a problem where none existed."

"Or you solve a problem."

"Tamorov would wonder why we were questioning two of his caterers."

"Let him wonder." Gorsky continued, "We should at least have told Tamorov to tell those two to leave."

"And if they were embassy watchers, they would have gone directly to their vehicle and called the FBI, who would have sent aircraft and boats to watch Tamorov's house. And we would not be here now."

Gorsky thought about that. Yes, it was a difficult situation with difficult choices, and Colonel Petrov had made the choice to do nothing. And that may have been the best choice. Still... He said to Petrov, "We should have taken them inside and killed them."

Petrov smiled. "There are times, Viktor, when killing solves problems and times when it creates problems."

"The more people you kill, the fewer problems you have." He explained, "People cause problems."

Petrov again smiled. "You are a simple man, Viktor. I like that."

Gorsky did not reply.

Petrov thought about all of this. It was possible, he conceded, that those two could have been the embassy watchers who had followed them from New York. And if that were true, then they had seen him and his two companions and the prostitutes board the amphibious craft and sail out to sea. But that was all they saw, and all they knew. They could not know where he was going, though it would seem obvious because of the ladies that they were going to another party. And as Petrov also knew, the embassy watchers only watched, then reported to the FBI, who, as in the past, would be slow to react to the missing Russian diplomats.

Or more likely this man Depp was simply a day worker hired off the street and not very good at his job. The woman, however, seemed more intelligent, though equally inept. In any case, the mission had begun. They were aboard *The Hana*, and there was no turning back. Especially after they began shooting everyone.

Petrov said, "We have more immediate things to think about, Viktor. Do not let your mind become distracted."

"Yes, Colonel." Gorsky turned and left the stateroom.

Petrov resealed the blue wrapping paper around the MP5 and looked at his watch. Within fifteen minutes, the decks of this royal yacht would be running with blood. But that was nothing compared to what was going to happen when *The Hana* sailed into New York Harbor in the morning.

CHAPTER NINETEEN

Colonel Petrov left his stateroom and went into the hallway where Gorsky was waiting. Both men carried their gift-wrapped MP5 submachine guns, and stuffed in their pockets were extra magazines and *The Hana*'s deck plans. Under their loose-fitting polo shirts they each carried the small Makarov pistol in a holster clipped to their belts in the small of their backs. Each man also carried a sheathed commando knife.

Petrov whispered to Gorsky in Russian, "I want no bodies—dead or alive—going overboard." He made sure Gorsky understood, "I want no corpses that can be traced to this boat washing up on the shore with bullets in them. All evidence of our presence here and what we did will be vaporized in New York Harbor."

Gorsky was annoyed that Petrov thought he needed to explain this, as though he, Gorsky, was little more than a killer with no thought of the finer details of the job. "Yes, Colonel."

Petrov continued, "Remember, we cannot communicate with our cell phones, and we cannot use the crew's handheld radios or the intercom system, which can be heard by everyone. So we must act independently, but in concert." He asked, "Are we clear about our assignments?"

Gorsky nodded.

"And do you know this ship as well as you know your own house?"

"Better, since I have not been home in half a year."

Petrov smiled and asked, "Are you feeling confident, Viktor?"

"I am, Colonel."

"Good. Well, it is time for us to deliver our gifts." He reminded Gorsky, "Fire low." He and Gorsky shook hands, and Petrov said, "We will meet on the bridge when we are finished."

Petrov walked toward the stern of the yacht and ascended a staircase to the main deck.

Gorsky walked in the opposite direction, through the officers' quarters where there was a vestibule with a small elevator and a spiral staircase that connected all the decks. Gorsky climbed the spiral staircase to the bridge deck.

Vasily Petrov saw a deckhand at the top of the stairs, coming toward him. The man stood aside at attention and said to the prince's guest, "Good evening, sir."

Petrov didn't want to kill him there, but he noted the man's face and build, as he had done with the stewards and crew he'd already seen. The next time he saw those faces they would be dead or a second from death. And if he didn't see one of those faces, it meant the man was hiding and needed to be found.

He asked the deckhand, "Where are you going?"

"To dinner, sir."

The man, about thirty years old, had an accent and looked Slavic, so Petrov asked, "Russkii?"

"No, sir. Bulgarian."

Petrov nodded. "Have a good dinner."

"Thank you."

Petrov ascended to the main deck where the ladies had gathered earlier for champagne and a dip in the pool. No doubt the prince had watched them from the salon deck above, and perhaps he had already made his choice. Or several choices. Petrov smiled.

He passed through double doors that led to a wood-paneled bar area adjacent to the dining room.

Standing around the bar were seven men, somewhat better dressed than he was—the four Saudi guests and the two Chinese businessmen, and also Prince Ali Faisel, his host, who saw him enter and said, "Welcome, Vasily."

"I apologize for my lateness."

"Come join us."

But Vasily Petrov did not move from what would be his firing position.

Petrov also noted the bartender, whom he recognized as the steward who'd served them in the salon, and another steward, Karim, the one in traditional Arab garb who was the prince's personal bodyguard and who was now serving hors d'oeuvres. He wondered if the man was armed. To the right of the bar was the entrance to the long dining room, partly separated by frosted glass partitions, where two other stewards were making last-minute preparations for dinner.

"Come. What do you drink?"

"Mineral water," Petrov replied, but did not move to the bar, and the six guests looked at him quizzically, as did the prince, who said to Karim, "Don't you see that this man has a package? Take that from him."

The steward set down his hors d'oeuvre tray and hurried toward the Russian guest.

The prince inquired, "And where are Viktor and Pavel?"

"Directly behind me." Petrov glanced behind him, though not to look for his compatriots, but to be certain no one was there. Then, as Karim reached for the package, Petrov tore the wrapping paper from his submachine gun and fired a single round, low, into the steward's groin, throwing him to the floor.

The men at the bar, not having heard the silenced gun, could not process what their eyes had just seen, and they stood, looking at the bleeding steward, then at Petrov, then at the weapon in his hands.

Petrov aimed low so as not to hit the glasses and bottles behind the bar, and fired a long, traversing stream of 9mm rounds, from left to right into the tightly packed men, who all went down, some thrown against the bar, others falling where they stood. Only the bartender remained standing, dazed and frozen, looking at Petrov with terror in his eyes as he threw out his hands in a protective gesture and shouted, "No!"

Petrov fired a single round through the man's chest and he fell back, crashing into the glasses and bottles behind him, then dropped behind the bar.

Petrov moved quickly through the entrance to the dining room, where the two stewards were hurrying toward him. It was obvious that they'd heard glass breaking, but not the muffled sound of the shots or the bodies hitting the carpeted floor.

The stewards stopped and stared at Petrov, then noticed the weapon at his side as Petrov brought it up with one hand and fired a round into each man's abdomen. Both men doubled over, then dropped to their knees on the marble floor, holding their bleeding wounds. Petrov stepped closer and fired a round through each man's head, then spun around and walked back to the bar area.

None of the seven men on the floor appeared to be dead, though there was blood everywhere. Petrov drew his silenced pistol and went from man to man, putting a bullet in each one's head, coming last to the prince, who was sprawled on the floor with his back to the bar, his hands pressed against his spurting wounds, moaning loudly. The two men made eye contact, and Petrov said, with sincerity, "You have given your life to defeat America, and you will be praised throughout Islam as you ascend into Paradise." Petrov smiled, and added, "I, unfortunately, will get no credit." He squeezed the trigger and put a bullet into Prince Ali Faisel's forehead.

Petrov did not forget the bartender, and he came around the bar and saw the man lying on his back with a pool of blood around him, and no further bleeding from his motionless chest. But to be sure, he fired a bullet into the man's throat.

He then went to Karim and searched him for a weapon, finding only a dagger, reminding him of an American expression: "Don't bring a knife to a gunfight."

Petrov checked his watch. Four minutes from start to finish.

He put a fresh magazine into his pistol, and another into the submachine gun, which he wrapped in the bartender's towel.

Now on to the galley.

* * *

Viktor Gorsky came to the vestibule at the top of the spiral staircase. To his left was a door whose brass plaque read, in English, CAPTAIN, and to his right was a door whose plaque said SHIP'S OFFICE.

Behind him was the elevator door, and ahead was the bridge, where he saw two men in white officers' uniforms sitting in high-backed pedestal chairs at the long instrument panel. The man on the left had swiveled his chair toward the man on the right, and they were speaking. Neither man was Captain Wells.

Gorsky also noticed that on the bulkhead to the right of the bridge opening was an intercom and also the security pad that according to his briefing would activate a sliding bulletproof door. The bulkhead, too, was bulletproof. A good security feature in case of pirates or mutiny. Or assassins.

Gorsky strode into the light, airy bridge carrying his wrapped parcel, and the man whose chair was turned saw him and asked, in Irish-accented English, "Can I help you, sir?"

Gorsky recognized the man from the photos that Gleb had taken in Monte Carlo as Conners, the first mate. "I am looking for Captain Wells." He held out his wrapped parcel. "I have something for him."

"He's in his quarters, sir." He suggested, "You can knock."

"Yes, thank you."

The man on the right, who Gorsky recognized as Donato, the engineer, swiveled his chair and looked at Gorsky and at the wrapped object in his hands and said with an Italian accent, "His room is there." He pointed. "Captain."

Gorsky glanced over his shoulder, then stepped farther onto the bridge, trying to position himself and his shots to avoid hitting the instrument panel or the wraparound windshield that he knew was bulletproof, but would shatter.

Conners stood and said, "Here, let me show you."

"Thank you. That will make it easier for me."

Conners walked past Gorsky, who pulled his Makarov from

under his shirt and fired a bullet into the man's lower spine, sending him sprawling onto the deck.

Donato swiveled completely around and stared at his shipmate, facedown on the deck, blood spreading across his white shirt. He looked up at Gorsky, confused, then saw the pistol, which Gorsky fired at a downward angle into the man's groin, causing him to let out a surprised grunt. Gorsky watched as the engineer slid off his chair and slumped to the deck, holding his groin with both hands and moaning in pain. As the man tried to stand, Gorsky put a bullet into the back of his head.

Gorsky also put a bullet into the first mate's head, then without breaking stride he exited the bridge, pushing the button to close the sliding security door. Gorsky then walked to the captain's door and knocked.

"Come in."

Gorsky stuck the pistol under his shirt, opened the door, and saw Captain Wells, still in his uniform, sitting cross-legged in an easy chair in his spacious quarters, reading a book. Wells seemed surprised at the visit and said, "Mr.... Gorsky. Correct?"

"That is correct."

"How can I help you?"

"Two of your officers, Mr. Conners and Mr. Donato, were kind enough to show me around the bridge, and I wanted to thank you."

"No need to thank me, Mr. Gorsky."

"I have here a gift"—he held up his package—"for your officers. Where may I find the other officer?"

Wells seemed a bit confused and said impatiently, "I believe Mr. Lentini is in the ship's office. Right behind you."

"Thank you. And I wanted to assure you that my ladies will not trouble you on your last voyage."

Captain Wells looked into the eyes of Viktor Gorsky and knew something was very wrong. But before he could think about how to get to his gun, the Russian pulled a pistol and fired a round through the book and into the captain's chest. Captain Wells, still holding the book, looked down at his chest and Gorsky fired a bullet into the top of Captain Wells' head. "Bon voyage."

Gorsky turned and left the captain's quarters, closing the door behind him. He crossed the vestibule, and knocked on the door of the ship's office.

"Come in."

Gorsky stuck his pistol under his shirt and opened the door. The ship's navigator, Carlo Lentini, dressed in his whites, was sitting at a computer keyboard. Without looking up, the man asked, "Yes?"

Gorsky did not reply, and the officer turned his head toward him and asked in Italian-accented English, "Who are you…?" Then, "Oh…" He stood and said, "How may I help you?"

"You may sit, Mr. Lentini."

The officer hesitated, then sat and waited for the guest to say something.

Gorsky asked, "What are you doing?"

The navigator looked at his unannounced guest, and there was something in the man's tone and manner that troubled him. He replied, "I…I am entering in the ship's log."

"And where will the officers dine tonight?"

"We dine tonight in the captain's quarters."

"And who will have the watch?"

"A deckhand will take the watch."

"And who will bring you your dinner?"

"A steward. Why—?"

"When?"

"Soon."

"Good." Gorsky looked at his watch and said, "Make a final entry in your log, Mr. Lentini." He pulled his small pistol from his belt and said, "All ship's officers were killed by twenty-one hundred hours…" He fired a single shot into the navigator's chest, which spun the swivel chair around, and Gorsky put another round into the base of the man's skull. "…and dined in hell."

Gorsky left the ship's office, closed the door, and took up a position in the vestibule behind the spiral staircase, near the elevator, waiting for the steward and the deckhand.

Hunting people, like hunting game, had two basic elements—stalking and waiting in ambush. He preferred stalking, but sometimes one needed to wait. Killing was an art. Being killed, not so much.

Vasily Petrov slung his submachine gun, wrapped in the bartender's towel, over his shoulder and walked quickly past the two dead stewards and through the long dining room whose table was set for ten. He noticed through the large windows that the sea was calm, though there was a fog coming in from the south. This could be a problem for the rendezvous with the fishing trawler and for the trawler's lifeboat with only Captain Gleb onboard to find *The Hana*. But they had made provisions for a bad-weather rendezvous, and Petrov was confident that Gleb and the nuclear device would be aboard *The Hana* within the hour. He hoped that Gleb had been fully briefed about the corpses all over the ship.

Petrov passed through the butler's pantry and entered the main galley.

The four kitchen staff were putting garnish on ten appetizer plates, which appeared to be some sort of pink creamed fish. Petrov disliked French food and he was glad he didn't have to eat this.

One of the kitchen staff saw him and tapped the chef's arm and nodded toward the door.

Chef André, a tall thin man, looked up from his food preparation and said, "Yes?"

Petrov knew that the galley would be a problem; it was filled with tightly packed steel equipment, open flames, and propane tanks. Not a good place to fire an automatic weapon. Also, the five kitchen staff—three men, one woman, and the chef—were spread out and moving quickly as they went about their duties.

"Monsieur, may I help you?"

"His Highness has permitted me to see your kitchen."

"Yes? What do you wish to see?"

"A photo, s'il vous plaît." Petrov held up his cell phone. "It will go quickly," he promised.

The chef hesitated, then, realizing it would be better to accommodate the prince's guest than to protest, he motioned his three male staff and the woman to stand with him in the aisle between the cutting table and the food locker.

They all assembled, closely packed in the narrow aisle, and Petrov raised his cell phone. If anyone noticed or wondered what it was that he had slung in a towel over his shoulder, they didn't ask. "Smile!"

He would have actually snapped the photo, but he'd removed the battery from his phone so that the Americans could not track his signal.

"One more, please."

Everyone smiled again, though the chef, André, looked impatient.

Petrov dropped the phone into his pocket, then swung the submachine gun to his front, pulled off the bar towel, and fired a low sweeping burst of rounds into the posed group, who for a half second didn't understand what it was in his hands that was spitting flames. In fact, the woman was still smiling when she was hit. The ricochets pinged off the tile floor and kitchen equipment. Then everything was silent.

Petrov put the weapon on single shot and stood at the feet of the five white-smocked people who were spurting blood from their legs and abdomens. They were all alive, and Petrov began with the woman, who was starting to cry out in pain, and fired a bullet into her head. Then in quick succession he gave the other four what André would call the coup de grâce.

He found a bigger towel to wrap his submachine gun and slung it across his back, then went to the stove and shut off the gas under the pots and saucepans. He smelled something unpleasant and looked through the glass door of the raised oven and saw mutton chops roasting in a pan. Who could eat this? He shut off the oven and left the galley.

Now on to the crew quarters.

Viktor Gorsky waited for the steward and the deckhand.

He carried his submachine gun, still gift-wrapped, under his left arm, leaving his right hand free to draw his pistol, which was in his trouser pocket. So far, this had all been handgun work; not the type of work where one needed a submachine gun. That, however, would change in the salon with the ladies.

Gorsky heard the hydraulic whine of the elevator and stood off to the side of the door.

The door slid open and a food cart appeared, followed by a white-coated steward who pushed the cart across the vestibule toward the captain's door, not seeing Gorsky, who was behind him.

The steward glanced at the closed security door to the bridge, then knocked on the captain's door and waited. He then moved, without the cart, to the bridge door and pressed the intercom button. "It is Abdi. Dinner." He waited a few seconds, and Gorsky could tell that Abdi was perplexed and didn't know what to do. Ring again? Or push the entry pad to open the bridge door, which Gorsky guessed was rarely, if ever, closed.

The steward pulled his handheld radio from his pocket and was about to make a call, but Gorsky said, "Excuse me."

The steward turned with a start, then, recognizing a guest, he relaxed, though he didn't know where the man had come from. The staircase perhaps.

"Yes, sir?"

"I am waiting for the deckhand who will stand watch."

"He should be on the bridge."

"He is not."

The steward looked at his watch and said, "Perhaps a few minutes. Why—?"

"I will wait."

Gorsky knew he could shoot the steward there and then, without concern that the round would pierce the bulletproof door or bulkhead and strike something vital on the bridge. But he didn't want a dead man in the vestibule when the deckhand arrived, so he said, "The captain awaits you."

"I have knocked—"

"Please." He motioned toward the captain's door and the food cart.

The steward hesitated and looked at the Russian standing on the far side of the staircase railing with a wrapped object under his arm, then returned to the captain's door and knocked again. He glanced at the guest, shrugged, and said, "Perhaps he is in the ship's office."

"He is not."

Clearly the steward was finding this situation unusual, and he reached again for his radio. Gorsky reached for his gun.

The sound of footsteps came up the spiral staircase, and the steward said, "That will be Malkin." He seemed relieved, Gorsky thought, that someone else would take charge of this situation. The steward had many guests to attend to. Or thought he did.

The head and shoulders of a man wearing the blue shirt of a deckhand appeared on the spiral staircase. As the man stepped into the vestibule, he glanced at the closed door to the bridge, then noticed the steward at the captain's door and asked, "Why is the bridge door shut, Abdi?"

The steward shrugged, then nodded toward the guest near the elevator, noticing that he had laid his package on the floor.

The deckhand, Malkin, turned and saw Gorsky. "Yes, sir?"

Gorsky drew his pistol and held it in a two-handed grip, steadied his aim, and fired a round at the center mass of each man, both of whom were thrown back against the wall. The deckhand slid slowly to the floor, but the steward bounced off the wall and fell across the food cart.

Gorsky came quickly around the spiral staircase and threw open the door to the captain's quarters and pushed the food cart with the steward's body lying atop it into the captain's room, then grabbed the deckhand by his collar and dragged him into the room. Both men were still alive and Gorsky fired a bullet into each man's head, then exited the captain's room and closed the door.

Gorsky pocketed his pistol, retrieved his package, and moved quickly to the spiral staircase, descending three steps at a time toward the salon level. As he descended, he could hear music and women's laughter.

Vasily Petrov moved quickly from the main deck galley down to the tank deck, still carrying his MP5 slung across his back. He passed no one on the way, but in the narrow passageway that led to the crew's quarters a deckhand suddenly appeared, coming toward him. The man stopped and braced himself against the wall as the guest hurried past him.

Petrov suddenly spun around, pulled his pistol, and fired a bullet into the side of the man's head.

A serendipitous kill was as good as a planned kill, except in a hallway, which presented problems. Petrov looked around, then opened a door marked VALVE ACCESS, revealing a maze of vertical and horizontal pipes. He dragged the man across the floor and squeezed him into the tight space, then shut the door and continued toward the midship of the tank deck.

He could hear voices coming through a large door at the end of the passageway, and he conjured a mental image of the crew area deck plan: an open common space for recreation and dining, flanked by five small rooms on the port side for the chef and his kitchen staff, all of whom were now accounted for.

On the starboard side were two-man cabins that were the sleeping quarters of the seven deckhands and the seven stewards, and farther toward the bow was the crew's pantry and galley.

Petrov tried to determine how many men would be in the crew area. He had already eliminated four stewards in the bar and dining room, and he knew that one or two stewards would be with the ladies in the salon, where everyone should be dead by now if Gorsky was on schedule. That left one or two stewards unaccounted for—though they should not be down here because of the large number of guests onboard. Therefore, only deckhands should be in the crew area—except the one who was in the valve access room. So, with the ship at anchor, he might find the six remaining deckhands, including the Bulgarian, having dinner, which would make his life and their deaths much easier.

Petrov unslung his MP5 submachine gun and loosely re-wrapped it in the towel with his right hand in the folds, four fingers around the vertical grip and one finger on the trigger. He checked that the shell casings had enough room in the towel to eject, then let his arm fall at his side and opened the door marked CREW QUARTERS.

Four young men in white jeans and blue shirts sat around a table toward the rear of the large common room, eating their dinner as they watched a flat-screen television. None of them was the Bulgarian he'd passed earlier on the staircase. That man, therefore, was elsewhere, and so was the seventh deckhand. Perhaps they were in their rooms.

The television was showing a war film, and he heard American voices coming from the soldiers on the screen. They looked like brave young men, and they seemed confident as they fired at ill-dressed and bearded men carrying Kalashnikov rifles. Iraq, perhaps, or Afghanistan. There was a lot of blood. He wondered if the prince would approve of this movie.

One of the deckhands noticed him and said something to the other three men, who took their eyes off the television and stopped eating.

None of them stood, but at least one recognized him, because the man called out, in Russian, "Are you lost?"

Petrov remembered the man from the tender garage and replied, in English, "No. Are you?"

The man laughed tentatively, then asked, in English, "What do you have there, sir?"

"A gift from the chef for the crew."

No one replied, and Petrov asked, "Where are your mates?"

The Russian-speaking man replied, "You will find Malkin on the bridge, standing watch. As for Diaz, he just left to assist your ladies in the salon—in any way he can." He smiled.

The other three men laughed, and Petrov, too, smiled, knowing that six deckhands were now accounted for—Diaz dead in the valve closet, Malkin on the bridge and now similarly indisposed, and these four men a few seconds from joining their mates, leaving just the Bulgarian to find. Petrov asked, "And where is your Bulgarian shipmate?"

No one answered, and Petrov realized he had asked one question too many and the men were now staring at him and glancing at his towel-wrapped arm.

One of them asked, "What have you brought us?"

Petrov, still standing outside the door, glanced over his shoulder, raised his arm, and aimed the towel-wrapped submachine gun.

"Smert." *Death.* He fired a long burst at the men around the table, and the towel smoked and caught fire.

He ripped the towel off and flung it aside as he strode quickly into the crew area to the table where all the men had been knocked off their chairs and now lay on the deck in spreading pools of blood. Petrov flipped the MP5 onto single shot and fired into each man's head, then turned and looked at the table, which was covered with splattered blood, food, and broken dinnerware. He spotted an unbroken bowl filled with sliced apples, and he helped himself to a piece before checking the pantry and the crew's galley, which were empty. He then went from door to door and checked each room, but they were also unoccupied. The seventh deckhand, the Bulgarian, was still missing.

Petrov took a handheld radio from the belt of one of the crewmen and listened, but no one was communicating. Well, he thought, if Gorsky was having equally good hunting, *The Hana* was now a ghost ship. He put the radio in his pocket and found a pillowcase in a linen closet and put his submachine gun into it.

He looked again at the flat-screen TV. An American soldier with a sniper rifle was taking aim at a bearded man in a turban who held a Kalashnikov rifle. Yes, this was Afghanistan, but it reminded him of Chechnya. He pulled his Makarov pistol and fired two quick shots—one at the American sniper and one at the Islamist fighter. The screen transformed into a kaleidoscope of colors, then went black. Petrov smiled and walked out of the room.

Viktor Gorsky stepped off the spiral staircase onto the salon deck. A set of glass doors led to the long salon where a buffet dinner was laid out on the sideboard, though the ladies, still in their bikinis and cover-ups, seemed to be ignoring the food and enjoying the champagne that was being poured by two stewards. Soft music came from the wall speakers, and he recognized Tchaikovsky's *Swan Lake,* which he supposed the prince had requested for his Russian guests.

One of the ladies saw him and called out in Russian, "What do you have there, Viktor? Come in. Why are you standing there?"

He stepped into the silk-draped salon and his eyes scanned the twenty-meter-long room of floor-to-ceiling windows. To the left was the side balcony, which was now occupied by three of the ladies. At the far end of the salon was the al fresco lounge where another three ladies were smoking and drinking.

One of the ladies in the salon said to him, "Where is your lover, Viktor?"

The other ladies laughed, but when Gorsky looked at them they stopped laughing. Gorsky forced a smile and said, "He has left me for the chef."

The ladies laughed again, and one of them reached for the gift-wrapped submachine gun. "Is that for us?"

Gorsky held the blue package over his head and replied, "Yes. But you must earn it."

A steward walked over to him and asked, "Can I help you, sir?"

"I am just seeing that my ladies are being taken care of."

"They are, sir." He reminded the guest, "Dinner is being served in the dining room."

"Thank you."

"May I show you to the dining room?"

"In a minute."

Gorsky noticed that the other steward was on his handheld radio, apparently trying to call someone. Or someone had called him. But who was alive to call? Or to answer a call? In any case, it was time to act, before either of these stewards sensed that all was not right aboard this ship.

Gorsky called out, in English, "Ladies! I need your attention, please!"

The six ladies in the salon looked at Gorsky and he said, "I need everyone here." He said to the stewards, "Go get the others."

One steward went to the balcony, and the other who had been on his radio walked to the outdoor lounge.

One of the ladies asked, "What is it, Viktor?"

"Some good news."

She replied, in Russian, "We don't have to sleep with these Arab pigs?"

They all laughed.

Gorsky smiled.

The ladies from the balcony and the lounge were in the salon now, and the two stewards looked as though they were about to leave, but Gorsky said to them, "Please stay. This will take only a minute."

Gorsky stood motionless, looking at the twelve women, and a feeling of sadness came over him. He had killed women before, but not Russian women—only Muslim women who were enemies of the Russian Federation.

"Viktor! Why are you standing there? Are you drunk?"

He looked at the woman, Tasha, the one who had given her phone number to the American. He would have liked to question her about the man, but Colonel Petrov wasn't interested in any information that would abort this mission. And in any case, now that the killings had begun aboard *The Hana*, the mission was unstoppable.

The ladies were getting restless, and they were all probably drunk, Gorsky knew, and therefore more difficult to communicate with than usual.

One of them called out, "We want our cell phones back, Viktor."

They all joined in agreement. "Our cell phones. Give them to us."

He took a deep breath and said, "Yes, but first, the prince has a gift for all of you." He held up his package, and though it was poorly wrapped and oddly shaped, he said, "There are diamond necklaces in here. And the prince wants a photograph of all of you wearing them."

The ladies became excited and one of them called out, "Open it!"

"Yes, but now..." He motioned to the chairs around the coffee table. "You must sit and I will give them to you for the photo."

A few of the ladies seemed impatient, but they all moved to the seating area where Tasha took charge, seating six of the women, with three standing behind them, and three kneeling in front, including herself.

"Excellent," said Gorsky.

One of the ladies suggested to the others, "Take off your cover-ups so the prince can see his diamonds on our skin."

Everyone thought that was a wonderful idea and they pulled off their cover-ups.

Gorsky noticed that the stewards now seemed more interested in staying in the salon, and he said to them, "Please see that each lady has a glass of champagne."

One of the women protested, "Give us the diamonds, Viktor, and to hell with the champagne."

They all laughed.

"Please," said Gorsky, "the prince deserves a beautiful photograph."

This was becoming more difficult than his work on the bridge. But he knew it would be.

The stewards were handing out glasses and pouring champagne into them.

Gorsky stepped onto the ottoman and faced the ladies and the two stewards.

Thirty rounds in the magazine, fourteen targets. He would probably have to reload.

One of the women said to him, "Now give us our diamonds, Viktor." She stood and walked toward him, her hand extended.

He tore the paper from the submachine gun.

Tasha said, "What is...? Oh my God!"

Petrov quickly searched the tank deck—the engine room, laundry room, storage compartments, and all the belowdeck areas of the large ship—calling out, "Is anyone here? I am lost! Can anyone help me?"

But no one replied.

Petrov climbed a staircase to the lower deck where the tender garage and the swimming platform were located, as were the guest staterooms and the officers' quarters.

He went first toward the stern, calling out in the tender garage, "Hello! Is anyone here?"

He then moved to the glass doors that led outside to the swimming platform and noticed that the doors were bolted from the inside, meaning that no one had gone out to the swimming platform and abandoned ship by this route. He unbolted the doors and walked out to the platform.

The low clinging fog was getting thicker, and the sky was filled with stars, with a half-moon rising in the east. The sea, he saw, was still calm. Off in the distance, he saw the lights of a helicopter, hovering unusually low. He put this out of his mind and looked at his watch. Captain Gleb would be arriving in half an hour. And there was still work to do aboard *The Hana*.

Petrov left the swimming platform, rebolted the doors, and passed through the tender garage. He walked down the long, wide passageway between the ten staterooms, knocking on the locked doors and opening the unlocked ones, calling out, "Hello! Is anyone here?"

No one replied, except Dr. Urmanov, still locked in his stateroom. Petrov called to him, "Stay where you are!"

It would be good, he thought, if Gorsky had come upon the last deckhand. It would be bad, however, if this Bulgarian had seen the dead bodies and was hiding. Well, Petrov thought, they had anticipated this in their planning, and as long as the man had no access to the radios on the bridge, then for all Petrov cared he could hide like a rat until the ship exploded in a mushroom cloud.

But the thought of the bridge with all its communication equipment troubled him, though Gorsky should have finished his business in the salon and returned to the bridge by now. Petrov passed through the officers' quarters and took the elevator up to the bridge level.

Viktor Gorsky remained standing on the ottoman, surveying the carnage in the salon.

Yes, it was a difficult thing, and though he had tried to do it quickly, there were too many targets, and he had to go first for the men, and after he emptied his thirty-round magazine some of the ladies began running or crawling toward the exits, and he had to reload quickly and take them down, one at a time, with short bursts of fire. They had been terrified, and their screaming still echoed in his ears.

But at least he hadn't hit any of the windows, so there would be no outward evidence of violence onboard *The Hana* as it sailed into New York Harbor and lay at anchor through the night.

He stepped down from the ottoman, drew his pistol, and surveyed the nearly naked and still-bleeding women. A few were wounded only in the legs and were crying, or trying to crawl away, or imploring him to spare them. He went quickly from one to the other until his magazine was empty. He reloaded and continued.

He came to Tasha, who was lying on her back, a bullet wound in her abdomen and a grazing wound across her thigh. She was crying, though not so much from the pain, he thought, as from sadness.

He said, "I am sorry."

She looked at him and managed to say, "Why...?"

"Close your eyes, Tasha."

She shut her eyes and he fired a bullet into her heart.

He saved the two mortally wounded stewards for last, then went to the bar, washed his hands, and poured himself a flute of champagne.

Gorsky checked his watch. Twenty-two minutes since he had first walked onto the bridge. The operations officer in Moscow had estimated fifteen. But the desk idiots didn't know anything.

The stereo was still playing *Swan Lake,* which he liked.

Vasily Petrov exited the elevator into the vestibule of the bridge deck.

He held the MP5 in one hand, his finger on the trigger and the firing switch set to fully automatic.

He noticed that the bridge door was closed, and he wondered if Gorsky had closed it, or if the officers had been alerted and sealed themselves off. He felt his heart beating quickly in his chest, but then he saw to his left the bloodstains on the wall and floor near the captain's quarters, and he knew that Gorsky had been successful here, which gave him a sense of relief.

He moved quickly to the door marked SHIP'S OFFICE and pointed his MP5 at the door as he threw it open and dropped to one knee.

He saw that Gorsky had also been there, and he stood, closed the door, and went to the captain's quarters and threw open the door.

It took him a second to process what he was seeing, and he wasn't certain how this scene had come about and he didn't care, but he saw that the deckhand, Malkin, was now a confirmed kill. Sprawled across a food cart was a steward, and sitting in his easy chair was Captain Wells, staring at the book in his lap.

Petrov closed the door, then went directly to the bridge door and pushed the intercom buzzer.

No answer.

He pushed the entry pad, leveled his submachine gun, and dropped to one knee as the door slid open, revealing the two dead officers on the floor.

Petrov stood and went onto the bridge, moving quickly to the instrument console to inspect it for damage.

"I was very careful."

Petrov spun around to see Gorsky standing in the opening. He caught his breath and snapped, "That is a good way to get yourself killed, Gorsky."

Gorsky wanted to say, "You are the one who would now be dead." But he said, "I trust your quick judgment, Colonel."

Petrov did not respond to that, but asked, "Are you finished in the salon?"

"It is done."

"Good... so tell me."

"You can see this for yourself. All four officers, a deckhand, and a steward. As for the ladies... they are all gone, as are two stewards."

Petrov confirmed, "That accounts for all seven stewards."

"How do we get that number?"

"There were four with the prince and his six guests."

Gorsky nodded, and inquired, "And all the cooks were in the galley?"

"They still are." He smiled.

Gorsky, too, smiled, and asked, "Did you remember to shut off the gas?"

"I forget nothing, Viktor."

"Yes, Colonel." He asked, "And how was your visit to the crew's quarters?"

"Four, and one in the passageway."

They stood there a second, each waiting for the other to point out that a deckhand was missing. Finally, Petrov said, "So, unless you have forgotten a man you killed, there is one not accounted for."

Gorsky nodded.

"I actually passed him earlier on a staircase. A Bulgarian." Petrov added, "He said he was going to dinner, but he wasn't in the crew dining room." He smiled. "Well, he can't go far."

Gorsky pointed out, "He can, if he goes into the tender garage and takes the amphibious craft."

Petrov looked at the instruments on the panel that monitored the tender garage. There was no indication that anyone was opening the door and flooding the compartment.

Gorsky went to the security camera screen and pulled up the garage, but he couldn't see anyone there, and the amphibious craft sat in its chocks on the dry deck.

Petrov said, "I think we should not worry about one deckhand."

Gorsky didn't like his colonel's inattention to a problem. Petrov did this too often, and one day it would prove fatal to him. Or to the mission. He thought again of the man and woman at Tamorov's house. Problems—real or imagined—had to be addressed quickly and forcefully. He said, "I will go look for this man."

Petrov checked his watch. "Gleb will be here soon." He said to Gorsky, "We will follow the plan. I will stay here and secure the bridge, and you will go to the garage and open the door for Captain Gleb." He added, "Don't forget our nuclear physicist on the way."

Gorsky nodded.

"I will call you on the public address system when I see Gleb's craft approaching." He smiled. "No one else will hear me."

Gorsky ignored the joke and reminded Petrov, "The deckhand will hear you. And if he is Bulgarian, he will speak or understand some Russian."

"Well, then, Viktor, see if you can find him on your way to the garage." He smiled again. "You have as good a nose for finding the living as a cadaver dog has for finding the dead."

Gorsky did not reply.

Petrov was feeling suddenly better, and he said to Gorsky, "You did a good job, Viktor."

"Thank you, Vasily. Yourself as well."

"The pieces are almost all in place. We now await our new captain, and our cargo. And then we sail for New York."

Gorsky nodded. The colonel's optimism was perhaps justified. They were more than halfway toward the successful completion of the most important military mission that Russia had mounted since the Great Patriotic War against the Germans. For the colonel, this meant a promotion to general and a comfortable position in Moscow for the rest of his life. And of course, his father would be proud of him. As for Gorsky, he had been promised any assignment he asked for—as long as it was in Russia. Neither he nor Colonel Petrov would ever be allowed to leave Russia again. Not after what they did in New York. They would take that secret to the grave with them.

Petrov said, "I will remove these corpses from the bridge so they don't upset Captain Gleb. You will now go to the garage—"

The beating sound of helicopter blades penetrated into the nearly soundproof bridge, and both men looked through the windshield and saw the lights of a helicopter off their port side, at about two hundred meters altitude, traveling west.

Petrov said, "A commuter helicopter from the Hamptons."

Gorsky did not reply, though he knew that a commuter helicopter would not fly that low or be this far from land. But perhaps it was a Coast Guard helicopter, looking for a boat lost at sea.

Petrov said, "Go. Gleb will be here shortly."

Or, Gorsky thought, the Coast Guard was looking for *them*.

"Go!"

Gorsky stared at the retreating lights of the helicopter as it disappeared, then pulled his pistol, turned, and left the bridge, taking the spiral staircase down to the lower deck. He hoped he would find the deckhand trying to escape on the amphibious craft. Or maybe the man had put on a life vest and gone overboard. That's what he would do. Or perhaps the deckhand would do what most sailors would do—come to the bridge to see if the officers were there. Well, there *was* an officer there—Colonel Petrov of the SVR.

As he descended to the lower deck, Gorsky began to realize that all was not well. A deckhand was missing, and a helicopter had just flown by. These facts were not related, but it was possible that the helicopter was related to the two caterers, who he still believed were not caterers.

The mission control officer in Moscow had given them a way to abort this mission, even at this point. But that was not going to happen with Colonel Vasily Petrov in command. Colonel Petrov had dreamt too long about sitting in the private jet having coffee as a nuclear fireball engulfed New York City. That was the only way Colonel Petrov was going home.

CHAPTER TWENTY

Viktor Gorsky, with his pistol in his hand and his submachine gun slung across his chest, moved through the passageway between the staterooms.

He came to Urmanov's door, knocked, and called out in Russian, "It is time, Arkady."

The door opened slowly and Dr. Arkady Urmanov stood there, a blank expression on his face.

"Take your bag, Doctor."

Urmanov retrieved his overnight bag.

"Do you have your gun?"

Urmanov tapped his bag.

"Good. Follow me, please."

Urmanov closed his door and followed Gorsky down the passageway. As they passed beneath the bar area on the main deck above, Gorsky saw blood trickling down the wall. Urmanov saw it, too, and hesitated, but Gorsky took his arm and propelled him forward.

At the end of the staterooms, they came to a set of ornate doors marked GARAGE and BEACH CLUB.

Gorsky opened one door, revealing the two docks and the amphibious craft sitting on its chocks on the dry deck. Beyond the garage, through glass doors, was the swimming platform, which was illuminated, and the light reflected off the fog that lay over the platform.

Gorsky looked around to be certain he was alone, then moved into the garage and motioned Urmanov to follow him.

The public address system came on and Petrov, speaking in Russian, said, "Good evening, Doctor."

Urmanov was momentarily startled, then looked around for the source of the voice.

"You are on camera, Doctor. I can see you, but can't hear you. Wave to me."

Urmanov raised his arm without enthusiasm.

Petrov informed Gorsky, "I see a small craft on the radar, two hundred meters south on a direct course for The Hana."

Gorsky nodded in acknowledgment.

"Prepare to open the door."

Gorsky walked along the dock to the port side of the yacht where a catwalk connected the two docks, and stopped at an electrical panel that controlled the shell door, the pumps, and the lights.

"One hundred meters," Petrov announced. "I can now see him coming out of the fog and he is signaling with a red light. I will return the signal."

Gorsky knew that Petrov was now turning the bridge lights off and on—the signal to Captain Gleb that *The Hana* was secure.

"Open the door," Petrov ordered.

Gorsky engaged the switch, marked in English SHELL DOOR. He could hear the hydraulic sounds as the huge door on the starboard side of the forty-foot-beamed yacht began to rise slowly from its top hinges.

The sea rushed in like a waterfall, running at high speed across the garage deck and lapping against the two parallel docks, then washing up against the hull beneath the connecting catwalk where Gorsky stood. The amphibious craft began rising from its chocks.

Gorsky could smell the ocean and feel the damp fog entering the flooding compartment.

Petrov said, "Welcome our new captain with the underwater lights."

Gorsky found the switch, and the rushing seawater in the compartment suddenly lit up, reminding Gorsky of their own arrival aboard *The Hana*.

The waterfall flattened as the water level in the compartment reached the sea level, creating a smooth, uninterrupted passageway of water from the ocean into the ship.

Gorsky looked at Dr. Urmanov on the dock, staring at the gaping hole in the hull of *The Hana*. Gorsky wondered what the man was thinking. Maybe about the two million Swiss francs. Or the Siberian exile. Or the blood running down the wall. If so, these were not unrelated thoughts. In any case, they would soon see if the nuclear device had a problem. Or if Dr. Urmanov had a problem.

Gorsky heard the sound of the approaching boat's engine, then saw the red bow light of a small craft coming through the fog.

The red light got closer, and the engine stopped as the bow appeared out of the fog and the craft slid silently through the doorway and into the compartment.

Gorsky turned the switch and the shell door began to close. He walked quickly back to the dock and stood beside Urmanov.

The lifeboat from the Russian fishing trawler floated between the two docks, and at the helm was a gray-bearded man who reminded Gorsky of the late Captain Wells, except that this man was wearing a blue quilted jacket and a green knit cap.

In the center of the lifeboat was a black tarp, and beneath the tarp was a rectangular object.

Captain Gleb surveyed his surroundings, then looked at Gorsky and Urmanov and shouted, "Throw me a line!"

Gorsky threw a line to *The Hana*'s new captain.

Petrov's voice came over the speaker: "Welcome aboard The Hana, Captain."

Gleb did not acknowledge the greeting and secured his craft to the dock. He drew a knife from his boot and cut the ties holding the tarp, then flung the tarp into the water.

Sitting on the deck of the small craft was what looked like a large black steamer trunk.

Petrov's voice boomed over the speaker: "Doctor Urmanov! Behold your creation! Behold your monster, Doctor!" Petrov laughed.

Gorsky smiled, then looked at Urmanov, who seemed in a trance. He knew a problem when he saw one.

Gleb patted the black trunk and said, "Here it is, men. You don't have to sign for it. It's all yours." He laughed.

Gorsky regarded Gleb. The man sounded as rough as he looked.

Gleb stepped onto the gunnel of his craft carrying a large overnight bag, and jumped onto the dock. He stuck out his hand to Gorsky. "Captain Gleb."

They shook hands and Gorsky said, "I am Viktor." He indicated Dr. Urmanov. "This is Arkady."

Gleb smiled. "Let me guess who is the physicist and who is the SVR assassin."

Gorsky didn't find that amusing.

Gleb said to Gorsky, "You, sir, have blood on your hand and a bit on your shirt." He looked at Urmanov. "And you, sir, look like a man who wouldn't kill a fly. Well, not with a swatter." He cocked his head toward the nuclear device and laughed again.

Neither Gorsky nor Urmanov responded.

Captain Gleb lit a cigarette and informed his compatriots, "I saw two helicopters out there, flying patterns. And the trawler's radar saw two high-speed craft, running west." He exhaled a long stream of smoke. "Where is your boss?"

"On the bridge."

Gleb drew again on his cigarette, then nodded toward the black trunk. "Leave that alone until I speak to him. I have a message for him."

"You can give it to me."

"He can give it to you if he wants to."

Petrov's voice came over the speaker: "Captain, I need you on the bridge. Doctor, I will join you shortly. Viktor, stay with Arkady."

Gleb flipped his cigarette into the water, grabbed his bag, and started toward the door.

Gorsky called to him, "There is one deckhand not accounted for."

Gleb stopped. "How did that happen?"

"That is no business of yours."

"It is if I run into him." He asked, "Is he armed?"

"That is not likely."

"Well"—Gleb drew a Grach from under his coat—"I am."

"Do you know how to use that?"

Gleb laughed and said, "SVR men are all assholes." He turned and walked through the door.

Gorsky watched him moving down the long passageway. Captain Gleb, he understood, was a man who knew that his skills were crucial to the mission, which made him feel free to say what he pleased. Even to an SVR officer.

Well, Gorsky thought, as soon as Captain Gleb was no longer indispensable, then he would become disposable.

Gorsky turned and looked at the black trunk in the lifeboat, then looked at Urmanov. They made eye contact and it seemed to Gorsky that Dr. Urmanov had guessed his fate.

Gorsky smiled at him. "Cheer up, Doctor. You are about to earn your two million Swiss francs."

Urmanov looked away and stared at the nuclear device.

Gorsky said, as if to himself, "Yes, many fates hang in the balance tonight, and tomorrow morning will see two bright suns. God's and man's."

CHAPTER TWENTY-ONE

Vasily Petrov stood on the bridge and followed Gleb's progress on the video monitor. Petrov saw that Gleb had his gun drawn, meaning Gorsky had told him about the missing deckhand, though Petrov noted that Gleb had obviously not been trained to walk tactically with a weapon. Also, it had apparently not occurred to Captain Gleb that his SVR-issued Grach, like Urmanov's Makarov, did not work. The SVR did not give dangerous weapons to potentially unreliable people.

Petrov switched to the garage camera and saw that Gorsky and Urmanov had boarded Gleb's craft, though, as per instructions, they had not opened the lid of the trunk.

Petrov heard Gleb on the spiral staircase and turned toward the open door.

Gleb glanced around the vestibule, noticing the blood near the captain's door, then entered the bridge.

Both men, holding guns in their hands, looked at each other. Finally, Gleb stuck his Grach inside his jacket and put his overnight bag on the bloodstained deck.

Petrov said, "Welcome."

Gleb nodded and went to the long, wraparound instrument console, moving from left to right as he read the instruments and gauges. He glanced at the radar screen, then went to the security monitor and pressed the labeled buttons, going from camera to camera, looking at the carnage in the crew's common room, the bar and dining room, the galley, and finally the salon.

He asked, "Where is my friend Captain Wells?"

"In his quarters."

Gleb nodded, still staring at the image of the dead prostitutes lying in the salon. "Who are they?"

"It doesn't matter."

"They look like Russian girls."

Petrov did not reply.

Gleb asked, "And why would I think my fate will be different?"

"Because I need you."

Gleb looked at Colonel Petrov. "Until what point?"

"Until we anchor in New York Harbor and you sail The Hana's amphibious craft from this yacht to the pier in Brooklyn."

"And then?"

"Then we drive to the airport and fly home."

Gleb stared at Petrov. "There is an American expression—three can keep a secret if two of them are dead."

Petrov did not respond.

Captain Gleb asked, "What happens to Arkady when you no longer need him?"

"You ask too many questions, Captain."

"You should ask some of your own." He pointed out, "After Arkady finishes his business, I am the only man needed to complete this mission."

"Captain, it would take a better man than you to kill me. Or Viktor." He advised, "Do not provoke me."

Gleb lit a cigarette and looked at the blood-covered chair and the blood on the floor. "This is nasty business."

"Did anyone tell you otherwise?"

"The money is good." He asked, "And you?"

"The money is not so good."

Gleb smiled. "I will buy you a new car in Moscow."

"I assure you, we will never see each other again."

Gleb changed the subject and asked, "Do you think this seaman is still onboard?"

"Where else would he be?"

"He should be in the ocean wearing a life vest." He added, "A sailor is taught how and when to abandon ship."

Petrov thought about that, but did not reply.

Gleb continued, "From here, it could take him about ten hours to reach shore. If he didn't die first from hypothermia." He added, "But he could be picked up by a passing ship."

"Let us assume he is not a factor."

"Let us assume he is." He informed Colonel Petrov, "We saw two high-speed craft on the trawler's radar. And we observed two helicopters flying what appeared to be search patterns."

"Then they are searching for a ship in distress. They are not searching for The Hana."

"Well, you would know more than I on that subject."

"I would and I do."

Gleb told Petrov, "A man named Leonid from your fine organization who is on the trawler has a message for you."

Petrov did not reply.

"He says that if you believe the mission is compromised, you should go to the default plan. I have brought with me five kilos of plastique—" He nodded toward his overnight bag. "We can blow a hole in the ship's hull and sink The Hana and her secrets. You and I and your man Viktor, and also the physicist, will board my craft and sail to the trawler, which will take us and the black trunk home."

"That is not what I came here to do, Captain."

Gleb shrugged. "The decision is yours. But consider that the Americans may be looking for us."

"Well, then we have sat here too long." He said to Gleb, "It is time to get underway."

Gleb went to the radar screen and said, "Come here." He pointed to the screen. "See this blip? You see how fast it is moving?"

Petrov did not reply.

"Why would a craft travel at forty or fifty knots in this fog?"

"I have already told you why."

Gleb looked at Colonel Petrov. "Well, I see you are a stubborn man. Or a brave one. Or perhaps...well, driven by your love of the Motherland. Or something else."

"They are not paying you two million Swiss francs to psychoanalyze me."

Gleb laughed. "All right. Then we set sail for New York." He said to Petrov, "I will turn off all the deck lights and the bridge lights, and you will go through the ship and turn off all the interior lights that can be seen through the portholes."

"Why don't you use the circuit breakers?"

"Because that will cause the emergency lighting to come on." He said to Petrov, "I know a few things about ships, Colonel." He also reminded Petrov, "I am in command of this ship."

Petrov did not reply.

"And while you are at it, remove the prince's ensign from the stern." He asked, "Can you do all that?"

"I can, if it makes you feel better, but I am sure they are not looking for us."

"Let us act as though they are, and let's not make it easy for them." Gleb continued, "I will turn off the yacht's AIS—the Automatic Identification System—which will make us disappear from the Coast Guard's monitors and their computers." He added, "We won't disappear from radar, but we will be only a blip, without an identification tag." He added, "Not all craft are required to have AIS. So that will not raise suspicions with the Coast Guard."

Petrov nodded.

"I will also shut off the GPS and radar and navigate by compass. I will leave one radio on to monitor police and Coast Guard traffic."

Again, Petrov nodded. The original plan did not call for *The Hana* to hide. The prince's yacht was in the Coast Guard AIS system, and it was on a pleasure cruise. They were to make the two-hour run to New York Harbor at 4 A.M., then enter the harbor at dawn. But the situation seemed to have changed—if Gleb and Leonid's suspicions were valid.

Gleb continued, "I will head south, to the edge of the shipping lane, so that we will not appear on radar as a lone ship between the shore and the shipping lane."

Petrov had no reply.

Gleb went on, "But we will be traveling faster than that very slow line of ships waiting to get to Ambrose Buoy, and that may draw attention. So perhaps we should keep pace with them."

Petrov considered all this, then said, "In my business, Captain, we rely on speed." He told Gleb, "If they are looking for us, they will find us if we give them the time. So we need to be ahead of them. And you need to sail now directly to New York at full speed." He added, "The Hana can make twenty-five knots, which will put us at the entrance to New York Harbor in less than two hours."

Gleb thought about that, then replied, "I think a slower approach, near the shipping lane, is better. It is easier to hide in a crowd."

"Do you watch soccer, Captain?"

"I do."

"Then you know that if the ball progresses slowly toward the goal, the defense is in place and the ball is not likely to get into the net."

Gleb drew on his cigarette.

"But if the ball moves quickly, before the defense can react, then there is only the goalkeeper between the ball and the net. So if you believe that the Americans are looking for us, you will now set sail and we will arrive at the goal before the defenders are in place."

Gleb pointed out, "This is not a soccer game, Colonel. This opposing team has guns."

"All the more reason to run faster."

"And radiation detectors."

"Which is why we are going to sink your lifeboat in the flooded compartment."

Gleb stayed silent, then said, "We may get to the goal, but we may find the entire opposing team waiting there for us."

Petrov replied, "We only need to get close." He reminded Gleb, "This ball explodes."

"Yes, it does. But perhaps you are forgetting our escape plan—our sail in the amphibious craft from The Hana to the pier in Brooklyn, and our car ride to the airport."

Petrov did not reply immediately, then said, "You and Viktor may be making that trip by yourselves."

Gleb looked at Petrov. "Well, you can kill yourself if you want. But we may all be killed or captured before then."

"I assure you, Captain, you will be on that flight to Moscow."

Gleb stared at Petrov, then said, "When an SVR man makes me assurances, I can be sure of only one thing."

"You can be sure that if you don't get this ship underway quickly, Captain, you are no longer needed."

Gleb took a deep breath, lit another cigarette, then said, "I am just pointing out some problems that you should consider, Colonel. And I am reminding you that we can still safely abort this mission by sinking this ship." He added, "The trawler will remain on station for another thirty minutes."

"Thank you for reminding me. Now, we will get underway. And if you refuse to do so, we will indeed sink this ship, and when we get to the trawler, my colleague Leonid and I will hold a very short summary court-martial and execute you on the spot. So now you have your choice of how you wish to die—doing your duty, or not doing your duty."

Both men made eye contact, then Gleb stared out the windshield, smoking his cigarette. "Well, this fog helps."

"Get underway, Captain."

Gleb replied, "Hoisting an anchor is usually a two-man operation, but since neither you nor Viktor are available, I can do it myself, but it will take some time—"

"Quickly."

Petrov took a flashlight from the bridge and left Captain Gleb to his duties.

As he walked into the vestibule, he heard a noise and looked over his shoulder to see the bridge door sliding shut.

CHAPTER TWENTY-TWO

Vasily Petrov slung his submachine gun over his shoulder and went first to the captain's quarters, then to the ship's office where he had dragged the bodies from the bridge, and shut off the lights, barely noticing the corpses as he thought about Gleb the man and Gleb the bearer of bad news.

As for Gleb the man, Petrov had expected a strong personality—Gleb was a ship's captain and a commander of men, and he had agreed to this dangerous mission. As for Gleb's suspicion that the Americans were looking for *The Hana,* Petrov did not believe that. And regarding Gleb's other paranoia—that Petrov was going to kill him—well, that was understandable, though ironically it was not true, though it could become true.

Petrov drew his Makarov pistol and took the spiral staircase down to the salon, noting the location of the fourteen bodies on the floor so he could step around them when all the lights were out.

He also noted the bullet wound in Tasha's heart, and this made him think again of her caterer friend at Tamorov's house.

Even if this man, Depp, was an embassy watcher, how could he connect the amphibious craft and its occupants to *The Hana*?

Petrov had told Tamorov that they were going to a party in East Hampton and would return in the morning. So even if the FBI questioned Tamorov, that was all Tamorov knew. And if there was some suspicion that the amphibious craft had sailed out to meet a ship, how would anyone know which ship? And if the Americans were looking for the amphibious craft, they would not see it on the water or on the deck of a ship.

Petrov switched on his flashlight and began shutting off the lights in the salon. Outside, the deck lights were going off, and he could feel the vibration as Gleb started the ship's engines.

He went outside and descended the exterior staircase to the main deck. He could now hear the sound of an anchor being raised. They would soon be underway.

Petrov moved to the stern where the prince's ensign flew from a staff, and he drew his knife and cut the flag loose, letting it fall into the sea.

He looked out over the stern, noting that the fog was low, barely reaching the main deck. The sky was clear and the half-moon was overhead. Out in the distance to the south he could see ship lights—tankers and cargo ships—waiting in a line that stretched for over a hundred miles from the open ocean to the security checkpoint at Ambrose Buoy, which was ten nautical miles from the entrance to New York Harbor.

It must be frustrating, he thought, for those ships' captains and crews to sail halfway around the world at good speed, only to be slowed to a crawl at this bottleneck; very unlike incoming aircraft that needed to land on time. And yet for all the Americans' obsession with airport security and efficiency, they had still not perfected seaport security or efficiency. And thus a ship with evil intent could slip through. And would. Soon.

Petrov thought, too, of the aftermath of the nuclear explosion in New York Harbor. Not only would the New York seaport be shut down for a decade or more, but every other seaport in America—and probably Europe—would be shut down, as were the airports after September 11. And when the American seaports reopened, the lines of ships waiting to dock would stretch back to their home ports as each arriving ship was boarded and searched at length, costing the Americans great amounts of time and money. In fact, world commerce would be disrupted for years, and American imports and exports would slow to a trickle. And all of this would happen as a result of the trauma and devastation caused by Saudi Prince Ali Faisel's nuclear attack on New York. Petrov smiled.

He took a last look at the ship's lights on the horizon. Well, he thought, those ships would be fortunate if they did not get into New York Harbor before 8:46 A.M. And those ships that did would not be so fortunate.

The Hana began to move.

He turned and walked quickly into the bar area.

He surveyed his earlier work and wondered if the missing deckhand had seen this. And if he had, had that caused him to jump overboard? Or to hide? In either case, the man was not a threat to the mission unless he was picked up by a passing ship, which was unlikely with this blanket of fog on the ocean.

Well, he thought, if the deckhand was still onboard, he would be in his familiar surroundings on the tank deck below, which was a maze of storage rooms and infrastructure, providing many places to hide like a bilge rat. But Petrov would deal with that later.

Petrov looked down at His Royal Highness, Prince Ali Faisel. Ambition is a noble trait, but if you wear it like a crown, people will see it and use it for their own advantage. That was what he would have told His Highness if they had actually had that breakfast meeting to discuss their common problems.

Petrov looked at the diamond-encrusted watch on the prince's left wrist, now covered with dried blood. In the end, death is indeed the great equalizer. Ali Faisel, though, was a man of faith—professed or real—and though he did not get his Russian prostitutes here on his wife's namesake yacht, he was by now in Paradise, enjoying the virgins.

Petrov continued into the dining room, stepping around the bodies of the two stewards, then moved on to the warm galley where the unpleasant smell of mutton had been replaced by the unpleasant smell of the cooks' blood.

He shut off all the galley lighting, then used his flashlight to guide him to a passageway that led to the main deck vestibule where the spiral staircase and elevator were located.

There was only one other door in the vestibule, a teak door that led to the prince's suite and that Petrov knew had a bulletproof core. In the door was a peephole and above the door was a security camera. The prince, like all men with money and power, thought about his enemies. Unfortunately for him, he also thought that Colonel Petrov, the enemy of his enemy, was his friend.

Petrov tried the handle on the door, finding it unlocked. He held his handgun to his front and threw open the heavy door as he dropped into a crouch.

He thought it unlikely that the deckhand would pick the prince's suite to hide, but he called out in English, "Is anyone there? Please help me." He smiled. "The Russians are murdering everyone onboard."

There was no reply.

Petrov stood and entered the sitting room of the suite, which was dimly lit by a few lamps. He went quickly through the sitting room, the bedroom and dressing room, then the large bathroom, finding only more gilded extravagance, and also some photographs of the prince's many children, though none of his wife—or wives.

It occurred to Petrov that there might be some people, including Americans and Saudis, who could not bring themselves to believe that Prince Ali Faisel, who loved life and all it had to offer, had become a suicide bomber. On the other hand, the Americans did not think that deeply when it came to ascribing evil intentions to those who followed Islam; all Muslims were capable of all things.

And the prince's own coreligionists were equally unthinking, and they would believe what they wanted to believe; that every Muslim—even a decadent royal, and especially such a sinner—could be touched by the light of God and become a martyr for Islam.

Yes, there could be some speculation and doubts about Ali Faisel ending his life in a nuclear holocaust. But that line of thought would go nowhere in the hysterical aftermath of the attack.

Petrov turned off the lights in the prince's suite and descended the spiral staircase to the lower deck.

He began first in the quarters of the three officers whose doors were unlocked. Again, he didn't think that the deckhand would choose a dead-end room in which to hide, so he moved quickly through the officers' rooms.

As he went through the staterooms, his thoughts returned to the Americans. If they were looking for a ship at sea at night, they would rely more on radar and infrared scanning than on a visual sighting. They loved their technology. And on that subject, they had very sophisticated radiation detectors that were effective at great distances. And *The Hana* was now emitting radiation, though not for long.

But then he had another thought…a thought that he had been pushing to the back of his mind. Arkady Urmanov. Known to the Americans as Pavel Fradkov, the Russian Federation's U.N. delegate for Human Rights. It was possible, he conceded, that the American State Department—or the FBI or CIA—had identified Pavel Fradkov as Arkady Urmanov, a nuclear physicist, whose specialty was miniature nuclear weapons.

But if they had made that identification, why had they allowed Urmanov into the country? Or allowed him to stay? Obviously, the Americans wanted to see why he was here—and if they knew why, then the mission was compromised. And if it was compromised, then Moscow would blame Colonel Petrov for insisting that Urmanov be sent to New York under an alias with diplomatic cover. And if *that* was true, then he, Colonel Vasily Petrov, had no future in Moscow.

It also occurred to him that if the FBI had questioned Tamorov, then it was possible that the rich oligarch may have been cooperative, to protect his money and his American visa. It was also possible that Tamorov had recalled that Petrov wanted to be introduced to Prince Ali Faisel. But would Tamorov make the connection between the prince and the prince's yacht, and the amphibious craft that had taken them from the beach? Possibly.

Petrov stopped in the passageway to collect his thoughts. He still had the option of scuttling *The Hana* and returning to Moscow via the fishing trawler. But what awaited him in Moscow? Not a promotion to general. Not his father's congratulations. *The future of Russia has been placed in your hands, Vasily.* And if this mission failed because of him, what awaited him in Moscow was possibly a firing squad.

He leaned his back against the wall and drew a long breath. There was really only one option left. Complete the mission—at any cost.

Petrov continued through the passageway between the guest

staterooms, finding most doors locked, which he opened by firing one or two rounds from his Makarov.

He then proceeded toward the ornate doors at the end of the passageway that led to the flooded tender garage, noticing the blood on the wall as he passed by.

Yes, there was only one option left for him. And the two things that he needed to complete his mission had just arrived. Captain Gleb and the bomb.

Come home in glory. Or do not come home.

Vasily Petrov was no longer sure that he was coming home. But if he did not, his father would know how his son met a glorious end.

CHAPTER TWENTY-THREE

Vasily Petrov entered the garage, which was dimly illuminated by indirect lighting and by the underwater lights on the flooded deck.

Tied to the opposite dock was the amphibious craft that would take him, Gorsky, and Gleb from *The Hana* to the pier on the Brooklyn waterfront—though if he eliminated Gleb, he was sure he could operate the craft himself. As for finding the pier, he had been there twice, once by car and once by boat, and he had flown over it in a helicopter, so he knew he could find it even at night because of the large boathouse that covered the pier. That was the plan. But the plan might have to change.

Tied to the dock in front of him was the lifeboat from the fishing trawler, and sitting in the center of the boat's deck was a black trunk.

Petrov motioned for Gorsky and Urmanov to stay in the lifeboat, and he walked along the dock to the catwalk, out of earshot of the two men, and used the intercom to call the bridge.

Gleb answered, "Captain."

"Vasily. Report."

"Well, we are underway, as you see. I have plotted a course twenty nautical miles from shore, close to the shipping lane. It will take us a few more minutes to get up to speed, and if I can get twenty-five knots out of the engines, we will be approaching the entrance to New York

Harbor at the Verrazano Bridge in less than two hours—depending on tides and currents."

Petrov checked his watch. That would put them outside the harbor at about midnight. Perhaps earlier if the currents were with them. And if the Americans were waiting for him, he would proceed at full speed straight into the harbor, and as *The Hana* got within a hundred meters of Manhattan Island, he could manually detonate the device.

Like an Arab suicide bomber.

But that might not be necessary. He needed more information.

Gleb said, "I saw another helicopter heading east. Also two high-speed craft on the radar." He pointed out, "If I see them, they see us."

"They don't know what they are looking for."

Gleb didn't reply to that, but said, "The fishing trawler will remain on station for five more minutes. If he doesn't get a radio signal from me, he will head back to Saint Petersburg."

"I hope he has had good fishing."

"Well then, the die is cast."

"It was cast a long time ago in Moscow." Petrov changed the subject and asked, "Why did you close the bridge door?"

"So I don't get a bullet in my back."

"I assume you are referring to the deckhand."

Gleb did not reply.

"Have you locked the door?"

"That is the procedure if there is a danger onboard."

Petrov knew that the bridge door could be locked from the inside without a code, but it could not be opened from the outside without entering the code. So Gleb had effectively locked Petrov out, and he had a reasonable excuse to do so. Petrov said, "I will have full access to the bridge."

"When you come up, bring me some coffee."

Petrov didn't reply to that and said, "You can communicate with me through the ship's speakers. I am in the tender garage."

"I see you on the monitor, and if that thing you're working on starts to smoke, I'll be in the water." He laughed.

Petrov shut off the intercom and walked quickly along the dock to the lifeboat and jumped in.

Gorsky stood and said, "I assume you have not found the deckhand."

Petrov shook his head, then put his hand on the black trunk. "This now deserves our full attention." He looked at Gorsky and Urmanov. "Are we ready?"

Gorsky nodded. Urmanov did not.

Petrov said to Gorsky, "Unlock the trunk."

Gorsky knelt before the trunk, which had a conventional hasp and padlock securing the lid, as though it was actually a steamer trunk, though the combination lock and hasp were made of titanium alloy, as was the trunk itself.

Gorsky, from memory, entered the six-digit combination. He heard a soft click and pulled the lock open.

Petrov said to Urmanov, "The honor is yours, Doctor."

Urmanov stared at the black trunk, then stood and put his hands on the sides of the watertight lid. He lifted the heavy, lead-lined lid until the two steel arms locked into place.

Petrov, Gorsky, and Urmanov looked down at the device, which filled the entire trunk. Engraved in the lower right-hand corner of the cast aluminum face was RA–115, followed by –01, which designated this device as submersible.

Petrov and Gorsky exchanged glances and nodded. Yes, this was exactly like the device they had trained on, except this one had a plutonium core, about the size and shape of an American football.

The size of the fissionable core never failed to impress Petrov. It was difficult to imagine how anything that small could produce a fireball the size of six sports stadiums, rising over five hundred meters into the air and generating temperatures of over ten million degrees Celsius, consuming everything within the firestorm, and igniting anything combustible within another half kilometer, melting steel, glass, and flesh.

And then there was the shock wave that would travel at the speed of sound, tearing apart buildings and throwing people and vehicles into the air like leaves in a storm.

And what followed would be much worse: a radioactive plume, riding on the prevailing winds, sickening everyone it came into contact with. Petrov remembered the Chernobyl nuclear reactor meltdown. People were still dying from the effects of radiation poisoning almost two decades later.

Petrov stared at the aluminum face of the device. Its four corners were secured by sunken screws whose heads needed a special tool, which Urmanov had in his tool kit to unloosen them if necessary. Also in the tool kit were instruments that Urmanov would need if there was a problem with the device. Petrov and Gorsky could arm the device without Urmanov, but they were not authorized to remove the face and expose the inner workings of the miniature nuclear bomb.

Ironically, Petrov knew, it was not the plutonium core or even the electronics that presented a problem; it was the two detonator caps and the conventional high explosive charges packed around the plutonium—to compress it and give it the critical mass it needed to achieve fission—that could explode if improperly handled. Thus the age of gunpowder met the nuclear age in this trunk. And Dr. Urmanov, nuclear physicist, had an understanding of both, plus an understanding of advanced electronics if a problem arose.

Mission control had told Petrov that the device had less than a five percent chance of malfunctioning. Urmanov was needed to lower that to zero percent.

If, however, Dr. Urmanov could not seem to solve the problem, then there were ways to help him remember the intricacies of the device he invented.

Petrov again looked at the aluminum face of the device. It had no knobs or dials, no switches or meters, only small, color-coded ports into which electronic leads could be inserted.

The timer clock was internal and not shown in a display window, but would be shown on the handheld arming device that lay in plastic wrap on the surface of the aluminum face.

Petrov picked up the arming device and unwrapped it, letting the four color-coded wires fall free. Except for the dangling wires, this arming device looked like a large satellite phone. And in fact, signals could be sent to Moscow, and also to the nuclear device. He asked Urmanov, "Did you remember to bring your arming device?"

Urmanov reached into his bag and retrieved the backup arming device.

Petrov said, "We will use the one that came with the package."

He inserted the lead from his black wire into the hole that had a black circle around it. He looked at the electronic display screen on his handheld device and said, "Battery is fully charged and all electronics are reading normal."

He turned the device toward Urmanov and Gorsky and they both nodded, and both repeated, "Normal."

He then plugged the green wire into the green port and looked at his display. "Radiation level is within normal range," meaning there was no radiation leak and no depletion of the plutonium, which was critical if they were to achieve a ten-kiloton yield.

He turned the remote device toward Urmanov. "Correct?"

Urmanov nodded.

The public address speaker crackled and Gleb's voice filled the garage. "Helicopter across the bow at three hundred meters distance and four hundred meters altitude, proceeding south." He added, "He has a searchlight, and the beam passed briefly over us."

Petrov glanced at Gorsky, then said, "If they are looking for the amphibious craft"—he nodded toward the amphibious craft five meters away on the opposite dock—"they would need X-ray vision, like Superman."

Gorsky smiled, but he was concerned.

Petrov looked at the open trunk. It was now emitting enough radiation to be detected, but it would emit less when the lid was closed, and almost none when it was submerged. But now they were exposed and needed to hurry through the arming sequence. Petrov still did not think that the Americans were thinking the unthinkable. But they might discover this radiation source by accident if they had their detectors turned on and if someone in a helicopter or boat noticed the detector's flashing red light or somehow heard its audible alert over the sound of their engines.

He said, "We will continue."

He plugged the yellow wire into the yellow port and a digital calendar appeared on the screen. He set the date for September 12, then switched to clock mode. He pushed the hour button on his control and stopped at 08. He then advanced the minutes to 46.

September 12—08:46. He pressed the Set button and said, "That will be about the time we are over the Atlantic, enjoying our coffee."

Gorsky nodded, though he was no longer sure they would be on that private jet. But Colonel Petrov seemed sure, as though there were no helicopters flying overhead and no high-speed craft on the sea. Gorsky glanced at Urmanov. Now that this was a minute away from becoming real, Urmanov had become almost catatonic.

Petrov plugged the last wire—the red one—into the last port and said, "We will recite the arming code." He put his finger on the electronic display that now showed numbers from zero to nine and said, "Seven."

Gorsky repeated, "Seven."

Urmanov said, "Seven."

Petrov pushed seven on the screen, then said, "Three."

"Three."

"Three."

Petrov pressed three, then said, "Nine."

They went through the eight-digit arming code, until the last number, which was known only to Petrov. He pushed the number, which was zero, and the displayed code disappeared, replaced by the word ARMED.

And, Petrov thought, that was all there was to it. He held up the arming device so that Gorsky and Urmanov could read it, and he said to Urmanov, "So, Doctor, there were no problems and we did not need you after all."

Urmanov did not reply.

Petrov continued, "You designed a very reliable weapon. I congratulate you."

Again, Urmanov had no reply.

Petrov unplugged his four lead wires, then took Urmanov's backup arming device and ran through the procedure again, then said, "I am satisfied." He looked at Urmanov. "And you?"

Urmanov nodded.

"Good. So we have a hundred percent certainty that nuclear fission will occur tomorrow at zero eight forty-six hours." He looked at Urmanov. "Correct?"

Urmanov replied, "Nothing is one hundred percent certain."

"Some things are." He glanced at Gorsky, who nodded.

Petrov removed the four wires from the nuclear device. Clipped to the underside of the upraised lid was a long coil of copper wire, which Petrov removed. On one end of the wire was a long copper needle, and on the other end was a black rubber ball. Petrov stuck the long needle into a waterproof port on the right side of the trunk, then tossed the ball overboard into the water. This was the external radio antenna, necessary if Petrov needed to send a signal from his arming device to the submerged nuclear device. There were only two signals he might have to send: a shutdown of the timer clock, which he had no intention of sending; or a signal to advance the time of detonation. And that might be a signal he would need to send.

He put his handheld arming device into remote mode and tested the signals sent through the radio antenna. His display screen showed all the data—battery and electronics, radiation, detonation time, and status: ARMED.

Satisfied that he had control of the timer clock, he said to Gorsky, "You may lower the lid."

"No!"

Petrov and Gorsky turned toward Urmanov, who was standing near the helm of the boat, a gun in his hand. Petrov noticed he was shaking almost uncontrollably.

Gorsky said to Urmanov, "You told me your gun was in your bag. I don't like people who lie to me."

Urmanov waved his gun and said in a quavering voice, "Move… away from the trunk."

Petrov and Gorsky exchanged glances, nodded, and moved toward opposite sides of the lifeboat.

Urmanov took a step forward, pointed his 9mm Makarov at the aluminum face of the nuclear device, and pulled the trigger.

There was a dull thud as the hammer hit the firing pin block.

Urmanov again pulled the trigger.

Gorsky suggested, "You need to re-cock it. Pull back on the slide." He stepped toward Urmanov. "Here, let me show you." He snatched the gun out of Urmanov's trembling hand, cocked it, and put the muzzle to Urmanov's forehead. He pulled the trigger, and again the hammer made a dull thud.

Urmanov sank to his knees, his hands covering his face and his body heaving.

Gorsky said, "I believe someone filed down your firing pin." He tossed the gun into the water, then grabbed Urmanov by his shirt and pulled him to his feet. Gorsky took a step back, then drove his fist into Urmanov's solar plexus.

Urmanov let out a grunt, doubled over, and again sank to his knees, holding his abdomen.

Petrov glanced up at the security camera, wondering if Gleb had seen any of this. He said to Gorsky, "I think we have shot enough people today. Tie him to the dock." He told Urmanov, "You will be the first to see the nuclear explosion—the second it happens."

Gorsky nodded appreciatively and dragged Urmanov off the boat and onto the dock.

Petrov closed the watertight lid on the trunk and snapped the padlock onto the hasp. He pulled his Makarov and fired eight rounds into the hull and watched as water spurted from the bullet holes. He gathered Urmanov's bag and the two arming devices and jumped from the sinking boat onto the dock.

Gorsky had taken a coiled line from the dock and bound Urmanov's arms to his side with his hands behind his back, tied to a cleat. Urmanov was now in a sitting position, facing the boat with his legs dangling in the water. Gorsky said to him, "You can stare at your bomb until eight forty-six tomorrow morning. Then you should close your eyes so you are not blinded by the incandescent flash." He crouched beside Urmanov and asked, "Were you trying to destroy the device? Or detonate it?"

Urmanov did not reply.

"Well... perhaps you yourself don't know."

Petrov said to Gorsky, "Shut off the lights, but leave the underwater lights on so we can monitor this space."

Gorsky went quickly to the connecting catwalk and turned off the indirect lighting, leaving the garage bathed in the shimmering underwater lights.

Petrov watched the lifeboat as it sank under the weight of the nuclear device. No air bubbles rose to the surface, indicating that the trunk was indeed waterproof. The lifeboat settled on the deck of the garage beneath two meters of water.

Petrov took a last look around the garage. "It is done."

Gorsky agreed, "It is done."

As they were leaving, Urmanov shouted, "*You* are the monsters! Monsters!"

Petrov stopped and turned. "*We* are monsters? Perhaps, but you, Doctor, *you* are the monster's creator. Think about that as you wait for your creation to kill you." He added, "Good evening."

Petrov and Gorsky left the garage and closed the doors behind them.

PART IV

CHAPTER TWENTY-FOUR

We made the border crossing from the Shinnecock Nation to Southampton, and my former trainee suggested some shortcuts to Tamorov's house, trying, I suppose, to make herself useful.

She asked, "Are you still angry?"

I didn't know if she meant angry at her or angry at Buck, but thinking back on all those conversations with her when she was conning me, maybe I felt a little foolish, and thus angry at myself. I mean, if they'd sent a guy instead of a good-looking woman I would have just clocked him.

Ms. Faraday advised me, "Anger gets in the way of good judgment and good performance."

"I liked you better when you were a clueless trainee."

"No you didn't." She changed the subject and told me, "I can see why Buck wanted me to work with you."

"Then you can also see why I don't want to work with either of you."

"Well, you should know that it was Buck who first got onto this." She explained, "About two months ago, the Russian Foreign Ministry notified the State Department that Pavel Fradkov was to be assigned to the Russian U.N. Mission. Buck's job is to vet these guys. He's one of the last of the SDI Cold Warriors and he knows all there is to know about the former Soviet Union. He even wrote a memo on Vladimir Putin from when Putin was a KGB officer, saying to watch this man closely."

Clearly Ms. Faraday was impressed with old Buck, which colored her perception of him, just as mine was colored by his double-cross in Yemen.

She went on, "So Buck saw the photo of Pavel Fradkov in the diplomatic visa application that the Russians submitted to the State Department, and though Fradkov had aged and altered his appearance, Buck recognized him as Dr. Arkady Urmanov, a nuclear weapons physicist from the days of the Soviet Union."

"Buck is smart," I agreed. "But whoever let the nuke guy in the country was not so smart."

"Sometimes we can turn these guys. We actually have a program where we buy Russian nuclear physicists and give them a job in the U.S."

"How about Gorsky and Petrov? Do you have jobs for them?"

She didn't reply for a second, then said, "We—someone—wanted to see what they were up to."

"Well, now you know."

She had no response to that and asked me, "What happened in Yemen?"

I was sorry I'd lost my cool with Buck while she was standing there. "I may have misinterpreted what happened."

"I'm sure you did." She let me know, "Buck is a patriot."

So was Adolf Hitler. And so is Vasily Petrov.

I ended the conversation by calling Scott Kalish. He answered, and I said, "I'm driving, on speaker with a Federal trainee, Ms. Tess Faraday."

"Okay, I'll speak slowly." He let me know, "I'm at Timber Point," meaning the Suffolk County Marine Bureau Headquarters. I felt guilty about pulling him away from his Law and Order reruns. I asked, "How's it going?"

"Not so good. I thought this amphibious craft would show up someplace." He tried to assure me, "In addition to the sea-and-air search, we've issued a BOLO—be on the lookout—to the Bay Constables and local PD for all the marinas, yacht clubs, public docks—"

"The craft is sitting on the deck of a ship by now, Scott. You need to find that ship."

"Hundreds of ships out there." He let me know, "We have all four of our choppers flying search patterns, using infrared thermal imaging, and the Midnight Sun—the searchlight. But none of the choppers have spotted the amphibious craft you described, either on the water or onboard a large ship."

This was not looking good.

Kalish continued, "I've got ten harbor units deployed and they're running search patterns east and west of Tamorov's house, from the shore out to the Fairway—the shipping lane—which starts about twenty miles offshore." He further informed me, "Basically we're covering about a thousand square miles. And the search area is getting bigger as time passes."

"I understand that." I let him know, "The Coast Guard has been called in to assist."

"Okay, we'll coordinate." He reminded me, "We don't even know how fast this ship is traveling or what direction, or what it looks like."

"It looks like it has an amphibious landing craft on its deck. If it's covered with a tarp, use the infrared imaging."

"Thanks for the tip."

I ignored the sarcasm and informed him, "We have some info that this ship is heading west, destination New York City."

"How do you know that?"

I know that because if there's an atomic bomb onboard, New York City is ground zero, as Buck so vividly explained. But in the world of compartmented information, I wasn't sure I could share that with Scott Kalish, so I glanced at Tess, who shook her head.

I said to Kalish, "I can't say. But trust me on this."

"Okay... we'll concentrate on westbound ships."

"Good. And call your counterpart in the Nassau County Marine Bureau and ask them to begin a sea-and-air search to pick up where yours ends. Also, someone will need to call NYPD Harbor." I further suggested, "Get the rest of your fleet out."

There was silence on the phone, then Kalish said, "I don't mind helping you out, John, but this has turned into a budget buster." He asked, "How important is this? And am I covered?"

I again glanced at Tess, who held out her hand for the phone and I gave it to her.

She said, "Captain Kalish, this is Tess Faraday of State Department Intelligence."

He didn't reply, probably wondering how the trainee got promoted so fast.

She continued, "We have reason to believe that the amphibious craft rendezvoused with a ship that could be harboring a number of armed terrorists."

There was a few seconds of silence, then Kalish said, "I thought this was about an amphibious craft with a bunch of Russian hookers onboard, going out to a party ship."

"I can't say anything further, Captain, but I will have someone in Washington contact you directly."

"That would be good. Soon."

Tess handed me the phone and I said to Kalish, "So that's the deal, Scott. This got big and ugly."

"Okay...but for all we know, the target ship could be a hundred miles south of the shipping lane. Or it could be at anchor, waiting to make its run."

"That's true..." Basically we had no information, and what information we had was old by this time. I said, "It would make sense that this ship is Russian registry." I asked, "Can you find out what Russian ships—commercial or private—are due into the Port of New York?"

He thought a moment, then replied, "Yes and no. Yes if the ship has its Automatic Identification System transmitter operating. Then the Coast Guard can look on a screen and see the location of every approaching vessel, with all its info—its name, where it's from, its cargo, and so forth."

"Sounds good."

"But if the ship is up to no good, it might turn off its AIS transmitter." He added, "Like an aircraft would do if it was up to no good. But the difference is that aircraft will show up on radar as unidentified, but the sea is not so well covered by radar." He further added, "A ship at sea can theoretically disappear by going electronically silent."

"I understand." But I still didn't understand how Petrov thought he could get a ship emitting radiation past all the patrol craft, or past the old harbor forts that were equipped with very sensitive radiation detectors. I couldn't use the word "nuclear," so I asked, "How could a ship harboring terrorists get past all the checkpoints? Give me some scenarios."

"Okay... well, a ship can theoretically slip past the Coast Guard and past the Ambrose checkpoint if it has shut off its AIS transmitter. And I suppose it can go right into the harbor unseen, especially at night." He added, "But eventually the ship has to dock somewhere to unload the terrorists."

Actually the ship only had to make it into the harbor, then detonate the nuke as it approached Manhattan.

Scott Kalish, however, was thinking it was a boatload of guys from Sandland, armed with AK-47s and hand grenades or something, so he said to me, "I'm not understanding Russians and terrorists in the same sentence."

"Not all terrorists are named Abdul." I further clarified my bullshit, "Maybe saboteurs would be a better description."

Kalish still wasn't satisfied and he said, "I'm not getting a clear picture of the threat or the mission."

"I'll get back to you on that."

He continued, "I assume if there are terrorists—or saboteurs—onboard this ship, we need to approach with caution and be prepared for an armed confrontation."

"That's a good assumption."

"I would have appreciated this information sooner."

"Right. Well, now we're sure."

"Well, I'm still not sure about the mission or the threat."

I really wanted to be straight with Scott, but you don't want to yell "atomic bomb" and scare the crap out of everyone—especially if you're not sure. But I kept coming back to Arkady Urmanov, who was not in America to get a job. Though it was still possible that he was just partying with his pals tonight.

Kalish asked, "Anything further?"

I glanced at Tess, who was looking at me as if to say, *Don't say it.*

"John? Anything further?"

Time to make an important decision. The code name for a radiation detection operation is Radiant Angel, which Tess might not know, so I said to Kalish, "Pray that a radiant angel will guide you."

There was a silence, then he asked, "Are you serious?"

"Don't worry about the budget." A nuclear takedown of Manhattan will cost a lot more. "That's all I can say, Scott."

"Holy shit..." He pointed out, "If I'd known this, I'd have made sure everyone was glued to their radiation detectors."

Join the compartmented information club, Scott. I looked at Tess, who didn't seem happy with me, then I said to Kalish, "I just got the word."

"Okay...well, in a way, this makes finding this ship easier... but...geez..."

To change the subject, I asked him, "Any luck with Tasha's cell phone?"

No reply. His head was still in Nukeland. "Scott?"

"No...but the commo people are working on it."

"Okay, I'm on my way to Tamorov's. I need two county detectives to meet me on Gin Lane. They should look for a black Dodge minivan and my black Chevy SUV." I also told him, "I may want to get aboard one of your choppers or boats later."

"Okay...you can rendezvous with either at Shinnecock Coast Guard Station. Just let me know."

"Will do."

I was about to hang up but Scott informed me, "I'm getting a report here...hold on."

"Good news, I hope."

"It is...if you're the guy we're looking for." He told me, "There's a fog rolling in from the south." He added, "Typical this time of year."

"Keep me posted." I hung up.

Tess said to me, "You handled that well. Until you mentioned the unmentionable."

"He needs to do his job."

"Then someone else will make the decision to tell him. Not you."

I informed her, "When you and Buck asked me to work with you,

you knew what you were getting." I strongly suggested, "Call your people in Washington and tell them to call Scott Kalish."

She took my phone and began sending a text, telling me, "Buck is on his way to the Shinnecock Coast Guard Station. I'll advise him to also go to Timber Point and see Captain Kalish in person."

"Tell Buck he needs to be straight with Kalish."

She sent the text to Buck and asked me, "What do you think Kalish's chances are of finding an unknown ship on the high seas?"

"Not good at the moment. But at some point the target ship will get into range of a radiation detection device."

"Can't radiation be shielded with lead?"

"Yes and no."

"Tell me about yes."

"Well...from what I remember from a Nuclear Emergency Support Team class I took, if the device is encased in lead it may not emit enough gamma rays to be picked up by a detecting device—from a distance. But you will get a reading up close."

"How close?"

"Depends on the amount of radiation being emitted, the sensitivity of the detector, and the thickness of the lead shield." I also informed her, "The best shield is water, so the big scare is of a nuclear device riding underwater on the hull of a ship that might slip through."

She didn't reply to that, then asked me, "Can we get all shipping stopped at sea?"

"All legitimate ships will comply with a radio call from the Coast Guard. Unfortunately, the one ship we want stopped is not going to comply. Or respond."

"All right...can we block the harbor?"

I'd played that scenario in my mind and replied, "It's difficult to physically stop a large ship that's intent on entering the harbor." I let her know, "We have police and Coast Guard craft that can pull off a combat boarding of a large hostile ship going full speed ahead, but it's not easy—especially if there's armed resistance."

"Can't the ship be...like, blown out of the water?"

She was asking questions I'd already asked myself, and the

answers were not good. I informed her, "Even a Coast Guard cutter doesn't carry a gun big enough to stop a large ship, and all the shore batteries guarding the approaches to New York Harbor were deactivated after World War II. You'd need a Navy warship to be in the area—or jet fighters." I added, "In any case, do we want to fire on a ship that may have an atomic device onboard? Or fire on the wrong ship by mistake?"

She thought about all that, then said, "You're telling me that a ship with a nuclear weapon onboard could sail directly into New York Harbor and detonate."

"Well...it's possible. Especially if it was a ship that looked legit. Or if it was on a suicide mission."

She thought a moment, then said, "Whoever planned this in Moscow understood that seaport security has some holes in it."

"Big enough to sail a ship through."

Tess stayed quiet, then said, "Maybe, as Buck said, we are misinterpreting what we see."

"We'd all be happy to be proven paranoid."

She didn't respond and we drove in silence. Indeed, it was hard to believe this was happening. It seemed like an abstract problem in a training exercise. *Find the nuke, Detective. We gave you some clues. Think. Is Abdul smarter than you?*

No. But Ivan could be.

Holy shit.

CHAPTER TWENTY-FIVE

As I drove along Gin Lane I could see the ocean fog rolling in. What else could go wrong tonight? Well, I was about to find out.

I drove past Tamorov's gates, and up ahead I saw a Chevy sedan parked in the street. As I got closer, my headlights picked out a man and a woman talking to Steve and Matt.

I pulled over and got out, leaving the Blazer running. Tess followed.

The guy, a middle-aged man wearing a young man's sports jacket and jeans, introduced himself as Suffolk County Detective Phil Florio, and the lady was Detective Beth Penrose. I actually knew Detective Penrose, having once worked with her on the Plum Island case. In fact, we had become romantically involved, as they say.

"This is a pleasant surprise," I said sincerely.

"Nice to see you," she replied, though she didn't mean it.

This was a bit awkward. I mean, it didn't end well, and may not have ended at all, except that Kate came into the picture and I had to stop double-dipping, so I'd made The Call and explained the problem to Beth, who did not seem to understand the solution. I would have told her in person, but she carries a gun.

Detective Florio asked, "You know each other?"

Neither of us replied, which was a clue for all the detectives standing there that this was not a happy reunion.

Also, Beth must have known from Kalish or Florio that she'd be meeting me here, and if not, she'd just heard it from Steve and Matt.

But she apparently hadn't told anyone that she knew me. Nor had she recused herself by explaining, "I slept with that asshole for a year and he dumped me for some FBI slut." I would certainly recuse myself from any assignment that brought me into proximity of an ex, but women... Well, they're into drama. Sometimes revenge.

Anyway, Tess took advantage of the silence to introduce herself. "Tess Faraday, State Department Intelligence."

Matt and Steve, like Scott Kalish, seemed surprised that Tess had come up in the world in the last few hours.

I said to my team, "I'll explain later." I asked them, "Any word from the home office?"

Matt replied, "Just a few texts." He let me know, "I told them you were on a meal break."

It sounded like my FBI colleagues at 26 Fed didn't know they were in a possible nuclear blast zone. Well, it's not in my limited job description to tell them. Also, that's compartmented information. Sorry, boys.

Beth asked me, "How can we help you, Detective?"

I looked at her in the light of the Blazer's headbeams. It had been about six years since I'd last seen her. She looked the same and she still favored her tailored, almost masculine pantsuit, white blouse, and sensible shoes. Not particularly sexy, but professional. On the plus side, she still looked like she was smuggling balloons.

"Detective?"

"Sorry, Beth. What was the question?"

"All my friends call me Detective Penrose. Why don't you do the same?"

Why don't I just call you bitch?

She asked again, "How can we help you?"

"Have you been briefed?"

Phil Florio replied, "We were told you're here on a Federal surveillance, and the target, a Russian dip, went in this Russian guy's house, then sailed off in a boat with some guests, and you want to question the owner of that house. Georgi Tamorov."

"Correct." I let them know, "Tamorov is having a party, and there are about thirty Russian guys in there, maybe not all U.S. citizens, plus about a dozen Russian hostesses." I added, "The Russkies who took off in the boat had another dozen escorts with them."

Detective Florio smiled. Detective Penrose rolled her eyes.

I further briefed them, "As I'm sure you've heard, Ms. Faraday and I were in there undercover with the caterers, so we know the layout."

Tess added, "Everyone is naked."

"Right. So we don't need to pat them down."

Matt and Steve laughed. Even Beth and Tess smiled. And Detective Florio seemed anxious to get to the party.

I said, seriously, "I counted eight Russian security guys in there, dressed in black, and they may be carrying—and there could be more I didn't see."

Detective Penrose asked, "Do you expect any resistance?"

"I expect that the hired security guards will decide not to be heroes."

Tess advised, "But, as you know, have a plan to kill anyone who poses a threat to you."

I think I created a monster.

Florio suggested, "Maybe we need more people."

"We can handle it." I also informed them, "There are about fifteen caterers on the premises, mostly English deficient, and a few household staff, similarly challenged."

Detective Penrose asked, "Do you have a warrant of any sort?"

"We don't need one." I explained, "We've been invited onto the premises."

She knew me well enough to know I'd invited myself. I said to everyone, "Here's the plan. Tess and I go in first with our vehicle and gain entry at the gate, followed by Phil and Beth…Detective Penrose. Matt and Steve bring up the rear and they secure the gate, the guards, and the dogs—bring your Mace—then Steve goes down to the beach. I don't want anyone leaving the party. Especially if they're naked." I asked, "Any questions?"

Detective Penrose had a question. "What are we looking for?"

"For the record, we're looking for drugs and underage females. Also illegal aliens and unlicensed guns."

"And off the record?"

Tess answered, "That's classified information."

Beth ignored her and looked at me. When we parted, I was working for the Anti-Terrorist Task Force, and sometimes I'd share a few things with her, and maybe that's what she was thinking now. Finally, she asked me, "Do you anticipate any arrests?"

"That's why you're here, Detective." I advised everyone, "Bring enough cuffs and zip ties. Okay, time is of the essence. Ready?"

Everyone nodded, though I could see that they all thought we could use more muscle and maybe a more detailed plan of attack. But if there's one thing I learned from the Feds it was that they overplanned and overmanned. People know their jobs, and less is more. Especially when the clock is ticking. "Let's go."

I got behind the wheel of the Blazer, and Tess jumped in beside me.

As I turned the vehicle around, Tess asked, "What's with you and Detective Penrose?"

"What do you think?"

"I think you must run into a lot of old girlfriends."

"Detective Penrose was pre-marriage."

"Okay."

As I waited for the other two vehicles to get behind me, I asked Ms. Faraday, "You ever do anything like this before?"

"Only in my fantasies." She asked, "Can I borrow five hundred dollars?"

"Just stick close." A nice feature of these surveillance vehicles is that you can deactivate the airbags, which I did. "Seat belt."

I glanced in my rearview mirror, then hit the accelerator and got to Tamorov's gates in a few seconds. I cut hard left into the closed iron gates and busted through them, waking up the two security guards. I continued up the long driveway past the line of parked cars, and in my rearview mirror I saw the unmarked Chevy right behind me. The Dodge minivan had stopped and Steve and Matt were out and I could see them holding up their creds, guns drawn, screaming at the two Russian security guys who didn't know whether to shit or go blind. The two Dobermans were trying to eat Steve, but he hit them with Mace.

There are less confrontational ways to gain entry, but I like the gangbuster method. It puts everyone—cops and suspects—in the right head. Also, it's fun.

I crashed through one of the closed garage doors, which unfortunately was the one opposite the Jag, which more unfortunately I hit, driving the nice car into the concrete wall.

Tess screamed, "Are you crazy?"

"The caterers have arrived." I jumped out of the Blazer and ran to the service door where the two Russian security guys from the kitchen had appeared, drawn there I suppose by the sound of the crashing objects. They seemed surprised to see us again, and more surprised when Tess pointed her Glock at them and I shoved them back into the storage room and yelled, "FBI! Down! Down! Hit the floorski!"

They understood that we hadn't returned with the mushrooms and they got down on the floor where I frisked them and relieved them of two MP-443 Grachs—standard Russian military-issue.

Detectives Penrose and Florio arrived and they zip-tied both guys as Tess and I ran into the kitchen with our guns drawn.

Dean also seemed surprised to see us, and the catering staff appeared frightened but not surprised to see the Anglos back with guns. They always knew we were trouble.

I said to Dean, "Party's over. Collect your people, leave your stuff, and vamoose."

The staff seemed relieved this wasn't an immigration bust and they dropped what they were doing and streamed past us toward the door. "Don't step on the Russians," I said.

I said to Dean, "Great party. What's the bill?"

"Uh…"

"I'll get you twenty thousand from Tamorov. If you keep your mouth shut about this."

He nodded.

Florio and Penrose came into the kitchen and Tess and I led them into the service corridor. I informed them, "There were three or four security guys on the deck."

I haven't had this much fun since my shoot-out in Yemen.

We came onto the deck, where the Beatles were singing, *Sergeant*

Pepper's Lonely Hearts Club Band. A fog shrouded the beach and a sea mist had settled on the deck, where half the tonga torches and hurricane lamps had gone out.

The party had reached the stupefied stage and no one seemed to notice us, so I sent Beth to the sliding glass doors that led into the house, and Florio went to the staircase that led down to the beach.

Most of the male guests were zonked out in chaises, and six guys were floating naked in the pool. Two other gentlemen were in the steaming hot tub with two hostesses. In addition to the twelve young ladies who'd gone out on the boat, there seemed to be another eight or ten ladies missing, and an equal number of men, so I assumed they were all upstairs having a happy meal.

I looked around and spotted the four security guys at the far end of the deck, sitting around a cocktail table, smoking and joking.

Only two catering ladies were on the deck, retrieving dirty dishes, and the two bartenders were staring off into space. I caught the attention of the two ladies and motioned for them to leave.

I needed to find Dmitry and Tamorov, but first you need to go for the guys with the guns, so I said to Tess, "Stay here and cover," and I grabbed a metal tray and walked quickly along the rail, past Florio. I caught a glimpse of Steve standing in the fog down on the beach, gun drawn. Beth was still standing near the glass door with her gun at her side, watching me. A few heads turned toward me, and one guy yelled to me, "Vodka!"

The party's over, asshole.

I got to the end of the deck where the four security guys were sitting around the low cocktail table. One of them puffed on his cigarette, then looked up at me in the dim light, and I could see recognition in his face. He asked me, "Where you go?"

To answer his question, I hit him between the eyes with the metal tray.

That seemed to get everyone's attention, so I held up my creds, pointed my Glock, and shouted, "FBI! On the fucking floor! Down! Down!"

Nobody went for their gun, though they did hesitate, so to overcome the language problem I demonstrated my verbal command by throwing the stunned gentleman on the deck. "Down!"

The other three men slid off their chairs and lay facedown on the wooden deck.

Florio came over and relieved the men of their guns while I covered him. He had a pocketful of zip ties and he bound the four guys' hands behind their backs.

Meanwhile, the Beatles were asking, *What would you do if I sang out of tune?*

All the commotion had roused the sotted guests and they started to stand, which is not what I wanted, so I yelled, "FBI! Down! Get down!"

Florio and Penrose joined in. "Police! Get down!" Florio shoved one guy back into his chaise, and Beth Penrose pushed a tipsy gentleman into the pool, which gave her an idea for how to corral the crowd, and she shouted, "Everyone in the pool! In the pool!"

Steve had run up from the beach and he got right into the action by rolling a wheeled chaise and its occupant into the swimming pool. The Russians must have thought they were back in the USSR.

Bottom line, even through their alcoholic haze, Tamorov's guests understood this was an FBI and *politsiya* bust, and they complied with our shouted commands to get into the pool, including the two naked couples in the hot tub. The two bartenders, however, remained at their post in case anyone needed a drink.

Meanwhile, I was looking for Tamorov and Dmitry, but the light was bad, and the air was so misty it was hard to see clearly. Maybe they were upstairs with the girls playing hide the pickle.

But then I saw Dmitry staggering toward the pool, and I would have collared him, but he had no shirt, so I shoved him into a chair and said, "Stay there, Dmitry."

He was surprised that I knew his name, but then he recognized me and his surprise turned to confusion. "Who is happening?"

Hard question to answer, but his English was good enough for him to answer my questions.

Tess tapped me on the shoulder and pointed, and I turned to see Georgi Tamorov, fully clothed, trying to sneak into his house.

I came up behind him and asked, "Where you going, Georgi?"

He turned and looked at me. "What do you want here?"

"I want you."

"I have done nothing wrong."

"That's for me to decide."

Tess was beside me now and I said to her, "Frisk him and take him inside. I'll be along shortly."

I found Dmitry where I'd left him and motioned for him to follow me. He stood unsteadily and I escorted him to the hot tub and pushed him in.

I looked across the sprawling deck. Everything seemed to be under control. The pool was full of Russians, including all the cuffed security guys, and standing at poolside were Steve, Phil Florio, and my old friend Detective Beth Penrose, who was either regretting our breakup or happy she wasn't dating a psycho.

The bartenders remained behind the bar, in the tradition of bartenders all over the world who see crazier things than this and just zone out.

A few lamps flickered on the tables, and the tonga torches spluttered. The fog got thicker, and steam rose off the pool filled with naked and half-naked people, like a scene out of The Inferno.

And somewhere out there on the ocean was a ship that held a radiant angel, Lucifer himself, the Angel of Light and of Darkness, sailing in the night toward eight million souls.

The Beatles were singing, *We all live in a yellow submarine*... I stripped down to my shorts and got into the hot tub with Dmitry.

CHAPTER TWENTY-SIX

Limo drivers overhear things, so I asked Dmitry, "Where did Colonel Petrov go?"

"Speak no English."

"I have two questions for you, Dmitry—who is happening and where is Petrov?"

He shook his head.

Well, I'm not a big fan of enhanced interrogation, but if time is short, and there are lives at stake, you gotta do what you gotta do. So I got his neck in an armlock and forced him under. He thrashed like a wounded walrus, and when I let him up he seemed ready to have a conversation. I started with a softball question. "When do you expect Colonel Petrov back here?"

He drew a deep wheezy breath, then replied, "He say tomorrow."

Actually, there might be no tomorrow. But Dmitry didn't know that, though he knew other things that I needed to know.

"Has he called you since he left?"

He shook his head.

"Did you call him?"

"He say no call. No text. Phone is off."

Meaning Petrov's phone had no battery and was therefore not transmitting its location. Well, if true, that was not conclusive proof that Colonel Petrov was up to no good. The SVR guys sometimes pulled their batteries, plus they changed cell phones regularly.

I asked Dmitry again, "Where did Petrov go?"

Dmitry hesitated, then, remembering his breathless experience, he replied, "He say... party."

"Where is the party?"

"He say... how you say...? East Hampton."

East Hampton? Well, that blew a lot of theories. Like the theory that Petrov rendezvoused with a Russian ship carrying a nuclear device onboard, headed for Manhattan. I might as well go home.

But if that amphibious craft carrying three Russians and twelve party girls had docked or run ashore in East Hampton, Scott Kalish would have found it by now.

"Please... I tell you—"

"Shut up." To test Dmitry's truthfulness, I asked him, "Who were the two men with him?"

He hesitated again, then replied, "Pavel Fradkov," using Arkady Urmanov's alias. "Viktor Gorsky."

"Have you ever driven them before?"

"No."

"What are their jobs?"

"I do not know." He reminded me, "I am only driver."

"What were they talking about in the car?"

"I... not listen."

I pushed his face a few inches from the water and held it there. I knew that Dmitry was racking his brain for something that would save him from another near-death experience, and I hoped he came up with something.

Finally he said, "I hear... one word..."

"Repeat the word, please."

He stayed quiet a moment, then said, "Yakut. How you say this?"

"How the hell do I know?"

"Yakut. The big boat for rich."

"You mean... a yacht?"

"Yes. Yakut. Fradkov speak this in car. Colonel say not to speak this. So now I tell you."

I asked Dmitry, "Is that where Petrov's boat went? To a yacht?"

"I think."

"Was this yacht going to East Hampton?"

"Please, I do not know."

"A Russian yakut?"

"I do not know."

"What is the name of this yakut?"

"I hear only yakut."

Okay, so if Dmitry was to be believed, the amphibious craft took Petrov and his companions to a yacht. And maybe the yacht was going to East Hampton. So why would anyone think there was anything sinister about that? Well, maybe because of the passengers—an SVR colonel with a license to kill, an SVR assassin, and a nuclear weapons scientist. The most innocent people in that amphibious craft were the prostitutes.

I asked Dmitry, "What is Petrov's cell phone number?"

He hesitated, out of fear or loyalty, but then he recited the number.

"And Fradkov and Gorsky's numbers."

"I do not know. If I know, I tell."

Sounded reasonable. Well, if I had more time I would have spent it with Dmitry to see if he could remember anything else about his passengers' conversation during the long car ride. But my time as a loose cannon was probably running out, and I needed to speak to Georgi Tamorov before the Feds got their act together and showed up. And quite frankly, if I spent any more time in the hot tub with Dmitry, my colleagues would start to wonder about me.

I released my hold on Dmitry, but before we parted, I said, "Your friends in the pool will tell Colonel Petrov that you spoke to the FBI. But we can protect you if you continue your voluntary cooperation. The choice is yours. Siberia or Brighton Beach."

He nodded.

I climbed out of the hot tub and Beth walked over to me as I squeezed water out of my tighty-whities. I informed her, "This gentleman, Dmitry, works for the Russian U.N. Mission as a driver. He is a potential government witness, so he needs to be kept incommunicado, away from his compatriots."

She glanced at Dmitry still standing in the tub and said to me, "This must be important for you to engage in that kind of interrogation."

"Dmitry's not complaining." I added, "It's important."

I knew she wanted to tell me, "You look good in wet underwear," but she controlled herself and motioned for Dmitry to come out of the hot tub.

Meanwhile, I pulled on my pants and polo shirt and gathered my shoes and socks and my holstered Glock.

To further compromise Dmitry in front of his compatriots, I pointed him toward the bar and said, "Go get yourself a drink."

He didn't need to be told twice and he scooted off.

Detective Penrose reminded me, "You're in my jurisdiction. Follow the rules and the law."

"I always do. Meanwhile, I need your assistance."

"What's this about?"

"This is sensitive compartmented information."

She reminded me, "You used to confide in me."

"I also used to call you Beth."

She looked at me. "Please call me Beth."

"Well...all right, Beth." I confided in her, "There may be a nuclear device on a ship headed for Manhattan."

She took that in, then glanced around, as though trying to fit this party into a nuke on a ship. Finally, she said, "The Russians?"

"They're not all about fun."

"I'm not understanding..."

"Call Scott Kalish. But first get some uniforms here, and a prisoner bus. I want everyone brought in for questioning—but not about nukes. The beef is prostitution and consorting with prostitutes. Also we got guys with guns, probably unlicensed."

She nodded, but said nothing, still thinking about the nuke.

I continued, "Also, do visa checks, immigration status, and so forth, and look for drugs, and seize all the cell phones. And ask the young ladies here if they've heard from their friends who took off in the amphibious craft. And see if you can find my and Tess' Nextels that were taken by the security guys. Also see if Dmitry remembers any more about where Petrov went."

She informed me, "This is going to be a legal mess—and an international incident."

"That should be the least of our problems tonight."

She nodded, then said, "I need to call the FBI."

"You should first determine if there's a Federal beef here." I advised her, "They don't like to be called on Sunday."

"How much time do you need to play Lone Ranger?"

"Two hours."

"One."

"Okay. And thanks for your help."

As I headed toward the house, I heard her call out, "See me before you leave."

I acknowledged with a quick wave as I slid open the glass door.

And now for Georgi Tamorov. But first, a call to Scott Kalish with a possible lead. Colonel Petrov and his pals had sailed off to rendezvous with a yacht. A *yakut.* But why? Party? I hope so.

CHAPTER TWENTY-SEVEN

Georgi Tamorov was sitting on a white couch in his spacious contemporary-style living room, looking very pissed off, and Tess was sitting opposite him, legs crossed, staring at him. It appeared that Mr. Tamorov was being uncooperative. I hoped he would talk to me. In fact, I knew he would.

The air-conditioning was set to simulate a Russian winter, and the transition from the hot tub was a shock. Fortunately, I spotted a warming station—a bar—in an alcove off the living room, where I threw my shoes and my Glock and helped myself to Mr. Tamorov's French cognac. I picked up the phone on the bar and dialed Vasily Petrov's cell phone, hoping if Petrov saw the Caller ID from Tamorov's phone, he'd answer. But there was a short recorded message in Russian and the phone went dead.

I gave Tasha's phone another try, but I got the same message as last time. I pictured guys all over New York waiting for Tasha's callback. They might be waiting a long time.

I used my cell phone to dial Scott Kalish. He answered and I said, "I'm at Tamorov's with your two detectives, interviewing witnesses."

"Anything good?"

"You first." I took a swig of cognac. Hypothermia is dangerous.

"Okay, I've got the Nassau County Marine Bureau out looking, and I've got the rest of my units deployed, as per your request, and I'm in contact with the Coast Guard, and I've alerted NYPD Harbor."

"Good." He sounded a bit tired and strained, so I said, "You're doing a great job." I asked, "Have you met Buck Harris yet?"

"Yeah. He dropped in." He let me know, "Looks like he escaped from an assisted living facility."

"What did he say?"

"Not much. Like, this is really important. He forgot to mention the nuke thing, so I brought it up and he didn't deny it, but then he said we never had this conversation."

I guess that was Buck's way of being straight with the local police. The FBI has the same problem. The CIA has no problem; they speak to no one, except to lie. As for State Department Intelligence…well, they got off to a bad start with me.

Kalish continued, "I also got a conference call from Washington, from people who didn't fully ID themselves. They wanted me to know that I was doing an important job and that I was serving my country, and that they were a hundred percent behind me."

"Wonderful."

"Yeah, but meanwhile, they're not telling me squat about a nuke, and I didn't bring it up, but somebody said there could be terrorists onboard the target vessel. I guess that's the cover story. So I should take any and all action, using all available resources to locate and intercept the target vessel."

Sounded like they were taking this very seriously in Washington. I took another swig of the cognac. "What else did they say?"

"Well, unfortunately there are no naval vessels in the immediate area, but the Coast Guard will take the lead in a boarding if they're close by. Otherwise, it's my show—if they give me the go-ahead. Also, Washington has notified Customs and Border and also Coast Guard headquarters in New York City, and I told them I'd given the NYPD Harbor Unit a heads-up." He added, "So we have the Atlantic Ocean covered between here and New York Harbor."

"Good. And I might have something for you."

"I'm listening."

"Okay, I spoke to Petrov's driver, a guy named Dmitry, who says that his boss and his friends went to a party in East Hampton."

"I'm positive that amphibious craft would have been spotted by now if it went ashore anywhere." He also let me know, "Actually, I just heard from our commo people—they just IDed a hit on Tasha's phone. Maybe twenty minutes after you saw the amphibious craft leaving the beach. The signal came from six miles out, almost due south of Tamorov's, then it went dead."

"I *told* you they went out to sea."

"Good guess. Now we know they went six miles out. But that's all we know."

"Well, I have something else for you." I told Kalish about Dmitry overhearing one of his passengers saying something about going to a yakut—yacht.

"All right...so are we looking for a yacht?"

"If we believe Dmitry. And if there was nothing lost in the translation. And this yacht must be big enough to hold a twenty-five-foot amphibious craft, twelve hookers, three Russian guys, maybe other passengers, and the ship's crew."

Kalish suggested, "That sounds more like a party than a nuclear attack."

"That's what it's *supposed* to look like, Scott." I urged him, "Think nuke, not nookie."

"Okay." He asked me, "Is your witness reliable and truthful?"

"He appeared to be giving truthful answers." I confessed, "I held his head underwater."

"I should do that with my supervisors."

"Me too. So if we believe this twenty-five-foot amphibious craft was taken aboard a yacht, not only is this a big yacht, it may not be a sailing ship. It's probably an ocean-going motorized vessel. Correct?"

"Probably." He asked, "Whose yacht is this?"

"Not mine. Yours?" I asked him, "How big would a yacht have to be to take a twenty-five-foot craft onboard?"

"Maybe...at least a hundred and fifty feet. Maybe closer to two hundred."

"Good. Easy to spot with the amphibious craft on deck."

Kalish stayed silent a moment, then informed me, "People who own a yacht that big, especially one of those newer, half-billion-dollar super yachts, usually have what's called a tender garage below deck."

"That sucks."

"Also, FYI, some of these super yachts even have submersibles—a small submarine—for exploring. Even cars and helicopters. So that's something to think about."

"Right."

"Okay, I think I'm getting a picture of this ship. I'll put the word out to the search units. Maybe they've already spotted something like this."

"That would be good." I asked, "How fast is this two-hundred-foot yacht?"

"Maybe…twenty, twenty-five knots." He added, "Depends on a lot of factors."

"So where is it now?"

"John, I don't know its speed, or what route it's taking. I don't know if it's lain at anchor for a few hours. Also, I have to check winds, currents, and tides."

"Assuming the best conditions, how close is it to New York Harbor?"

He did some quick math and replied, "If it started at Southampton, maybe a half hour after you saw the amphibious craft heading out to sea, and if this ship—this yacht—took the direct ocean route at twenty knots, it could be approaching New York City now."

Shit.

"Or, since we're apparently now looking for a private yacht, you should also know that private vessels are allowed to sail through the Long Island Sound and down the East River or the Hudson as a route to New York Harbor. The good news is that would add hours to its sail time to New York—the bad news is that it more than doubles our search area."

"Right…well, then we have to get the Sound covered."

"I guess we do. So I'll call my counterparts in Connecticut and also notify the Coast Guard in New Haven." He asked, "How did I become the admiral?"

"Enjoy the moment. The Feds will soon throw you overboard. Meanwhile, you have intel they don't have. A two-hundred-foot motorized yacht."

"I will share that information with all agencies."

"Don't mention my name. That came from your conversation with Detective Penrose, who is going to call you. I've told her about Radiant Angel, so you can tell her everything you know."

"Understood." He added, "I hear that you know her."

"We worked a case together." I continued, "I'm assuming this yacht is Russian registry, so see if you can find out if a Russian yacht has requested a berth in New York Harbor."

"I can ask. But if this yacht and its crew and passengers are up to no good, they're not advertising their intentions."

"But get ahead of the Feds and check it out."

"Will do." He also informed me, "There's another possibility that we consider when we run these security scenarios in training sessions."

"Is this bad news?"

"Well…not good news." He told me, "This yacht could have already docked in New York Harbor, like yesterday or this morning, and if so it would have been cleared at Ambrose, then cleared by ICE at the pier. Then the captain can ask to go out on a short pleasure cruise." He continued, "If that were the case, when the yacht returns to New York Harbor he can skip the checkpoint at Ambrose and proceed directly to his assigned pier. And sometimes the ship's captain decides not to pick up a harbor pilot."

"Sounds like a security lapse."

Kalish explained, "It's sort of a courtesy for pleasure craft so the ship doesn't have to wait hours at Ambrose with all the cargo ships or wait for a pilot. Especially if it's a pleasure craft from a friendly nation."

I wasn't sure Russia was a friendly nation, which gave me another thought, though it was stuck somewhere in the back of my mind.

Kalish continued, "Also, if the ship is just out for a short cruise, sometimes it isn't re-boarded by ICE when it returns to the pier."

"What if the ship picked up something at sea? Like drugs, or maybe a small suitcase nuke?"

"Well, they still have to go through Immigration and Customs if they leave the ship."

I thought about all that and said, "I don't think they intend to take the nuke ashore. In fact, they may not even dock. They could blow the nuke in the harbor."

"Right...if there is a nuke."

"Think worst case." I asked, not altogether rhetorically, "How the hell could this happen?"

"Well, seaport security is not like airport security. Everyone involved with seaport security has to evaluate every situation and decide what level of security is appropriate for each ship, and for the ship's passengers and crew." He further added, "We have what we call trusted cargo carriers, and trusted pleasure craft flying the flag of friendly nations, and so forth. Otherwise, the boat traffic into New York Harbor would be backed up to Europe and South America."

"Okay...I understand that." And I also understood why the Russians would choose this method to deliver a nuke. I said to Kalish, "But in this case, if we're looking for a radiation source—"

"Then it doesn't matter if the ship is flying the flag of the Pope. If the detectors light up, all hell breaks loose."

"Right." I asked Kalish, "Do you think a ship can shield its radioactive signature?"

"The Feds tell me no."

"Good answer." But we both knew otherwise.

Kalish said, "I'll check with the Coast Guard to see if they've got an inbound private yacht in the AIS system." He assured me, "There are a lot fewer super yachts than cargo ships or tankers coming into New York, so if you're right about a yacht, this narrows it down. Also, I'll check with ICE to see if maybe a yacht put into New York Harbor, then went out on a cruise."

"Right." Well, I was feeling a bit more confident that someone would find that yacht. Assuming Dmitry was telling me the truth. But maybe Dmitry had been more interested in air than asylum. That's the problem with enhanced interrogation.

But if Dmitry *was* telling me the truth, then the search was getting focused. The bigger picture, however, was still blurry. It didn't make sense for Petrov to board a Russian yacht with a nuke onboard, because if he got stopped at sea and a Russian-made miniature nuke was found, Petrov and his government would have a lot of explaining to do. And if the nuke detonated in New York Harbor, there would be Russian fingerprints all over the explosion, and we'd be looking at World War III.

This made no sense when I'd first heard about a nuke from Buck, and it still made no sense. So I tried to put myself in Colonel Petrov's head, and in the head of his SVR and Kremlin bosses, and I said to Kalish, "I'm thinking that this yacht is *not* Russian. As you suggested, it could be from a friendly country that would be extended some courtesies regarding security."

"I don't think friendly countries carry nukes into New York Harbor."

"They probably don't know they have a nuke onboard, Scott."

"Right…lots of contraband is smuggled aboard trusted ship carriers—usually hidden in crates of provisions." He added, "Or this yacht could rendezvous at sea with a Russian ship…and Petrov would tell his host that they're taking aboard a hundred kilos of caviar or something, compliments of the Russian government." He informed me, "Drug smugglers do stuff like that."

There were a lot of possible scenarios, including Petrov and his killer Gorsky hijacking the yacht, then taking the nuke aboard, along with a Russian sea captain. I mean, piracy was not out of the question for a man like Petrov and his organization.

I said, "Look, Scott, we might be wrong about some of this, but what we know for sure is what I saw—Colonel Petrov, along with an SVR assassin named Gorsky and a nuclear weapons scientist named Urmanov and twelve ladies, took off in an amphibious craft out to sea. And now I just found out about a yacht."

"And this is the first I'm hearing about a nuclear weapons scientist."

"Now you know why I'm worried."

"And now I'm worried."

"And when you find the yacht, we'll know if it's a party ship or a nuclear weapon delivery system."

He didn't reply.

I told Kalish, "I'm about to interview Georgi Tamorov. If I get anything out of him, I'll call you."

"Hold his wallet underwater."

I gave him Petrov's cell phone number to try to locate the signal and said, "I'm sure it's as dead as Tasha's, but try."

"Will do."

"Okay, talk to you—"

"One more thing... look, if my guys find this ship or this yacht, and we attempt to board, and if there's a nuke onboard, what stops somebody from getting desperate and lighting the fuse?"

"What do you want me to say?"

"Say they don't want to commit suicide."

"I can't say that."

"Say *something*."

"Okay. I don't want that ship sailing into New York Harbor with a nuclear bomb onboard and the timer ticking."

There was silence on the phone, then Scott said, "I need to let my people know what this is about."

"If you do that, it will go viral and cause mass panic."

He didn't reply.

"We need to find that yacht while it's still at sea."

"Okay... If it's still in my area of operation, I will find it. If it's someplace else, someone will find it."

"Right." One way or the other. I had another thought—another theory that I'd been kicking around in my mind—and I shared it with Kalish. "Look, tomorrow is September twelfth. So maybe this attack is supposed to look like an Islamic terrorist repeat of 9/11."

"Okay..."

"Follow my reasoning. Today, September eleventh, we have a heightened security alert, making an attack more difficult. Also, it's a Sunday and there are a lot fewer people in Manhattan to kill."

"Right."

"Islamic extremists are into symbolism, anniversary dates. Right? So the nuke could be set to detonate at eight forty-six A.M.—the same time, if not the same day, as the first plane hit on 9/11. Or maybe nine oh-three A.M. when the second plane hit—when there will be hundreds of thousands of people making their Monday commute into Manhattan. So maybe we have some time."

"I hope you're right."

"Meanwhile, I'd like to join the search. Can you get a high-speed unit to meet me at the Shinnecock Coast Guard Station?"

"I have a twenty-seven-foot SAFE boat that can make fifty knots."

"Call him in."

"I'll let you know when he's a half hour out. But call me after you speak to Tamorov."

"Will do."

He asked me, "How the hell did this happen?"

"Nothing has happened yet. And we're going to make sure it doesn't."

"I've got a daughter in Manhattan."

I thought of Kate, who would be flying back from Washington late tonight—or hopefully tomorrow. I also thought of the millions of people who lived and worked in the potential blast zone, and the millions more who would be affected by the radiation and fallout. The real question was, How could anyone do this?

"John?"

I remembered when the first plane hit the North Tower, and I thought, *Thank God it's only this, and they don't have a nuke.* And my second thought was, *Not this time.* And if my reasoning was correct—that this was a Russian attack, made to look like an attack from an Islamic country—then everyone would have no problem believing that Abdul finally did the unthinkable.

I said to Scott Kalish, "Call your daughter."

I hung up and walked into the living room where Tess was keeping Tamorov company. This asshole was my last play before I got on a boat and went out to find a ship that might be carrying a nuclear weapon guarded by a couple of trained killers.

Nobody asked me to do that, and nobody would expect me to do it. In fact, I got put out to pasture because I wasn't a team player. And because I bent the rules until they broke. So why was I doing all this again? All I really needed to do according to my dead-end job description was text 26 Fed: Target has left last known location, whereabouts unknown, call Suffolk County Marine Bureau for more. And, by the way, get your asses out of that building.

That's what I should do, then go on a 10-63—a meal break—and have a beer at Sammy's Seaside Grill and hope things turn out okay. But that's not what I was going to do. And why not? Well, because Colonel Vasily Petrov was my responsibility today and I lost him. And in my NYPD head, I'd like to call in a 10-91—"Condition Corrected."

Also, to be totally honest, I wouldn't mind showing those assholes at 26 Fed—including Tom Walsh—who I was. Kate, too. Right?

CHAPTER TWENTY-EIGHT

I threw my shoes, socks, and my holstered Glock on the coffee table and sat in a comfortable leather chair, facing Georgi Tamorov. We looked at each other.

He was about mid-forties, fairly trim compared to his porky friends, and he had a thin face with dark narrow eyes. He was not handsome, but women found the bulge in his back pocket irresistible. He was still wearing shorts and his silly Hawaiian shirt, but he'd lost his sandals somewhere. He may have been drunk earlier, but the events of the last half hour seemed to have sobered him up.

I asked Tess, "This guy have a cell phone?"

"Not when I frisked him."

I looked at Tamorov. "You throw it in the pool?"

He didn't reply.

I asked Tess, "Cat got his tongue?"

"He wants to call his lawyer."

I looked at Tamorov. "You can't call your lawyer if you don't have a phone." I asked, "Where is it?"

No reply.

I tried a compliment. "Great party. Love your caterers."

At this point, the suspect usually says something like, "I knew all along that you were a cop," which they say because they're feeling stupid about getting conned. I recently had the same feeling. But

Tamorov didn't say anything, and I couldn't determine if he or Petrov had any suspicions about the two caterers who were now sitting with him. In the end, though, it didn't change Colonel Petrov's plans, though it did change mine.

I got down to business and informed him, "As you may have guessed, this is a raid. A joint operation by the FBI and the county police, code-named Revenge of the Caterers."

He didn't respond to that, but asked me in good English, "Do you have a search warrant?"

"No, but I have a caterer's license."

He wasn't amused and said to me, "I must see your credentials and your search warrant."

I tapped my Glock on the coffee table. "See?"

He kept his eyes fixed on me.

I informed Mr. Tamorov, "Not only do I not need a warrant, but you have no right to remain silent."

"I wish to call my attorney."

"He'll tell you what I'm telling you, Georgi. You're in a lot of trouble—but you can get out of it if you cooperate."

He didn't reply.

I'd established that he was married with children, and with men of substance and standing you go right for the family jewels. So I told him, "I understand that your wife is in your townhouse in Tribeca. So I'm going to call her and tell her you've been arrested for engaging the services of two dozen prostitutka, and you got a blow job in the pool where she swims." I added, "Then you'll really need to call your lawyer."

His impassive face showed a little concern. Even oligarchs are afraid of their wives. Right?

"However," I continued, "I can make all this go away."

Our eyes met, and he tried to get a measure of me. To help him with that, I said, "You have to decide who you're most afraid of—me, Vasily Petrov, or your wife."

"I am afraid of no one."

"Come on, Georgi. You're afraid of your wife."

"Americans are afraid of their wives."

He could be on to something. More importantly, I got him talking.

I also informed him, to put him on the defensive, "Every gun here better be licensed. And every foreign national better have a valid visa."

"I have no knowledge of that."

"I hope you have knowledge of everything in your house when we search it."

"I need to see your search warrant."

"When I find it, I'm going to roll it up, put a coat of oil on it, and shove it up your ass."

He had no response to that.

I pulled on my socks and shoes, but left the Glock on the coffee table. There was a crystal cigarette box and ashtray on the table, and a silver table lighter. I said to him, "Smoke if you want."

He looked at the cigarettes, and I'm sure he needed one, but his experience in his homeland told him not to go anywhere near the gun.

"Go ahead," I urged. "Reach for the cigarettes."

He sat back on the couch and stopped trying to stare me down, and he looked off into space.

I let him know, "You can answer my questions here, or you can answer them at 26 Federal Plaza in Manhattan."

He must have had a law degree or something, because he said, "Prostitution is not a Federal crime."

"Right. But assaulting a Federal officer is. That's me."

"I have not assaulted you."

"You tried to bite my toes."

He seemed confused, but then he understood that I was crazy and he was fucked. But he was a smart guy so he called my bluff and said, "If you allow me to call my attorney, I will accompany you to your headquarters." He added, "I have done nothing wrong."

Well, I didn't have time to go to 26 Fed, and I certainly didn't want to be there when the building disappeared in a nuclear firestorm. But apparently that was not a concern for Georgi Tamorov. I could deduce, therefore, that Mr. Tamorov had no idea what his three U.N. guests were up to tonight. Or I could conclude that Colonel Petrov and his pals were not up to anything. But I think I was past that point. I was believing the unbelievable, and thinking the unthinkable.

I said to him, "You understand this is about Colonel Petrov."

He understood that, though he'd hoped it was about prostitutes, unlicensed guns, and expired visas. He seemed a bit uneasy now, so this was the time to reveal the true nature of the suspect and of the crimes under investigation.

I said, "As I'm sure you know, Vasily Petrov is not actually a Human Rights delegate to the United Nations. He is an SVR colonel, and a killer."

No response.

I continued, "We have information that he is in this country to do harm, which is why we followed him from the Russian Mission to here." Actually, we follow everyone, but that was none of his business. I asked Tamorov, "Why was Petrov *here*?"

He realized that he needed to answer at least the easy questions and he replied, "For the party."

"Why did you invite him?"

"I... he is an acquaintance."

"How do you know him?"

"He was introduced to me... at a United Nations reception."

"By whom?"

"I don't remember."

"Maybe your wife will remember."

"By our U.N. ambassador."

"Did your ambassador mention that Vasily Petrov was an SVR assassin?"

"Of course not—"

"Or that his father, Vladimir, was a KGB general, and the head of SMERSH?"

"I did not know that."

"So I know more than you do?"

"It is no business of mine who this man is. That is your business."

"Do you understand the legal concept of guilt by association?"

No reply.

"You could be looking at twenty years in jail."

"I know nothing about this man."

"Bullshit. He's your friend."

"We are acquaintances." He added, "We are compatriots."

"No, you are co-conspirators in a criminal conspiracy to do harm to the United States."

"No."

"Maybe thirty years." He was on the run now, and I pressed on. "We'll seize all your assets in America and around the world. Your wife will be shopping at Kmart, and your kids will be waiting on tables in the Russian Tea Room."

He knew this was part bluff, but he didn't know which part.

He insisted, "I know nothing about this man." He also reminded me, "Colonel Petrov is a United Nations delegate vetted by your country—"

"And I'm Santa Claus." I said to Tess, "Get a car and we'll take Mr. Tamorov to 26 Fed."

She glanced at me, knowing we weren't going to 26 Fed, and we'd already seen that Mr. Tamorov didn't wet his pants when I told him I was taking him to Lower Manhattan. So Tess understood she was supposed to say something clever, and she said to me, "I think we can resolve this here if Mr. Tamorov cooperates."

"He's an asshole." I told her, "Cuff him."

She actually didn't have any cuffs, so she said, "Let me talk to him."

I glanced at my watch and said, "Five minutes."

Tess leaned forward and pushed the cigarettes and lighter toward Tamorov, who hesitated, glanced at me, then took a cigarette and lit up.

Tess assured him, "If you are cooperative, and if we can determine by your answers that you have no knowledge of Colonel Petrov's illegal activities in America, then you are free to remain here, at liberty, subject to further interviews with your lawyer present."

Not bad for an intelligence officer.

She asked him, "Do you understand?"

He nodded.

She got down to business and asked, "Who were the two men who arrived here with Colonel Petrov?"

Tamorov guessed correctly that we must know the answer to this, and that in any case he should know who his guests were, so he was quick to reply. "They are Petrov's U.N. colleagues. One is Viktor Gorsky and the other is Pavel Fradkov."

Also known as Dr. Arkady Urmanov, a suitcase nuke guy. But I was fairly sure Tamorov didn't know this. And if I'd told him that his three compatriots had sailed off to obliterate his Manhattan real estate along with Mrs. Tamorov, he'd be shocked. You can reveal some stuff to a witness or even a suspect, but you don't give them sensitive information, so Tess didn't mention nuking New York.

Tess asked him, "Where did that amphibious craft come from?"

"I do not know."

"You know it came from a ship. And that it was going back to the ship. And you knew the amphibious craft was coming. I saw that you knew."

He looked at both of us, and I was sure he was pissed off at Colonel Petrov, the pro, for not getting on to us and getting rid of us.

"Mister Tamorov?"

"Petrov told me that he had a party to go to."

"Whose party?"

"He did not say. But he mentioned East Hampton."

I said to Tamorov, "We've already checked this out. There has been no sighting of an amphibious craft filled with Russian hookers anywhere on the east end of Long Island." I assured him, "Someone would have noticed."

Tamorov shrugged. "I am telling you what he told me."

I said to him, "We know that Petrov sailed out to a ship at sea." I suggested, "Tell me about that."

"I have no knowledge of that."

"Did he tell you when he intended to return here?"

"Tomorrow morning."

"Can you call him?"

"I do not have his cell phone number."

"When we find your cell phone, we'll see if that's true."

No reply.

"Okay, so you invited him to your party, provided him with a dozen prostitutes to take with him to another party, and you don't have his cell phone number. Is that right?"

Tamorov thought about this, then replied, "Petrov is a man of few words and he shares very little."

"You need better friends."

"He is not my friend."

I nodded to Tess and she continued, "I know that Colonel Petrov is fond of alcoholic beverages. But tonight, neither I nor this gentleman nor anyone served him a drink." She asked, "Why is that?"

"I have no idea."

"Well then, I'll tell you—because he and Gorsky and Fradkov wanted to remain sober because they are on a mission tonight. A mission to inflict harm to my country."

Tamorov looked a little uncomfortable, and he replied, "I assumed they were...saving themselves for the other party. Yes. In fact, Gorsky said that."

I interjected, "Bullshit."

Tamorov was in a tough position, wanting to be cooperative enough to get us out of his house, and at the same time not saying anything that Colonel Vasily Petrov of the SVR would disapprove of if and when they met again. Tamorov was not protecting Petrov; he was protecting his own life. And that was the problem. Petrov kills.

I said, "Look, Georgi, you and I both know who Petrov is and I'm really sensitive to your concerns. But I want to assure you that I will take care of Colonel Petrov."

He looked at me and asked, "And will you also take care of the entire SVR?"

He had a valid point there, but I couldn't help saying, "When you dance with the devil, Georgi, you're going to get burned."

He got what I was saying and replied, "One cannot always refuse the invitation of the devil."

Right. Especially if you have relatives and oil wells in hell.

I told him what he already knew. "Colonel Petrov is not good for business."

He gave me a half nod.

Tess returned to the topic and asked, "What was in the luggage they took with them?"

"How would I know?"

I was positive that Petrov and his pals did not have guns with them in the car, so if they needed guns they picked them up here. And Tess knew that, too, so she asked, "Is it possible that one of your guests—or one of your security men—gave something to Petrov and the men with him?"

"How would I know this?"

He was annoying me, so I picked up the heavy silver lighter and shattered the ashtray, startling Mr. Tamorov and even Tess. I shouted, "Stop the bullshit! We know Petrov picked up guns here! And you know it!"

Tamorov didn't reply and just looked at the mess I'd made.

"You," I informed him, "are what we call a useful idiot. Understand?"

He understood. Better than being a co-conspirator.

"Maybe an accessory to a crime."

"No."

"You're also an asshole."

That was not an indictable offense, so he didn't argue with that.

"Last chance to come clean. Tell me about the ship."

He insisted, "I do not know of any ship."

I leaned across the table and looked him in the eye. "Yakut?"

He seemed confused by the word in his own language and replied, "I don't understand."

"You don't understand Russian?"

"I understand the word, but—"

"Do you own a yacht?"

"No."

"Do you have friends who own yachts?"

"No. Yes."

"Did you introduce Colonel Petrov to someone who has a yacht?"

He hesitated a second, then replied, "I do not recall making such an introduction."

"You need to think about this, Georgi."

He did not respond.

Tess asked him, "Was it Colonel Petrov who suggested that you have this party tonight?"

Good question.

Tamorov thought so, too, because a yes answer meant that all this was pre-planned, and that he, Tamorov, was complicit in something, even if he didn't know what it was. So he replied, "No."

Tess pressed on, "So it was just coincidence that your party was on the same night that a yacht was passing by? A yacht that Petrov had been invited to?"

"I do not know of any yacht." He added, "As I told you, he said he was going to a party in East Hampton."

I pointed out, "These people at your party were your friends, from *your* world. Not Petrov's. There were no other diplomatic people here. So why did you invite Petrov, Gorsky, and Fradkov?"

"I... Petrov and I sometimes have business to discuss."

"Yours or his?"

"He is a useful man for me to know. In Russia."

"Does he whack people for you?"

"Excuse me?"

"Look, Georgi, you're in deep shit, and it's up to your ears now." I looked at him. "I want a yes or no answer. Did Petrov ask you to have this party tonight?"

He understood that we both knew the answer to that, but he couldn't bring himself to say yes, though he didn't say no.

Well, if I could reverse-engineer this evening, it seemed that it started with a non-Russian ship that Petrov needed to deliver a nuclear weapon to Manhattan Island. It was hard to figure out how all this came about and it was hard to know how much of this was Petrov's bright idea, and how much was cooked up in Moscow. Probably Petrov had the idea, and Moscow had the suitcase nuke. All they needed were a few clueless idiots like Georgi Tamorov and a ship owner—who Tamorov probably knew—to pull it off, and to be sure there were no Russian connections to the nuclear explosion. Well, but there were—Petrov, Gorsky, and Urmanov—but only if American intelligence could connect those three Russians to a yacht that became ground zero in a nuclear explosion. And there was really no way to make that connection. Or so Colonel Petrov thought.

The plan seemed a bit complex to me, but it also had a certain simplicity to it. If the goal was for Russia to nuke Manhattan and make it look like someone else had done it, like the North Koreans or the Chinese—or an Islamic group, if this was supposed to look like a replay of 9/11—then it was a good plan. Not nice, but good.

I leaned toward Tamorov and said, "Look at me."

He looked at me and I asked, "What is the name of this yacht's owner? What country is he from, and what is the name of his yacht?"

"I do not know of any yacht."

"I know you do. And you know you do."

Georgi Tamorov took a deep breath, then said to me, "I mean no harm to your country." He waved his hand around the big room. "I enjoy my time here." He further informed me, "I am a Russian by birth, but I am a citizen of the world."

More likely a citizen of Switzerland for tax purposes. But I got his point, though that didn't mean he couldn't answer my question. "The name of the yacht. And the name and nationality of the yacht's owner."

"I do not know... but I will think about what you are asking."

Right. Lots to think about. Like, what to get in return. It's all about the deal. Not to mention who was most likely to ruin his life. Or end it.

He had no idea how serious this was, nor did he know that the clock was ticking and his window to make a deal was closing.

I said to him, "Information that comes too late is no information. Meaning you have nothing to trade." I asked him, "Understand?"

He nodded, but said nothing.

While I was contemplating inviting Mr. Tamorov for a dip in the hot tub, my cell phone rang and it was Scott Kalish. I took the call and Kalish said, "I have that SAFE boat for you, about twenty minutes from the Shinnecock Coast Guard Station."

"Okay."

"And before you ask, still no sighting. Also, I'm asking about all yachts that are due in or have already docked in New York. And I checked with the East Hampton Police and the Bay Constables, and rechecked with my people, and everyone's sure there is no amphibious craft full of hookers docked at a party anywhere."

"Right. Can't talk now. I'll call you later."

I hung up and said to Tamorov, "Here's the deal, Georgi—if Vasily Petrov blows something up tonight, or kills someone, you are in a world of shit. So think hard about what we've asked you, and maybe what we didn't ask you. And if you think of something, especially about a yacht, you tell a lady named Detective Penrose that you need to speak to me. Not your fucking lawyer. Understand?"

He nodded.

I picked up my Glock, and Tess and I stood. I instructed Tamorov, "Do not move. But before you're taken into protective custody, you will write a check for twenty thousand dollars to Hampton Catering. Actually, make it twenty-five."

Money he understood, and he said, "Perhaps I can write a check to each of you for a million dollars."

"I'll get back to you with my Swiss bank account number."

"I am serious."

"Good. I'll add bribery to the charges." I reminded him, "Think about who and what you're most afraid of." I looked him in the eye. "Time is running out."

I was about to leave, but then I decided that this was a situation that was desperate enough for me to break the rules and to share a great secret with this Russian. I moved close to him and said, "We have good reason to believe that onboard this yacht is a Soviet-made miniature nuclear weapon, heading for Manhattan."

Tamorov looked like I'd just hit him in the nuts.

Tess said, "John—"

I continued, "If this nuke detonates, you can say good-bye to your Manhattan real estate, your Wall Street investments, and also your wife, and your life."

He stared at me, trying I guess to see if I was lying, but he was smart enough to see that I wasn't. And smart enough to know that his pal Colonel Vasily Petrov was capable of mass murder.

I said, "The yacht."

He replied, in a barely audible voice, "I...made an introduction... but..."

"You introduced Petrov to whom?"

"To a Saudi prince. Ali Faisel."

Right. A Saudi prince. It all made sense now. Our sometimes friends the Saudis take the rap for the nuclear terrorist attack. Or Ali Faisel was complicit. Lots to think about and lots to figure out. And not much time to do either. "And the prince owns a yacht named...? What?"

"The Hana."

"Spell it."

Tamorov was staring at the floor now, and he spelled the prince's name and the name of the yacht, then said, "That is all I know."

I hope that's all I need to know. I said to him, "If you pray, Georgi, say a prayer for Mrs. Tamorov and for a million other innocent people."

He nodded, and I thought I heard him say, "My God."

"As my mother used to say to me, pick your friends carefully."

Tess and I left Georgi Tamorov to contemplate the results of his bad choices.

CHAPTER TWENTY-NINE

Out on the back deck, the Suffolk County PD had arrived. Phil Florio and Beth Penrose, as the first responding detectives, were in charge, and they were conversing with two uniformed sergeants.

Detective Florio seemed anxious to get a team together to go upstairs and bust the Ivans and their ladies, but I told him he needed to go to the living room and sit on Tamorov and not let him communicate with anyone.

Someone had found the audio controls and shut off the music, and I could hear the surf breaking on the shore. There was no sea breeze and the fog lay motionless over the ocean and the beach. The floodlights came on and reflected off the mist, adding more weirdness to an already surreal night.

I texted Scott Kalish: You are looking for a yacht named The Hana. Owned by a Saudi prince, Ali Faisel. Will call you later.

Tess asked me, "How did you know about a yacht?"

"From Dmitry, the driver."

She nodded, and came to the same conclusion I did. "The nuke would not be on a Russian ship. But it could have come from one."

"Correct."

"And this Saudi prince will look like a nuclear terrorist. Or he actually *is* a terrorist."

"It almost doesn't matter at this point. But we'll know when we find The Hana."

"I hope it's The Hana that we're looking for."

"It is."

"And that we're not too late."

I was fairly sure now that the attack was supposed to look like a jihadist follow-up to 9/11—or it actually *was*, if this Saudi prince was in cahoots with Petrov. I said to Tess, "I think we have until eight forty-six A.M. or nine oh-three A.M."

She looked at me, then nodded.

"Unless Petrov is spooked and goes early."

She had no reply.

Tess and I found Detective Penrose talking to a uniformed sergeant about how best to get a few dozen naked people out of the pool, dressed, cuffed, and into the waiting prisoner bus.

I said to Beth, "The homeowner, Mr. Tamorov, is inside with Florio. I have told Tamorov about Radiant Angel and he needs to be kept in strict isolation. The only phone call he's allowed to make is to you. Give him your card and instruct him to ask someone at the county lockup for permission to call you if he remembers anything further. Call me and I'll get back to him." I added, "And please be sure Mr. Tamorov writes a check to Hampton Catering. Twenty-five thousand."

"Does he get the police raid discount?"

Funny. Even Tess laughed. I also asked Beth, "Has anyone found our cell phones?"

"Unfortunately, the caterers grabbed the whole basket when you told them to leave." She scolded me, "You are not supposed to let anyone leave the premises."

"They had a tough day."

"Me too. And I'm still here."

"Well, I'm leaving. But please send someone to get our phones, deliver the check, and remind Dean Hampton to keep quiet. National security."

She reminded me, "You and Ms. Faraday and your team have to log in your presence."

Sounded like my wife. Another stickler for rules. Even when the world was about to blow up. "We'll be sure to log in and log out."

"Where are you going?"

"Just between us, I'm going out on a SAFE boat."

"I suppose that's better than having to deal with all this."

"I always know when to run from a shit storm."

"You usually run into a worse one."

"That's my M.O."

Ms. Faraday sensed a private moment coming, so she moved off to where Steve and Matt were speaking to another uniformed sergeant.

Beth and I looked at each other, and I said, "It's good to see you again."

She didn't reply.

She wasn't wearing a wedding band, but in this business you often don't. I said, "I married that woman."

"Congratulations."

"You?"

"Looking for a rich Russian."

"You came to the right place."

Well, that seemed to cover it, so I got down to business and asked, "Have you spoken to Scott Kalish?"

"I did."

"So you understand there are no rules tonight." I added, "I want all these people kept under wraps until at least noon tomorrow. Make up some charges."

"The FBI will be all over this in an hour."

Not to mention the CIA if they were working with the State Department. I advised her, "If my name comes up, you don't know where I went."

"All right. But can I mention that you appeared crazy as ever?"

"That's our secret." I added, "I'm sure we'll be in touch when you write your report."

"I'm sure the Feds will make you unavailable for the next ten years."

Longer, if the CIA whacked me. "Call me anytime."

"You don't have a phone."

I smiled. "You'll find it. Meanwhile, Tess and I are sharing Matt Conlon's phone." I gave her the number.

She told me, "I have discovered that you are with the Diplomatic Surveillance Group, and that your duties and responsibilities are very limited."

"My job is to keep the surveillance target in sight at all times, and to find him when I lose him. And that's what I'm doing."

"Don't get yourself killed doing it."

"Anything further?"

"No. I'll take care of this." She gave me her card. "Call me later and let me know what's happening."

"If you see an incandescent flash on the western horizon, you'll know what's happening."

"Don't say that."

"Talk to you later."

We both hesitated, then hugged for a brief second. "Careful," she said.

I walked toward Steve, Matt, and Tess, who saw the public display of affection. They were speaking to a patrol sergeant, and I motioned to my team to join me.

Steve informed me, "I just got a call from a supervisor, Special Agent Howard Fensterman. He says he knows you."

"We worked together in Yemen."

"He said you've exceeded your authority—"

"How does he know that?"

"Not from us. I told you, the last we texted was that you and the trainee were on a meal break."

"Okay." So the word had reached 26 Federal Plaza, probably through Washington, that there was a situation in progress. And somehow my name came up, and my name at 26 Fed causes concern for some reason.

Steve continued, "Fensterman said you are relieved of your duties and you are to report to him at 26 Fed with all due haste."

I didn't think I wanted to be at 26 Fed tonight. And neither did Howard Fensterman, who obviously didn't know he was in a nuclear blast zone. I mean, that's compartmented information. To the max.

Steve also told me, "Matt and I are also relieved. We're all going to see Fensterman."

Matt asked, "Are we getting fired?"

"Probably."

"Shit."

My boys looked at me as though I'd let them down and totally fucked up their second careers and their lives. I asked Steve, "And Tess?"

"Fensterman didn't mention her."

Right. Fensterman probably knew who she was. I glanced at Tess, and she understood that I wanted to let my team know what was going on, but she shook her head.

I assured Matt and Steve, "Don't worry about your jobs."

Matt said, "I don't think you can fix this one, boss."

Steve added, "Fensterman was really pissed."

"Well," I informed them, "he's going to be more pissed, because I'm not going to 26 Fed."

"You gotta go," Steve said.

Matt added, "We all have to go. Now."

Tess surprised them by saying, "John is not going to 26 Fed, and neither are you."

They looked at her, then at each other. Steve asked, "What the hell is going on here?"

I replied, "You don't need to know and you don't want to know."

Matt asked, "Where you going?"

"Can't say."

"We'll go with you."

I reminded my team, "You're done here. E.O.T. End of tour. Go get a drink." I suggested, "Sammy's in Southampton. Have one for me." I let them know, "Good job tonight." I shook hands with both men and assured them, "You're covered." I added, "Do *not* go back to Manhattan. That is an order."

Tess and I went into the service corridor to the kitchen where two uniformed officers were securing the scene and sampling the unserved desserts. We showed our creds and headed toward the service entrance.

There were four household employees in the kitchen, including the fat housekeeper, who saw me and shouted, "Yob vas!"

That's the thanks I get for slicing a hundred feet of kolbasa.

Tess suggested, "We can stop at Hampton Catering for our phones."

"The less commo we have the better."

"I've never heard that one before."

She never worked an unauthorized case with me before.

We walked through the storage room and into the garage.

Tess asked, "Do you think your wife has been trying to call you?"

"I don't know."

I inspected the damage to the Blazer. The front end was a little banged up, but the headlights were okay. The Jag was going to cost Tamorov big bucks. But that was the least of his problems.

Tess asked, "Is she staying in D.C. tonight?"

"I'm not sure."

"Maybe you should call her."

I'd thought about that—many times—and I said, "I can't do what we are telling other people not to do."

"This is your wife."

I did tell Scott Kalish to call his daughter in Manhattan, but Tess didn't know I'd had a weak moment.

Tess suggested, "Just tell her she needs to stay in Washington tonight. And tomorrow."

"I'm assuming the Feds will halt air traffic into New York at some point."

"Okay, but she could be at the airport now, ready to board."

I looked at Tess and reminded her, "There are a million people in the blast zone."

"We just told Steve and Matt not to go to Manhattan without telling them why. You can do the same for your wife."

This was none of her business, but I said, for the record, "Special Agent Mayfield is a stickler for rules and procedures and she wouldn't want special treatment."

Tess and I looked at each other. Finally, she said, "You have to live with that decision."

"And you don't." I moved to the driver's door. "And you don't need to come with me."

She didn't reply and went around to the passenger's door and got in.

I got behind the wheel, started the engine, and backed out over the broken garage door panels, and off we went down the driveway, now lined with police vehicles.

Two uniformed officers were at the gate and we showed our creds and logged out, then exited the oceanfront estate of Georgi Tamorov, whom I envied when I got here. Goes to show you.

I remembered a line that I'd read when I was a kid—a line about the nuclear war we all thought was coming. *The survivors will envy the dead.*

CHAPTER THIRTY

The United States Coast Guard Station is about six miles west of Tamorov's house, but the Shinnecock Inlet separates the beach road, so we had to go around the bay, and Tess navigated the foggy roads. What would I do without her? I'd use my GPS.

Tess seemed to be having second thoughts. She asked, "Are you sure we should be doing this?"

"What else would you like to do tonight?"

"Maybe our job is to stay with the police at Tamorov's, then work the case at police headquarters."

"Actually, I have no job." I suggested, "We can keep going and be at 26 Fed in two hours, as per orders."

She didn't reply.

"Or I can leave you at the Coast Guard Station."

"I'm with you."

I called Kalish, he answered, and I said, "Ms. Faraday is with me on speaker." I asked him, "Did you find the yacht, Scott?"

"I haven't, but I have some info for you about The Hana."

"Great."

I heard some paper shuffling and Kalish said, "Here's the scoop—The Hana is indeed registered to a Saudi prince named Ali Faisel, and is here in New York. The ship got cleared at Ambrose yesterday, around noon. It had arrived from Istanbul with a refueling stop in the Azores." He continued, "The Hana, with the prince onboard, picked up a harbor pilot, then docked at Pier 11 and was inspected by Immigration and Customs Enforcement, who found no problems or issues, and everyone onboard who had passports and a valid visa was cleared to disembark. Six crewmembers and five passengers, including the prince, left the ship, and everyone returned by three A.M. according to ICE."

"I hope they partied like there was no tomorrow."

"Not funny. Okay, then this morning, around nine A.M., The Hana's skipper, a Brit named Jack Wells, asked for a harbor pilot and for permission to leave the pier and go on an overnight cruise, within U.S. territorial waters, expecting to return about eight Monday morning."

The facts were starting to match the theories. I glanced at Tess, who was paying close attention. I said to Kalish, "Have the Feds check out the names on The Hana's manifest."

"Already being done, no red flags so far." He continued, "This prince has some sort of U.N. diplomatic status, plus, of course, he's a member of the Saudi royal family, so he's VIP."

"Where did you get this info on Ali?"

"A reliable source." He confessed, "The Internet."

"What's the Internet say about The Hana?"

"Not much, but I did get some info from a luxury yacht website." He read, "Built in Ancona, Italy, by CRN Shipyard, The Hana is two hundred and twenty feet, with a forty-foot beam, and weighs in at six hundred and thirty tons, powered by two twenty-one-hundred-horsepower engines, and has a cruise speed of twenty-one knots and a max speed of twenty-five knots. It can sleep a crew of about twenty, plus four officers, and will accommodate ten to twelve overnight guests."

I guess the twelve hookers sleep with the twelve overnight guests—or they're all sleeping with the fishes.

He continued, "Here's the interesting part—it has a float-in garage space below deck for two twenty-five-foot tender craft."

"Does it say anything about an amphibious craft?"

"No, just the max length of the tender craft."

"Well, the length is right." I recalled something Kalish had said earlier and asked, "Does this yacht have a submersible craft?"

"I don't see that on this website. But some of these yachts are built in semi-secrecy, and some are retrofitted later."

"Okay. Well, this sounds like what we're looking for."

"Where did you get the name of the yacht?"

"From Tamorov. But I can't directly connect this yacht with Petrov, though it looks like a no-brainer."

"Right. And the yacht seems to fit the profile we discussed—friendly nation, good creds, previously cleared at Ambrose and cleared by ICE at the pier, out for a cruise, and holds up to two twenty-five-foot tenders." He asked me, "What more evidence do you need?"

"None. I need the yacht."

"I don't understand why Petrov and his pals didn't just meet The Hana at its pier this morning before it set out on its cruise."

"Because the Diplomatic Surveillance Group is up Petrov's ass 24/7, and we would have seen him boarding, and even if he gave us the slip he'd still have to go through security at the pier. And obviously he wants no connection between him and The Hana."

"Right."

"What else have you done for me tonight?"

"Well, now that we have the name of the ship, we were able to tune in to The Hana's AIS transmitter to find its location."

"But it wasn't transmitting or you'd be aboard by now."

"Correct." He also told me, "It's illegal to shut off the transmitter."

"The transmitter could be out of service."

"It could be, but then The Hana would have radioed this fact to the Coast Guard, but they haven't. Also, the Coast Guard has decided not to call The Hana on the hail and distress channel, so as not to tip them off."

"Right."

"And finally we have no signal from The Hana's GPS."

"Well, that just about nails it, Scott. No GPS signal and no transmitter signal. The Hana is hiding."

"It would appear so." He added, "We've seen this M.O. with drug smugglers."

"Right." And for all I knew, *The Hana* had rendezvoused with a

South American ship and taken a ton of Colombian marching powder aboard, and this had nothing to do with Russians or nukes. This wouldn't be the first time I was investigating one crime and discovered another. In fact, there was really nothing to conclusively link Petrov and his pals to *The Hana,* or to a nuke. Except that Tamorov introduced Petrov to the prince, and if everything looks like a coincidence, it isn't.

Kalish informed us, "This fog is not helping, but we're using infrared imaging now that we have an idea what this ship looks like. And we also know we're not looking for an amphibious craft on its deck." He also let us know, "By now the search area is thousands of square miles, and quite frankly even with every available craft from every agency out there, it's not easy looking for an electronically silent speck in a fog-shrouded ocean at night. And if The Hana is hiding it probably has all its lights off." He added, "But if you're right about the nuke, we do have the radiation emission going for us."

Unless Petrov had a way to shield his nuke. I said, "I think we'll have more luck as the shipping lanes narrow and funnel into New York Harbor."

"Right. But you don't want that ship getting that close."

"Correct." That's a goal-line defense, and it wouldn't take much to get *The Hana* into the end zone. Or it was already there.

Kalish speculated, "By now they could know we're looking for them, and their first clue would be if they noticed helicopters flying search patterns overhead, or saw high-speed craft on their radar, or saw we were using the Midnight Sun. And a bigger clue would be if The Hana was monitoring police search and rescue frequencies." He added, "But of course no one is using the name Hana on the air, so Petrov and his pals could think they were seeing and hearing a search and rescue. Or a drug interdiction."

"Hope so." But Vasily Petrov, a.k.a. Vaseline, might have guessed we were looking for him. A sane man would have dumped the nuke overboard and aborted the mission. But no one who intends to murder a million innocent people is sane.

Kalish asked me, "You think this Saudi prince is in cahoots with Petrov?"

"I don't know. Could be that Petrov hijacked the ship. Or conned the prince. Or the prince is complicit. I don't know."

"Okay...so we don't know how many hostiles are onboard."

"Correct."

Tess asked Kalish, "How many crew would it take to run a ship of that size?"

"Three for a long cruise. But for a short run, like to New York Harbor, one person could do it if he knew how to steer, navigate without GPS, and set the engine speeds."

Tess said, "So this captain, Jack Wells, or one of his officers, could sail The Hana by themselves?"

"Theoretically," Kalish replied, "but why would they? Unless they were in cahoots."

I didn't think any of *The Hana*'s crew was in cahoots. But you never know what money can buy. Or how much cooperation you could get from a man with a gun to his head. It was also possible that the officers and crew were clueless about what was going on. The last possibility was that Captain Wells and his officers were no longer in charge of the ship, and Petrov picked up a Russian sea captain and crew along with the nuke.

There were a lot of unknowns here, and as someone once said, you need to know how many unknowns there are that you don't know about. On the other hand, you can get lost in weeds if you go down that path. To simplify this, all we needed to know and to believe was that a yacht named *The Hana* was headed to Manhattan with a suitcase nuke onboard. It was amazing, I thought, how something so small could alter the course of history.

Vasily Petrov, however, must understand by now that his mission was compromised. But maybe he saw it as a challenge. Or maybe he was so crazy that he couldn't understand that all the odds were against him. Or were they?

Tess said to Kalish, "I assume the Coast Guard and all Federal authorities are up to speed on this."

"I have shared all this information."

"And what did they suggest?" she asked.

"Nothing." He let us know, "We have a good relationship with the Coast Guard, but sometimes with the Feds they suck in information like a black hole and nothing comes back."

I advised him, "Don't take it personally."

"Right. They can't help themselves. And they're not helping me much."

"But they want you to help them."

"They appreciate my assistance."

"That's all you need to know, Scott. And I mean, that's *all* you need to know."

"Right." He also let us know, "The thinking is that this ship—The Hana—is no longer in my area of operation. It could be much farther west by now, close to New York Harbor. But the Coast Guard has asked the Suffolk County Marine Bureau to continue the search in our area in case The Hana is lurking around in the fog, waiting to make its run."

"Good thinking. And I hope that's the case."

Scott Kalish and I both knew through long experience with the Feds that they needed you when they needed you. And the minute they didn't need local law enforcement, you were dropped like a cheap date, and you never heard another word about the case until you read about it in the papers. Well, two can play that game.

He asked me, "Where are you?"

"About ten minutes from the Coast Guard Station."

There was a silence, then Kalish said, "I was told that the Diplomatic Surveillance Group is no longer part of this operation." He concluded, correctly, "I think that means you."

"Probably. But Ms. Faraday has deputized me to join her on the SAFE boat."

"Can I have that in writing?"

"No."

"Well..."

"Who's in charge here, Scott? You or the Feds?"

"This is a joint operation."

"If the worst happens with this joint operation, which joint gets blamed?"

He didn't reply, so I added, "And if this has a happy ending, you'll be lucky if you get a one-line mention in a press release or two words at a press conference."

"That doesn't matter." He let me know, "I don't think you can get aboard my SAFE boat, John."

Time to call in my I.O.U. "Did you phone your daughter?"

"I didn't tell her *why* she needed to come home tonight."

"But I assume she's on her way."

"Right..."

I changed the subject and asked him, "Does that website have a photo of The Hana?"

"Yeah. Plus plans of its five decks."

"Did you send that out to all the units?"

"Everyone."

"Good. Please make sure there are printouts of this info at the Coast Guard Station."

"All right." He let me know, "You did a good job. But if I were you, I'd let it go."

"You're not me."

"And you're not *me*. And I don't need you out on one of my units." He asked me, "What is your purpose?"

"You're breaking up."

"Do you think you're going to take part in a combat boarding?"

"Why not?"

"Are you trained to do that?"

"Why don't you just find The Hana? And let me worry about what I'm going to do."

He didn't reply to that, but said, "You owe me dinner."

"Ecco's," I said, naming a restaurant in the nuclear blast zone.

He knew the place and replied, "We hope."

"Speak to you later. And thanks."

"Anytime, except not next time."

I hung up and Tess said, "He made a good point. About you not being authorized, or trained—"

"You're staying at the Coast Guard Station."

"I am not. If you go, I go." She did ask, however, "What *is* your purpose? What is driving you?"

"I'm driving myself." I turned the steering wheel. "See?"

She said, with some insight, "You don't have to prove to your bosses—or to your wife—"

"You're out of line." I should have left her with Buck. I said, "For the record, you did not approve of my actions, and chose to stay at the Coast Guard Station."

"You're not getting all the glory, Mr. Corey."

"There will be none, I assure you."

She put her hand on my shoulder and said, "We will finish this together."

I didn't reply.

She changed the subject and asked, "What was that about Scott Kalish's daughter?"

"She lives in Manhattan."

"Sounds like you both discussed it and you said it was okay to tell her to get out."

Ms. Faraday has a deductive mind. She should be a detective.

"You need to call your wife," she reminded me.

"Later."

She continued, "If, as you said, Petrov is spooked, he will advance the time, and there will be no later."

"Or he could abort the mission." I added, "There is a lot we don't know, so don't make assumptions. In fact, aside from the fact that we're not sure we're dealing with a nuclear threat, we don't even know the target, if there is one." I reminded her, "We only *assume* it's the financial and government districts of Lower Manhattan."

"What else would it be?"

"The East Coast of the United States is what we call a target-rich environment. For instance, there's the nuclear submarine base in Groton, Connecticut, which the Russians would love to see vaporized."

"But if you're saying that it's supposed to look like Islamic terrorists—9/11, Part Two—then the target is once again Lower Manhattan." She suggested, "Don't overthink this, Detective."

"Right."

I know never to underestimate the enemy, but I also know never to overestimate him. Somewhere in between was the sweet spot, the place where facts, clues, logic, instinct, and experience come together to form reality.

In any case, I had no other goose to chase tonight, so I either chased this one or I went for a drink. End of tour.

Tess said, "I need to call Buck."

"He knows everything we know, and probably more. And if Buck wants you to know what he knows, he'll call you."

"Okay...but I need to tell him we're going out with a search unit."

"That's the kind of call you make after the fact."

She thought about that and concluded, "You have a problem with authority."

"No problem."

She said, again with some insight, "Your NYPD days are over. You need to adjust your thinking and your attitude or get out."

I think that decision had already been made for me. But if I was going out, it would be in a blaze of...well, something.

As I drove through the fog, it occurred to me that *The Hana* could be in New York Harbor now, with its timer ticking down the last few minutes. Well, when we got on that SAFE boat, if I saw the western horizon light up it wouldn't matter that I got it right if I got it right too late.

CHAPTER THIRTY-ONE

Ms. Faraday got us on the right road, and up ahead I could see the lights of the Coast Guard Station through the mist.

My Nextel—actually Matt's Nextel—chimed and I looked at the message: Corey, call me ASAP—Fensterman. Apparently he'd learned I had Matt Conlon's phone.

Tess asked, "Who texted?"

"Fensterman."

She didn't waste her breath telling me to call him.

FBI Supervisory Special Agent Howard Fensterman, as I recalled from when he was the legal attaché in Yemen, was big on rules and procedures, chain of command, and all that, so I would be hearing from him again, but he wouldn't be hearing from me.

There was a twelve-foot chain-link fence around the Coast Guard Station and I pulled up to a call box at the gate and picked up the phone. "John Corey, FBI."

The electric-powered gate rolled open, and the watchstander, a young woman in a blue uniform, stepped out of a nearby building as I pulled ahead and lowered my window.

I handed my and Tess' creds to the young lady, whose nametag said, "Mullins," and she asked me, "Sir, what is your business here?"

"We're meeting a county police harbor unit."

She handed our creds back, and having met Buck Harris awhile ago, she asked, "What is going on tonight?"

Tess replied, "Ship lost at sea."

Seaman Mullins didn't ask why State Department Intelligence or the FBI was interested in this, but she did glance at the portable radiation detector on the console, then said, "Okay...please proceed to the boathouse," and gave us directions.

The old Shinnecock Coast Guard Station was picturesque, especially in the swirling mist, and we drove past a few white-shingled buildings toward a brick boathouse where an illuminated American flag hung limply from a tall pole.

I parked near the boathouse and we got out. Tess pocketed the PRD, though there would be one on the SAFE boat.

There were no Coast Guard vessels at the docks, and I assumed they were all deployed looking for *The Hana*. In fact, there didn't seem to be anyone around, but at the end of the second finger dock was a Secure Around Flotation Equipped craft—a SAFE boat.

My Nextel rang and the Caller ID read 26 Fed.

It kept ringing and went into voice mail.

Again, Tess did not bug me about returning the call. She had come aboard the good ship Corey. I wish I could get my wife to do the same.

We walked to the boathouse and entered the cavernous, dimly lit interior.

A man and a woman wearing bulky blue-and-orange float coats were standing at a coffee bar on the far side of the room. On the back of their coats were the words, "Suffolk Police," and slung over their shoulders were MP5 submachine guns. They turned as we approached, and I said, "John Corey, and this is Tess Faraday."

The guy introduced himself as Sergeant Pete Conte and the woman was Police Officer Nikola Andersson. We all shook hands and Sergeant Conte said, "So we're going yacht hunting."

"Right. Thanks for the ride."

"No problem."

Conte was about late thirties, and his face was weather-beaten from long hours at sea. Nikola Andersson had a prettier face and looked too young to be a police officer, but maybe I'm getting older.

In any case, Marine Bureau duty, as I knew, was good duty until it wasn't. Sunny summer days on the water were nice. Cold winter nights, looking for bad guys, weren't so nice. No job is perfect.

Conte looked at his new crew and asked, "You have any experience or training boarding a hostile craft?"

I assured him, "I used to ride the Staten Island Ferry."

He laughed, and Officer Andersson smiled.

Conte knew from Scott Kalish that I was former NYPD, so we were brothers and all was good. He wasn't sure about Ms. Faraday, however, and he asked her, "Are you coming along?"

"No," I replied.

"Yes," she corrected.

Sergeant Conte suggested, "You get that straightened out." He asked, "Coffee?"

I inquired, "You got a head on that SAFE boat?"

"Nope. But we got a bucket."

That was good enough for Tess and she poured herself a mug of black coffee.

Conte informed us, "We topped off with U.S. government gas, so we can be out for about five hours, give or take."

"Good." I asked him, "You have some printouts for me?"

He reached into his float coat and extracted some folded papers.

I put them on the coffee bar and looked at the website printout in the dim light.

The color picture of *The Hana* showed a big, tall, gleaming white yacht with *Hana* in gold letters on its fantail. In the background was a sandy beach, blue skies, and palm trees. I noticed, too, a flag flying from its stern with what looked like a royal crest of some sort. It's good to be a prince.

I flipped through the deck plans and saw that *The Hana* had five decks, many staterooms, a long dining room, a huge salon with balconies, and a spa tub. Vasily Petrov should be enjoying life rather than plotting to nuke a city. Asshole.

I looked at the schematic of the lower deck and saw the two-dock tender garage toward the stern of the ship. The garage had a door in the side of the hull, and I remembered that Kalish said it was a float-in garage, and I pictured the twenty-five-foot amphibious craft with Petrov and his pals sailing through the open door and into the yacht. The ladies must have been excited. I wondered if Petrov intended to escape from *The Hana* using the amphibious craft. Or was he going down—or blowing up—with the ship?

I still couldn't figure out if this was a suicide mission or if Petrov had an escape plan. And even if Petrov was willing to die, I wasn't sure the men with him were so anxious to give their lives for Mother Russia. I wondered, too, about the fate of the twelve ladies.

I turned my attention back to the ship plans and noticed that in the stern near the tender garage was something labeled "Beach Club," and I pointed this out to Conte and Andersson.

Conte informed us, "Most of the big yachts have that." He pointed to the plans, "This is a swimming platform, just above sea level. You can have chairs and stuff and you can swim off the platform. Unless the boat's moving."

I looked again at the so-called beach club, and I could see on the plans that it had a doorway that led to two staircases going up to the next deck.

"That swimming platform," I said, "is the way into The Hana."

Conte agreed. "Better than trying to toss grappling hooks twenty feet up to the main deck."

Andersson reminded us, "First we have to find the target ship." She asked me and Tess, "You have any new info?"

Tess replied, "The latest is what you know. It's a yacht named The Hana and we have these specs on it, so we're hoping it will be sighted or picked up by infrared."

Sergeant Conte said, "I doubt if this ship is still in our police district."

I replied, "We don't know that, but I do know that we will be available to assist when the target is located."

"Right." Conte asked, "What is the threat assessment?"

"Intel says there are at least three armed terrorists aboard."

"What are they doing on a Saudi prince's yacht?"

"They may have taken over the ship and they may have picked up some other people at sea. But we don't know."

"How many crew aboard?"

"Maybe twenty or more, and maybe some guests. Plus twelve hookers."

Conte looked at me and asked, "What's this about?"

"It's about whatever Captain Kalish told you it's about."

"He said it was Russian U.N. guys and Russian hookers going out to a party boat. Then it became terrorists."

"Right."

"He also said pay close attention to the radiation pager."

"Correct."

"We looking for a nuke?"

Tess replied, "There may be radioactive material aboard the target craft. Maybe enough to make a dirty bomb." She added, "There is a potential for radiation exposure, but we're assuming the radioactive material is contained."

Conte nodded. Officer Andersson looked concerned.

Okay, I thought, better to admit to a small nightmare than a big one. Sounds more believable than denying the whole thing. Ms. Faraday knew how to bullshit.

Conte pointed out, "Well, if the target ship is emitting radiation, it can't hide."

"Right." So why hadn't any of the search boats or aircraft detected a radiation source? Well, because they weren't looking for that until about an hour ago. But now . . . I looked at *The Hana*'s plans again. The tender garage. I asked Conte and Andersson, "Can this ship sail with the garage flooded?"

Conte replied, "According to the notes on The Hana, the ship is seaworthy with the garage flooded."

Well, that might be the answer. I wasn't sure how the nuclear device got aboard *The Hana*, but I was fairly sure now how Petrov was keeping it from emitting detectable radiation. It was underwater.

Conte had come to a similar conclusion and said, "Holy shit. You think this radioactive material could be in the flooded garage?"

"Makes sense."

He thought about that, then told us what we already knew. "That's what we're always worried about. A nuke riding underwater on the hull of a ship."

"Right." Or in this case, inside the ship, in a flooded compartment.

Every time I started to doubt that this was really a nuclear attack, something else popped up and pointed in that direction. Buck was right. The Russians had a plan.

I said to Conte, "You should call Captain Kalish and advise him of this possibility, and tell him to put that out to all parties."

"Right." He added, "This is a game changer."

Conte used his cell phone to call Kalish, and while he was giving Kalish the bad news, Tess announced, "I need to hit the head."

Andersson pointed. "Over there."

Tess asked me, "Can I borrow your cell phone?"

"No."

She hesitated, then said, "Don't leave without me."

Don't tempt me.

She walked toward the restrooms.

My Nextel radio blinged and I heard a voice say, "John, this is Howard. Are you up?"

I decided to stop these annoying calls and I moved out of earshot of Conte and Andersson and replied, "Up."

"Where are you?"

"On the way to Manhattan."

"What's your ETA?"

"About two hours."

"I want to see you when you get here."

"I got that message."

"Where are Conlon and Lansky?"

"They're somewhere behind me."

"Why do you have Conlon's phone?"

"I dropped mine in the toilet."

"Okay... I can't reach Lansky."

"Bad reception out here." Or he's in a noisy bar. Or he's not taking your calls.

"I call and text out to the Hamptons all the time."

"Howard, I don't run Nextel. File a complaint."

"Where is Tess Faraday?"

"Where she usually is. In the ladies' room."

"I thought you were on the road."

"Pit stop."

"Okay. I'll see you in two hours."

"It's Sunday night, Howard. Go home. This can wait."

There was a silence, then Howard Fensterman asked me, "What's this about?"

"If you don't know, I don't know."

"Okay... look, I owe you a favor from Yemen. So I'll go to bat for you if you're straight with me."

"If you want to do me a favor, go home."

"I've been instructed to wait for you."

"Let's meet halfway. You live on Long Island, right? Pick a place."

"The place is 26 Fed. Be in my office—two hours, latest."

"Copy."

He signed off.

Well, hopefully that took care of Howard Fensterman for the next two hours. Longer if 26 Fed disappeared. I liked Howard, despite some crap in Yemen, and I wanted to get him away from the blast zone, and I tried, but... Well, maybe this will all become moot. One way or the other.

Which reminded me. I dialed Kate's cell phone and it went right into voice mail, so maybe she was still at the Sheraton in D.C., sleeping, with her cell phone off—or she was airborne, heading home.

I left a message: "Kate, I'm using one of my guys' cell phones, Matt Conlon. Call this number as soon as you get this. Important." I added, "Love you."

I tried our home number, but it went into the answering machine, and I left the same message.

It occurred to me that if we didn't connect tonight, one or both of us might not be receiving or sending any further messages in the morning. We had both missed taking the elevator up to the North Tower minutes before the plane hit. So we were sort of on borrowed time. Luck is often the result of missing your plane or your elevator, and fate is what the gods give you when you run out of luck.

I moved back to the coffee bar and asked, "Are you guys the whole crew?"

Conte was off the phone and replied, "The SAFE boat has a two-man crew, three in bad weather, with bench seats below deck for twelve personnel." He asked me, "You want more people?"

I did, but I didn't want to wait for them, and also extra people meant a slower speed and more fuel consumption. "We can handle it."

"Is your friend coming along?"

She thought so. And actually it might be better if she wasn't left behind to rat me out. Also, I could see a situation—if we were lucky enough to find and board *The Hana*—where I could use another gun.

"Detective?"

And to be honest, I sort of…well, I was getting used to her. I said, "She's coming."

"What's she doing in there?"

"Is there a pay phone in the ladies' room?"

Officer Andersson replied, "No."

While I was contemplating an unwise remark about women in the ladies' room, Tess appeared, and said, "Ready to go."

"Then let's go," said Sergeant Conte, and we exited the back door onto the illuminated dock. He said to me, "Kalish thinks you could be right about the flooded garage. He'll put that out to all agencies."

"Good."

He asked me, "Are we talking about radioactive material? Or a nuclear bomb?"

"Radioactive material."

He didn't respond for a second, then said, "Well, whatever it is, if it's underwater, it's not going to be lighting up the PRDs. So we have a problem."

"Right."

The night had grown colder, but there was no wind, so the basin was calm and the fog just sat on the water. The SAFE boat also sat motionless on the water, and the only sound was our footsteps on the concrete dock.

As we got closer I could see the small boat that was going to take us out on the ocean. The hull was aluminum, surrounded by what looked like a huge blue inner tube with the words "Suffolk County Police" in white.

The cabin took up about half the twenty-seven-foot deck, and on the roof of the cabin I recognized a radar tower, a Forward Looking Infrared Radar antenna, and a GPS and VHF antenna. There was also a spotlight, floodlights, blue police lights, a public address speaker, and a foghorn, but unfortunately no naval cannon to blow *The Hana* out of the water.

Conte walked down the aluminum gangway and stepped onto the port side gunnel, followed by Andersson. Tess and I followed, but before we jumped aboard, Tess said to me, "Last chance."

"That ship came and went."

I hopped onto the gunnel and put my hand out for Tess, who took it, and I pulled her aboard. We looked at each other for a moment, then I entered the cabin.

The gray cabin had aft, port, and starboard doors that Conte said were weathertight and sound resistant, as were the windows. The cabin was upholstered to further deaden the sound of the big outboard engines, so the ride should be relatively quiet, according to Conte, who was probably engine-deaf.

Conte said, "Put on your float coats."

Tess and I found the bulky float coats on the two rear seats and slipped them on.

I noticed two Kevlar vests draped over the backs of the two forward seats, and Conte apologized for not having two more bulletproof vests aboard. "Nikki and I didn't know we were having company." He added, "You may take a bullet, but you won't drown."

Cop humor is sick and dark. I felt at home.

I asked, "Any more MP5s laying around?"

"You want guns, too? This is the basic cruise package."

Funny. But not the answer I wanted.

Conte sat in the air-ride captain's seat and Andersson entered the cabin and sat in the navigator's seat. She said to Tess and me, "This is going to be a bumpy ride at fifty knots. As you can see, there is one air-ride seat behind me, and one not so comfortable jump seat behind the captain."

Tess offered, "You take the air-ride seat, John. You're older."

I sat in the jump seat.

Conte turned the breaker switches on and fired up the twin 225-horsepower Mercury engines.

Conte and Andersson went through a checklist, looking and listening for normal operations of the radar, GPS, FLIR, and engine readings.

Everything seemed okay, and Andersson left the cabin and cast off, then re-entered, took her seat, and leaned out the port side pocket door and cast off the remaining line from the mid cleat. "Clear." She said to us, "Seat belts."

Tess and I strapped ourselves in as Conte engaged both engines and maneuvered away from the dock while Andersson sounded the horn to signal we were leaving the berth.

Andersson monitored the radar, depth finder, and GPS as Conte ran parallel to the Ponquogue Bridge, then cut southeast running a high-speed course through the fog.

As promised, the cabin was relatively quiet if anyone wanted to say anything.

In less than five minutes we passed through the Shinnecock Inlet and we were out into the North Atlantic.

Conte pushed the throttles forward and said, "Hold on." The rear of the boat squatted and the bow stood almost straight up, then settled down to a forty-five-degree angle as the boat reached fifty knots, nearly sixty miles an hour.

Conte called back to me, "I have a search pattern we can run unless you've got something else in mind."

Actually, I did. "Head due west."

He cut to starboard and we began running along the shore, about twelve miles out.

The sea was getting choppy and the SAFE boat was bouncing and slapping the water.

"Hold on," cautioned Officer Andersson.

To the south, I could see the lights of a long line of cargo ships and tankers in the shipping lane, heading west toward Ambrose Buoy, with a final destination of New York Harbor.

At fifty knots, the SAFE boat could be passing under the Verrazano Bridge and into the harbor in less than two hours. I checked my watch. It was half past midnight, and September 11 had come and gone without incident. This was the time when every law enforcement officer and citizen in New York usually let out a sigh of relief. But I wasn't sure about September 12.

PART V

CHAPTER THIRTY-TWO

At 11:55, less than two hours after *The Hana* had gotten underway, Colonel Vasily Petrov stood on the bridge as Gleb sailed the ship under the Verrazano Narrows Bridge, following in the wake of a large cargo ship.

Petrov was surprised that inbound shipping had not yet been halted, making him think that the Americans were not certain what was happening. Or if they were, they had not expected *The Hana* to get this far, undetected, and they were still searching on the ocean.

As a last defense against a shipborne nuclear attack, there were two old fortresses on both sides of The Narrows that once guarded the harbor with cannons, but now guarded it with radiation detectors. These detectors, like the ones at sea, would remain silent.

Petrov said to Gleb, "Apparently we are a step ahead of the opposing team. They are still playing on the field and have not organized their defense here at the goal."

Gleb did not reply, and glanced at his radar screen.

They were in the huge harbor now, and within twenty minutes they would be close to the southern tip of Manhattan Island. But Petrov knew it was now impossible to anchor the ship and leave the timer set to 08:46 hours.

He wasn't certain how the Americans had reached the conclusions that they had, and even if the American intelligence services could connect him and his compatriots to *The Hana*, it did not necessarily follow that Russia was complicit in the nuclear explosion; it would appear that he and Gorsky, and also Urmanov—whom he hoped they knew only as Fradkov—had boarded the prince's yacht thinking they had been invited to a party, which was why they had brought the prostitutes. Prince Ali Faisel, however, unbeknownst to his Russian guests, planned to become a nuclear suicide bomber, and he had invited the Russians aboard so that the Americans would believe it was the Russians, not the Saudis, who were behind the attack. Which of course was true, but not obviously so.

As Petrov knew, almost any event could be interpreted in several ways—especially if one created a hall of mirrors, where truth and reality were distorted. And not only distorted, but vaporized, leaving no physical evidence so that even the Americans with their famous forensic science would be left with nothing to examine except radioactive ash and rubble.

Yes, he thought, the Americans would be filled with doubt. Who was responsible for the attack? The Russians? The Saudis? Or someone else? And that doubt would divide them and lead to dissention and inaction, which would be a terrible humiliation on top of the attack itself.

Gleb looked at his radar. "There are two small craft a kilometer ahead that could be police boats heading in our direction."

Petrov stared at the radar screen. He knew he could order Gleb to make a high-speed run to Manhattan, ignoring any security craft in the area, and when they were close to the shore, he would send a radio signal to the nuclear device and advance the clock to detonate in minutes.

Gleb, however, might refuse to continue toward the security craft—or he might put on a life jacket and jump overboard. Or Gleb might even try to surrender the ship to the Americans, though Petrov would kill him before he could do that. In fact, Petrov would kill all of them by detonating the device. But he needed to get closer to Manhattan Island, so he needed another plan. And he had one.

He said to Gleb, "We will sail The Hana now to the pier that we will escape to later in the amphibious craft."

Gleb did not reply.

Petrov continued, "The pier is a construction project—a new waterfront recycling facility with a boathouse." He informed Gleb, "We will hide The Hana there until we can proceed to Manhattan."

"It is not easy to hide an eighty-meter yacht, Colonel."

"The boathouse is large enough to hold three ships of this size, and it has solar panels on its roof that will confuse infrared scanning devices." He also informed Gleb, "The construction site is surrounded by a security fence and there are construction barges blocking the view from the harbor." He assured Gleb, "I have chosen this site carefully."

Again, Gleb did not reply, but turned starboard toward the Brooklyn waterfront and switched on his GPS, saying, "We cannot leave this on for more than five minutes."

As they got closer to the shore, Gleb asked, "What is your plan?"

"The plan is the same. In a few hours we will sail to the tip of Manhattan and anchor The Hana with the timer set for eight forty-six. We then sail from The Hana aboard the amphibious craft back to the recycling pier where our car is parked on the street." He pulled a set of keys from his pocket. "A black Ford Mustang."

Gleb looked at the keys, but had no reply.

Petrov continued, "We then drive to JFK Airport and board our private jet for Moscow."

Gleb pointed out, "We would be very lucky to get The Hana all the way to Manhattan without being seen. We would be more lucky to get into the amphibious craft and sail to the pier. And even if we do, and we get as far as our car, you can be sure that the airport will be closed and there will be no private jet for us." He looked at Petrov and said, "The mission has been compromised."

"You are in command of the ship. But I am in command of the mission. Do as I tell you."

"Yes, Colonel." Gleb proceeded at ten knots toward the Brooklyn shore, dividing his attention between the GPS, his radar, and the windshield.

Petrov glanced at Gleb. The man was correct, of course. And by now Gleb was thinking that this could become a suicide mission. And he was also correct about that. But as long as Gleb believed there was an escape, he would follow orders. In fact, however, after they got underway again, and as they were approaching Manhattan Island, Petrov would detonate the nuclear device.

He understood now that there was no escape and that he would die here. But it would be a quick death. A nanosecond. And a million people would die with him. That was a far better fate than the one that awaited him in Moscow if he failed. And far better than spending his life in an American prison.

So, yes, the mission was compromised, but not fatally so. The mission just needed some adjustments. The goals had not changed: destroy Lower Manhattan and destroy all evidence of who had perpetrated the attack.

Gleb slowed the yacht to a few knots, and coming up on their right—less than six kilometers from the southern tip of Manhattan Island—was the huge construction project and the massive steel boathouse extending over the pier and into the water.

Gleb shut off his GPS, then brought *The Hana* around and reversed the propellers. He switched on his infrared camera and watched his aft video screen as he sailed in reverse between two construction barges, then maneuvered the yacht under the steel boathouse, a few meters away from the concrete pier.

He shut down the engines and lit a cigarette.

Petrov looked through the wraparound windshield. It was dark inside the boathouse, and they were a hundred meters from the entrance, so any passing security craft would not be able to see them unless they used a searchlight and also had a clear line of sight between the construction barges.

The boathouse had solid vertical walls on either side of the pier, and the roof provided overhead concealment from passing helicopters. Also, as he told Gleb, the entire construction site was surrounded by a security fence so Petrov knew that police cars could not enter.

Gleb drew on his cigarette, then asked, "Can you signal Moscow for instructions? To let them know the mission has developed problems?"

"Yes, I will do that."

But of course he would not signal Moscow. Nor would Moscow

signal to him. He always understood that he was not a guided missile—he was a ballistic missile; once fired, there was no further guidance from those who launched him on his mission. There was no fail-safe and no callback. The very least he was expected to do was to detonate the device—anywhere—and destroy all evidence of the murders onboard, and of his country's involvement in the nuclear attack. And that now included destroying himself. And he had sworn to his superiors—and to his father—that he would do this, if necessary.

He put his hand in his pocket and felt the arming device.

If a boat appeared or if a police patrol got through the security fence and approached them from the land he could advance the timer clock and at least destroy a large area of the Brooklyn waterfront. The winds were from the southeast and the radioactive plume would pass over Manhattan Island. That was not what he had hoped for, but it was good enough. His superiors in Moscow and his father would understand that he had done his best, and he would receive his promotion posthumously.

Gorsky appeared on the bridge and asked, "What is happening?"

Petrov replied, "We will wait here." He added, "There are two patrol boats in the area."

"There will be more later."

Petrov did not respond.

Gleb shut off the one radio they had left on to monitor the police frequencies. "We are now deaf and blind. But so are they. We have disappeared."

Gorsky looked at Petrov. "What is your plan?"

"To wait."

"For what?"

"For the right time."

Gorsky did not reply, but Petrov knew that Gorsky—and Gleb—must have realized that the escape plan was either no longer possible, or at best very difficult.

An easier escape plan, however, *was* possible and obvious, and Gorsky said, "We are already at the pier we planned to escape to. So we should reset the timer clock for an hour from now and leave this ship and go to our car, and to the airport—"

Gleb said, "The Americans will soon be closing all airports."

Gorsky looked at Petrov. "We can drive to our residence. Or even to Tamorov's."

Petrov saw that Gorsky, like Gleb, was becoming concerned. Viktor wanted to live to kill again. Petrov said, "We wait here."

Gleb said, "I like Viktor's plan."

Petrov looked at both of them. "I did not come all this way to destroy a few abandoned piers and a recycling center."

Neither Gorsky nor Gleb replied.

Petrov said to them, "It is obvious from what we saw on the radar and what we heard on the radio that the Americans are concentrating their search on the sea. They have no indication that we are already here, and they wish us not to be here, so they continue their search on the ocean, substituting hope for intelligence. They continue to look for our radiation, but they will not detect it." He concluded, "Soon they will institute a desperate defensive plan and use all their available craft to block The Narrows. They will look out to sea, but we are already behind them. We are in the goal zone."

Gleb glanced at Gorsky, but neither man had anything to say to Colonel Petrov, who now seemed distant and remote.

Petrov stared through the windshield into the darkness, then said, "We can pick the time when we wish to move, and nothing can stop us from sailing the last few kilometers to Manhattan Island—to the financial heart of the beast." He added, "And then we return home to glory and gratitude and with pride."

Neither Gorsky nor Gleb inquired about the escape, but each man was thinking similar thoughts: Colonel Petrov's plan did not include an escape.

Petrov changed the subject and said to Gorsky, "I assume you did not find the deckhand."

"I did not." He added, "He must have gone overboard earlier."

"Or," Petrov said, "he has eluded you."

Gorsky had no response, but he went to the security screen and switched from camera to camera, looking at the images of the lifeless ship. He stopped at the tender garage, where he could see Urmanov tied to the dock, his chin resting on his chest.

Gleb said, "You should be kind and put him out of his misery."

Petrov replied, "I would have done just that, but he tried to betray the mission and the Motherland."

Gleb understood that this was a message meant also for him, and he did not reply. He deeply regretted having gotten involved with the SVR, but no one else was offering him two million Swiss francs for captaining a ship. He put his hand in his pocket and felt his gun, which gave him some comfort.

Colonel Vasily Petrov seemed at ease now. He had seen the towering skyscrapers of Manhattan. And soon, if all went well, he would see them again. And that would be the last thing he saw on this earth. Most importantly, no one on this earth would ever see those skyscrapers again.

PART VI

CHAPTER THIRTY-THREE

After about ten minutes at sea, Conte asked me, "What do you have in mind?"

I didn't know where *The Hana* was, but I knew where it was going. "New York Harbor."

Sergeant Conte informed me from the captain's chair, "I am not authorized to cross jurisdictional lines." He made sure I understood, "We are not going to New York Harbor."

I anticipated that response and reminded him, "You are authorized to cross jurisdictional lines when you are in hot pursuit." I assured him, "That's the law."

"I know the law, Detective. I just don't see the hot pursuit."

He had a valid point, so I tried another approach. "I am a Federal law enforcement agent, and Ms. Faraday is a Federal intelligence officer. We have no jurisdictional boundaries in the war on terrorism."

"I need to speak to a supervisor."

"Call Captain Kalish."

He reached for his radio, but I suggested he use his cell phone so the rest of the world couldn't hear the conversation—or hear that I was on the SAFE boat.

He got Kalish on the phone and explained why he was calling, then handed me his cell phone.

Kalish asked me, "What the hell are you doing?"

"I thought Sergeant Conte just explained that."

"Look, I've already stuck my neck out for you—"

"I appreciate that and I hope you took credit for my theory about how the radiation is being hidden—"

"And if what you think is going to happen actually happens, then neither you nor my officers want to be there when it happens."

"We're going to the harbor to make sure it doesn't happen."

"I assure you, this operation can proceed without you."

"I lost my surveillance target, Scott. Now I need to find him."

"Get over it. And put Conte back on."

I looked at Sergeant Conte, who was dividing his attention between piloting the boat and trying to decipher my end of the conversation about going to the harbor to make sure something didn't happen. Officer Andersson, too, seemed all ears.

Tess was looking at me, and I couldn't tell if she approved of a trip to nuclear ground zero. Maybe I should have asked her.

Kalish said, "John? Put Conte on."

"Scott, let me explain the situation to Pete and Nikola and put this to a vote."

"A *vote*? We don't vote. I vote. And I vote no."

Time to pull rank. Or call in a favor. Unfortunately, I didn't have any rank to pull, and Scott and I were even on favors. So I appealed to his sense of duty. "Look, Scott, you understand how important—"

"Please put Sergeant Conte on or I'll radio him and everyone can hear what I have to say."

Tess asked me for the phone, and since I didn't want Kalish on the radio, I handed it to her.

She said, "Captain Kalish, this is Tess Faraday. I'm putting the phone on speaker."

"Good." He said, "Conte, turn the unit around."

Sergeant Conte called out, "Roger that." He reduced his speed and began a wide starboard turn.

Tess said to Kalish, "Captain, we believe this event is not going to happen until eight forty-six A.M. or nine oh-three A.M., and I think you agree with that."

"I might agree, but I'm not going to bet anyone's life on it. So you and Detective Corey and my officers can run search patterns out in the ocean all night." He added, "That's an order."

The SAFE boat was heading east now, back toward where we started.

Tess went on in a calm and reasonable tone of voice, "I'd like to explain the situation to Sergeant Conte and Officer Andersson, and see if they will agree to take us to the harbor."

"Last time I saw them, they didn't look suicidal."

That seemed to get Conte's and Andersson's attention, and they exchanged glances.

Tess said, "All we're asking for is a quick ride to New York Harbor. When we get there, Detective Corey and I will transfer to an NYPD Harbor unit or a Coast Guard cutter, and your unit can return to your area of operation."

Kalish was silent, then asked, "How do you know you won't get to the scene at the time it happens?"

"John and I are willing to take that risk, and we'd like to ask your officers if they are also willing."

I had to admit that Tess was handling this well. Plus, she had balls, and Kalish appreciated balls.

Kalish stayed silent again, then said, "Okay... lay it out and have Conte call me back."

Tess hung up and handed the cell phone back to Conte, who asked us, "What the hell is going on?"

I replied, without bullshit, "We believe there's a ten-kiloton suitcase nuke onboard The Hana."

Conte had no reply to that. Andersson stared at me.

I continued, "I believe it's set to detonate at either eight forty-six A.M. or nine oh-three A.M., and you understand why. But I could be wrong about the times."

Conte nodded, and so did Andersson.

I briefed them on the highlights of what we knew, though the background wasn't as important to them as the words "suitcase nuke," "New York Harbor," and "8:46 A.M." Or "9:03 A.M." Or earlier, if Petrov was spooked.

Conte and Andersson listened, then Andersson asked, "Are you sure about this?"

Tess replied, "Not sure, but... almost sure."

Conte said, "Holy shit." He stared through the windshield. "Holy *shit.*"

Neither Tess nor I said anything, and we let them process all this.

Finally, Nikola Andersson turned in her seat and asked Tess and me, "Why do you want to go there?"

I replied, "I don't actually *want* to go there. But I need to be there." I explained, "This guy Petrov is my responsibility tonight."

Tess added, "And my organization is partly responsible for letting these people into the country."

Conte pointed out, "The Suffolk County Police Marine Bureau didn't let them in." He looked at his partner, and Andersson said, "If you're just looking for a one-way ride, I think we can do that." She asked Conte, "Okay?"

He hesitated, then said, "Okay."

I felt obligated to remind them, "We could be sailing into a mushroom cloud."

Conte replied, "Understood." He added, "We won't hang around after we transfer you to another unit."

"Fair enough."

Before he even called Kalish, Pete Conte began to come around.

Well, I thought, be careful what you wish for, especially if you have a death wish. Actually, I didn't, but I do have an ego problem, and I was pissed at being marginalized by those pompous asses at 26 Fed. Screw them and their quiet end. Also, of course, I was doing my duty and protecting my country. It's not all about me. Well, maybe it is.

I looked at Tess, who was looking at me. I said to her, "I should have let you know what I wanted to do."

"Believe me, I figured that out long before I got on this boat."

Am I that obvious? While I was thinking about that, Conte called Kalish on his cell phone and reported, "Heading west."

"Copy." Kalish asked, "Anything further?"

"Negative."

"Godspeed."

So that was it.

We headed west toward New York City, making fifty knots, and the SAFE boat practically flew over the water.

The fog was thinning, and I spotted two other Suffolk County Marine Bureau vessels and one helicopter as we continued toward New York Harbor.

The radar showed other craft in the vicinity, including the long line of commercial shipping on the Fairway heading to Ambrose Buoy. I noticed that the blips on the radar were not moving, so apparently shipping had been halted.

I got a text on my cell phone and read Kate's message: <u>Conference went overtime, then we all went to late dinner. I'm beat, phone off, going to bed. Speak tomorrow. Love, K.</u>

Okay, so she was still in D.C., which was good. And I'd be able to speak to her in the morning. Maybe.

I did recall, however, that my message to her said it was important that she call me. And she didn't seem curious about why I was using someone else's cell phone. I guess she was really tired.

Marital ignorance is bliss, but willful ignorance is just stupid. Detectives want to know things, but unfortunately I wasn't having much luck today locating either my surveillance target or my wife. In fact, this was turning out to be one of those days where I couldn't find my ass with both hands.

Tess asked me, "Who was that?"

"My wife." I added, "She's staying in D.C. tonight."

"Good." She said, "I should call Buck. To let him know where I am."

"If you let him know where you are, you won't be here much longer, and neither will I."

Tess was catching on to the Corey way of doing things, and she nodded, then said, "If he wants to talk to me, he'll call."

"Correct." Same with my wife.

I considered sending Kate a return text, or calling her hotel room, but I had more pressing issues than an AWOL wife. I'd settle this in the morning. If there was one.

Conte set a course that brought us closer to the south shore of Long Island where the fog had dissipated and the ocean was calmer. We were maintaining fifty knots and Conte said we'd be at the Verrazano Bridge in less than ninety minutes.

I stared out at the western horizon. I said to Conte, "If you see a flash of bright light—"

"We turn around and go home."

"Correct."

Within half an hour we were in the operational area of the Nassau County Police Marine Bureau, and I could see their units on the radar running search patterns. I spotted the navigation beacon on the Jones Beach tower about three miles away, then the lights of the city of Long Beach stretching along the coast.

We crossed an imaginary line and entered New York City's borough of Queens, and in the distance across Jamaica Bay I could see aircraft taking off and landing at Kennedy Airport. I was surprised that Washington hadn't halted inbound air traffic, as they had done on 9/11, but apparently the threat, in their minds, wasn't as clear or imminent as it was in mine. There is always something lost in translation between the men and women in the field and those in the capital. In any case, I was glad that Kate wasn't flying in tonight.

Ten minutes later we were off the coast of Brooklyn and I spotted Brighton Beach, where I'd thought this surveillance was going to end this morning. I saw the lights of Coney Island and the landmark twenty-five-story-high parachute tower, where I used to scare the crap out of myself as a kid. A few minutes later we turned northwest into Gravesend Bay, and there in front of us was the illuminated Verrazano Bridge spanning The Narrows between Brooklyn and Staten Island—the entrance to New York Harbor.

I could also see at least a dozen watercraft between us and the bridge, and Conte reduced his speed, then checked his radar screen and told us there were Coast Guard cutters and NYPD Harbor units all around us. Also, we could see and hear helicopters overhead.

It was obvious that there were enough boats at the entrance to the harbor to accomplish the mission, and we all knew that our SAFE boat was not going to add much to the effort. But we also understood that there were times when just showing up was enough.

Conte reduced his speed again and asked me, "You want to transfer to a unit here, or in the harbor?"

"The harbor."

He looked at Andersson, then said, "Okay."

We passed under the mile-long Verrazano Bridge and entered Upper New York Bay. We were now in the blast zone.

The fog was patchy in the bay and sat in clumps like gray islands. I didn't see any other watercraft nearby, but helicopters circled overhead.

Conte further reduced his speed to ten knots and Andersson divided her attention between the radar and the radios, monitoring the marine and police channels.

I could make out the lighted skyline of Lower Manhattan, about three miles straight ahead. Well, I told Howard Fensterman I was on my way to Manhattan, and I kept my word.

To the west was the shoreline of New Jersey, miles of commercial shipping piers and warehouses. To the east was the Brooklyn waterfront, more miles of warehouses and marine terminals where cargo ships sat at their docks.

I looked around the bay at the far shorelines and the towering skyscrapers and the squat warehouses that made up the Port of New York. It took over three hundred years to build this. It would take about five seconds to destroy it.

Through a break in the fog off our port bow I caught a glimpse of the illuminated Statue of Liberty, standing tall in the harbor. And in the distance, where the Twin Towers once stood, I could see the Twin Beams—two vertical columns of searchlights that were lit every September 11 since 2002 as a memorial and remembrance of the September 11 attacks. Tess, too, noticed them, and so did Conte and Andersson, but no one commented.

Conte reduced his speed to five knots, then looked at his radar screen and said, "There are not many units operating in the harbor. What they're doing is relying on the helicopters, and they're using the available watercraft to play goal-line defense at The Narrows."

"Right." A good strategy if *The Hana* was still on the ocean. But if Petrov was already in the harbor, then he was already in the end zone, ready to spike the ball.

Conte asked me, "You want me to raise an NYPD unit?" I didn't reply and he asked, "Or hail a Coast Guard vessel?"

"Why?"

"*Why?* So you can transfer and I can get out of here."

"I thought you wanted to stay."

"Where did you get that idea?"

"You've come this far."

Conte looked at Andersson, then said to her as though I wasn't there, "Who is this guy?"

I informed them, "I don't think I'm welcome aboard any other vessel."

"Why not?"

"It's a long story."

"Well, then," Conte suggested, "let me run you ashore while you're telling me the story."

Tess interjected, "Let me make some calls to get permission to board a Coast Guard vessel."

I didn't want to board a Coast Guard vessel, or any other vessel where I was persona non grata and would probably wind up in chains. I wanted to board *The Hana,* and I could do that only from this boat. I said to Conte and Andersson, "Let's give it an hour here in the harbor. Then if we still haven't located the target ship, Tess and I will transfer to another vessel." I added, "One that's sticking around."

Conte got that I'd challenged his manhood: show balls or chicken out?

He looked at Andersson again, and she said, "I'm okay with waiting."

Conte said to me, "I'll go you one better, Detective. We'll stay here until you tell me you want to leave."

Well, boys will be boys—especially in front of girls. And the girls, too, seemed okay with looking death in the eye. I said, "You got a deal."

I looked at my watch. It was 2:35 A.M.

The good news was that if the nuke blew before 8:46 A.M., we wouldn't feel a thing. And I wouldn't have to go to 26 Federal Plaza to get fired.

CHAPTER THIRTY-FOUR

We took up a position about half a mile southeast of Battery Park off the tip of Manhattan Island. About a half mile south of us was Governors Island, separated from Brooklyn by Buttermilk Channel. Farther up the East River I could see the Brooklyn Bridge and the Downtown Heliport where a chopper was taking off, and also Pier 11 where *The Hana* had docked Saturday morning before sailing out on its fateful Sunday cruise.

If this was a football game, we would be playing safety near the goal line. Unfortunately, the nuclear football didn't need to get into the end zone to score a touchdown.

A half hour passed, mostly in silence except for radio traffic, which was minimal because of the Russians' listening post at their residence in the Bronx. Most communication was being done by text, or e-mails on laptop computers, and occasionally by a direct cell phone call to an individual, though even that commo was not secure. My guess, however, was that Petrov's mission was so secret that no one at the Russian listening post even knew about it, so they weren't monitoring for a problem, nor was anyone at the Mission or the 'plex in communication with Petrov. Vasily was on his own, and I wondered if the assholes in Moscow who planned this could stop him.

The protocol here would be a direct call from the president to Putin saying we know what you're up to. But no one in Moscow was going to admit to a nuclear attack, nor would Moscow risk a traceable communication to Petrov to try to stop the show. At this point, the Russians needed to be certain that *The Hana,* the nuke, and Petrov did not fall into the hands of U.S. authorities. Meaning the nuke had to detonate. And Colonel Vasily Petrov had been chosen as the man to do this.

The SAFE boat's twin Mercs were idling, and now and then Conte would give them some throttle to keep the craft from drifting out with the tide. We couldn't drop anchor because if we got an alert it would take too long to hoist it up.

Conte suggested that we take up a position in Buttermilk Channel so that if the nuke blew in the harbor, we'd be protected by Governors Island from the direct blast. I said, "So instead of frying, we'll have the air sucked out of our lungs. Sounds good."

We stayed where we were.

Howard Fensterman texted me: <u>Where are you?</u>

I texted him: <u>I'm with your wife. Don't come home.</u>

Tess saw the text, smiled, but then said on a related subject, "You should leave a message at the Sheraton telling your wife to call you first thing in the morning."

I didn't recall telling Tess that Kate was at the Sheraton, but I did recall Buck mentioning it, though Tess had been out of earshot.

"That's what I would do," Tess advised, "in case you don't connect in the morning."

Meaning in case I'm reduced to nuclear ash in the next few minutes. Well, I wasn't sure I should take marital advice from an unmarried woman who had concocted a whole jealous husband. I let her know, "This phone is almost dead." I turned it off.

It occurred to me that Tess Faraday, an intelligence officer, was trying to share with me some intel about Kate.

In fact, Kate's trips to D.C., probably with Tom Walsh, and her lack of communication at home and on the road, could be interpreted as suspicious. Plus, of course, my new job put me conveniently out of the office.

I asked Tess, "You have anyone you need to send a message to?"

"No."

I asked Conte and Andersson the same question and they said they'd already done that via e-mail.

Well, to paraphrase D. H. Lawrence, we had built our ship of death and we were ready for our long journey to oblivion.

Conte was reading a chain of e-mails on his laptop and he informed us that all commercial and private ships coming into the Port of New York had been halted, and scheduled outbound ships were encouraged to leave the harbor ASAP, though I didn't see many of those on the water or on the radar. Cargo ships at their piers, waiting to load or unload, were not being ordered to leave, Conte explained, because that would be logistically complex, not to mention highly unusual.

Apparently whoever was running this operation in Washington was trying to play it down the middle; stay calm and carry on, but be prepared to kiss your asses good-bye.

I noticed, too, that in the great tradition of bureaucratic communication, none of these messages directly mentioned the nature of the problem—though you'd have to be an idiot not to understand that the threat was a weapon of mass destruction. To be fair, however, you don't want to put that out in plain English for other people to see and hear.

On that subject, I also knew from classified briefings and memos that there were two opposing schools of thought regarding alerting the populace that an attack from a WMD was imminent. One school of thought said an alert to evacuate a heavily populated area would cause pandemonium, and injuries and death, possibly in excess of the attack itself.

Theory two said that it was morally indefensible to not alert the population.

To take it a step further, if there was no alert, and the nuke blew, a lot of people in Washington would have a lot of explaining to do. And if there *was* an alert, leading to panic and chaos, and the nuke didn't blow—or didn't exist—there would be unnecessary deaths and injuries. Not to mention great embarrassment.

Tough call.

Well, I didn't know which theory Washington was going with tonight, but if I had to guess I'd say they were still arguing over the word "imminent."

Conte showed us an e-mail that said: To reiterate previous instructions, U.S. Coast Guard craft will take the lead in any attempted boarding of target vessel.

I didn't think that was going to go over big with the NYPD Harbor units. But when the Feds are on the case, as we all knew, everyone else stands back and applauds.

Conte received a text and said to us, "All security craft will leave the harbor at zero eight-fifteen hours and proceed to Gravesend Bay. Or earlier if fuel is an issue."

I glanced at the fuel gauges and saw that indeed fuel could become an issue, and Andersson confirmed, "Even at idle, we're not going to make it to eight-fifteen."

Was that good news or bad news? I mean, at what point do we haul ass out of here with enough fuel to make it out of the harbor? Also, apparently I wasn't the only one who had figured out that you didn't want to be here at 8:46 A.M.

In truth, however, 8:46 A.M. had no meaning any longer. By now, of course, Petrov knew that we were on to his game, and I had no doubt that he would advance the clock. I had no idea where he and *The Hana* were hiding, but I was sure Petrov was going to detonate the nuke as soon as he felt we were closing in on him. By now, however, he had turned off all his electronics, including radar and radios, so he was basically deaf, dumb, and blind, and I pictured him aboard *The Hana* using only his eyes, ears, and instincts to determine when to make his move. Also, by now he must have understood that he was not going to survive this mission, so he, like us, was preparing himself for his final journey. And also, like us, he was not going to lose his nerve at the last minute; Colonel Vasily Petrov was about to sail into history.

Conte looked at a new text message and informed us, "Due to a credible terrorist threat, all flights into Kennedy, Newark, and La Guardia have been diverted. Also, all public transportation into Manhattan has been suspended, and all bridges and tunnels will be closed."

So there would be no inbound rush hour this morning, and that would save a lot of lives if the worst happened. But there were still a million and a half people who lived in Manhattan and another few hundred thousand visitors and tourists, plus a few hundred thousand people who lived and worked along the shorelines of Brooklyn, New Jersey, and Staten Island, and apparently there was no plan to attempt an evacuation.

Conte received a text saying: Search continues in New York Harbor and all adjacent waters for target ship. Threat level remains high.

Well, I thought, that was one way of saying to everyone, "Stay awake."

It was like a stakeout where the hours pass and what you're looking for and waiting for doesn't happen. You start to second-guess the information you acted on, and you start to wonder if the bosses got it wrong again. And with each hour that passes, your mind goes from hypervigilance to a sense that this isn't real anymore. And it's at that moment when the shit hits the fan.

If I could put myself into the heads of everyone in the White House Situation Room, I'm sure that a bunker mentality was taking hold. Some people would be arguing that the threat was either overhyped, or had passed, or it had never existed.

Also, someone would point out that New York Harbor was blocked, as were the East and Hudson Rivers, and all waterways were being patrolled, and there was no sign of the target ship. Plus, police patrols had checked out all docks and piers in Manhattan, Brooklyn, and New Jersey. More importantly, someone would argue, there had not been a single radioactive hit since this operation began. And that was the real problem. Though I hoped everyone had gotten the word about *The Hana*'s flooded garage and they understood why *The Hana* was not emitting radiation.

But when you get tons of negative information, that causes a false sense of security, not to mention a comfortable sense of denial.

There's not a lot to do in a small ship's cabin while you're standing around waiting for a nuclear explosion—or hopefully an alert that the target has been spotted—so Conte and Andersson played with their electronics, monitored their instruments, and pulled up New York Harbor on Google Earth. Tess scanned the water and shorelines with binoculars, and I stared out at the Manhattan skyline, and the

Statue of Liberty, and the Twin Beams. Now and then Tess, Conte, or Andersson would offer some theories about the whereabouts of *The Hana.*

The possibilities were reduced to four: Petrov had long ago aborted the mission and *The Hana* was on its way across the Atlantic. Or two, it was under the Atlantic, scuttled. Three, there never was a mission or a nuke, and Petrov was aboard *The Hana* having a party with the prince and the prostitutes, probably off the coast of Atlantic City. The fourth possibility was that *The Hana* with Petrov and the nuke had found a good place to hide, either in the harbor or out on the ocean, and we would be seeing the yacht and/or the fireball very soon.

Conte pointed out, "We're not contributing much to the operation."

I replied, "We don't know that yet."

Conte shrugged, then smiled and said, "Hey, I've never seen a nuke detonate. I can tell my grandkids about it someday."

Cops, as I said, have a sick sense of humor.

So we waited.

At 4:15 A.M. Nikola Andersson informed us, "We now have a low-fuel situation."

I asked, "How long can we idle?"

Andersson replied, "Maybe... fifteen minutes. Then we need to head out." She added, "We have a five-gallon gas can onboard."

"Kill one engine," I suggested.

Conte said, "I'll kill both. We'll drift out with the tide, then restart if we get an alert."

He shut down both engines, and the night became very quiet, except for the sound of helicopters overhead.

We began to drift south, away from Manhattan Island.

Conte said, "We're doing maybe three or four knots, so it will take over an hour to reach The Narrows."

Well, we were still in the game, but backing out slowly—though with enough fuel to charge back in if we got the word.

The cabin was getting claustrophobic, so I exited and climbed along the gunnel onto the bow. Ms. Faraday decided to join me, and we sat cross-legged on the foredeck. Behind us the skyline of

Manhattan was retreating, and ahead, about five or six miles away, I could see the lights of the Verrazano Narrows Bridge on the horizon. The old fort on Governors Island was passing by on our left, which reminded me that the entire harbor and the entrance to the harbor were covered with radiation detectors and none of them had lit up, and none of them would if I was right about the nuke being submerged in *The Hana*'s flooded garage. And if everything went wrong tonight, this place would be radioactive for two or three decades.

Tess asked, "What do you think?"

"About?"

"The Hana. Petrov." She asked, "Did we get this wrong?"

"I hope so. But I don't think so."

"Then where is he? How do you hide a two-hundred-foot ship?"

I looked at the long piers sticking out from the coastline of Brooklyn. I knew there were about forty or fifty of them, some abandoned and derelict, and some hidden in basins that were formed by breakwaters.

The New Jersey waterfront was also lined with piers, active and inactive, over a hundred of them, running from Bayonne near The Narrows up the Hudson River for about fifteen miles.

There was lots of revitalization construction along the shorelines that made up the Port of New York, so there were lots of places for a two-hundred-foot yacht to hide along the waterfront on a dark, foggy night. And even with an air, sea, and land search of this size and intensity, there was so much ground clutter on the radar screen that a stationary ship along the waterfront might well go undetected. Plus, the harbor itself was huge—maybe close to thirty square miles.

I never met Vasily Petrov, but I felt, after watching him for months, that I could get into his head. And if I were Vasily Petrov, I would have made a high-speed run to the goal line before anyone else knew there was a game in progress. I said to Tess, "He's here. In the harbor."

She wasn't so sure and said, "What I think is that The Hana is out on the ocean, electronically silent, ready to make its run through The Narrows." She added, "I remember you said it would be difficult to stop a big ship that was going full speed ahead from entering the harbor."

I didn't reply.

She continued, "Assuming Petrov is prepared to give his life to accomplish this mission, all he has to do is plow through those security vessels around the bridge, and he's in the harbor. Then he keeps going full speed ahead and within…what did you say? In less than twenty minutes The Hana is at the tip of Manhattan." She added, "There are not many security vessels inside the harbor."

"Correct. But the vessels at The Narrows will pursue and carry out a boarding."

"I'm sure Petrov has the ability to detonate the nuke anytime."

"Right."

She stayed silent, then asked, "So why are we here?"

I hate when people ask questions like that.

"John?"

"We are here to let Petrov know we are here. We are here to force his hand and make him detonate the nuke prematurely, before he gets close to Manhattan. We are here to remove any thought he has of escaping the blast or escaping a bullet." I added, "But mostly we and everyone else are here because this is our job."

"And maybe we're here to pray."

So we sat there on the bow of the SAFE boat, knowing that any second could be our last. Well, there are worse ways to make an exit.

Tess was looking up at the sky, which was clear and starlit. The moon was low on the western horizon and moonlight sparkled on the bay.

In fact, it was a nice night. The harbor was calm, the shore lights reflected on the water, and the misty fog was…well, romantic.

Tess took my hand.

Neither of us spoke for awhile, then she said, "Will you buy me a drink tonight?"

"Of course."

"You can bring your wife if you'd like."

"And you can bring Grant."

She laughed softly, then said, "If you bring Kate, I'll bring Buck."

"Is that a threat?"

She squeezed my hand. "I'm frightened."

"We're all frightened. It's okay."

"What's your favorite bar?"

"All of them."

"I'll take you to the Yale Club if you promise to behave."

"I'll take you to a Russian nightclub in Brighton Beach if you promise not to behave."

"It's a date."

She put her arm around me and I did the same. I could only imagine what Pete and Nikola were thinking.

Well... what difference did it make at this point?

Conte opened the front window of the cabin and said, "I hate to interrupt, but for what it's worth, a helicopter just got a radar blip moving on the water near the Thirtieth Street Pier... but no radiation. So maybe it's an outbound cargo ship."

I knew the Thirtieth Street Pier, because the NYPD had once used that Brooklyn pier to store vehicles that had been towed, abandoned, or stolen and recovered. But now it was being converted into a modern recycling facility—so there shouldn't be any ships using the pier.

Last time I saw this facility, a huge steel boathouse bigger than three football fields was being constructed to enclose the pier. On the land side of the project was construction equipment and material, surrounded by a twelve-foot chain-link security fence. It occurred to me that an NYPD patrol car checking out the waterfront could not possibly see the far end of the enclosed pier, which was nearly three hundred yards from the fence. And it was very possible that an NYPD Harbor vessel, even with a searchlight, might not see a ship sitting inside the huge, unlit enclosure, especially if construction barges were moored at the end of the pier. To add to all this, the roof of the steel structure was covered with photoelectric cells that would confuse any helicopter's infrared devices or penetrating radar. Maybe I should have thought of this sooner.

I said to Conte, "Let's check this out."

"Right." He fired up both engines and reminded us, "We are relying on choppers in the harbor, and almost all the security vessels on this operation are blocking The Narrows or are on the Hudson and East Rivers—so it appears on radar that we are the only sea vessel in this immediate area."

"Our lucky day." I pictured in my mind the Google Earth image and said, "Buttermilk Channel is the most direct route from the Thirtieth Street Pier to the tip of Manhattan."

Conte turned the SAFE boat and headed for the mouth of Buttermilk Channel, which ran between Governors Island and the Brooklyn waterfront. If the radar blip was *The Hana,* Petrov would be heading toward us from the opposite direction.

As we approached the mouth of Buttermilk Channel, Conte called out to us, "I see it on radar—target is gaining speed...on a course for Buttermilk."

Tess knelt on the bow of the SAFE boat, staring straight ahead. She glanced at me and I put my hand on her shoulder. "If this is him," I said, "he won't detonate in this enclosed channel."

She nodded.

The SAFE boat continued at about twenty knots through the channel, which was widening as it neared the end of Governors Island.

Ahead was a gray wall of fog spanning the thousand-foot opening to the channel, and as we approached, the huge bow of a gleaming white ship suddenly cleaved through the fog bank, followed by the rest of the towering ship, coming straight at us.

We had found *The Hana.*

CHAPTER THIRTY-FIVE

We were on a collision course with the ship and Conte cut hard to starboard. Tess and I flattened ourselves on the bow and clung to the rail as the SAFE boat heeled sharply to the right. I yelled into the cabin, "Come around!"

Conte continued his turn and within a minute we were behind *The Hana,* which was making about ten knots as it continued through the channel toward Manhattan Island. We closed the distance quickly, though we were now riding in the big ship's wake and bouncing badly.

I shouted to Conte and Andersson, "I'm going to board!"

They both acknowledged and Conte increased his speed.

Tess said, "*We* are going to board."

Right.

We were less than twenty feet from *The Hana*'s stern and I got up on one knee, holding on to the rail and calculating my jump from the bow to *The Hana*'s swimming platform. My float coat was heavy, but it might come in handy if I misjudged.

As we got closer, I could see the glass doors at the far side of the swimming platform, which I assumed were locked. Every police vehicle carries a Halligan tool—a multi-purpose crowbar to pry open doors and smash glass—and I called into the cabin, "You got a Halligan?"

"Right here!" said Andersson, and she passed me the tool through the open windshield.

She also grabbed a bulletproof vest and an MP5 submachine gun with an extra magazine and passed them to me. I flung the vest to Tess and aimed the MP5 at *The Hana*. I fully expected hostile fire from the yacht, but I couldn't see anyone on the darkened ship. I wanted to think that Petrov and his pals didn't know they were about to be boarded, but whoever was captaining this ship must be watching us on their rear video camera.

The bow of the SAFE boat was a few feet from the swimming platform, and as I waited for the bow to drop, I called to Tess, "Cover me!"

"No, you cover *me*." She stood, flung the Kevlar vest onto the swimming platform, then jumped.

I called into the cabin, "When I jump, get out of here!"

Conte called back, "Good luck!"

I slung the MP5 over my shoulder, and as the bow dropped again I saw Tess kneeling on the platform, gun drawn, facing the doors. My turn. I might get shot, but I wouldn't drown. I jumped and hit the wooden platform and shoulder-rolled toward the glass doors, then sprang to my feet and swung the Halligan tool at the door, but the security glass didn't shatter. I thrust the tapered end of the Halligan between the double doors, rotated the tool inward, and the door popped open. I drew my Glock and dropped to one knee, then glanced over my shoulder and saw the SAFE boat heading south, out of the harbor. We were on our own.

Tess came up beside me carrying the bulletproof vest and I said, "Put it on."

"Swap you the vest for the MP5."

"Put it *on!*"

She slipped off her float coat and put on the vest, and we scanned the interior of the ship.

This was the float-in tender garage and I saw that it was indeed flooded, and it took me a second to realize that the source of the illumination was underwater lights. To the left and right were staircases that rose to the main deck, and also to the left was a catwalk running along the hull connecting the two docks. At the closest dock I could see the amphibious craft that I last saw heading out to sea with Petrov and his friends. Well, we were on the right boat.

We moved in a crouch farther into the ship. Across the flooded garage, near the opposite dock, I noticed something dark under the water, and as my eyes adjusted to the light I recognized it as a submerged boat. I whispered to Tess, "You got that PRD?" She took the radiation detector from her pocket and I could hear a faint beep, followed by another, and I saw the red light flash intermittently, indicating a weak reading, which I'd expect if the nuke was submerged and had a lead shield. So there was little doubt in my mind that we were in the presence of a radiant angel.

Tess said, "That's got to be it. But how do we—?"

"Get down!"

We dropped into a prone position and I pointed my Glock at where I'd seen movement on the opposite dock.

A man was sitting on the dock with his legs dangling over the side, and even in the dim light I recognized him as Arkady Urmanov.

Tess and I exchanged glances, but before we could decide on our next move, Urmanov called out, "Help me!"

That wasn't what I expected to hear, but I replied, "Okay. Where—?"

"I am tied. You must free me."

So if I could figure this out, Urmanov had done his job of arming the device and he was now one witness too many, and for some sick reason Petrov decided that Urmanov should die by his own creation. Petrov was a tough boss.

"You must pump out the water! To your left. On the walkway. The switches for the pump."

I looked at the catwalk and I could see control panels on the hull.

"Untie me!"

One thing at a time, pal. I said to Tess, "Stay here and cover."

She got into a kneeling position, and I rose to one knee and was about to make a dash for the catwalk, but another movement caught my eye. The door on the far side of the tender garage had swung open, and I saw a figure crouched in front of the door. But before I could swing my Glock toward the figure, I saw muzzle flashes, but heard no sound. Well, I know a silenced weapon when I don't hear one, and I hit the deck and shouted to Tess, "Down!"

Arkady Urmanov let out a loud cry, followed by a moan.

I aimed my Glock at the place where I'd seen the flash of the automatic weapon and popped off five rounds, which echoed in the huge space.

Tess did the same, and we rolled away from our firing positions and popped off the rest of our magazines, then rolled again as we reloaded.

There was no flash of return fire, so whoever was shooting was not giving away his position. Or maybe we hit him. I glanced at Urmanov across the flooded garage, and I could see that he was slumped forward. I was pretty sure he was dead, and so were my chances of Urmanov disarming the bomb.

Tess was about twenty feet away, flat against the deck, pointing her Glock downrange, but maintaining fire discipline until a target presented itself, as was the guy who shot at us. Petrov? Gorsky? In either case, they were both trained killers, and killers know when to play dead. Meanwhile, the nuke was sitting about thirty feet away in a sunken boat that I could see but couldn't get to. And I was sure the timer was no longer set for 8:46 A.M.

I looked up at the catwalk where Urmanov said the pump switch was located, and I would have made a dash for it, but standing there was Viktor Gorsky, who shut off the underwater lights, throwing the garage into total darkness.

I knew he was already gone but I fired anyway to draw his fire, and a second later Gorsky returned the fire and I could hear the rounds smacking into the wooden deck around us as Tess and I shot at the muzzle flashes.

Gorsky's firing stopped and I lay motionless, listening for Tess, hoping she was alive and Gorsky was dead. I called out softly, "You okay?"

"Yeah." She suggested, "Use the MP5."

They tell you never to reveal the automatic weapon until you see the target, then you surprise the guy. Gorsky was using his, but it was silenced and he probably had lots of ammo, and I did not.

While I was weighing the pros and cons of bringing out the big gun, another burst of rounds cut through the darkness and I could hear them buzzing over my head. A round smashed into the glass door behind us, confirming that even pros tend to fire high in the dark.

Okay, so Gorsky was obviously alive and not leaving. But if he intended to escape the explosion, he had to leave at some point. But if he was on a suicide mission, then we'd all share the one-time experience of nuclear oblivion. But I didn't come this far and get this close to the nuke to have it blow up in my face. All I had to do was get to it. Which meant getting to the catwalk and pumping the water out of the garage. Which meant getting rid of Gorsky and his automatic weapon.

And then what? Well, I took a Bomb Squad class on how to disarm a conventional bomb. *There are three components you look for when faced with an unknown explosive device: the power source; the explosive charge; and the detonator.*

How much different could a nuclear bomb be?

Most sophisticated explosive devices have a collapsible circuit. If you cut one wire leading to the charge, it collapses the other circuit, setting off the charge. But if you can remove any one of the three components...

Right. Easier said than done. Gorsky had this entire open area covered by a silenced automatic weapon, and the nuke itself was covered with water. We had come to a standoff, and in this case with the timer ticking, a standoff was as good as a win for Gorsky and Petrov.

But Vasily Petrov was an impatient and impulsive man and he did not see it that way, because I heard his voice boom out over a speaker, "Kill them!"

Gorsky, who understood that he'd checkmated the intruders, did not fire, and Petrov yelled again, "Kill them!"

It's not a happy occasion when someone is yelling, "Kill them!" and you see muzzle flashes followed by the sound of bullets impacting around you. I mean, this asshole couldn't see us, but if you spray enough bullets downrange, eventually you're going to hit your target. Time to get out of here.

I retrieved the Halligan tool and whispered to Tess, "We have to get around this guy. We split up and take the staircases. Meet you on the main deck."

"Okay..."

"On three. One, two"—I tossed the Halligan tool into the air over the water—"three!" I heard the Halligan hit the opposite dock, followed by rounds impacting far behind us as we sprinted toward the left and right staircases.

I reached the top of the stairs in about three seconds and saw Tess already there, gun drawn covering the rear deck.

There was some moonlight left, and some illumination came from the Brooklyn waterfront, which was sliding by on our right. I figured we'd be out of the channel and near the tip of Manhattan in about fifteen minutes—or less if this ship picked up speed when it cleared the channel.

There was a helicopter overhead, so we weren't alone, but we were as good as alone until someone made the decision to board *The Hana*. Conte and Andersson had by now transmitted a sit-rep, but bureaucracy and chain of command being what they were, the order to commence a combat boarding could take ten or fifteen minutes, followed by a detailed plan of operation, and by that time the show would be over.

Tess asked, "What now?"

"If we can't get to the nuke, we have to get to the asshole who controls the nuke and the other asshole who's steering this ship, and one or both of them will be on the bridge."

I got rid of my heavy float coat and moved quickly to the doors that according to the deck plans led to the bar and dining room. I held my Glock in my right hand and the MP5 in my left, and motioned to the door, which Tess threw open. I burst inside the barroom, but before I had a chance to shoulder-roll, I tripped over something on the floor and found myself staring into the face of someone with a third eye in his forehead.

Vasily Petrov turned away from the image on the video monitor. Even in the dim underwater lights of the garage, he recognized the man and the woman. Viktor was right; he should have killed them at Tamorov's house.

Gleb said, "It appears that we have been boarded, Colonel."

"Viktor will kill them."

"He has not killed them. He has only managed to kill Arkady, who was not a moving target with a gun."

Petrov ignored the sarcasm and stared through the windshield, fixated on the lighted skyline of Lower Manhattan. He would have enjoyed seeing the post-apocalyptic photographs and news footage of the nuclear wasteland, but that was not to be, though his father would see them and be proud of his son's sacrifice.

Gleb had set the autopilot on a course to bring *The Hana* to the ferry terminal at the tip of Manhattan, so Gleb was no longer needed. But Petrov wanted more speed, so he said, "Full speed, Captain."

"How do we get off this ship?"

Petrov was prepared for the question and replied, "We don life vests and jump." He added, "When we come ashore, we will go to our car—or find a taxi to take us to the diplomatic residential complex in the Bronx, where we will be safe." He glanced at Gleb to see if he was believing any of that.

Gleb pointed out, "We will not get far in the water before the Americans capture us, or the explosion kills us."

"I know what I am doing, Captain."

"And *I* know what you are doing."

Gleb turned on the radar and looked at the screen. There were now four craft within a few hundred meters of *The Hana*, and overhead he could hear a helicopter. He said to Petrov, "We are surrounded by hostile craft, and there are at least two Americans with weapons onboard." He looked at Petrov. "It is over."

Petrov stared at the Manhattan skyline.

"It is *over*, Colonel."

"It is within reach, Captain." He took the arming device from his pocket.

"Yes, if we intend to die in a nuclear explosion. I do not." He said to Petrov, "Give me that thing in your hand."

Petrov looked at Gleb and saw that Gleb had his pistol pointed at him.

Gleb repeated, "Give me that thing in your hand."

Petrov held out the arming device. "Do you mean this thing? Or..." Petrov drew his Makarov from his pocket. "...this one?"

Gleb pulled the trigger on his pistol and was surprised to hear a dull thud.

Petrov said, "We seem to have a problem today with malfunctioning guns." He aimed at Gleb's face and fired a bullet between his eyes. Gleb's head snapped back and he fell to the deck.

Petrov pocketed his pistol and took Gleb's place at the helm. He looked at the autopilot light. The ship's speed and course were set, and if he did nothing, *The Hana* would continue toward the tip of Manhattan Island at ten knots. But if he pushed the throttles forward for more speed, the autopilot would disengage and he would have to steer the ship himself. He wanted more speed, but he didn't want to cancel Gleb's pre-set course, in case he had to leave the bridge—or if he was killed. All he had to do now was reset the timer on the nuclear device.

The autopilot display showed that *The Hana* at this speed would be close to the tip of Manhattan in less than fifteen minutes. He looked at the clock on the dashboard: 06:11. He reset the detonation time on the arming device to 06:27, then did the same with the backup device. He dropped the two arming devices on the deck and put a bullet into each one, sealing not only his own fate but the fate of the City of New York. He would have also put a bullet into his own head, so he didn't have to wait for death, but he wanted to watch the skyline getting closer as the minutes ticked off. Perhaps, he thought, there would be a moment of incandescent beauty at the instant of nuclear fission. This was the way to die.

Well, I thought, if you gotta die, it's good to die in a bar.

I didn't know who these people were, but I knew they were in the wrong place at the wrong time.

With Tess close behind, I led the way into the dining room, and I saw two more bodies on the floor. I also noticed that the table was set for ten, but the guests were still lingering over cocktails.

I pulled the deck plans from my pocket and Tess shone her penlight on them. I could see an area marked VESTIBULE where there was an elevator and a spiral staircase that connected the decks toward the front of the yacht, and we headed quickly in that direction, guns drawn.

We got to the vestibule and I unslung my MP5. You never take an elevator in a tactical situation, and I whispered to Tess, "I go up the stairs face first, you follow ass first."

I climbed the stairs, two at a time, my MP5 to my front, and Tess followed, climbing the stairs backwards, covering our rear with her Glock pointed at the base of the staircase.

I had no idea how many hostiles were aboard this ship, but there was a minimum of two. Petrov and Gorsky. And there was probably a Russian skipper aboard. There could also be a few other SVR killers who came aboard along with the Russian captain and the nuke, but maybe not if Moscow wanted to limit the number of people who knew about this. Which was why we found Urmanov waiting to die. So hopefully the only other Russians aboard were the party girls, and based on what I saw in the barroom, the party was over.

And then there was the crew. Maybe twenty of them. Where were they? Could Petrov and Gorsky have whacked them all? If so, Petrov was the worst ship passenger since Count Dracula.

I reached the vestibule on the salon deck and dropped to one knee as I swept my MP5 around the dark space. The ship was very quiet and I could hear my breathing.

Tess backed up the staircase and into the vestibule, her Glock still pointed down the stairs.

The next deck was the bridge where the ship's office and captain's quarters were located, and I stood and moved toward the spiral stairs.

Tess, however, moved toward the glass doors of the salon and motioned me to follow.

Well, you're supposed to check out everything to make sure you're not leaving hostiles behind you, but in my head I heard a timer ticking.

Petrov's handheld radio beeped and Gorsky said, "I am not sure they are still here."

Petrov replied, "In any case you must stay there and guard the device and kill anyone else who comes aboard from the swimming platform."

Gorsky did not reply immediately, then said, "The Americans will start boarding over the sides, and in force—"

"I see no craft from the bridge," though he did see them on the radar.

"But they know who we are, Colonel, and why we are here."

"It is too late for them, Viktor."

Again, there was a silence, then Gorsky said, "It is also too late for us."

Petrov did not reply.

"Are we going to die?"

"Yes, we are going to die."

Gorsky said nothing, so Petrov advised, "Be brave. Stay at your post—as Captain Gleb is doing." He reminded Gorsky, "We cannot be taken prisoner. We cannot betray our country." He assured Gorsky, "Your family will be taken care of. If you do your duty."

Again, Gorsky said nothing, and Petrov had nothing more to say to him, so he signed off and turned his attention to the radar and the windshield, confident that Viktor Gorsky would do his duty. And if not, it didn't matter because there was literally nothing that could stop *The Hana* at this point, except perhaps a naval cannon. But even if the Americans had a warship in the area, would they take the risk of firing on the ship that they suspected had a nuclear device onboard?

Petrov stared at the approaching skyline, then glanced at the Statue of Liberty in the harbor. "Yob vas."

I followed Tess into the long salon. She stopped and took a deep breath. "Oh my God..."

So as it turned out, Tasha and her friends were just throwaway props, easily expendable in the pursuit of some psychotic goal of world domination. Well, Buck and I agreed on another thing—the Russians needed closer watching.

There was nothing more to see there, so we returned to the vestibule and approached the spiral staircase carefully, knowing that at least one person was on the bridge deck—and also knowing that these people carried submachine guns and knew how to use them.

We listened for a sound at the top of the stairs, but all I heard was that ticking in my head.

I made a tactical decision and said to Tess, "The only chance we have of stopping this fucking nuke from leveling Manhattan is if we split up. I go back to the tender garage, kill Gorsky, pump the garage dry, and try to disarm that thing. You go up to the bridge and see if you can get rid of whoever is up there and turn this ship toward the middle of the harbor." I looked at her in the dim light and I could see she understood that this was our only play. She nodded.

"And if you get a chance, jump ship."

She looked at me and our eyes met. "Well…nice working with you, Detective."

"Yeah. You too." I promised, "I'll buy you that drink later."

She started up the spiral staircase toward the bridge, and I moved quickly down the stairs to the lower deck.

Well, there are good plans and there are desperate plans. Petrov, too, had a desperate plan that obviously included dying for his country. He could have stopped the ship and raised the white flag, or he could have jumped overboard. But he wasn't doing that, so neither were we.

Tess Faraday stopped near the top of the spiral staircase, noting that the bridge door was closed and that the other two doors in the vestibule were also shut.

She climbed the last few steps and swept the vestibule with her Glock, noticing blood trails on the floor that led to the captain's quarters and the ship's office, and she understood that dead bodies had been dragged into the rooms. Nothing in there to check out.

She turned toward the bridge door. Behind that door, as Corey said, was the asshole who controlled the nuke and the asshole who controlled the ship.

She took a deep breath, hit the entry pad, and dropped into a low crouch with her Glock aimed at the door, ready to empty her nine-round magazine. This could all be over in a minute.

But the door did not slide open.

She stepped back, aimed at the door, and began firing.

Tess felt a sharp pain in her arm and realized she'd been hit by a ricochet, and that the door was armored. "Damn it!"

An intercom speaker near the entry pad crackled, then a voice with a Russian accent said, "I am watching you on the camera. Where is your friend?"

"Open the fucking door and put your hands in the air!"

"I can't hear you. Push the intercom button."

Tess hit the intercom button, took a deep breath, and said, "Listen... we know what you're doing, and we know this is not an attack by the Saudis. We know all this, and if you want to start fucking World War Three—"

"Shut up."

"Look... Colonel Petrov... think about—"

"Shut up."

"Asshole!" Tess took her finger off the intercom button and began kicking at the door. "You bastard! Stop this!"

There was no reply, but then Petrov's voice came through the speaker. "You will be dead in thirteen minutes."

I ran through the dark passageway on the lower deck between the staterooms, and at the end of the passageway were the double doors that led to the garage—and to Viktor Gorsky and the nuke.

I gripped my MP5 in my right hand and threw open a door, then dove into a prone position and scanned the darkness.

I could hear the blood pounding in my ears, but that was all I could hear, and I could see nothing except some moonlight coming through the doors that led to the swimming platform across the flooded garage.

Okay, I'd outflanked Gorsky, but where was he?

If I couldn't see him, he couldn't see me. But he had to have heard me diving through the door and hitting the deck, so he knew approximately where I was, and I expected to see the flash of his MP5 and hear the bullets smacking into the deck around me—or into me. I tried to control my breathing, but it sounded too loud. Someone had to make a move. But time was still on Gorsky's side, and he didn't have to do anything. Unless he'd decided he didn't want to be standing at ground zero when the nuke blew. So maybe he'd put on a life vest and gone off the swimming platform, leaving me alone with the nuke. File that under wishful thinking.

I rose slowly to one knee and suddenly the underwater lights came on, and I turned quickly toward the catwalk. And there was Viktor Gorsky, not twenty feet away, aiming his submachine gun at me.

I knew I was dead, but Gorsky seemed to hesitate for half a second, or maybe the light momentarily blinded him. I used that half second to dive over the side of the dock into the water, just as I saw the flash of his muzzle and heard the bullets impacting on the dock where I'd been.

I sank to the bottom of the illuminated water and saw bullets coming at me, but they lost their velocity before they traveled a foot into the water.

I found traction on the submerged deck and I half walked and half swam toward the catwalk. I was running out of breath, but if I surfaced for air I'd be inhaling hot lead.

Gorsky kept firing into the water, desperately trying to overcome the laws of physics. He was losing his cool.

I got under the catwalk and hoped that Gorsky would not think of the only thing he could do to save his ass, which was to jump off the catwalk and join me in the water. But he didn't think of that fast enough and I extended my arm until the submachine gun was out of the water and aimed straight up at the catwalk's floor grate and squeezed the trigger, hoping the MP5 really could fire when wet.

I felt the submachine gun bucking in my hand, and I looked up through the water to see Gorsky lying facedown on the catwalk, hopefully with a few rounds in his balls and up his ass. Surprise!

The water around me was turning red, and I surfaced, took a deep breath, then reached up and grabbed the edge of the catwalk.

Gorsky's face was right above mine, and his eyes were open, staring down at me through the grate, and his lips were moving. I put the muzzle of my MP5 to his mouth and pulled the trigger.

Now for the nuke.

Vasily Petrov stared at the video monitor. Was it possible that Gorsky was dead? He kept staring at the dim image on the screen, then watched as the American climbed out of the water and onto the catwalk, then found the switch to the pumps, then the switch to the overhead lights. The garage brightened and Petrov continued to stare at the screen as the man Depp searched Gorsky's body, then ran to the dock toward the submerged lifeboat—and the nuclear device.

It was not possible that this man could disarm the device even if he was trained. There simply wasn't enough time for the water to recede and for him to get the locked trunk open.

Petrov looked at the clock on the dashboard. Then back at the image on the screen.

The time until detonation was so short that Petrov knew he needed to do nothing...but the American had found Urmanov's tool kit...so perhaps he needed to go below and kill this man. But first he needed to kill the woman outside his door.

Tess stood in the vestibule, her gun drawn, staring at the bridge door, thinking about how to get to Vasily Petrov and whoever else was on the bridge.

Petrov's voice said, "I can see my man Gorsky on the monitor. He has killed your friend in the garage."

Tess felt her stomach tighten.

"It is finished. Save yourself. Go!"

Tess aimed her Glock at the intercom, fired, and silenced it. "Bastard!"

She looked up at the eyeball video camera in the ceiling and fired three rounds into it. "Fuck you."

She also noticed a skylight on the ceiling, and she moved under it, seeing that it was hinged. It was about ten feet above her head, impossible to reach, but there must be a ladder.

She looked around, then saw a lever next to the elevator buttons, marked ROOF HATCH. She pulled the lever and a collapsible steel ladder fell from an overhead compartment.

Tess slapped a fresh magazine into her Glock and began climbing the ladder, which would take her to the roof above the bridge, and also to the sloping windshield where she could lie flat over the edge of the roof, look into the bridge, and empty her Glock into Vasily Petrov.

I stood on the catwalk and hit the switch marked PUMPS, and heard them engage. I found the light switches, turned them on, and the garage brightened.

I also noticed a switch marked SHELL DOOR, which I assumed opened the door in the hull. I glanced at the amphibious craft tied to the dock. That was a way out of here if the pumps didn't work fast enough to get the water below the nuke. The question was, How fast was that amphibious craft and how big was that nuke? I hoped I didn't have to find out.

I also hoped that Tess was having better luck on the bridge, but I could feel that the ship was still moving forward, meaning that the bad guys were still in command.

I quickly searched Gorsky's body to see if he had something, like a remote control device, or a code to stop the clock, but all he had on him was a small pistol and a knife. As for extra MP5 magazines, apparently he'd used them up murdering everyone. I pocketed his pistol.

The water level was dropping, and I came down from the catwalk and ran along the dock to the submerged boat. I glanced at Urmanov, whose slumped body was soaked in blood. Another asshole who'd made bad decisions.

I noticed an overnight bag on the dock, and it looked like the one Urmanov had carried to the amphibious craft. I knelt and opened it, finding an aluminum box that I also opened and saw it was filled with small precision instruments, which were obviously for the suitcase nuke.

I looked at the black trunk, still underwater. Maybe another two or three minutes before I could get to it. I jumped into the half-submerged boat and examined the trunk, noticing now that it had a hasp and combination padlock. "Damn it!"

I also noticed a wire coming from the side of the trunk, and I followed it visually and spotted a black ball floating in the water. This, I guessed, was the antenna that would pick up radio signals from a remote control and transmit the signals to the device; and Petrov undoubtedly had the remote, so there was no question now that the asshole had reset the time from 08:46 to…now.

I left the wire plugged into the trunk, thinking that if Tess could get onto the bridge and get hold of the remote, and if she or I could figure out how it worked, we might be able to stop the clock. Not likely, but…Well, I was due for a break. But I actually needed a miracle.

The water had dropped to an inch above the trunk. I moved off to the side, knelt in the cold seawater, pulled my Glock and put the muzzle right above the water. I aimed at the combination lock and fired three rounds.

The bullets hit the lock and it swung on the hasp, and I fired four more rounds, then grabbed the damaged lock and pulled. It held fast.

"Damn it!"

I sat in the submerged boat, waiting for the water to drop a few more inches. Seconds, minutes, inches.

The speaker crackled, and Petrov's voice said, "What are you doing, Mr. Depp?"

I looked toward the catwalk where the public address speaker was mounted on the hull. "Fuck you."

"I can see you, but I cannot hear you." He suggested, "Come to the catwalk and use the intercom. I need to speak to you."

"No, asshole, you need to die."

"I cannot hear you, Mr. Depp."

"The name's Corey!" I flipped him the bird, then I looked at the trunk. The lid was now above water.

Petrov said, "I have killed your lady friend."

I took a deep breath, then unslung my MP5 and pointed it at the top of the trunk.

Petrov's voice was a bit urgent. "Do not shoot at the device. You could detonate it."

Or stop the clock. Well... either way was okay. Tess would agree. "Save yourself."

I shifted my aim to the lock, which was now clearing the water, and emptied my last MP5 magazine into it.

Petrov had no comment.

I knelt and pulled at the lock, which still held. "Damn it!"

I remembered the Halligan tool I'd tossed here to draw Gorsky's fire, and I saw it lying on the dock. I jumped onto the dock, grabbed the tool, and jumped back into the half-submerged boat. I shoved the tapered end between the lock shank and the hasp and twisted, reminding God that it was time for a break. The lock shank held, but the hasp ripped loose from the trunk. "Thank you." I tossed the lock and hasp aside and lifted the heavy lead-lined lid until its supporting arms locked into place. And there in front of me was the bomb.

There were no dials, no switches, and no ticking clock. Just a smooth metal faceplate, secured by four recessed screws or bolts. The four color-coded ports were obviously for leads and wires attached to the arming device, which, more obviously, I did not have.

Okay, so back to basics. I pulled my Glock, stood, and pointed it at the shiny metal faceplate of the nuclear device.

I expected to hear from Petrov again, but the speaker was silent. He could have jumped ship, but I didn't think that was part of his plan. And maybe he was lying about Tess and she'd whacked him... but the ship was still moving forward, and I didn't hear anyone's voice on the speaker. Not Petrov's and not Tess'.

I took a deep breath and squeezed on the trigger, wondering if I'd hear the sizzle of fried electronics, or the Big Bang. One way to find out.

Tess scrambled up the ladder and slid quietly across the white fiberglass roof, between the radar tower and the antennas.

Up ahead she could see the skyline of Manhattan, maybe three miles away, and getting closer. A pink dawn was visible on the eastern horizon. It was going to be a nice day.

She saw a helicopter overhead flying in slow circles, and a few hundred yards off the port side was a Coast Guard cutter, keeping pace with *The Hana,* and to starboard was an NYPD Harbor craft, also running alongside the yacht.

She waved her arm, hoping they knew that a female agent had boarded the hostile ship. *Don't fire.*

Tess held her Glock in both hands and propelled herself over the edge of the roof until she was staring down through the windshield into the dimly lit bridge. She saw a body on the floor, and it wasn't Petrov's, who was off to her left, looking down at the lighted video screen on the instrument panel. She held her Glock at a downward angle and took aim.

Petrov suddenly looked up and saw her face staring at him a few feet away, and he went for his gun.

Tess fired three rounds into the windshield, realizing instantly that they weren't penetrating. Petrov returned the fire, with the same results.

They looked at each other for a moment through the fractured glass, then Tess jumped to her feet and emptied her magazine into the fiberglass roof, above where Petrov was standing, but she realized the roof was also bulletproof. "Damn it!"

She scrambled back to the hatch and dropped ten feet to the vestibule floor, then reached into her pocket for a full magazine.

Before she could reload, she was aware that something was moving, and she looked toward the bridge to see the door sliding open. Standing there was Vasily Petrov, pointing his pistol at her.

"Bitch!"

Tess saw a flame spit out of his silenced pistol, and felt something hit her in the chest, knocking her back against the elevator.

He fired again, and again he hit her in her Kevlar vest, knocking her off her feet.

Petrov seemed momentarily pleased, then confused.

Tess dove for the spiral staircase as Petrov fired again. She went over the railing and dropped to the deck below.

Petrov was at the top of the staircase and he fired again, this time hitting her in the left thigh.

She rolled as she slammed a magazine into her Glock and emptied it up the staircase, then ran into the salon and sprinted across the bloody carpeting, tripping over a body, then getting to her feet and continuing until she reached the outdoor lounge.

She was aware that she was covered with blood and that some of it was hers, but it wasn't gushing, though the wound was starting to throb. She took a deep breath and looked back into the salon, but she couldn't see Petrov.

As she moved down the outside staircase to the main deck, she saw a large ship about three hundred yards off the starboard side. The ship had a strange bow and she realized it was an icebreaker. They were going to ram *The Hana* and sink her—her meaning *The Hana*, but also meaning *her*. Well...it was a smart move. Maybe the only move left.

She had no idea where Petrov was, but she hoped he was following her so she could kill him before the nuke did.

Tess moved cautiously down to the main deck, then to the staircase that went down to the garage, and began to descend. The wound in her thigh was now sending sharp pains down her leg, and she held the rail with one hand and her Glock in the other.

There was no good reason to descend into the flooded garage, except to see for herself if Corey was dead. And if he was, that meant that Gorsky was alive, and she would also kill him.

Before I fired into the nuclear device, I had a lucid moment and remembered Urmanov's aluminum box. I'm not good with tools, but I evolve fast.

I found what looked like a screwdriver, except that the tip had a very odd shape with three prongs. I looked at the four holes in the corners of the metal faceplate, which I assumed held recessed screws, and I put the screwdriver in one of the holes and twisted, but it didn't budge. *Shit.*

I was about to give up on this idea, but then I thought that this being a Russian suitcase nuke, it was not user friendly, so I twisted clockwise, which is supposed to tighten a screw, and I felt it turn.

I quickly removed all four screws, but there was no place to get a grip on the recessed steel faceplate to lift it off. Then I noticed a narrow notch on the right edge of the plate, big enough to get a knife blade into. I took my pocketknife—Swiss Army—and extended the blade, which I slid into the notch and levered the faceplate up an inch, enough to get my fingers under it. So if I lifted it, would it blow?

One way to find out. And I did, and it didn't.

I threw the faceplate into the water and looked down at the inside of a nuclear suitcase bomb. *Holy shit.*

I'm a little squeamish about radiation exposure, but I understood that this was not my immediate problem.

...if you can remove any one of the three components... I looked for the digital countdown clock, one of the items that could possibly be removed, but there was no such thing. The clock must be internal, part of the electronic circuitry, not visible to human eyes. Petrov, of course, had the remote arming device and he could see how many minutes we all had left, but I could not.

I looked for the power source, but I didn't see anything that looked like a battery, so it must be buried deep in the electronic bowels of this monster.

The third component was the explosive charge...but this explosive was made up of two elements: the nuclear core and the conventional high explosive that was wrapped around the core. And all of this was contained in a beach-ball-sized metal globe, which I was staring at, and there was no way to get into it. Nor did I want to.

Two electrical wires led into the globe, one on each side—and those wires led to the detonators buried in the high explosive material. And the wires came from a battery that I couldn't see, and somewhere in the circuit was the clock, which I also couldn't see. *Damn it!*

Okay...now what? Cut a wire? *If you cut one wire leading to the charge, it collapses the other circuit, setting off the charge.* Not a good idea according to my Bomb Squad instructor.

I felt sweat forming on my forehead, but my hands were very steady if I wanted to do something with them.

Then I understood that this was actually a win-win situation. If I got lucky and disarmed the bomb, all was good. But if I blew it, this far from the city, then the damage would be…well, acceptable. So if I removed myself from the equation, then I knew what I had to do. I grabbed both wires leading to the metal globe, understanding that they had to be pulled simultaneously—if one was pulled first, the other circuit would probably collapse in a nanosecond and send an electrical charge into the detonator, which would blow the high explosives, and the nuclear core would achieve critical mass and do its fission thing.

I tugged on both wires to sort of rehearse, then I heard a voice in my head, and the voice said, *Submerge the electronics, stupid.*

Then another voice said, "John!" That voice sounded more like Tess than God.

I stood and looked at her on the opposite dock, and saw blood on her left pant leg. "You okay?"

"I'm okay…Petrov said that Gorsky killed you."

I wasn't sure how she'd had a conversation with Colonel Petrov, and I didn't care, but I cared about his health, so I asked, "Is he dead?"

"No. He's…he may be following me."

Shit.

She started limping toward the catwalk, and I asked her, "Who's steering this ship?"

"I don't know…I saw a dead man on the bridge."

Well, he wasn't steering. So either Petrov was steering or the autopilot was. I informed her, "Gorsky is dead. On the catwalk."

"Good."

"How far are we from Manhattan?"

"Maybe…less than a mile."

So we had maybe five minutes—or less.

She moved across the catwalk and stepped over Gorsky like he was dog turd. She looked at the nuke as she came toward me on the dock and exclaimed, "You got it open!"

"Right."

"Do you know what to do?"

"I do."

"Thank God."

I was about to dash to the catwalk and open the shell door, flooding the garage and submerging the nuke, which, if it was like my cell phone, would die quickly.

But Vasily Petrov had other ideas and he said, "Put your hands up and move away from the device." He was standing at the double doors and aimed his MP5 at Tess. "Or I will shoot her."

He was going to shoot her anyway, but he wasn't going to shoot at me standing in front of the nuke, so I knew I could try to pull my Glock. Or pull the detonator wires.

"Move away!" He raised his submachine gun and pointed it at Tess, who knew the same trick I knew, and she dove over the side of the dock, but the water level was less than two feet now and she took a hard fall, though Petrov lost sight of her.

I used the opportunity to pull my Glock and pumped my remaining two rounds at him, then the gun clicked empty.

Petrov was down but not out, and he got to one knee, blood all over his arms and shirt. He raised his MP5 and aimed it at me, but hesitated because of the nuke behind me, which he did not want to blow prematurely, though I did, so I said, "Shoot, asshole!"

He didn't shoot, but he stood and staggered toward the edge of the dock and looked down at Tess, who I could see from the boat, lying in the water. She'd been hurt in her dive off the dock and I knew she'd lost a lot of blood.

Petrov aimed his submachine gun down at her, and before I could pull the small pistol that I'd taken from Gorsky, Tess raised her Glock and put a bullet into Petrov, who tottered on the edge of the dock, then fell on top of Tess, who brought her arm around and fired another bullet into the side of Petrov's head, splattering his brains out the other side. Can't get deader than that. *Das vidanya, asshole.*

The water around her and Petrov was red, and I needed to put a tourniquet on her wound, but my only job now was to open the shell door and flood the compartment. I started to climb out of the boat and onto the dock.

A voice with an Eastern European accent said, "Please help me."

I turned my head toward the voice and saw a guy coming from the double doors, dressed in blue denim. His shirt was open and there was blood on his chest and he was gripping his abdomen with both hands. "Who are you?"

"I am Mikhail. A seaman." He also assured me, "A Bulgarian. Not Russian. All my mates are dead. I am wounded. Please—"

"Turn around and get down on the deck." I started to reach for Gorsky's pistol, but Mikhail had a similar gun and he pointed it at me.

"Do not move."

What the...?

Mikhail informed me, "To be more truthful, I am not wounded. Also, I am a colleague of the late Colonel Petrov and the late Viktor Gorsky. Along for the cruise to see that all went well."

I stated the obvious: "It didn't."

"I see that." He continued, "Also I am here to eliminate all witnesses—including my colleagues."

"Done that."

"Thank you." He, too, stated the obvious: "And now it is your turn."

Well, I was totally pissed that this guy snookered me. That doesn't happen often, but once was all it took. I glanced at Tess, but she was still lying on her back in the receding water with Petrov still on top of her. *Shit.*

To make sure Mikhail understood the situation, I told him, "In a few minutes, there won't be any witnesses, including you, asshole."

He replied, "I have reduced the speed of the ship." He held up what looked like a cell phone. "And I have given myself another ten minutes to leave the ship." He nodded toward the amphibious craft. "But before I leave, I wish to know from you what you and the CIA know about Operation Zero, and how you discovered this."

I didn't like being mistaken for a CIA guy, but I didn't make an issue of it and asked, "What's in it for me?"

"A quick bullet to your head. The alternative is several bullets to your abdomen." He assured me, "Very painful."

I already knew that from the last time I got shot in the gut, but I didn't find either alternative very attractive or persuasive.

Mikhail sensed this, and he continued along the dock to get into a position to fire without hitting the nuke behind me. "What do you know?"

"I know you're a dickhead and you're going to die." I glanced again at Tess, but she wasn't moving.

Mikhail now noticed that the trunk was open, and this disturbed him. "Turn around and close the lid."

So my options were reduced to two—go for my borrowed gun, or turn around and pull the detonator wires, which would either blow the nuke prematurely or kill it right before this asshole killed me.

People are morbidly drawn to looking at dead bodies, and Mikhail made the mistake of glancing at Urmanov as he passed him, and I pulled Gorsky's gun from my pocket at the same time as Mikhail looked back at me.

I don't know who would have gotten the first shot off, because all of a sudden I heard a deafening crash and the sound of tearing metal, and the ship rolled sharply to port. I was knocked off the boat and into the water and momentarily stunned, but I jumped to my feet, moved quickly to my left, and aimed my pistol at the dock above me.

Mikhail suddenly appeared with his gun aimed at where he'd last seen me. I popped off three rounds, discovering that Gorsky's pistol was silenced, at the same time that Mikhail discovered that my aim was good.

I could hear water rushing into the ship, and *The Hana* was starting to list to starboard. Obviously we'd been rammed. The good news was that the nuke would be underwater. The bad news was that this ship was sinking fast.

I ran to Tess, who was now trying to get out from under Petrov's dead body.

I pulled him off and helped her to her feet. She did not look good, but her head was clear and she said, "I saw an icebreaker..."

"Right. Let's go."

I lifted her onto the dock, then climbed up and got her to her feet. "I'm going to carry you to the swimming platform." I reminded her, "Your float coat is there. Ready?"

"John, the nuke..."

I assured her, "The electronics will fizzle. Let's go."

But she kept staring at the nuke. "It might take too long for the water..."

I could hear the sea rushing in from about midship, but I didn't see any water coming into the garage. So with the extra time that Mikhail had given us, I went back to Plan A and ran to the catwalk, shut off the garage pumps, then hit the switch marked SHELL DOOR.

I heard a hydraulic sound, and watched as the door on the starboard side began to swing out, letting in the sea. A wall of water ran into the garage, making the ship list more to starboard, and I thought we were going to capsize. Was this a good idea? But the nuke was completely covered with water now, and if it was really like my cell phone, it was dead. If not, we were.

The amphibious craft was rising with the water, and I called to Tess, who was limping toward me on the tilting dock. "Stay there!"

I ran across the catwalk to the opposite dock, jumped into the amphibious craft, and released the two lines.

I looked at the dashboard, which seemed simple enough, like a lot of sports boats I'd been on. I started the engines, pushed off from the dock, and turned the wheel hard. The amphibious craft came around in the tight space and I maneuvered it to the forward dock where Tess was kneeling. "Jump in!"

She slid into the seat beside me as I headed for the open shell door.

The water inside the garage had reached the level of the water outside, so we didn't have to sail against the incoming sea. That was the good news. The bad news was that *The Hana* was listing so badly now that the top of the door opening was only about four feet from the water, and the headroom to clear this ship was getting tighter as the ship continued to tilt. I gunned the engines and said, "Duck!"

As we shot through the open door, the windshield of the amphibious craft clipped the top of the opening and ripped it off, sending the windshield flying over our heads.

When I looked up, we were out in the bay where the dawn was breaking.

I put some distance between us and *The Hana*, in case the nuke was still alive, then I looked back at the big yacht, which was almost on its side, a few degrees from slipping under.

Off in the distance I spotted the icebreaker, heading out toward The Narrows, mission accomplished.

I didn't see any other ships around, but an NYPD helicopter hovered overhead and his loudspeaker blared, "Stay where you are!"

I cut the engines and we both stood. Tess put her arm around me and we waved, trying to look friendly.

Tess turned toward the rising sun. "Long day."

"I hope you learned something."

I took off my shirt and tied it tightly around her thigh as we watched *The Hana* disappear under the water, taking its secrets with it. At least until it was raised. Then it remained to be seen what secrets were made public. I know how these things work.

I looked at the Manhattan skyline, about half a mile away, still standing, but still in the center of a lot of people's crosshairs.

The Twin Memorial Beams, which go on at dusk on September 11 and off at dawn, went off. Until next year.

Tess put both arms around me and we looked at each other, then kissed for the video camera in the chopper. I guess I could explain that later.

She lay down on the bench seat and I knelt beside her. "You okay?"

"I need a drink."

She probably needed a pint of blood, but I said, "We have a date."

I heard engines approaching and looked up to see a Coast Guard cutter and an NYPD Harbor craft heading toward us.

So, situation corrected. Surveillance target in known location. End of tour.

Holy shit.

CHAPTER THIRTY-SIX

So the FBI put me on paid administrative leave, which they sometimes do during an ongoing investigation into a serious case or incident. This has the dual benefit to them of getting rid of me while still keeping me under their control. As a contract agent, I could have just resigned, but they were going to terminate my employment anyway, so why bother?

Kate finally made it home, oblivious to my bad day on the job. Normally I'd share some of this with her, but this was sensitive compartmented information that she had no need to know. She did, however, have some unclassified information for me that she could share; she had been offered a reassignment to FBI Headquarters in Washington. Or did she *ask* for the reassignment? I don't know and I didn't ask.

The following day, after I visited Tess in the hospital, I told Kate that I had been placed on leave, pending, I told her, an investigation of me losing an important target. Kate seemed concerned, maybe because this brought up the question of me going with her to Washington. But as we both knew, my non-job was still in New York, so officially I had to stay here. I could, however, put in a request to spend my free time—which is every day—in D.C. But Kate and I agreed that a little separation would be good for both of us while we were going through career transitions.

And did I mention that her boss, Tom Walsh, was also being

reassigned to Washington? My detective instincts told me this was not a coincidence.

Regarding the events under investigation, there was a complete news blackout on that, except for the cover story that a yacht of Saudi Arabian registry had suffered a serious collision with another boat in New York Harbor and had gone down with loss of life. Salvage operations were underway. All of this is true, confirming once again that the best lies are lies of omission, and about ninety-nine percent of what happened has been omitted.

Geopolitics is not my strong point, but I understand why the government is not calling this a thwarted nuclear attack, perpetrated by the Russians. I mean, American-Russian relations are shitty enough without accusing them of nuclear terrorism, which wouldn't improve things much, and might restart the Cold War. I'm sure Washington is going to get its pound of flesh from the Russkies, somewhere, somehow, but in the meantime we're still focused on Abdul, which is an easy sell to the public, and Ivan still looks like a potential ally. At least that's my take on this. But who knows what the hell is going on in Moscow and Washington?

Well...I think I know what's going on in Washington. Kate is fucking Tom Walsh. That's what's going on. But I could be wrong.

And what's going on in New York? Well, as it turns out, Tess, like most State Department people, lives in Washington, but she, too, is on paid leave—medical, in her case—so she has some time on her hands and State doesn't care where she spends it, though they care who she spends it with. Therefore, we're not supposed to have any contact, but we see each other whenever she's in New York, which is most weekends. Screw the Feds. What are they going to do? Fire us? We know too much. On second thought, maybe we know *too* much. But that's another subject.

As for Georgi Tamorov, the State Department has pulled his U.S. visa, forever, and he'll never see his Southampton mansion or his Tribeca townhouse again. I don't know if he cares, but I do know that if he steps foot in Russia again his next address will be an SVR prison. He's a man without a country. Maybe he can buy one.

Scott Kalish, as I predicted, got no ink, except for a confidentiality statement that he had to sign in triplicate. Same with Pete Conte and Nikola Andersson. I owe them all a dinner. Maybe Dean Hampton can cater it at my place. I've had an official-looking award made up for Dean at Sir Speedy and I need to present it to him.

As for Steve and Matt, I took care of that with Howard Fensterman, who got wind of what almost happened and understood that I had tried to warn him to get out of town. So he owed me a big favor, and he saw to it that Steve and Matt got new five-year contracts with the Diplomatic Surveillance Group with promotions to team leader. Hopefully my boys learned from the master—me—how not to do that job. I'm not supposed to have contact with Steve and Matt either, but we've gone for beers at McFadden's on Second Avenue a few times. I don't know if that constitutes contact. I'll check.

And then there's Buck Harris, who has once again thankfully disappeared from my life. I did, however, get a verbal message from him through a third party—Tess—and she said he said, "We continue to appreciate your silence and we trust it will continue." He also let me know, "I look forward to seeing you again."

My reply, through the same third party, was, "We're even. Let's keep it that way."

But Tess likes the devious old coot, and she wants us all to be friends. Right. I have to remember to tell Paul Brenner to remove Buck from his hit list. I'll get to that soon.

Meanwhile, since Tess and I are not allowed to discuss the incident that we were involved in together—even with each other—we talk about things like my past and my future. As for my past, Tess would prefer if I didn't call Beth Penrose again. Ever. As for my future, Ms. Faraday has invited me to dinner at her parents' palatial estate in Lattingtown. Can't wait to get checked out and talk about my future.

So, what do I want to do with the rest of my life? I'm not sure, but I know someone will make me an offer. That's usually part of the shut-up deal. I see myself as a contract agent again, working for the Feds in dangerous countries, risking my ass for crap money, like I did in Yemen. Can't be any worse than the quiet end job I had.

Tess thinks I have a death wish, but I don't; I do, however, enjoy a little excitement. I mean, the only thing worse than someone shooting at you is no one bothering to shoot at you.

Sometimes I walk past the Russian U.N. Mission, which is in my neighborhood, and I think back to that Sunday morning of September 11. If Kate hadn't been in Washington, I probably wouldn't have worked that day. And if I hadn't worked that day... Would another DSG guy have followed Colonel Petrov into Georgi Tamorov's party? Hopefully yes, but would that have led to the same outcome in New York Harbor? We'll never know any of that, but what I do know is that it was a damn close thing.

I think, too, about Vasily Petrov, and I wonder what motivated him to commit mass murder and attempt an act of unspeakable evil. I'm sure he never saw himself as evil; he saw himself as a patriot, doing a good and noble thing for his country. We have guys like that, too. And they say *I'm* crazy?

I thought, too, about Mikhail, the assassin of the assassins. I'll bet Petrov and Gorsky would have been really surprised when Mikhail popped up and announced that he was going to whack them. Good job, boys. Now here's your reward. The SVR has a tough H.R. office.

I mean, Petrov and Gorsky risked their butts for their country, probably for the same crap pay I get, and what do they get in return? A bullet to shut them up.

Well, Tess and I saved Mikhail the trouble, and we also saved Petrov and Gorsky from a final disillusionment. Assuming they had illusions to begin with. There's a lesson here for me, too. But I think I already learned that lesson.

On a happier note, I took Tess to Rossiya one night, a Russian nightclub in Brighton Beach, where the late Colonel Petrov's girlfriend, Svetlana, is a chanteuse. Tess didn't want to go, having just had an unpleasant experience with some Russians, and she said all the guys there looked like Petrov and Gorsky. But you can't fight your demons unless you go looking for them, and after a few vodkas she got into the right head and we ate Russian food and danced all night and we heard Svetlana sing. She has good lungs. Later we took a stroll on the boardwalk and watched the sun come up.

Do I miss Kate? Yes, I do. But I'd rather try to figure out how to defuse a weapon of mass destruction than try to figure out how this marriage reached critical mass and blew.

Meanwhile, life goes on. And every day is new. And one day, if I live long enough, I'll come to a quiet end. And that's okay if I can look back and say, "I did good."

THE END

Acknowledgments

As with all of my novels, I've taken advantage of the patience and good nature of friends and acquaintances to assist me with facts, technical details, and inside information that a novelist needs but can't find in books or on the Internet.

And as always, here is my disclaimer: any errors of fact regarding the procedures or professions represented in this novel are either a result of my misunderstanding of the information given to me, or a result of my decision to take literary license and dramatic liberties. Also, in some cases I have been asked to alter classified information given to me in confidence.

First among these friends who have helped is Kenny Hieb, a.k.a. John Corey. Kenny, like Corey, is a retired NYPD detective, formerly with the Joint Terrorism Task Force, and currently with another Federal organization that needs to go unnamed. Thanks, Kenny, for your assistance and, more importantly, for your work in keeping us safe.

Next, I'd like to thank Pete Conte, Suffolk County (NY) Police Officer, Marine Bureau. Pete has been very generous with his time and very giving of his vast knowledge of police work on the high seas. In exchange for all this, I have given Pete a cameo role in this book. And again, whatever errors I've made in this regard are mine alone.

Also on the high seas, many thanks to my friend Bruce Knecht, yachtsman and author of *Hooked, The Proving Ground,* and *Grand Ambition,* for steering me in the right direction on my voyage of super yacht discovery. If I hadn't read Bruce's wonderful *Grand Ambition,* I could not have created *The Hana,* which is central to this story.

Thanks, too, to John Kennedy, Deputy Police Commissioner, Nassau County (NY) Police Department (Retired). John's a member of the New York State Bar, and patron (with me) of many local bars.

John has helped me with all my John Corey novels and he brings to this task a unique combination of skills and knowledge as a police officer and an attorney. If I make up too much stuff, John revokes my literary license.

And, now on to my publishing team. Many thanks go to my editor and friend, Jamie Raab, president and publisher of Grand Central Publishing. Jamie somehow finds time to run a company and edit my manuscripts, and she wears both hats with style and confidence.

Thanks also to my longtime friend Harvey-Jane Kowal, a.k.a. HJ, who has once again come out of retirement from Hachette Book Group to work on this, her thirteenth DeMille book. This comes under the category of "Glutton for Punishment." HJ knows her grammar, punctuation, spelling, and fact-checking, and she makes me look good on the printed page.

Forgetting to thank your agent at the back of the book is like forgetting to thank your defense lawyer as you walk out of the courtroom a free man. Imperfect analogy aside, I want to thank my team at ICM Partners, Jennifer Joel and Sloan Harris, not only for their hard work, but also for their smart work. Authors with good agents suffer fewer suicidal and homicidal urges.

This book was made possible by my two dedicated and hardworking assistants, Dianne Francis and Patricia Chichester. I write all my novels by hand, and there are only two people on the planet who can read my scrawl and put it into typed form, and for that I am very grateful. Dianne and Patricia are also my first readers and fact-checkers, and nothing goes to the publisher that is not perfect. Thanks, too, for keeping my schedule and my life organized.

Another early reader of the manuscript is my son, Alex, who as a screenwriter gets straight to the heart of the storyline and the characters. Screenwriters tell a story with an economy of words and they reveal their characters through dialogue, and I have learned much from Alex, making me feel good about the Yale tuition. Thanks, Buddy.

For a different perspective on the manuscript I always turn to my daughter, Lauren, a psychologist. Dr. Lauren is able to analyze my characters, and through them she can analyze the author and offer help for all of us.

And, penultimately, I want to thank the beautiful Ethel Kennedy, who is truly a radiant angel on earth. Ethel inspires me to be charitable and it's starting to work.

The best is last, and that is my wife, Sandy, who is an example to me and to all who know her of courage and optimism. Perfect wife, perfect mother, and perfectly beautiful, inside and out.

The following people have made generous contributions to charities in return for having their name used as a character in this novel: **Nikola Andersson**—East End Hospice; **Scott Kalish**—Boys & Girls Club of Oyster Bay–East Norwich; **Howard Fensterman**—Crohn's & Colitis Foundation; **Dean Hampton**—Robert F. Kennedy Center for Justice & Human Rights.

I hope they all enjoy their fictitious alter egos and that they continue their good work for worthy causes.

To contact the author, please visit his website,
www.nelsondemille.net